ISLAND INTERLUDE

As though she could hear Craig's thoughts, she turned back to look at him, not really expecting him to be there. But he was—every granite-hard inch of him. She'd spent the most erotic moments of her life with him, and now she ached for more time in his fantasy world. Time to touch him, kiss him, have him fill the hollow in her mind and the void in her soul. To have him entombed in her body again and again. Needing nothing more to convince her, she yielded to her strong desire to have him possess her completely as she turned around and ran toward him.

With his eyes piercing into the dark at the vision of beauty floating his way, he sat up, hoping she was running to him and into his lonely arms. Landing on top of him, she pushed him back onto the sand. He felt a powerful rush of love and warmth. He felt complete.

Holding on to her in desperation, Craig pressed his body in to hers with an urgency he'd never experienced before. His desperate need for her momentarily frightened him, as all the answers to his questions became crystal clear—so clear that he could almost see his feelings etched in the air. He was crazy in love with Sambrea Sinclair. The stunning revelation felt wonderful and awesome—it also had his body shaking atop the sand beneath him.

The pleasure she felt was immeasurable as his mouth opened to surround a bronzed nipple, his fingers branding her creamy flesh with sizzling caresses. Having him pressing against her with such urgency made her want to devour his nakedness.

BOOK YOUR PLACE ON OUR WEBSITE AND MAKE THE ARABESQUE ROMANCE CONNECTION!

We've created a customized website just for our very special Arabesque readers, where you can get the inside scoop on everything that's going on with Arabesque romance novels.

When you come online, you'll have the exciting opportunity to:

- View covers of upcoming books

- Learn about our future publishing schedule (listed by publication month and author)

- Find out when your favorite authors will be visiting a city near you

- Search for and order backlist books

- Check out author bios and background information

- Send e-mail to your favorite authors

- Join us in weekly chats with authors, readers and other guests

- Get writing guidelines

- AND MUCH MORE!

Visit our website at
http://www.arabesquebooks.com

ISLAND INTERLUDE

LINDA HUDSON-SMITH

BET Publications LLC
http://www.bet.com
http://www.arabesquebooks.com

ARABESQUE BOOKS are published by

BET Publications, LLC
c/o BET BOOKS
One BET Plaza
1900 W Place NE
Washington, D.C. 20018-1211

All Kensington Titles, Imprints, and Distributed Lines are available at special quantity discounts for bulk purchases for sales promotions, premiums, fund-raising, and educational or institutional use. Special book excerpts or customized printings can also be created to fit specific needs. For details, write or phone the office of the Kensington special sales manager: Kensington Publishing Corp., 850 Third Avenue, New York, NY 10022, attn: Special Sales Department, Phone: 1-800-221-2647.

First Printing: May 2002
10 9 8 7 6 5 4 3 2 1

Printed in the United States of America

This book is dedicated to my two sons: Gregory Lee Lewis Smith and Scott Brian Smith—AKA Justified. You are both so very dear to my heart. May your lives always be filled with the joy of love and laughter. May God bless you and keep you always!
I love you deeply!

ACKNOWLEDGMENTS

AAFES
NEX
Options For Youth
Lupus Foundation of America
Black Advocates in State Services
1st Personnel Group—Ft. Lewis, WA
SFC Cynthia Hamilton—Fort Lewis, WA
I Corps EO Staff Office—Ft. Lewis, WA
MSG Drusilla Smith—Ft. Sam Houston, TX
NAACP National Health Division
National Black Nurses Association
La Jolla Pharmaceutical Company
Blacks In Government—Inland Empire Chapter
Department of Social Services—San Bernardino County
Amanda McHenry—AHMCH's Greeting Cards
Grace Blount
Georgia Knox
Geraldine Crumpton
Dr. Leticia Wright—*The Wright Place*
The Citizens of Winnsboro, Louisiana

A very special thank-you for your tremendous support!

ONE

Performing their celestial ritual, the silver moon and the blue stars polished the Hawaiian skies with dazzling light. Twinkling in unison, heaven's crown jewels lovingly embraced the purple, velvety sky. The Oahu waters were warm, yet the beach was deserted, with the exception of one figure, a lovely, willowy, curvaceous figure.

The tiny grains of sand felt cold and mushy under her bare feet, yet Sambrea Sinclair walked on with no apparent direction. Carelessly, she tossed her sable-brown hair over her shoulder. Her large sand-and-sable eyes glistening with tears, she looked back at her tiny beach bungalow, where a single candle still flickered on the sill of a large picture window, the only flicker of light in her dismal life. Though the sky was awash with brilliant light, she could only relate to the light of the single candle, a candle soon to be burnt out. As burnt out as her life was quickly becoming.

Lost in her thoughts, Sambrea walked another quarter of a mile before turning back toward the bungalow. Pulling the hood of her jacket up over her head, she crossed her arms against her chest. A sudden crunching noise crashed into the stillness of the night, causing her to turn and look behind her.

Seeing the figure of a tall, dark male closing in on her at what appeared to be a menacing pace, her pulse began to race and her feet began to move rapidly. The tall figure also picked up speed, drawing alongside of her before she could even attempt to escape. A viselike fear gripped her insides as the tall stranger fell into step beside her, but her feet couldn't seem to move any faster. Praying with fervor for protection against harm, she continued on. Although it felt as if she were moving in slow motion, she was making some progress.

"You don't have any reason to run." The male voice was deep and sultry. "I'm just here to protect you. You should never walk the beach alone, especially at night."

Ready to defend herself, if necessary, she stopped abruptly. Slowly, she turned to face the intruder. His eyes, black as a starless night, shimmered with midnight magic. Enthralled by his beautiful eyes, she stifled a gasp. "I've been walking this beach for many, many years now. Alone, I might add. I don't need a protector." Her tone held undisguised sarcasm.

Her discomfort grew when he slid his hand into hers with ease, yet she didn't pull away.

As he resumed walking, his magnetic draw pulled her along with him. "What's your name?" The tone of his voice was sexy, hypnotic.

"Sam . . . Sambrea Sinclair." Her voice was as cool as the sea breeze, belying the slight wariness she felt deep down inside her gut.

"I like them both. In fact, I love your unusual but very pretty name. My name is Craig Caldwell. I live a couple of miles down the beach. I've seen you out here many times before, but it always concerns me when I see you here after dark."

Don't let it," she countered quickly. "I own this tiny section of the beach—and you're trespassing, Mr. Caldwell. Didn't you see the posted signs?"

"I don't pay any attention to signs. You may own this land on a piece of paper, as I do mine, but we can never truly own what doesn't belong to us. Neither you nor I created this magnificent seascape. It all belongs to the Creator."

This was crazy—to be walking along the beach holding on to a stranger's hand as they argued over property rights. Yet his Havana-brown hands were so gentle and soothing, she quietly admitted to herself. It felt as though his fingers had reached inside of her to illuminate her tormented heart.

His hands moved up to her golden-brown face, touching her cheek with such tenderness. "You seem so sad to me, Sam. Do you want to talk about it?"

"No," she retorted sharply, "there's nothing to talk about. I've got to be going. Thanks for whatever it is you imagine you're doing for me."

Laughing, he spun her around before she could retreat. Without warning, his mouth took possession of hers. Much to her surprise, she didn't feel at all threatened. In fact, when his arms tightened around her, she felt fiercely protected.

Dropping to his knees, he drew her down in front of him, tasting the salty sea mist clinging to her luscious, melon-colored lips. While she thought she shouldn't, she found herself enjoying his exploring mouth too much to offer a single objection.

Physically, he held her away from him, drawing her emotionally nearer with his dark, penetrating gaze. "Have you ever made love to a stranger, Sambrea Sinclair?" Though the laughter in his tone said he was joking, she somehow got the feeling he was dead serious.

"Oh, please! What planet do you reside on? Did you just drop in out of the Twilight Zone, or do you live on Fantasy Island?" Making love to him was the farthest thing from her tumultuous mind. Yet the idea intrigued her—overwhelmingly.

"I reside on planet Earth most of the time, but I've been known to take a trip to the moon every now and then. No, I haven't been to the Twilight Zone yet, but I'd love to be your fantasy, Sambrea. Haven't you ever imagined yourself making love to someone you've never met, or perhaps to someone you may only have dreamed about? As beautiful as you are, I guess you don't have to indulge yourself in such mindless fantasies."

He certainly wasn't lacking in the beauty department, either. He was only drop-dead gorgeous. "Craig, I guess this has been nice, but you're either a drunk or merely insane. I'm not interested in getting involved with either personality defect."

He smiled. "I never touch alcohol, but I am quite insane. I lost my sanity the moment I first laid eyes on you." Although she figured she should be wary of him, she couldn't stop herself from cracking up. "Laugh if you must, but I speak the truth. Go on home now, Sam. I'm not interested in being made a fool of."

He sounded so seriously injured. Could he be that sensitive? She'd met very few men who knew the meaning of sensitivity, let alone the experience of it. Her sand-and-sable eyes grew bright with bewilderment. Looking into his midnight orbs, she tried to name the particular emotion she saw bleeding through.

Without thinking, she ran her fingers through his silky hair. His hair was as black as his eyes. "I wasn't trying to make a fool of you, Craig. You have to admit that this entire scenario is kind of strange. Are you really that sensitive?" She caressed his Havana-brown cheek as if she'd known him for years. Realizing the provocation in her actions, she quickly pulled her hand away from his smooth, clean-shaven face.

He laughed inwardly at her obvious reaction to what she'd done. *"Everyone* is sensitive. There are some of us who are just too embarrassed to admit it. But I'm not embarrassed by anything, Sambrea. If I were, I'd find life itself one gigantic embarrassment."

As his hands suddenly entwined in her hair, pulling her

in closer to him, she found herself relaxing her head against his rock-solid chest. His succulent lips, as full and moist as the ocean, kissed her until she trembled. As his kisses numbed her brain, he almost made her forget she was kissing a total stranger.

Scared of what could easily happen between them, she gently shoved him away. "I have to go. I can hear my phone ringing."

Her lie was obvious to him as he lazed his finger down her arm. "I hear bells, too, but they're not coming from any phone. Maybe one day you'll be able to admit that the ringing you're hearing isn't coming from the telephone, either. Good night, Sam."

She couldn't respond. He had totally blown her mind. Along with the midnight magic in his eyes, she saw how his teeth sparkled with some sort of white magic. Everything about this beautiful black man appeared magical, she marveled, pulling herself away from his hypnotic gaze.

Kicking up sand, she ran toward the bungalow, forgoing her nightly swim. Turning around for a last glance at the handsome Havana-brown face with the sparkling midnight eyes, she discovered he'd disappeared as quickly as he'd appeared. *Maybe he resides at the bottom of the ocean.* Her eyes filled with wondrous awe as she peered into the night.

Seconds later, safe inside her bungalow, she ran to the window, where the candle was flickering low. Her sand-and-sable eyes searched the darkness for any sign of him, unable to see anything other than the huge white waves sloshing haphazardly against the sandy shore. Certain that he was gone, and eager to perform her nightly swimming ritual, she returned to the beach. Wiggling out of her cut-off jeans and short sleeve top, she dropped them on the snowy white towel. Wading out into the water until it was waist high, she dove into the warm Oahu waters, hoping to forget the amazing encounter she'd just had, hoping to block out

the impressive image of the gorgeous brother with the un-
forgettable eyes and granite physique.

The water swirled around Sambrea's nudity, engulfing
her in its caressing warmth. Her spirits were lifted by the
titillating romance with the ocean as she swam until she
felt sure she'd have one heck of a deep sleep.

Emerging from the water, she felt that nothing could disturb her peace on this glorious night. Then she saw him.
Standing next to her discarded clothing, she saw the body
that looked as though it had been carved from the finest
marble. Knowing she couldn't get to her clothes without
passing near to him, panic arose in her throat. A dizzy feeling seemed to alert her to the potential danger ahead, but
her most basic instincts seemed to tell her something different.

Sensing her disquietude, Craig picked up the towel and
carried it to the water's edge. Handing her the large white
fluff of lint, he turned his back. "You are one hard-headed
broad." Ignoring his barbed scolding, she pushed past him.
"Not so fast, missy. You're going to hear me out whether
you want to or not." He spun her around like a top. "There's
a few things that you obviously don't know about, but I'm
here to enlighten you." Calmly, though his eyes stormed,
he explained the danger she'd unwittingly placed herself in.
He then informed her of some serious incidents that had
occurred on the private beachfront properties. It seemed that
a night predator was on the loose in the otherwise quiet
beach community.

"Thanks for the hot news flash. I'll remember to keep
my doors bolted and my fifty-seven Magnum next to my
bed. That is, when I'm not concealing it under my clothing." Her cutting remarks revealed a strong air of defiance.

He glanced at her sharply. "It wouldn't have helped you
out tonight since you're not packing it. You're a stubborn
wench, but that's how I like my women. It makes the challenge that much sweeter."

"Well, you'd better go find one of your wenches and challenge her. You're hardly a challenge to me, Golden Boy." Jeering at him with her eyes, she laughed out loud.

"Is that so? Why don't we just find out, Sam." Pulling her into his arms, he crushed his lips down over hers. Attempting to ward him off, she kicked at his legs and the towel fell away, exposing her nudity. He gasped for air. "God, you're beautiful! I thought you were beautiful with your clothes on, but this is ridiculous. You are one mesmerizing sea nymph."

Filled with embarrassment, she felt herself blush. "Looks can be deceiving, Craig Caldwell. Don't make me show you how ugly I can get."

Picking up the towel, he whirled it in the air to call a truce. While wrapping it around her nude body, his hand accidentally brushed against her bare breast. The contact seared him, nearly making him lose his self-control. With the towel snugly in place, Craig drew her down to the wet sand. As his tender hands warmed her heart, his touch felt so good she didn't want him to pull away his heat. Anything that felt this good had to be right, she pondered through the haze in her brain. Returning his ardent kisses, she ran her hands over the well-toned body, loving the hardness that felt so wonderfully soft.

As his engaging mouth chipped away at her sanity, she moaned, purring inwardly with pleasure. Her entire life was falling to pieces, yet she suddenly felt whole again. Unable to help herself, she got totally caught up in his whirlwind fantasy.

He pulled her head against his chest with infinite gentleness. "Oh, Sam, Sam," he whispered onto her lips, "you are indeed a wild fantasy. You taste just as sweet as you look."

The look in his eyes caused an intense heat to stream through her. Wondering what it would feel like to have him make her body an extension of his own, she closed her eyes. She couldn't help thinking how loving him back could come easy for her.

Craig's excitement grew as he thought about them making love in the wet sand. Though completely caught up in his wild fantasy, he knew it was just that, a fantasy. However, if he had his way, he would make it a fantasy for her too. He couldn't stop imagining himself caressing every inch of her firm flesh.

Her shyness surfaced as he drew her closer and closer to him, making her wish she were enshrined inside his body. If her life was going to go up in flames, then her body at least deserved to be tortured with a pleasurable burning. A ravenous burning, a burning to forever last, a burning to last past eternity.

Fearing that he could read her erotic thoughts through her eyes, Sambrea found it hard to look at him. Her musings had caused embarrassment and shame to set in—and it didn't look as if they'd go away anytime soon. Like he'd said, nothing embarrassed him. She watched him covertly. Looking as though he'd been utterly fulfilled by a woman's love, he smiled like someone who'd just finished having an amazingly intimate tryst in the sand.

During her covert glances, she realized he couldn't seem to take his eyes off her, either. What she saw there in his eyes caused her to leap to her feet. "I've really got to go, Craig." Unable to look directly at him, her heart thumping wildly inside her chest, she turned to walk away.

Craig wouldn't think of letting her go home alone, even if it was just a short distance. He quickly pulled himself up from the sand. "I'm coming with you." When she raised certain objections, he wasted no time in making his reasoning perfectly clear. Much to her dismay, he took hold of her arm and escorted her to the bungalow. In complete silence, they walked on until they reached her door.

She finally got the nerve to look directly at him. "Good night, Craig. Thanks for walking me to my door."

He kissed her forehead. "I'd like to come in for a minute or two."

Sambrea frowned. "I don't think that's such a brilliant idea. We're still virtual strangers, Craig." *I'd like to keep it that way.*

He smoothed her wet hair back from her face. "That's what I'm trying to change here, Sam. I don't want us to be strangers. If nothing else, we are neighbors, you know."

Sensing that he wasn't at all a threat to her safety, and too tired to fight him on the issue, she graciously conceded. Moving inside, she allowed him to follow her into the cozy warmth of her private space, which was encompassed in a dazzling array of soft pastels.

Loose pillows, colossal in size, were casually thrown on the rose-beige carpet in the living room. There was very little furniture, but it was explicitly tasteful. The winter-white leather recliner looked comfortable and well-used, as did the matching sofa and two armchairs. Indentations of resting heels marked the leather hassock.

She motioned for him to have a seat. "Excuse me, please. I really need to get into some dry clothing before I catch my death. A quick shower wouldn't hurt either."

Imagining himself joining her under the brisk flow of water, he simply nodded.

While she went off to shower, Craig got acquainted with Sambrea's surroundings, hoping to learn as much as he could about her. As though he had every right to do so, he went into the kitchen to brew up a pot of tea. In his caring way, he thought Sambrea should have something warm to drink after her swim. For sure, he didn't want her to catch a chill.

The minuscule kitchen held all the modern conveniences along with shiny new appliances done in smoky black. Looking around him, he saw shiny, copper-bottomed pots and pans hanging from an overhead rack. As a nature lover, he admired the bushy green plants filling the windowsills.

The colorful ceramic ornaments adorning the glossy ecru walls added a nice touch of brightness. A microwave oven was stationed atop the black and white ceramic-tile counter.

There wasn't enough water in the world to wash away the shame and guilt she felt. How could she have even considered such a thing? She'd actually entertained the idea of making love to a perfect stranger, which was preposterous. And on the beach, no less. Not only that, she wailed inwardly, she had dared to allow the same stranger into her home. He could be out there planning to rob her blind. Sambrea was sure she'd taken leave of all her senses.

All of her assets were on hold because some idiot was trying to take her livelihood away, now another idiot had almost succeeded in taking away her sense of good judgment and moral values. With growing inner antagonism, she finally decided that she was the idiot.

Craig stood at the doorway of the bathroom. "Sam, are you ready for a cup of hot tea?"

A cup of hot tea! She bristled inwardly. Oh, how she would like to tell him what he could do with his hot tea. Knowing she had only herself to blame for him even being inside her home, she felt that she had no recourse whatsoever. "I'll be out in just a minute."

After snatching a thick terry robe off the hook on the bathroom door, she nestled into it, tying the belt snugly around her waist. He'd practically seen every inch of her. Why should she even bother to cover herself up? Still, he had turned around when he handed her the towel. She gave him credit for at least showing her that kind of respect. He could've just as easily kept the towel away from her. He was definitely a lot bigger and stronger than she was.

Once Sambrea tackled the length of her hair with a large comb, she left it to dry on its own. Discarding the damp robe, she dressed in another pair of cut-off jeans and a plain

white T-shirt. Squaring her shoulders, she took a deep
breath and headed for what should've been the comfort of
her own living room. With Craig Caldwell out there, she
didn't know what to expect.

Observing things from the doorway, she immediately noticed that Craig had lit another candle to replace the burned-
out one. Hugging one of the large pillows, he rested on the
floor. As her anger gave rise to disapproval at seeing him
looking so darn comfortable in her private space, Sambrea
stepped into the room.

He looked up at her and smiled. "How was your shower,
Sam? You look refreshed."

She gritted her teeth. "I feel refreshed." She felt anything
but that. "I needed that shower pretty badly."

He pulled another pillow closer to where he lay. "Come
down here with me, Sam. The tea is starting to cool."
Tiredly, she dropped down beside him, thinking she should
be at least a little fearful of him. But she wasn't fearful,
and she wasn't able to explain that, either. Picking up one
of the black-and-gold mugs, Craig lifted it to her lips. After
taking two sips of the hot, minty-tasting liquid, she pushed
it away. "Don't you like it, Sam?"

"The tea is just fine, Craig. I guess I'm just not in the
mood for it. I've got to go to bed and get some sleep. I
have an important early morning appointment. It's already
very late."

He looked rather dejected. "Are you asking me to leave,
Sam?"

"I didn't think I posed a question, Craig. I merely stated
a fact. But if you need a more direct approach, yes, I'm
asking you to leave."

He sulked for a moment. "I get the feeling you're regretting the time we've shared tonight. It's been good, Sam.
There isn't any reason for you to feel regretful. We're two
adults who decided to spend some time together. I obviously

needed to be with someone tonight and I somehow think you needed company, too."

She clicked her tongue. "How princely of you! We may have needs, Craig, but we really don't know a thing about each other. It was irresponsible of me to let you into my home. I've always considered myself a sensible woman, but what sensible person invites a stranger into her home, someone she's never laid eyes on before? If you can honestly answer that for me, I'd be eternally grateful."

His body language showed signs of impatience as he sighed. "A very sensible woman named Sambrea Sinclair. Don't slay yourself over this, Sam. There's a first time for everything. I hope it won't be our last time to get together like this. It feels good. I like being with you."

She raised an eyebrow. "Are you sure you don't drink alcohol? Your brain is besotted with something, Craig. I'd like to have some of whatever it is. Maybe it will help me get rid of the guilt. Guilt that you're obviously not feeling."

He made direct eye contact with her. "What do I have to feel guilty about, Sambrea? As far as that goes, you shouldn't be feeling that way, either. Guilt is a terminal illness. It's very unhealthy to carry it around. Besides, we haven't done anything wrong. Strangers having an undeniable attraction to each other isn't anything to feel guilty about. We shouldn't even be having this type of discussion since these are all moot points you've been trying to make."

Why does he have to speak with such common sense wisdom? "I don't want to bother with this," she spouted impatiently. "I'm going to bed. You can let yourself out. See you around, Craig Caldwell." Tramping into the bedroom, she prayed she'd never have to lay eyes on him again. The man with the sexy midnight eyes was way too dangerous. After lighting a candle, she slid in between the pastel sheets. Feeling sure that Craig meant her no harm, she tore out of the jeans and T-shirt and tossed them to the foot of the bed.

Seconds later, as a shadow fell across the door, she looked up and saw Craig looming there. The candle and the moonbeams shining through the open window illuminated his striking figure. He looked like a magnificent idol of some sort—black, beautiful and strong.

Like a thief in the night, he approached the bed and sat down on the edge of the mattress. "I came to tuck you in. Then I'll leave." His eyes grew tender as he smoothed her satiny hair back, brushing his mouth lightly against hers.

Anticipating the sweet taste of his moist kisses on her thirsty mouth, she closed her eyes. Kissing her deeply, he laid his head against her breasts. She didn't so much as offer a whimper in protest. Holding her close, he stroked her hair until she fell into a deep slumber.

At home in his own bed, Craig Caldwell knew he couldn't even begin to sleep. This was the most bizarre thing he'd ever done in his entire life. In all his thirty years there'd been many bizarre happenings, but tonight was the most eccentric of all. Tonight he'd finally come face-to-face with the woman he'd fantasized about, had pined over for months. Sambrea Sinclair was the only woman he'd ever felt totally helpless around, the only woman who often came to life in his dreams. While he considered himself an extremely disciplined man, something about Sambrea had caused him to lose all of his finely honed skills in self-control. He could've controlled himself around any other woman, but this woman was something else.

This woman seemed to beckon to him via his soul. When she'd arisen out of the ocean like a sea nymph, he'd truly lost it. Every detail of her beautiful body was emblazoned in his brain. The mystical Sambrea Sinclair was as beautiful, as compelling—and as mysterious—as the deep seas. In reverence of her native-girl beauty, he succumbed to the black abyss of sleep.

TWO

The morning sunlight flooded into the room, cascading its warmth onto Sambrea's golden-brown face. Moaning, she turned over. Noticing the light of day, she catapulted into a sitting position. Looking at the clock, she screamed. It was now ten-thirty. Her appointment at the bank had been for eight A.M. Large teardrops streamed from her eyes. "I've blown it." Her sobs came brokenly. "I've lost it all. All because I chose to fantasize with some oversexed, muscle-bound jock."

Through her tears she saw that Craig Caldwell had covered her up with the lightweight blanket she kept at the bottom of the bed. She didn't know exactly when he'd let himself out, since she'd fallen right off to sleep. When she'd awakened at two-thirty, he'd already done another disappearing act. Smiling now, she finally admitted to herself that what she'd felt from him, with him, had been deeply satisfying. Then she shuddered, thinking about what could've happened to her had Craig been the sexual predator that he'd spoken about. How could she have been so stupid as to entertain a perfect stranger in her home? Had she been that needy for conversation, for the warmth of human contact?

Climbing out of bed, she retrieved her robe and trudged into the bathroom. Standing at the sink, she noticed the mirror wasn't very kind to her this morning. Her face was pale with anguish, which made her look like a refugee from the lost world of Atlantis. How she'd escaped from the fabled world at the bottom of the sea would forever remain a mystery. How she'd managed to further strengthen the ominous threat hanging over her company like a dreary rain cloud was becoming painfully clear. Beautiful Craig Caldwell had walked into her life and had immediately usurped her ability to think clearly, logically.

Sambrea decided to put in a call to the bank, but no sooner had she picked up the phone than she put it back down again. A phone call would never do. Making an appearance at the bank was the only possible solution. She owed Mr. Barker, the bank manager and her father's long-time business associate, at least that much. If he turned her down cold, then so be it.

Sambrea had just about everything a twenty-five-year-old woman could possibly want. Her father, the late Samuel Sinclair, had been a shrewd business tycoon. He had inherited the company—it had been passed down through generations of Sinclairs. He had amassed a fortune, but he'd made some seriously bad business decisions before his untimely death. In hopes of recouping the company's heavy financial losses, Sambrea was desperately trying to hold on to what was left of the family business. When the decision was made to sell some of the company's shares on the open market, De La Brise had become vulnerable to a hostile takeover.

De La Brise, French for 'of the breeze', was a private yachting operation that catered to the romantic adventurer by providing magnificent sunset dinner cruises throughout the Hawaiian Islands. The elaborate yachts were also leased out for private parties and business functions. Fully staffed with topnotch personnel, De La Brise not only promised first-class service, it also delivered on that promise.

Freshly showered and fully dressed now, Sambrea saw her own rather charming reflection. She felt really comfortable in her cute white linen sundress as she checked herself out in the mirror. Noticing how striking the white dress looked against her golden-brown complexion and sable-brown hair, she smiled. Though she always got very dark in the summer months, she worked hard at maintaining an even skin tone all year round.

After covering her full lips with a glossy tangerine lip color, she combed her long lashes with dark brown mascara. A light stroke of copper-brown blush enhanced the natural color of her high cheekbones. Brushing her hair until it shone, she started to tie it back but thought better of it. She loved her hair to swing free and loose.

At five-foot-six, Sambrea was sensuous yet willowy, with a firm, well-rounded derriere and high, shapely breasts. Despite her earlier tears, her sand-and-sable eyes glowed with the aftereffects of the delightfully intimate dreams she'd had of Craig in the early morning hours. Still assessing her mirrored image, she saw that it was quite a change from what the looking glass had revealed just a short time ago.

Once Sambrea put the top down on her white Mustang convertible, she slid behind the wheel. She then sped onto the road that would take her to downtown Honolulu, where the bank and headquarters of De La Brise were located.

Twenty minutes later, she turned into the parking lot of the Hawaiian International Bank. Before going inside, she pondered the situation. Since she was already terribly late, she decided to go to her office before facing Amos Barker. It was just two blocks away.

As she stepped into the comfort of the executive offices, Richard Henry, her right and left arm, best friend and confidant, rushed up to greet her. She tossed him a heartfelt smile. "Good morning, Rich."

Richard Henry, a great-looking middle-aged man, medium in height and build, had a smile sexy enough to bowl over any woman. His smooth, mahogany-brown complexion was kissably soft. Dark-brown eyes flashed with fiery flecks of amber as he smiled back at Sambrea.

Richard kissed her cheek. "Boy, am I glad to see you. I thought you'd never get here. I've got some great news, Sam."

Richard propelled her down the corridor and into her private office, which she felt in danger of losing. The office provided her with an excellent view of Diamond Head and the Pacific Ocean. Its leather furnishings were of fine quality and comfortably plush. Since Sambrea was a fan of most water sports, large pictures of the same hung on the glossy walls in polished brass frames. An array of elephants in many different sizes and materials could be found throughout the office, symbolic of the sorority she'd pledged at the University of Hawaii.

Rubbing her forehead with an open palm, Sambrea plopped down on the ivory-beige leather sofa. "Okay, Rich, give it to me straight."

Grinning, he sat down. "We've got a reprieve, honey. For some unknown reason, the people who've been buying up large shares of our stock are reconsidering their position. If I knew who the sons-of-sea-horses were, I'd kiss them."

Her brows furrowed. "You've got to be kidding! This is all so strange to me, Rich. Why would they reconsider, especially after all the trouble they've gone through jockeying for position? You might be willing to kiss them, Rich, but I'd give them a swift kick where it would hurt the most. I'd kick them so hard their precious family jewels would never be the same again. Assuming they're all men, of course. These idiots have all my assets tied up."

Richard frowned. "You're playing this *assets on hold* thing right down to the bone marrow. While some assets are tied up, we still have a surplus of funds to keep us in operation for some time to come. Besides, you're the one who ordered us to stop paying the bills, Sambrea."

"Don't remind me, Rich. I'm trying to use some clever strategy here. If they take us over, they're going to get most of it anyway. But if De La Brise gets into even more debt maybe these idiots will just go away. It might be working already if they're reconsidering. I want us to appear destitute."

Taking her hand, Richard kissed the back of it. "You're going about this the wrong way, Sambrea. But I'll let you do it your way." He laughed. "As if I had a choice. But, Sam, we need to appear strong and solvent, not weak and destitute. What would you do if you were face-to-face with the people who are responsible for all your inner turmoil?"

She smiled devilishly. "Refer back to my earlier comment, Rich. My feet could use a good workout."

"Well, you better get those feet ready." He glanced at his watch. "You've got about twenty minutes before you get to execute those swift kicks."

Looking incredulous, Sambrea's mouth flew open. "Say what?"

"Get with it, girl! You're going to meet the men whom your feet desire." Richard had barely finished his comment when a light knock came on the door.

Joe Walls, Sambrea's private secretary, stuck his dusky-brown head inside the door. "You got company, Sam," he drawled lazily. "There are three finely tailored suits out here waiting to see your highness." Joe loved to harass her in a joking manner.

Sambrea and Richard laughed heartily. She positively loved Joe. Like Richard, he was her dear friend and confidant. Joe Walls, with his husky, teddy-bear-like build, dusky-brown hair, and malted-milk complexion made her laugh like crazy. It was Joe who'd taught her laughter was the best medicine simply because it didn't have any negative side effects. Often overdosing her, he gave her large doses of laughter every single day. Joe had become her fun and relaxation guru over the years.

"Should I show them in, Sam?"

Sambrea looked around her office, noting the untidy mess she'd left—and had warned Joe not to touch. She frowned. "Show them into the boardroom, Joe. If they're as finely tailored as you say, they won't fit in with this new decorative mess I've created."

Joe smiled. He threw his hand up in a farewell gesture as he backed out the door.

She turned to Richard. "I've got to collect my wits. As always, I need you, pal. Three tough suits against one delicate dress is hardly what I call equality."

Richard brushed her cheek with his fingertips. "You're anything but delicate in business matters, Sam. Someone should've warned those guys to wear hardhats. Let me get my jacket and I'll come back and escort you to doomsday." He closed the door behind him as he left the privacy of her office.

Walking over to the window, Sambrea stared out at the ocean. Getting to meet the people who were trying to do a takeover of De La Brise overwhelmed her. She wanted to cry, but now wasn't the time for her to dissolve into a quivering mass of blubbering jelly. Her entire life was built around the company. She'd lived and breathed De La Brise since she was a small child. From the time she entered kindergarten, she'd been a daily fixture in Samuel's office. In many ways the company had become her whole life, especially after Samuel passed away. Running the company was the only real life she'd ever had, the only life she'd come to know, the only life she ever really wanted.

Samuel Sinclair wouldn't have allowed this to happen, she thought sadly. These people wouldn't have dared to try something like this if he were alive. Though he'd ended up making some bad investments, he'd been a tough nut to crack, she recalled with fondness.

Before she became too emotional over the wonderful memories of the days she'd spent with her father at the company, she stepped inside the small powder room adjoining her office and flicked on the light. Looking into the mirror, she took special note of the haunted look that had now come to roost in her eyes. Sighing with discontent, she picked up a rubber brush and straightened her wind-blown hair.

After minor repairs to her other delicate features, she went out of her office and toward the reception door to meet up with Richard. She had just stepped into the corridor when Richard shot out of his office. Together, they walked toward the boardroom, prepared to fight to the death to maintain the independence of De La Brise.

Sambrea and Richard entered the mammoth room; it, too, overlooked the Pacific, and was shiny with highly polished hardwoods and plush leather furniture. Sambrea's eyes immediately went to the two impeccably dressed men seated at the long conference table. After coolly scrutinizing the two strangers for a few moments, her eyes shifted to the tall black man who stood at the window with his back to her.

This suit was inconceivably impeccable, and the rest of his attire was equally dashing, Sambrea noticed. It looked as though his clothes had been tailored right on his lithe body. Neatly cut, carbon-black curly hair caressed the neckline of his barely pink silk dress shirt. She couldn't help noticing the hand passing through the curls was slender and soft—its fingers, long and sensuous. He wore it all so well, she reflected quietly.

Sambrea knew exactly to whom all these extraordinary personal assets belonged, even though she'd only seen him in the darkness of a moonlit night and by the light of a single candle.

As Craig Caldwell turned around, casting his hypnotic midnight gaze upon her, the air grew thin. She suddenly felt light-headed. Clutching at Richard's arm for support, her grip was like a steel-trap. She saw that Richard was somewhat puzzled by the obvious look of disdain she was so sure her expression carried. Regaining control, she flashed an even white smile at the three visitors.

"Gentlemen, it's nice of you to pay us a visit here at De La Brise. I'm Sambrea Sinclair, CEO. This gentleman with me is De La Brise's Assistant CEO, Richard Henry."

With her face cracking from the forced smiles, she walked around the room and extended her hand in an enthusiastic manner to all the men but one. She completely ignored Craig's outstretched hand. He chuckled inwardly at her blatant snub, knowing exactly what she was reacting to. *If only she knew the truth.* But he doubted that she'd listen to it or recognize it even if it sang a love song in her dainty ears.

Snatching Sambrea's attention away from Craig, a man with sandy-brown hair rose from his seat. His mahogany-brown eyes were somewhat startling. Sambrea thought the chiseled cleft in his chin was rather sexy. "I'm Paul Rochelle." Smiling, he pointed to his associates one by one. "This is Mike Arlington. The other gentleman over there by the window is Craig Caldwell."

Sambrea allowed her eyes to slowly rake over Mike's slender body, drinking in his darkly tanned complexion, wavy rust-brown hair, and java-brown eyes shining like morning sunbeams.

Burning with jealousy at the way her eyes seemed to seduce Paul, Craig Caldwell stared coolly at Sambrea. "I believe I've already met the lady."

"You have?" Richard asked. Startled by the news, he looked from Craig to Sambrea.

"Yes, I have. In one of my wildest fantasies," Craig shot back.

Mike and Paul laughed. Uncomfortable with the offhanded remark that had "sexist pig" written all over it, Richard cringed.

Sambrea sent Craig a chilling glance. "It's nice to know

somebody has fantasies. In my opinion, they're highly over-rated. And *I* would certainly know. Now that the fantasy is truly over, let's get into the reality of this situation." Although she'd made another sharp point, only Craig really understood her intentional barbs. His appearing amused by it all made Sambrea's insides burn like fire.

Continuing on, Sambrea ignored the laughter in Craig's eyes. "Let's start with you telling us who it is that you represent. Why are you here today? And what exactly do you hope to accomplish?"

"Why don't we all sit down," Richard offered. "The coffee is fresh if anyone would care for some." When no one appeared interested in the offer, Richard shrugged. He then waited for everyone to be seated before taking his own chair.

Eyeing her intently, Craig Caldwell sat down at the opposite end of the table from the seemingly untamable Sambrea Sinclair. He thought it was much safer for them to keep each other at a reasonable distance for the duration of the meeting. If looks could kill, he'd already be dead. Quietly, he observed the undisguised criminal intent in the beautiful sand-and-sable eyes of the stunningly gorgeous CEO of De La Brise.

"I'm usually the spokesman for the group," Paul informed Sambrea. "To answer your questions, Miss Sinclair, we represent Caldwell and Caldwell Incorporated. Craig Caldwell, whom you've just met, is owner and Chief Executive Officer. We're here to negotiate the buyout of your company. We'd like to acquire De La Brise as part of our entertainment conglomerate. Instead of a takeover, Mr. Caldwell has decided to make you a very sound offer, Miss Sinclair."

Having had no idea of Craig's part in all this, her eyebrows shot up at the announcement of his official title. Though reeling from the unbelievable discovery, she quickly regained her composure. "I see that you don't mince words,

Mr. Rochelle. But then again, neither do I. *Hell no* to any offer you might put on the table. Since we're on the subject of hell, I'll see you all burn there before I concede my company to your conglomerate, which is nothing but a cover-up for a renegade piracy operation." Sambrea's riveting gaze nailed Craig right to his chair. "Do you need a more direct approach, Mr. Caldwell?"

Pushing her chair back from the table, she stood up tall and erect. "Excuse me, gentlemen. I'm afraid I have other pressing matters to attend to." Calmly, gracefully, she walked out of the room, leaving her peers in a state of confusion. All of the men except for Craig seemed totally confused by her premature departure. Wondering if Craig and Sambrea had really met before, Richard glanced over at the man who'd just rained havoc on his lady boss.

Though Craig Caldwell remained cool and calm on the outside, his insides quivered. It was a rare feeling for him, but he found himself in complete awe of Sambrea Sinclair's masterful strength and direct approach. The *direct approach* certainly had a familiar ring to it. As he thought about the kisses they'd shared the previous evening, amusement was aglow in his midnight eyes.

Sambrea's nerves felt stretched to the absolute limit as she entered her private office. Craig Caldwell had set her up, had used her in the worst possible way—and that made her seriously angry. He'd purposely kept her up half the night so she would miss her appointment with the bank. Their rendezvous had been by pure design. He was the worst kind of slime, she thought maliciously. His motives had been self-serving from the onset. But hadn't he warned her about dangerous predators lurking on the beach?

He may have won this battle but the end of the war would crown her victorious, she vowed silently. She looked as though she could annihilate Craig with a mere glance.

* * *

"Well, gentlemen, I don't think we're going to be able to accomplish anything today. However, if you'd like to pass your offer on to me, I can give it to Miss Sinclair at the appropriate time. Otherwise, this meeting has been a waste of your valuable time," Richard said.

Craig jumped to his feet. "I don't waste time, Mr. Henry. Time is money. If you'll excuse me, I have a personal meeting to attend. I'll see you guys back at the office," Craig told Mike and Paul. "Have a good day, Mr. Henry."

With his jaw set tight, Craig Caldwell strode out into the corridor, where he asked an unsuspecting staff member to direct him to Sambrea's office. Having no intentions of leaving the offices of De La Brise until he talked with Sambrea Sinclair, he was determined to make her listen to him no matter how long it took. But he knew she wasn't going to let him smooth things over between them without putting up a ferocious fight.

Craig came face-to-face with Joe Walls. "I need to see Miss Sinclair."

"I'm afraid that won't be possible, sir. She's asked not to be disturbed. Would you like to make an appointment?"

Craig stroked his chin. "Yeah, sure. Right now." Craig passed Joe so fast that he was sure he smelled the rubber burning on his own shoes. Up for what would truly be a challenge, Craig stormed into Sambrea's office. The second their eyes met, a personal war was declared.

As though she needed a defense shield, Sambrea moved behind her desk and stationed both hands on her hips. "We're not having this conversation. If you don't remove yourself from my office, I'm calling security and have them throw your tight butt out of here."

He pointed a finger at her. "We *are* having this conversation, Sambrea. I know you feel betrayed, but I didn't know until this morning that you owned De La Brise. That's why

I came along with my crew. I never come to this sort of meeting. My people take care of everything."

She eyed him suspiciously. "Why not? Can't face the people you're stealing from? I never took you for a coward, Craig. Actually, I never took you for much of anything." She'd added that barb with the specific intent to inflict pain. "I can't believe a man like you wouldn't know all there is to know about a company he's trying to heist, right down to the spelling of the owner's first and last name."

He steeled himself against the onslaught of abuse that she seemed to dish out so easily. "My employees are extremely capable. And you're a poor liar, Sam, very unconvincing. You enjoyed the time we spent together every bit as much as I did. You stay in constant denial, don't you? Denial is as unhealthy as guilt. Are we going to handle this matter like the mature adults I know we are? Or are you going to insist that we act like errant children?"

She clenched and unclenched her tiny fists. "There's nothing to handle. You're not getting your dirty hands on De La Brise. That's a fact. I'll keep you tied up in court until you're too old to care anymore. Kindly remove yourself from my premises. Last warning, Craig!"

He shot her a look of exasperation. "Sam, if I don't take De La Brise from you someone else with a lot less scruples will. You need help, Sambrea. Whoever is handling your financial matters is leaving your tail badly exposed. It's being investigated, but, Sam, I need you to cooperate with me. There's a fox in the hen house—and it's feasting off of your chickens!"

She scowled. "I'm quite familiar with that concept, Craig. Danger was lurking on the beach last night, too, yet I locked it inside with me instead of locking it outside where it belonged. I'm sure my last statement is self-explanatory."

He slammed his fist down on the desk. "Not that again, Sambrea. I'm telling you, I didn't know it was your company until this very morning. Hit me, kick me, knock me down, but please don't call me a liar. A liar, I'm not. I have no reason to lie to you, or anyone else for that matter."

This was no good, she thought fearfully, not when he looked at her with those gorgeous midnight eyes. "Let's talk this over later, Craig. I have another meeting in half an hour. Are you familiar with Neptune?"

Unable to stop himself, he smiled broadly. "I was last night. Very familiar, I'd say." She hit him right between the eyes with a scathing glance. He held up his hand. "I know, I know, you're talking about the restaurant. I've never eaten there, but I know where it is. Are you inviting me to dinner, Sam?"

"I'm inviting you to dinner, Craig, but you're picking up the tab. I'll meet you there at seven-thirty."

His dark eyes grew soft and liquid. "Would it be too much to ask for a kiss? My lips sorely miss yours." Impatiently, she crossed her arms, ready to call security if he made one false move toward her. "Okay, Sam, okay. I know I'm pushing the envelope here, but I will taste your lips tonight. Count on it." Before opening the door, he turned around and winked at her.

Flustered, and enchanted with Craig at the same time, Sambrea dropped down in the chair. She had no intention of meeting him for dinner—she would've told him anything to get those devastating midnight eyes off of her. Believing nothing of what he'd said, she certainly didn't want to hear anything more from him. By the time the high and mighty Craig Caldwell realized what had gone down, she'd be long gone. Mischief danced in her eyes as she contemplated her next move.

Maui was looking real good to her.

She flew to Maui on a regular basis. The hotel she frequented there was quiet and very secluded. Her father's dear old friend, Tai Tanaka, was the manager. She needed to distance herself from Craig Caldwell, and halfway across the world probably wouldn't be far enough. He had the instincts and the mentality of a wild-game hunter. He'd sniffed her company out, hadn't he? Just thinking about his clever moves caused her irritation to grow.

"If he knows what's good for him, he'll quickly latch on to another scent. De La Brise will not be added to his financial stockpile," she swore under her breath.

Dwindling finances wasn't the only problem for her company. Personally, she could make it on very little, but she worried about her employees. De La Brise had been Samuel's baby and she would fight to the death for it. Samuel had given birth to De La Brise. He'd nurtured it until it had grown mature enough to hold its own against people like Caldwell. Yet something had gone terribly wrong. And it was solely up to her to right it.

Sambrea loved the company, she loved all of its challenges, but she didn't care one bit for this latest one. The latest challenge was far too sexy, far too charming and handsome, far too dangerous—and far too much man for a slip of a woman like herself to take on.

Yet take him on she would.

THREE

Because of the many matters she'd had to personally attend to, the remainder of the day was busy for Sambrea. Her least favorite task was calling on Amos Barker, whom she'd finally opted to talk with over the telephone. Assuring her he'd do whatever he could with board approval, Amos had been sympathetic to her situation.

At six o'clock she began to wind things down. Her flight to Maui was scheduled to depart at seven-thirty, the same time Craig would be expecting her at Neptune. She didn't have to worry about going home to pack since she kept an adequate wardrobe right there at the office.

At six-fifteen Sambrea brushed her hair and teeth and touched up her face. Removing a thin stack of files from her desk, she placed them in her leather shoulder-style briefcase. After retrieving her already-packed weekender bag, she took the elevator down to the lobby.

Just as she exited the building, Craig entered.

The look on his face showed his surprise at seeing her already down in the lobby. Her heart did a double flip as her eyes drank in his tailored-to-perfection magnificence.

He flashed her a dazzling smile. "Hi. I was just coming up to your office to pick you up. I don't like meeting my dates. Being an old-fashioned gentleman, I prefer to escort my companions from beginning to end."

"I see." Her voice was weak. "I'm afraid I'm not going

to be able to keep our date, Craig. Something very important has come up. If you'll excuse me, I have to be going."

His smile dropped to the ground. "You had no intention of meeting me, did you, Sam? You were on your way home, weren't you? You lied to me." In accusing her, he sounded as though he would've never believed her capable of lying to him, or anyone else, for that matter.

Sambrea stepped around his formidable figure. "You seem to have it all figured out, Craig. I don't see any reason to pass comment. Have a good evening."

Before she could take another step, he grabbed her by the arm, turning her around to face him. "I hope you don't think you're getting off this easy, Sam. You made a commitment and you're damn well going to keep it. Whatever you have to do will just have to wait. Neptune awaits us, darling!" Removing her briefcase from her shoulder, he placed it over his own. After getting a firm grip on her weekender, he took her by the hand and practically dragged her out of the building.

Completely ignoring her loud shouts of protests, Craig opened the passenger door of his car and gently shoved her inside. He locked the door with the remote on his keys, which made her fume. Her eyes spat hailstones his way as he settled himself into the driver's seat of the late model black Jaguar.

He looked into her hostile eyes, his smile taunting. "If the rage in your eyes is an indication of how you feel about me, I can see that I'm in big trouble." She didn't respond. "Oh, well, you can have it your way later, Sam. But I'll have mine right now."

Coiling his arm around the back of her neck, he drew her to him, kissing her thoroughly. Her clenched teeth had no effect on him whatsoever; continuing to kiss her, he held her in a heated embrace, making her sweat from the fire in his desire. Though she wanted to fight him off, Sambrea had no strength left. Just a glance from him caused her to go weak in the knees. If she continued to resist him, Sambrea rather suspected he'd grow even more determined to have things his way. She had an inkling that he always got what he was after.

Neptune was located in the Pacific Beach Hotel, and dining there was like having a romantic rendezvous beneath the sea. The lovely restaurant served delicious Continental cuisine and excellent seafood and offered a spectacular view of the fabulous 280,000 gallon three-story Oceanarium.

The uniformed waitress stood by patiently, ready to serve them. The young Hawaiian woman smiled in a friendly way before politely requesting their orders.

Sambrea hadn't spoken a word during the short drive to the restaurant. It didn't appear that anything was going to change now.

Noticing the waitress looking at him with a puzzled expression, Craig chuckled inwardly. "Sorry, miss, but she can't hear or respond to you. She's a deaf-mute." He kept his face totally straight. "I know everything she likes. I always order for her."

The waitress smiled sympathetically.

Making a liar out of Craig, Sambrea jumped up from her seat. "He's lying," she shouted. "He brought me here against my will. Please get some help." Sambrea giggled inside. Well, at least she'd told part of the truth. Craig *had* brought her there against her will.

The waitress didn't seem to know what to do; she stood there looking stunned. Sambrea suddenly felt bad, groaning in dismay as the waitress took off, running toward the kitchen area.

Sambrea was still cracking up at the look on Craig's face when the manager, who seemed to exercise extreme caution, approached the table. As the burly man stopped in front of their seating area, she looked up at him and smiled sheepishly.

Clearing her throat, Sambrea stood up and put her hand on the stout man's shoulder. "Sorry, sir, but this was all a bad joke. In very bad taste, I might add. I now realize it wasn't very funny. I shouldn't have upset your waitress like that. I hope you and your staff can forgive me and my charming companion."

The stout man scowled heavily. "*We* can forgive you. As for the cops, that's an entirely different matter. If you ever pull something like this in my restaurant again, I won't hesitate to call the police and have you removed from the premises. This is a very popular restaurant. Our patrons hold our staff to very high standards here at Neptune, just as we do our patrons."

Examining his name tag, Sambrea looked abashed. "I'm really sorry, Mr. Rogers. It won't happen again." Mr. Rogers grunted loudly with disapproval and walked away. Sambrea sat back down. "Looks like we got ourselves into one hell of a mess."

Craig shrugged his shoulders. "So, it's *we* now. *We* didn't do anything. You got yourself into this fine mess all by your lonesome. You made the waitress think I kidnapped you. That was a serious joke you played there, Sam. But you might enjoy being handcuffed by the police since you seem to be wild for crazy stunts."

Sambrea's eyes clouded with indignation. "Look who's talking. But that's okay. I handled it," she said haughtily. "I'd better go to the bathroom before the waitress comes back. I don't want to have a nervous accident. The menacing Mr. Rogers has left me a little shaken."

Craig grinned. *Ah, Sambrea, you are quite a handful, quite an intriguing challenge.*

Smiling to herself, she walked to the back of the restaurant, where she used the payphone to call a cab. She figured that Craig was probably still smoothing things over as she slipped out the front door. Once outside, she immediately howled out loud.

A smug smile was still on her lips as she let herself into the bungalow. She'd had fleeting moments of guilt, but when she thought of how much Craig had deserved it, she unloaded the unattractive burden with ease, heeding Craig's advice in the process.

Heading right for the bathroom, Sambrea changed into a swimsuit and a loose, flowing cover-up. Wishing she'd eaten first, *at Craig's expense,* she left the bathroom and went into the kitchen, where she prepared a tuna sandwich and a garden salad.

As she carried her meal into the living room, she heard the loud pounding of fists on the front door. She had no doubt that the banging came from Craig's powerful hands.

Opening the door, Sambrea greeted him with the sweetest smile. He was totally unprepared for that. "Hello." Her melodious tone completely dismantled his raging anger. "I've been expecting you," she said, then added under her breath, "I was hoping you'd get the hint and stay far, far away from me."

If he'd heard her, he didn't attempt a counter-attack, but stared at her incredulously. "I'll just bet you were! Why did you leave the restaurant like that, Sam? You made me look like a damn fool."

Stifling the laugher within, she lowered her lashes. "I'm truly sorry, Craig, but I had to get out of there. I was suffocating in your presence." Moving away from the door, she went into the living room and sat down on the sofa.

Following behind her, he dropped down close beside her. Another shock wave registered in his loins from being so near her, yet he found her closeness made him feel almost tranquil. "Suffocating? That was a heavy statement, Sam. Now will you please explain it?"

She shook her head. "I'm afraid I can't explain. I just can't seem to breathe when you're around, especially when you seem to enjoy making such a damn fool of me. You've done nothing but make me a fool from the moment we met, Craig Caldwell. Can't seem to forgive you for that."

So rueful was her attitude, he found it odd—especially for someone with so much spunk. The fact that there hadn't been any inflection whatsoever in the tone of her voice disturbed him a lot.

He draped his arm around her shoulder. Craig kept quiet for several moments as he studied her face. "I can't make you forgive me, nor can I make you believe me, Sam. But there's really nothing to forgive. I'm not guilty of anything. What I told you earlier was the truth. When we were together last night, I didn't know you were the owner of De La Brise."

She sighed with discontent. Did it really matter to him what she believed? Why should it matter? So far, everything had gone his way—and still was. "I'd like to go to bed now, Craig. I'm not capable of staying up much longer. I have to rest so I'll have enough energy to think about what's happening to me and De La Brise." She looked as dejected as she felt.

He brought her into his arms. "Oh, Sambrea, don't do this. Don't look at me like that. Everything is going to be just fine for you and the company. I promise."

As a strangled cry ripped from her throat, he felt an immeasurable amount of grief. A woman's cries had never before disturbed him so deeply, but these cries were quite different from any he'd ever heard before. These were Sambrea's cries—and he was indirectly responsible for them. Even though she thought him to be directly responsible for all her anguish.

Lodging her deeper within the comfort zone of his muscled arms, Craig stroked her hair and back as she sobbed brokenly. The magnetism of her lips drew his closer and he kissed her in a way that set her mouth on fire. As the fire spread to the rest of her body, Sambrea once again found herself helplessly caught up in his fantasy world, a fantasy world from which she had no intention of trying to escape.

Caressing the heat of her passion, Craig slowly peeled away the cover-up, surprised to find a wisp of a swimsuit underneath it. As a crazy, wild idea came to mind, he grinned.

With her head snuggled into his chest, he lifted her and carried her out to the beach. At the moment Sambrea didn't care what he did with her, as long as he made her feel the same way he'd made her feel the previous night. Even if he was going to drown her afterward, she wasn't going to offer any resistance.

Stripping down to his underwear, Craig carried her into the surf. Holding her tightly against his body, he effortlessly cut through the billowing waters. The ocean received them, then seemed to swallow them up. Sambrea wrapped her legs high around his waist as the waves bobbed up and down beneath them. Instantly, their movements became frantic. As they kissed and caressed each other, he stroked her legs and thighs. Then his hand reached down inside her bikini. Tenderly, his hand came to rest inside the blossoming flower of her intimate secret. As a large wave washed them ashore, he reached for his pants and removed protection from his wallet.

They made sensuous love in the shallow water, the surf gently lapping against their entwined bodies. Oblivious to the scratchy sand that was now their hot bed of pleasure, Craig fulfilled his fantasy. Feeling less shame than she'd felt before they'd actually made love, Sambrea snuggled her head into the crook of Craig's arm. She'd never felt such contentment.

After dusting the sand off her shoulders, his arm fell

across her back, squeezing her tight. "Are you having any regrets, Sam?" His tone was husky with passion.

"Not yet. And knowing me, I probably won't. After all, we're both consenting adults." *No, no regrets at all.*

"Are you having a hard time breathing, Sam?"

Looking up at him, she saw the mischievous twinkle in his midnight eyes. "I'm breathing just fine, Mr. Caldwell. But just give them time."

"Give what time?"

She laughed. "My allergies, of course. I'm seriously allergic to you, Craig. You come on me all of a sudden and then disappear without warning, the same as my allergies. Oddly enough, I haven't found a cure for them either."

He kissed her full on the mouth. "I may have come on you all of a sudden, but I don't think I'll be disappearing again. That is, not without a warning." He got to his feet, brushing the sand off his body. "Come on, Sam, we're going to bed. This entire day and night you've been putting me through an obstacle course I'm not sure I'll ever recover from." He gathered her into his arms. "May I spend the night in your bed?"

His question stunned her, yet excitement stirred in her breasts. "I don't think you should, Craig. Can't you see that we've really made this thing between us complicated? I can't love you in the bedroom and fight you in the boardroom. That won't work for me. If you stop and think about it, I don't think it will work for you, either."

"Who says it has to be that way? Sam, De La Brise is very vulnerable right now. Until I can find out what's going on, I can't withdraw. I won't withdraw. If I do, you could find yourself in major trouble. There's a simple way to settle this, Sam. That is, if you're willing."

"What would that be, Craig?"

"If we merge, Sam."

"Merge? As in joining our companies together?"

"Exactly. Though I had a little more than that in mind."

"Like what?"

"Like us getting married, Sambrea."

Of course he's joking, she thought fearfully. Marriage to Craig Caldwell would be insufferable. *Wouldn't it be? Marriage to anyone would be insufferable.* Just the thought of how strained her parents' marriage had been was enough to keep her forever single.

"Sorry, Craig. Marriage is not in my past, my present, nor is it in my future. Spinster-hood is much more appealing than the institution of matrimony. I don't want to live with someone I might possibly come to hate."

Jumping up from the sand, she quickly slipped into her cover-up. Taking off at breakneck speed, without looking back, she ran toward the bungalow and away from the man she more than desired. Craig had stirred something up inside of her, something she just couldn't face: the prospect of marriage. Not today, not tomorrow, not ever.

Having no strength to go after her, all Craig could do was watch her panicked flight. Sambrea had drained him physically and emotionally. What was it about her that made him want to protect her, to be with her at all costs, to have her in plain sight through every waking moment, to want to spend eternity with her? He didn't know for sure, but vowed to find out.

As though she could hear Craig's thoughts, she turned back to look at him, not really expecting him to be there. But he was, every granite-hard inch of him. She'd spent the most erotic moments of her life with him—and now she ached for more time in his fantasy world. Time to touch him, to kiss him, to have him fill the hollow in her mind, the void in her soul. To have him entombed in her body again and again. Needing nothing more to convince her, she yielded to her strong desire to have him possess her completely as she turned around and ran toward him.

With his eyes piercing into the dark at the vision of beauty floating his way, he sat up, hoping she was running to him and into his lonely arms. Landing on top of him, she pushed him back in the sand. He felt a powerful rush of love and warmth. He felt complete.

Holding on to her in desperation, Craig pressed his body in to hers with an urgency he'd never before experienced. His desperate need for her momentarily frightened him, as all the answers to his questions became crystal clear—so clear he could almost see his feelings etched on the air. He was crazy in love with Sambrea Sinclair. The stunning revelation felt wonderful and awesome—it also had his body shaking atop the sand beneath him.

The pleasure she felt was immeasurable as his mouth opened to surround a bronzed nipple, his fingers branding her creamy flesh with sizzling caresses. Having him pressing against her with such urgency made her want to devour his nakedness. He felt the softness of her hands as they gently massaged his manhood with an earth-shattering tenderness, working him into an ardent frenzy.

"Sam . . . Sambrea, I'm so glad you came back. I missed you, beautiful . . ."

Her wet kisses cut the line of verbal communication, yet she continued to communicate in so many other delicious ways. They were so tightly meshed together, even the small ripple-like waves couldn't invade the minute space between them. Sand was everywhere, in their hair, their mouths, and all over their nude bodies, but they didn't seem to notice or care. Nothing could deny them the exquisite pleasures that were theirs for the taking as he once again reached for his wallet.

Rolling her onto her back, he swept her nudity with midnight eyes. "Marriage to me would be wonderful. I'd be faithful to you. No one will ever love you the way I know I can."

"Can?" He hadn't said *"the way I do."* It wasn't possible for him to love her. He didn't even know her. "It's not open

for discussion, Craig. Tonight is ours. Tomorrow belongs to no one," she whispered softly against his parted lips.

He agreed that she was right about this night being theirs, but he wasn't ever going to concede the issue of tomorrow. Tomorrow was not promised, but should it come, he wanted to awaken alongside her, taking whatever part of her day she was willing to give him. After gathering up their clothing, Craig and Sambrea trudged through the sand, with his arm firmly planted around her slender waist.

In her bed, he stayed. In her arms, he slept.

Craig awakened with the sunrise. Finding himself all alone wasn't what he'd planned on. Dread filled him as he searched the bungalow for her. Realizing she was gone disappointed him bitterly. Hoping she was just out for a morning swim, he ran to the window. Looking up and down the seascape, he saw that the beach was devoid of human life.

Seagulls and other winged creatures swooped down on the shores, but Sambrea was nowhere to be seen. While watching the resident creatures dive and forage for food, he realized he was hungry, too, hungry for the taste and feel of Sambrea, hungry for the woman who filled him up from head to toe. Why wasn't she there to feed him? Why wasn't she there to further entice his voracious appetite, an appetite only she could satisfy? Why hadn't she conceded to forever with him? Hoping and praying she'd suddenly appear, he continued to stare out the window.

When his thoughts turned to the moment when he'd first discovered he loved her, he couldn't keep himself from smiling. Although the moment had caused him to tremble, he couldn't forget the undeniable peace that had also washed through his soul.

With her arms full of white bags, Sambrea stood outside

the bungalow. Using the tip of her shoe, she kicked lightly at the door, hoping Craig wasn't still asleep.

In the bedroom dressing, Craig had just about given up on Sambrea returning when he thought he heard sounds coming from outside the door. In his haste to respond to the noise, he nearly tripped on one of the throw rugs as he ran back toward the front of the bungalow.

Without further delay, he threw open the door. A brilliant smile deepened the midnight magic in his eyes when he saw Sambrea. A sigh of relief escaped his lips, voiding out the unpleasant feelings he'd had when he thought she'd run away from him again.

Mesmerized by his smile, Sambrea nearly dropped the bags she held in her arms. "It's about time," she scolded playfully. "I thought you'd never answer the door."

He reached for her cargo. "Here, let me help you with these. What have you got here, anyway?"

She sniffed one of the bags. "Doughnuts, cheese croissants, and steaming hot coffee. Smell." She lifted one of the bags to his nose.

He inhaled deeply. "Smells great, Sam. Where did you get all the goodies?"

She headed for the kitchen. "There's a small coffee shop right down the beach. It's called Morning Glory. I can't believe you live in the neighborhood and don't know about our favorite haunt. All the locals gather there."

Seated at the table, Craig accepted a rather large croissant from Sambrea. "I'm rarely around here in the mornings. I'm usually on the way to my office before the sun comes up and I'm out of town a good bit of the time." He took a bite of the freshly baked bread. "I only lurk on the beach on the nights I see you out there alone. I come out to make sure you stay safe."

She raised an eyebrow. "You mean you've actually followed me up and down the beach?" Thinking about all the times she'd swum in the buff, she felt the color rise in her cheeks.

Taking another bite of the croissant, he nodded. "Too many times to count. I always kept a safe distance. I didn't want to frighten you."

Sambrea studied him over the rim of her coffee cup. "What made you finally decide to approach me?"

Taking the cup from her hand, he took a sip of her coffee. "For one, the local news about break-ins in the community. As I mentioned to you that first night, a local female resident was sexually assaulted on the beach. I wasn't going to take any chances of that happening to you. You were my neighbor, my fantasy. I wasn't about to let you become the victim of a woman's worst nightmare."

Smiling wryly, she eyed him intently. "So you decided to make me a victim of your fantasy instead of allowing me to fall victim to a depraved predator? What's the difference between you making me a victim of your fantasies versus my becoming the victim of a rapist?"

Craig stood and pulled her up from the seat. Taking her by one hand, he led her into the living room and sat down on the sofa. Mindful of the cup of hot coffee she held he took it from her hand and pulled her down beside him. Stilling his desire to kiss her, he touched her cheek with the back of his hand. "Girl, if you have to ask me a question like that, I guess I haven't done such a good job at showing you the difference. However, I'm going to try and answer your question."

His eyes grew troubled. "I thought we'd already agreed that whatever we've done on the beach was by mutual consent. Since we've been together constantly, I'm puzzled. Have I been wrong in assuming that you and I came together because we wanted and needed each other? It even goes much deeper than that for me."

Her expression softened. "Oh, Craig, I'm sorry. That was an insensitive question. In no way do I think that you're a man capable of taking a woman against her will. You're right in your assumptions, but I can't explain why I gave myself up to the madness. All I can tell you is that I wanted you as much as you did me. It's the craziest thing I've ever done in my life. I pray to God that I don't do anything to try and top it."

Momentarily, he lost himself in his memories of the night. He could almost feel Sambrea beneath him, caressing him where he constantly burned like fire for her. In his mind, he was again tasting her where she'd never been tasted before.

Blowing into his ear, Sambrea brought him back to h with a start. "Is sex all there is between us, Craig?"

Looking deep into her eyes, he ran his thumb across lower lip. "Not at all, Sam. What's between us is wit' description. It's more complicated than anything you an could ever begin to figure out. If I were to try and define it, I'd start with the word *destiny*. Meaning: karma, inevitability, fate, predetermined. That's only the start of what's between us, Sambrea. It's not within our power to control it, or to stop what's happening between us. You and I would only be fooling ourselves if we somehow thought we could."

Awestruck, she stared at him. "Where do you come from? Do you rule over a kingdom at the bottom of the ocean? It's almost like you have some sort of magical powers over me. I felt your awesome powers the moment our eyes met. That alone scares me to death, Craig."

Craig chuckled, wrapping a strand of her hair around his finger. "Your majesty, you have those same magical powers over me. Where do you come from?"

Sambrea shook her head. "I honestly don't know anymore. Not only do I not know where I came from, I don't know where I'm going. I feel so lost at times."

He rested her head on his shoulder. "In that case, you need me to guide you. With me, you'll never feel lost. I will not lead you astray, I can promise you that. Will you follow me, Sam?"

To the ends of the earth. She breathed in deeply as his fathomless smile sailed beneath the surface of her heart. "I don't know. It's something I need to give much thought to." She only wished that she could voice her true feelings.

"Give it as much thought as you need to. But remember this, we are destined for oneness. If you don't believe me, ask your Higher Power. I'm coming back here tonight so you and I can figure out which prerequisites to take to master our destiny, my fair lady."

She jumped to her feet as he stood up. "Are you leaving now? You haven't finished your breakfast." She couldn't explain it, but she didn't want to let him go. The magical aura surrounding Craig caused her to do the absolutely unthinkable. As crazy as it seemed, he had somehow managed to consume all her power. That much she was certain of.

His hunger for her ravenous, he kissed her on the mouth. "You're all the breakfast I need, Sam. I'll stay awhile longer if you want me to. That's what you really want, isn't it, Sam? Do you want me here with you? Tell me now, Sam."

Tears pooled in her sand-and-sable eyes. "Yes."

FOUR

Just as the doorbell pealed Sambrea stole one last glance at her reflection in the mirror. Loving the way the cobalt-blue dress embraced her slender figure, she smiled. Luxuriously soft, the silk dress flowed gently about her waist and swirled loosely above her knees.

As the doorbell pealed again, she dashed out of the bedroom and into the foyer, taking a deep breath before opening the door to the man who stood on the other side, the gorgeous man with the magic powers and magical eyes. Looking good enough for her to devour on the spot, Craig wore impeccably pressed dark slacks and a heather-gray banded-collar shirt. Done in mixed stitches of black and gray on fine linen, a casual sports coat hung on one of his slender fingers. In the other hand, he held a beautiful bouquet of colorful flowers.

Stepping inside, Craig held the bouquet out for her to take. "These are for you, but I'm afraid I couldn't find a single blossom to match your beauty. I hope these will do until I can search the island over. Though I doubt there's a flower in existence that's as lovely as you."

Sambrea's breath caught in her throat, his poetic words deeply touching her soul. The flowers were magnificent, but not nearly as magnificent as the smile Craig cast her way. Craig was suave as could be, but she had to admit, he always came across as sincere.

"Craig, I've never seen more beautiful flowers." Leading him by the hand into the living room, she looked closely at the pretty blooms as they sat down on the sofa. "These aren't florist flowers. You've handpicked these somewhere, but where? You could get arrested for plucking them from a public place, you know."

He grinned at her, sticking his nose inside one of the delicate blooms. The sweet odor tantalized him, but it couldn't compete with Sambrea's engaging scent, especially when she wore no perfume at all. Sambrea's natural fragrances, fresh as spring's morning aromas, captivated him in so many inconceivable ways.

Taking the flowers from her hand, he placed the bouquet on the coffee table. *"From where* she has asked. What if I told you I grew them myself?"

She laughed from deep within. "**I wouldn't** believe you."

He gave a slight shrug of his shoulders. "I thought so. Will you apologize for calling me a liar if I can show you proof?"

Her lips curved into a slight smile. "You, a gardener! I would've never guessed it." *This* man *is truly amazing.* She cast a bright smile his way.

He kissed her gently on the lips. "I don't know why not. Haven't I tended to you like the sweetly scented flower that you are? However, a wildflower can survive without any nurturing from man. It only needs that which it receives from nature. Nature has showered you with extreme care, Sambrea Sinclair. You're the loveliest wildflower of all." He was so charming. If she hadn't been sitting, she would've swooned at his feet. She'd already come close to falling off the end of the sofa. Craig's poetic spirit seemed to keep her on the edge of her seat.

She exhaled a shaky breath. "I don't know about you, Craig Caldwell. You're some charmer, buddy. Are you like this with all the women?"

"Let me think about that while I put on some mood music. What about some Barry White?"

Sambrea's eyes widened. "Barry belts out a little more than mood music. The man is a master of seduction. Is it in your plans to seduce me?"

He gave both of her questions some thought as he turned on the stereo. Sitting much closer to her than he had been, he looked into her eyes. "Let's discuss your first question, Sam. Does it matter to you what I've done with other women?" He watched closely for her reaction just as the track "Don't You Want To Know" rustled into the room like autumn leaves blowing in the wind.

Feeling larger than normal, her ego surfaced. "I could care less what you've done with other women," she spouted off, wishing that particular Barry White track hadn't come on. She *did* want to know. She wanted to know everything he was willing to divulge about himself, and all that he wasn't willing to tell.

"That's interesting, especially since you initiated this conversation. I guess you didn't think before you spoke. You're good at that. At any rate, I'm going to answer you. There have been many women in and out of my life, but never has there been a woman that makes me crazy with desire. Nor has there ever been a woman I'd be willing to sell my soul to the devil for."

He kissed the side of her neck. "I pray that the woman of my most basic desires, of my strongest emotions won't force me into taking such drastic measures. I wouldn't want to ever offend the Creator I deeply believe in. Do you have any idea who that particular woman might be, Sambrea? Do you have any idea who creates the thunder in my heart when I'm with her and the rain in my eyes when we're apart?"

Unable to tear her gaze from the midnight eyes possessing her soul, Sambrea swallowed hard. She trembled as he stood up and pulled her to her feet. Guiding her to the middle of the floor, he took her in his arms. "You don't have to answer that." He was amazed by the undeniable love he felt for this woman he held. "We both know the woman is you." Drawing her in closer, he kissed her on each temple.

At a complete loss for words, she followed his lead. As he began moving slowly with the music, his hips oscillated slightly against hers, making sweat form between her thighs. As Barry crooned "There It Is," they fell under the spell of the hypnotic voice of the *maestro of love.*

He tilted her head back. "Do you still want to know if it's in my plans to seduce you?" Without giving her the chance to respond, he drew her lower lip between his teeth and sucked it gently. The sweet taste of her drove him insane, but he managed to keep himself in check.

Closing his eyes, he hummed "Baby's Home" along with Barry. As his fingers brushed her lips, she drew his forefinger into her mouth. Involuntarily, her eyes closed, too, just as he replaced his finger with his tongue.

Dancing to "Sexy Undercover," Sambrea's alluring moves caused his loins to ache. She was a great dancer, moving through the latest dance moves with ease. But he was glad when the "Time Is Right" came thundering from the speakers. Though it had a more funky, upbeat tempo, he pulled her into his arms, as though it were a slow song.

Laughing at his serious expression, she threw her hands up in protest. "I want to dance this one out. I can't get my groove on when you hold me this close."

His arms tightened around her waist. "You can do all the same moves right here in my arms. That way, I can feel all those sexy moves right where I need to feel them. Work it, girl. Work me into a frenzy."

Later, as they fell into a heap on the sofa, Sambrea couldn't stop giggling.

Emotionally full, Craig watched as she licked her lips without giving any thought to the type of effect that it might have on him. Though his physical needs urged him to take her to bed now, he fought hard to win the battle his body was waging against him.

"Are you thirsty, Sam?" As she licked her lips again, he almost conceded the battle to his aching need.

"I am, a little. There's some raspberry tea in the refrigerator. Want some?"

He pulled her up from the sofa. "Let's go into the kitchen. I hope you got something good to munch on. I'm hungry."

In the kitchen she opened two of the oak cabinets to give him the opportunity to inventory the shelves. While he scoped out the snack choices, she removed two tall glasses from another shelf and took the pitcher of recently brewed raspberry tea from the refrigerator.

A box of Ritz crackers caught his eye. Then he spotted an unopened jar of Cheese Whiz, two of his favorite snacks. Adding a can of tuna to his snack menu, he pulled a chair out from the table and sat down.

Sambrea stood over his chair. "Want some salad dressing for your tuna? I also have some whole-wheat bread."

"Just a can-opener. I like to eat my tuna dry, thank you." Pulling a face, Sambrea picked up the can of tuna and took it over to the sink. After opening the can with the electric can-opener, she took it back to Craig.

He stood up and pulled a chair out for her, kissing her before she sat down. Lifting the pitcher with one hand, he poured the cold liquid into the two ice-filled glasses and placed one in front of Sambrea as he sat back down. "Aren't you going to eat anything, Sam? It's getting late."

She pushed her hair back from her face. "I'm really not all that hungry, but I should eat a little something. I have a tendency to get faint when I go without eating for too long."

"We can't have that." Spreading a generous amount of cheese on a cracker, he held it up to her mouth. The bite she took was less than what a bird might manage to consume. He was amused by it. "Are you trying to preserve that dangerous figure of yours?"

She smiled at him. "Are you kidding? I normally eat like a horse. My father used to say my gluttonous appetite would catch up with me one day, but I don't think so. Now that I'm older and wiser I eat healthier foods. Lots of them. I'm a raw vegetable lover."

"You do look pretty healthy, Sam. I indulge in junk foods now and then. Like you, for the most part, I eat healthy. I also workout two hours every day in my gym at home." He looked at her thoughtfully. "Tell me something. How is it that your father ended up living in Hawaii? There are very few blacks settled here with the exception of those who are active duty or retired military members."

"There's more blacks here than you think. My father's great-great-grandfather, a native of the Caribbean island of Martinique, was a merchant marine. He settled here in the early 1900's. Back then he started a small island to island transport business. His small boat carried goods and some heavy equipment between the islands. The business grew and was passed down from generation to generation. As an only child, my father inherited it from his father, but he decided to change things. Instead of carrying goods and equipment, he decided to carry people wanting to be catered to. Sunset dinner cruises appealed to his romantic nature. Speaking of black men settling in Hawaii, what's your story? I'm pretty sure you're not a native, as I am."

He frowned. "It's a long one. I'll tell you about it someday." He looked as though he'd rather discuss anything but his reasons for coming to Hawaii. The reticent look on his face wasn't lost on Sambrea. "Do you know the history of your island, native girl?"

"I know enough. Would you like to hear some of it?"

He grinned lazily. "As much as you'd like to share."

She pulled out another chair and propped her feet up on it. "Let's see," she began. "I wasn't born on Oahu. I was born and raised on Maui. We moved here when my father decided to relocate the offices of De La Brise a few years back. In the early 1790s Kamehameha the Great trapped the defending army of the Maui King in Iao Valley, which was without an exit. Slaughtering the army, he sealed his dominion over the island, ruling the unified islands from 1803 to 1811. Kamehameha was sort of the first developer. At 728 square miles, Maui is the second largest island, noted for sugar cane, pineapple, cattle, and many other resources—natural and otherwise."

Craig applauded with enthusiasm. "Nicely done."

"Now that you know I'm somewhat educated in the history of my island, what about you? What world are you a native of, Craig?"

Craig stroked his chin. "The world is a native of me, Sam. The entire world was built on the backs of men like myself. Contrary to what people like to believe, slaves came in every color, race and creed, Sam. Among them were Africans, Egyptians, and Chinese, just to name a few. Slavery still exists in many cultures. Tyranny is still alive and well in the world, my beautiful island girl."

With deep admiration burning in her eyes, Sambrea placed her hand over his. "You're so wise, Craig. I admire you for that, but I'd still like an answer to my question. Where did you live before you moved to Hawaii? Or is that question too difficult for you to answer? I'm into direct approaches, you know."

His dark eyes flared intensely, burning a trail into her soul. "Nothing is too difficult for me, Sambrea, simply because I rely on a power much greater than myself. In tune with divine guidance, I'm the sort of man who never sits around and waits for things to happen. I make things happen. I've lived all over the world, Sambrea, but I moved here from New York."

His response surprised her. "I never would've guessed

that either. I don't hear that distinct New York accent at all when you speak. Were you there long?"

"Long enough." Popping a whole cracker into his mouth, he eyed Sambrea with curiosity. Quickly, he chewed and swallowed the salty snack.

The look she gave him was fraught with impatience. "Long enough for what, Craig Caldwell? And please be a little more specific."

"To do what I do best. Once I get what I'm after, I move on. I'm not one to put down roots for very long."

Fear invaded her entire body. "I see. But I find that strange. You own a house here, you claim to be a gardener of some sort, you have offices here—and you're trying to acquire other financial holdings based here, my company for one. Is that not putting down roots?"

Winking one midnight eye at her, he pursed his lips. "Not necessarily. It's not unusual for a man of my means to have more than one home, or to have offices in other parts of the world, as well as other financial holdings. As for the gardening, I love to be surrounded by beautiful things. You should've at least figured the last one out."

She felt herself blush. "I can see I'm not going to get much information out of you. For some reason or another, you don't seem to want to talk about yourself. Normally, when people refuse to talk about themselves, there's probably nothing about them worth mentioning. Or perhaps they have something to hide. Which category do you fall in, Craig? My father would've had you figured by now."

"I'm not a man that can be easily categorized, Sam. What about your mother? I haven't heard you mention her." Purposely, he once again made her the topic of discussion.

Sambrea stood up and began to clear the table. "It's a long story. I'll tell you about it one day," she shot back with indignation.

Turning her back to him, she walked over to the refrigerator and put the tea away. Discreetly, she swiped at the tears forming in the corners of her eyes. The subject of her mother was a sore one, one that had left her heart with a gaping, unhealed wound.

Breeze Sinclair had mysteriously disappeared from their home three years prior to Samuel's death. Sambrea was sixteen when her mother disappeared without a trace. It still wasn't known if Breeze Sinclair was dead or alive, Sambrea reflected. Breeze had been a very beautiful and stylish woman. She'd had exquisite taste in clothing and jewels. Everything about Breeze had been about the Sinclair wealth. Unfortunately, material possessions had meant more to her than her husband and daughter, Sambrea mused painfully. Breeze had often flown to Europe for extravagant shopping sprees, leaving a young Sambrea in the care of Samuel and anyone else willing to take over her responsibility to her child.

Samuel was able to afford the best care for Sambrea, but he felt that no one could care for his bundle of precious cargo better than he could. Fondly, Sambrea remembered him taking her everywhere he went and how much they'd doted on one another. When Sambrea grew older, she recalled how she and Breeze used to get into heated debates over Breeze's frequent absences. Sambrea's pleas had done nothing to alter things, yet she loved Breeze in spite of everything.

Though deep in thought over the response that echoed his own, Craig saw her hand go up to her eyes. Instinctively, he knew the subject of her mother had somehow injured her. *But why? Why had asking about her mother caused her pain?*

Getting up from the chair, he made his way across the room, where she stood stock still with her back to him. Pinning her against the refrigerator with his body, he used his nose to nuzzle the back of her neck. "Why are you crying, Sambrea?"

So much for discretion. "Who says I'm crying? I'm just tired and my eyes are burning from fatigue."

Deciding not to trespass on her private issues for now, he nibbled at her ear. "Do you want me to go home so you can go to bed? I rather thought we'd take a midnight swim together. That is your nightly ritual, isn't it, my beautiful Nereid?"

"Nereid?" She turned around to face him. "What does that actually mean, Mr. C?"

He smiled into her crystal eyes. "It means *Goddess of Nature.* It's the same as calling you my sea nymph. Neptune is one of many gods that's referred to as a sea god. But you and I know who the *real* God of the Sea is." He kissed the side of her ear. "Shall we go outside and create our own mysteries of the deep?"

Turning her around, he slid the zipper down on her dress, his breath catching when he saw that she wore nothing beneath the dress but a scanty piece of lace masquerading as underwear. Thongs had more material in them than what Sambrea wore. He hoped that she didn't go anywhere other than the beach dressed like that. If she got in a traffic accident—God forbid. He thought about the sanity of the male paramedics that might have to come to her rescue. Then he remembered that Sambrea swam in the nude. What she wore beneath her clothing, or didn't wear, revealed a woman who was totally uninhibited, a woman who wasn't ashamed to bare her intimate essentials.

Trying to locate his voice, he cleared his throat. "Should I get a couple of towels for us?"

Helpless against his dangerous allure, she found herself tugging at his fine leather belt. "Now that you know what I wear under my attire, I want to see what you have on under yours," she flirted shamelessly.

He removed her hand from his belt. "Not so fast, there, my lady. If you want to see what I have on under my clothes, you'll have to win the privilege. Got a deck of cards?"

"A deck of cards? What for?"

"A quick game of strip poker will stimulate us before we fire up the ocean, Sam."

She looked down at her golden brown body. "I'm practically standing here in the buff, and you're talking about stimulation? Either you're blind or impotent. Perhaps both," she charged with insolence.

Giving her one long, sexy look, Craig narrowed his eyes. "I think we both know I'm not impotent. If you're still not sure, come here and feel for yourself."

She declined the tempting invitation.

"Nor am I blind. I simply wanted to make you burn with yearning since you've already cast me into the incinerator of your burning sexuality. I just thought you should join me."

She shrugged her shoulders. "Oh, well, you stay in here and play strip poker with yourself. The sea has been making love to me a lot longer than you have." She ran off toward the bedroom. "For sure, it's not going to disappear with the sunrise," she taunted.

In a matter of seconds he came up behind her, just as she tied a full sarong around her body. "Is that an invitation for me to spend the morning-after in your bed?" He pulled her into his growing need.

"I refuse to incriminate myself." She broke his hold on her. Before he could pull her back into his arms, she was out the front door.

Running to the window, Craig watched as she ran like the wind. As the moonbeams raced through her sable hair, his eyes grew bright with moisture. As she undid the sarong and dropped it to the sand, he felt the front of his pants tighten. Watching her playing chicken with the surf, his heart grew as full as his eyes.

Unable to be away from her engaging warmth a second longer, he stripped down to the black jockey briefs he wore beneath his slacks. He'd wanted Sambrea to have the pleasure of removing them, but he'd played the wrong cards, figuratively speaking. Unfortunately for him, the idea of strip poker hadn't gone over very big with her.

Wanting him beside her, she came out of the ocean. Starting up the beach, she looked toward the bungalow. When the front door flew open, she smiled. *So he wears briefs.* She chuckled inwardly. *What a fabulous body.* As he ran toward her, his silky curls danced to the rhythm of the lightly gusting trade winds.

"Sambrea," he called out as he grew closer, "I'll race you into the surf. Take advantage of the lead you have. You're going to need it." He had changed his tone with the intent to intimidate.

The wind whipped her hair around her face as her legs carried her across the sand with lightning speed. Craig hadn't expected such quickness from her. He wished he hadn't given her the advantage, especially since he hadn't been able to overtake her yet. Laughing into the wind, he tried his best to catch up. When he was just a few feet away from her, Sambrea dove into the surf. As her head resurfaced, he heard her victorious laughter ring out over the water.

Just across the Pacific, on the island of Maui, Sambrea was stretched out comfortably on a colorful chaise lounge. As the blue waters gleamed under the early morning sun, the reflection was nearly as blinding as the tears swimming in her eyes.

She couldn't stop thinking of Craig Caldwell. He'd promised not to disappear on her, but she hadn't been brave enough to return the favor. Awakening at four in the morning, after one of the most romantic nights of her life, getting away from his smothering presence had been uppermost in her mind. When he was around, her own mind, body, and soul seemed to become her adversaries. Everything she thought she was rebelled against her when in close proximity to him. Distance was the only way to combat that rebellion. She'd even considered taking him up on his offer of marriage; as she recovered from a bout of temporary insanity, she knew that was the most asinine thing she'd ever considered.

Craig Caldwell had already enlightened her to the fact he didn't put down roots, which, in her opinion, made him a man who couldn't easily settle into matrimony. At least not with someone he'd just met and had already had his way with. Did he really want her? Or had his designs on De La Brise made him a willing candidate for a marriage of convenience? Would he really go as far as to enter into the bonds of marriage just to get her company?

Once he got his hands on her company, he'd move on. Just like he'd said, he never stayed in one place too long. The marriage would end in a quickie annulment. A worldly, debonair man like Craig Caldwell could never be satisfied with an unsophisticated woman like herself. Craig Caldwell defied the description of worldliness. He was so much more than just worldly. This man was the epitome of everything she thought a man should be.

Sambrea knew that most of her peers considered her a worldly woman, but her life was totally unsophisticated compared to the extravagant and insidious ways of those who moved around in the puissant circles of wealth and position. True, she'd had plenty of exposure to the finest things life had to offer, but Samuel had kept her sheltered from the unscrupulous practices of those living a fast-paced lifestyle. However, she'd seen more deception than he would've liked right in their very own home.

She thought of the many nights she'd heard Samuel begging Breeze to stay at home with her family. Breeze would refuse and a heated argument would ensue. It always ended with Breeze walking out on him. She'd stay away from home for days and sometimes weeks at a time. Because she stayed away so much she wasn't seriously considered missing for over a month. When she was at home, she often entertained handsome males much younger than herself. Breeze and Samuel had also had a bitter argument the day of her disappearance.

Picking up some financial statements she'd had Joe fax to her from the office, she read them over and over. But she understood very little of what she read. A bookkeeper she wasn't, but she didn't need to be since there was a complete staff of accountants at her disposal. Until now, she'd never questioned their abilities or loyalties where the company was concerned. With his detective-like probing, Craig had somehow placed doubt in her.

Feeling slightly irritated with herself, Sambrea slammed the folder shut and placed it back on the table. What was she going to do now? How could she do anything lying flat on her tail in Maui? Should she have let Craig investigate something that had nothing to do with him?

Yes, she'd done the right thing, she decided. For now, De La Brise needed to exploit his expertise. She needed to use him just as he'd used her, she told herself, bitterly justifying her actions in her mind.

FIVE

Shivering at the sudden and unexpected chill hanging in the air, a cold, tingling sensation running up and down her spine, Sambrea looked up to see what had blocked the sun from her body. Looking horrified, her mouth formed a scream but nothing came out. Silent screams pounded in her head, but there was nothing she could do to quiet them. Her mouth suddenly felt dry as cotton as she breathed in deeply.

"Hello, Sambrea. I hope I didn't frighten you." The familiar smooth-as-velvet voice haunted her. "You look as though you've seen a ghost."

Sambrea shook uncontrollably. Her mouth moved but she was mute. In fact, she had no control whatsoever over her entire physical and mental being. Finally, with a great deal of difficulty, she was able to close her eyes. When she opened them again, the tall, beautiful woman with the figure of a high fashion model was still standing there.

Breeze Sinclair enjoyed her daughter's helpless reaction, not to mention her obvious discomfort. Breeze's shrill laughter pierced the air and Sambrea covered her ears. "I've really shaken you, haven't I, Sambrea?"

As though in response to her question, a single tear ran unchecked down Sambrea's cheek. "Where have you been all this time?" Sambrea's voice was weak and her tongue felt as though it was tied in a million knots. Her stomach didn't feel much different.

"In the South of France, darling!" Breeze sounded as though she'd just returned from a lengthy holiday.

Sambrea cringed at her mother's response. "In the South of France? How wonderful for you," Sambrea quipped. "I can't believe you allowed us to think something terrible had happened. We thought you were dead, when all the time you've been off somewhere living a lavish lifestyle. How could you do something like this, Mother? Are you insane?" Sambrea was near hysteria. "What kind of monster are you?"

"Cut the theatrics, Sam." Breeze's tone was as cold as a winter storm. "You were just as glad to be rid of me as I was to be gone from here. You and I never did see eye to eye. I'm only here to ask a favor of you. Once it's granted, I'll get out of your life for good."

Sambrea blinked back hot tears. "A favor? You're out of your mind if you expect anything from me. A lot has happened since you left. One thing for sure has happened. I'm all grown up now. I'm no longer that naive little girl you used to do a major snow job on. And I'm sure you know Samuel is dead. There's nothing left here for you. Nothing at all."

"Oh, but you're wrong, Sambrea. There's plenty left— and we both know I'm talking about money. I'm just about totally broke, Sambrea. I came here to get what is rightfully mine. When I get it, I'll be out of here in a flash. You'll never have to see my face again."

Sambrea scowled heavily. "That is, until you're broke again. Do you know how many nights we sat up and waited for you, hoping you were just off somewhere on a shopping spree? I guess it never crossed your mind. I can't count the tears we wasted over you. It looks as though you didn't deserve any of our grief. How could you just waltz back into my life like nothing has happened, and without any prior warning? Mother, you are unconscionable. I want you out of here."

Breeze snorted. "Samuel may have left everything to you, but I deserve at least half of it. I lived with your father for a lot longer than I should have. I stayed with him for reasons you'd never understand. We fell out of love long before I decided to take matters into my own hands. Sambrea, Samuel Sinclair owes me big time."

Sambrea was too weak to carry on with this pitiful charade. Having been dealt a severe blow, she desperately needed to lick her open wounds privately, wounds that ran to the depths of her soul. Sambrea shook with fury. "The dead owe nothing. I owe nothing." Sambrea was disgusted by Breeze's gall. "You are absolutely vulgar."

"I'll concede you that much, Sambrea. But I'm not here to win your approval. You either write me a healthy check, or I'll help Craig Caldwell take it all away from you," Breeze menaced. "I understand that in just a few days he's been able to get closer to you than I was able to get in sixteen years."

At the mention of Craig's name a chilling reality raced through Sambrea's brain, leaving her numb with disbelief. *So, Craig is in cahoots with Breeze. What else is he involved in?* Her heart felt shattered beyond repair. Apparently, she'd fallen for the biggest con game around. Sambrea swiped at her angry tears. "How do you know Craig Caldwell, Breeze?" Calling Breeze *Mother* no longer worked for her.

Breeze tossed Sambrea a positively wicked smile. "Through many intimate encounters, Sambrea. Did you really think he was interested in you? Did you really think a sophisticated man like him could be seriously interested in someone as unworldly as you are, a plain Jane, so to speak? Craig and I are cut from the same cloth. We both love money and the power it wields. You could say that Craig and I have a business arrangement as well as an intimate one."

Sambrea had heard enough. Neither her ears nor her heart could bear to listen to any more. It was now that she fully realized she was hopelessly in love with a rat. A rat that wore impeccable attire, a rat that made exquisite love, a rat who'd somehow gotten under her skin, permanently.

Sambrea fought the tears. "Spare me the details. This conversation is terminated. I'm out of here." Seeing the look of triumph on Breeze's face, Sambrea grabbed the financial folders from the table. Following the brick walkway leading into the rear entrance of the hotel, Sambrea left Breeze alone.

Her entire body shook as she entered the hotel.

Tai Tanaka, the hotel manager and Samuel Sinclair's long-time friend, noticed how pale Sambrea looked the moment she came inside. She understood. She'd already had a nasty encounter with Breeze.

Tai, a small-built Japanese-American, had done a lot of business with Samuel over the years, and she had often been a welcome dinner guest at the Sinclair home when they'd resided on Maui. She had even helped Sambrea through her father's death, which was one of the many things that kept them in close contact with each other.

Tai put her arm around Sambrea's tiny waist. As Sambrea leaned into her, tears had already spilled from her sand-and-sable eyes. "Don't cry, Samiko," Tai soothed. "I can only imagine how you must feel." Tai's dark eyes held sympathy for the young woman she'd known since birth. "Would you like a cup of my special tea? I can take a short break."

"No, thank you, Tai. I guess you've already seen Breeze?"

Tai nodded and her jet-black hair bounced with body. "I

tried to send her away until I could prepare you for her sudden return. But . . . well, you know. Madame Sinclair has her own way of doing things. I don't know how she knew you were here visiting me. Can I get you anything at all?"

"A life preserver! It looks like I'm going to need one. I feel as though I'm drowning in a sea of anguish. Where do people like her come from? Where do they get all their unmitigated nerve?"

Tai sighed. "I don't know, Samiko. But we both know she won't leave until she gets what she came here for. She's a very determined woman."

"You're right about that, Tai." Breeze stood in the entrance. "I'll be checking in at the Honolulu Hilton very soon, Sambrea. I'll wait to hear from you when you get back." Breeze disappeared from the lobby almost as quickly as she had appeared, leaving her daughter bitter with anger.

Gritting her teeth, Sambrea shuddered. "Oh, this is impossible. She's impossible. I'd probably be better off if I just give her what she wants. I'm going up to the suite to lie down, Tai. *Big Foot* has just clobbered me over the head."

"Very well, my dear. I'll be right down here when you arise."

She smiled affectionately at Tai. "Thanks, Tai. You've always been there when I needed you. I'm grateful. Thank you for booking me a suite for a few days, especially on such short notice."

Unfortunately, rest was impossible for Sambrea. The flowers on the wallpaper appeared to cry, too. She looked around the room. The hotel's cheerfully decorated suites had always been a peaceful, safe haven for her. With so much inner turmoil, she didn't think she'd ever feel safe or at peace ever again.

Seeing Breeze alive had shaken her very foundation. Learning that Breeze was somehow involved with the same man she herself loved was too painful to cope with. Breeze Sinclair had once again found a way to shatter her daughter's very existence.

Sambrea thought about calling Richard and Joe but decided not to. They had enough to deal with at the office. Getting further entangled in her personal affairs was the last thing they needed right now.

A swim in the ocean was what she needed to relax. Eager to get lost in the exhilaration of the white foamy waves, Sambrea grabbed a towel from the linen closet and headed for the elevators.

Lazily, Sambrea drifted out into the deep water. The crashing waves knocked her about, yet she kept going further and further out. Escaping all forms of human life would set her free and hopefully afford her the opportunity to forget the only human she knew who sported midnight eyes. Until a giant wave dragged her under, nearly knocking the daylights out of her, Sambrea didn't realize she was entirely too far out. As she bravely battled with the menacing waves, her legs grew tired, and soon felt heavy as lead weights. As she went under for the third time, the water filled her lungs this time and breathing became difficult. Gasping for air, though nearly unconscious, she felt a pair of strong arms encircling her waist.

"Just relax and lie back. Let me do all the work. I'll get you back to shore safely."

The voice sounded familiar, but the water clogged in her ears made it difficult for her to hear clearly. Carrying her to the shoreline, her rescuer laid her on the sand. The tiny grains of grit never felt so good beneath her body.

A gentle hand pushed back the hair from her face. "Sambrea, Sambrea," Lawrence Chambers called out anxiously. A military brat who'd also grown up in Hawaii, he had been Sambrea's teenage heartthrob. When she didn't respond, he placed his mouth over hers and breathed life into her lungs. As she coughed and discharged a fair amount of water, he felt relieved. Turning her head to the side, he let the rest of the water run out from her mouth. Tenderly placing her head in his lap, he looked down at her colorless face. "I thought we'd lost you, Sam. Do you have a death wish? What possessed you to swim out that far?"

Her lungs felt like they were on fire as she sucked greedily at the air. Able to breathe much better now, she looked up at Lawrence. "That was . . . really . . . stupid . . . of me. I know . . . better than . . . to swim out . . . that far," she stammered painfully.

"That's nice to know, but it still doesn't answer my question. Something has to be bothering you for you to be so careless. Why weren't you able to see how far you'd gotten from the shore? You're well aware of the dangers of unexpected swells in these waters. You've lived here all your life, Sam. Maybe I should take you to the hospital and have you checked out."

Taking in several more deep breaths, Sambrea gave her heart and lungs a chance to further recover. She continued to breathe in and out. Several minutes passed before she even attempted to speak again.

"Lawrence, please give me a break. I'm fine and I've had enough traumas for one day. I hate to go inside hospitals. In case you haven't heard, Breeze has reappeared on the scene. She's alive and well . . . and has been living it up in the South of France. Since she and your mother were friends, I'm sure she'll be paying her a surprise visit. Maybe you should warn her so she won't get caught unaware like I did. I don't want her to have a heart attack when she thinks she's seen a ghost. Talking about needing a hospital. A near drowning is mediocre stuff compared to seeing Breeze again."

His gentle, dark brown eyes widened with disbelief. "You've got to be kidding, Sam! Your mother is alive? My mom will flip out over this. Like you and your father, my parents thought Mrs. Sinclair was dead." He shuddered. "My mother won't believe the horror in this story. She loved your mother so much."

Sambrea grimaced. "Very much alive. She has come to claim a nonexistent and undeserved inheritance. Samuel left her nothing because he thought she was dead. Breeze has an overabundance of gall. Always has."

Bands of steel embraced her. "I'm sorry, Sam. I know this has to be tough on you. I now understand why you were so careless out there. Your mind and emotions have to be running on empty. I think you need to go inside. This darn sun is blazing hot."

"I think you're right. Lawrence, would you like to go out to sea on the *Gentle Breeze* for dinner tonight? We could catch up on old times while we feast on scrumptious lobster and shrimp. I need a little fun and excitement. My treat." She coughed up more water, which made her feel much better. She felt sure that her lungs had completely cleared now.

"Yeah, right!" Looking concerned, he paused a moment. "Are you sure you're okay?" She nodded. "That's very generous of you, considering you don't have to pay a cent to dine on something you own. You're a cheapskate, Sam. You always have been, but I accept your invitation."

Almost fully recovered from her title bout with the ocean, she grinned. "It's nice to have influential friends, isn't it, Lar? The *Gentle Breeze* departs at six-thirty. Pick me up at six. That will give us plenty of time to get down to the docks."

As they walked toward the hotel entrance, it disturbed Sambrea to think of what might have happened had Lawrence not been on the beach. Though she was a strong swimmer, she'd been no match for the ocean. She always did need someone to look after her, she thought with deep sadness. Lawrence saw Sambrea safely inside the lobby before ambling on down the beach.

Recklessly, Craig pulled the rental car into the parking lot of the Hibiscus Court Hotel. Jumping out of the car, he ran into the lobby. Armed with the information Joe Walls had given him, he immediately took the elevator up to the eleventh floor. Joe had given him Sambrea's whereabouts for no other reason than his arrogant persistence. Joe would've warned Sambrea that Craig was on his way, but knowing Craig would see her no matter what it took, Joe let Craig talk him out of calling her. Craig Caldwell almost always got what he wanted. At the moment he wanted to see Sambrea Sinclair; wanted to see her every day for the rest of his natural life.

Hoping she wasn't going to fight him off, yet knowing the sort of stubborn willpower she possessed, he readied himself for a fierce battle. Since he'd already fallen in love with her, he realized how great the potential was for him to end up with a severely damaged heart. As far as he was concerned, she was every bit worth the risk.

Tai met Craig at the door of Sambrea's suite. She'd come up to the suite to check on Sambrea. "Aloha, sir. May I help you?"

"Aloha. I'm here to see Sambrea Sinclair. Is she in?" If Tai had been a man, Craig wouldn't have been too happy with who'd answered the door to her suite.

"Please come in. If you will kindly give me your name, sir, I'll see if she is free to receive you."

Craig briefly pondered Tai's request. "Jacob Ladder." He chuckled inwardly at the name he'd given. Sambrea wouldn't see him if he gave his right name, but he knew she'd be curious to see a man who carried a name like

Jacob Ladder. Seeing the stunned expression on Tai's face, he put his hand over his mouth to keep from laughing out loud.

"You may have a seat in the salon, Mr. Ladder. I will inform Miss Sinclair you're here to see her."

Craig wandered into the spacious living area. A grand suite, he mused. No expense had been spared in furnishing it. He gazed over at the cozy window-enclosed alcove overlooking the ocean. Entering the alcove, he took a seat on the beautiful caned-back floral print sofa. Two massive Papasan chairs of the same floral print looked comfortable and inviting. Everything in the room was beautifully appointed.

Just as Craig had thought, Sambrea couldn't wait to see the man who carried such a name. Dressed in white shorts and a blue tank top, she looked cool and relaxed, but she stopped dead in her tracks when she saw the imposing figure of Craig Caldwell. Shuddering with anguish, she looked at the man who had somehow taken her heart away without the slightest amount of force. Sambrea turned to walk away. Craig blocked her exit before she took another step. She pulled away from him, but her attempt was futile, as always.

He searched her face with somber eyes. "Why, Sambrea? Just tell me why? I thought everything was going fine between us. I thought we'd reached some sort of an understanding, thought we were in the process of building a good relationship. Don't you think you owe me an explanation?"

There was that word *owe* again. She bristled inwardly. Why did everyone think she owed them something? "If someone else tells me I *owe* them something, I'm going to scream. What makes you think I owe you anything? The sex was great, but I can live without it and without you. Sex is just a means to an end. Just because I had sex with you, it doesn't mean I have to commit my life to you. I'm sorry if you thought it was anything more than what it was.

Like you said, we needed each other. Nothing more, nothing less."

Pumping a bullet into his gut couldn't have hurt any more than the words she'd just spewed out at him, words that seemed to spout out like a hissing, erupting geyser of black tar.

He bit down on his lower lip, scrutinizing her so intensely that it made his eyeballs burn. "Is that all it was, Sam? Just good sex? If you believe that, then I feel sorry for you. It was much, much more than that for me. I don't know what or who has made you so bitter, Sambrea, but you need to find a way to release all that bitterness before it eats you alive. You're dying on the inside and you don't even know it. You're much too young to be filled with so much killer acid."

Knowing Craig was right about her, she choked back the tears. She was bitter. As bitter as thousands of bushel baskets of lemons. Life with its countless disappointments had made her embittered. All the disappointments that buried her under their leaden weight; just as her father's premature death still weighed on her so heavily. Now Breeze was back to heap more weight on her sagging shoulders.

Pulling her into the alcove, Craig planted her on the sofa and sat down beside her. "You're hurting terribly, Sambrea. I can see it in your eyes. Please tell me what's bothering you. I want to help you, sweetheart. Let me help you."

No longer could her tears be contained. Her eyes turned into a tropical rain forest as he held her close to him. The tears seemed without end, but it felt good to release them. She hadn't cried this way in years, not even when Samuel died. She thought she had to be stoic, thought she had to be tough, thought she had to prove she could handle all the problems that were now hers to deal with. What hurt more than anything is that she truly believed she had to do it all alone, that she didn't need anything or anyone to lean upon outside of her staff.

Crying wasn't the way to show her strength. Nor was it going to help her take charge of De La Brise and all the responsibilities that came with owning and running it. Stubbornly, she wiped away her tears.

Craig massaged her back. "Talk to me, sweetheart. It'll help if you can get it all out."

The phone rang and she was glad for the intrusion.

She could bare her soul to Craig, but what would it prove? It would just give him more ammunition to use against her. She couldn't get rid of the idea that he was her worst enemy. If he were somehow involved with Breeze, she'd never be able to trust him. However, she didn't want to come to hate him, either; she loved him far too much for that. There was a time that Breeze had confessed to loving Samuel, too.

Tai smiled delicately as she entered the room. "Excuse me, please. Samiko, may I speak with you for a moment?"

Sambrea stood up and walked toward Tai. Then the two women stepped out of earshot of Craig. "What is it, Tai?"

"Mr. Chambers called to say he wouldn't be able to sail with you this evening. He'll call on you tomorrow. Are you okay, Samiko? You look so distraught. Is it the gentleman?"

"I'm fine, Tai. The gentleman has been exactly that. Don't worry about me. Could you bring us some of your special tea, Tai? Mr. Ladder and I have a lot to talk about."

Sambrea laughed. "His name is not Jacob Ladder, Tai. His name is Craig Caldwell. At times he has the tendency to be awfully incorrigible."

Tai laughed. "Much like yourself," she said with genuine affection. "I feel relieved for the gentleman. It would've been a tough way to get through school with a name like that. I will go and prepare the tea, Samiko."

When Tai left, Sambrea returned to the alcove and her seat next to Craig.

"How did you know that I was here on Maui, Craig?"

He winked his right eye. "Radar, sweetheart. I always know where you are."

She gritted her teeth. "Thanks for being your usual vague self. What do you know about a woman named Breeze Sinclair?" she asked, jumping in with both feet.

"That she's desperate and possibly dangerous. Is she related to you, Sam? I ask because I know the company name means *of the breeze.*"

Not believing for a second that Craig didn't know Breeze was her mother, Sambrea snorted. "Oh, she's related to me alright, but I haven't seen her in years. She's my mother. Breeze tells me you two are very intimate. Are you?"

"Intimate isn't the word I would use to describe my non-existent relationship with one Breeze Sinclair. I just met her briefly. She came to see me at my office in Honolulu claiming to have an attractive business proposition for me, but I was too busy to take time to talk with her. However, my secretary did make an appointment for her next week."

"Why didn't you mention it to me, Craig? As you said, her name made you wonder if she was related to me. De La Brise was named for her. My father changed the company name when we moved here from Maui."

Hating to be put on the spot, Craig scratched his head. "I really didn't give it much thought at the time. I've been so busy trying to get you to trust me. You've given me the royal runaround for the past several days. Lady, you've done a serious number on me. In case you haven't figured it out, I'm in love with you, Sambrea Sinclair."

His confession hung in the air like a sunny day, warming her heart, yet it scared her to death. "I don't know what to say, Craig. I don't know how I'm supposed to feel. I don't know what to do." Somehow, as crazy as it seemed, she believed him.

"Don't worry about doing anything or saying anything. Give it time to sink in. Matters of the heart can string you out. I know. I've been strung out for days now. Whatever you do, don't let it chase you away. We'll never know what we can have together if you run away from it." He paused a moment. "You mentioned you hadn't seen your mother in years. Why not?"

Changing the subject might keep her from dwelling too much on his confession. He was unable to stand the thought of her running away from him again. He had her talking, which was good for her. If Sambrea stuffed anything else, he knew she'd self-destruct. Craig smiled as he saw Tai come into the alcove. Without disturbing them, she served the tea, and left the suite.

Sambrea didn't want to answer his question, but felt that she must. He deserved to know the truth about Breeze, especially since it seemed Breeze hoped to start an alliance with him. If he'd been honest with her—and she felt that he had—she needed to do the same. After all, he was the one who held the four aces.

"It's a long, ugly story, Craig, but I'll make it brief as possible. Breeze disappeared when I was only sixteen. I'm now twenty-five. We thought she was dead all this time. Today is the first time I've laid eyes on her since then. Breeze walked up to me today as though she'd been on an extended holiday. My father went to his grave thinking she was dead. It was a very cruel thing for her to do to us. What hurts the most is she never once expressed any sorrow over Samuel's death."

Hurting inside for Sambrea, Craig shook his head. "That's an incredible story. Why did she decide to come back after all these years?"

"I'll give you one clue. Money! She's broke and thinks she has a right to half of what was left to me. Does she, Craig? She deserted us. Does she have a right to anything?"

Craig exhaled. "I really can't answer that question for you, sweetheart. What was your relationship like before she split the scene?"

"Stormy, rocky, totally unpredictable. For years I truly

believed Mother loved me and that she just didn't know how to show it. But now I know she never did. If she did love me, how could she have left me like that?"

"Did your parents have a good relationship?" He palmed his forehead. "I guess that was a dumb question. No one walks out on a good relationship. I'm beginning to understand why you feel so bitter. You've been carrying the weight of burdens that should've never been placed on your shoulders. You're one class act, Sambrea. But you have to get rid of those burdens. Give them back to whomever they belong. They don't belong to you, Sam. Don't take ownership of them."

"Easier said than done, Craig. I've been carrying them for so long they've become a part of me." She sighed with relief. "I feel much better for having shared this with someone, even if that someone is trying to add to my burdens. Craig, if you take De La Brise from me it'll kill me. I'm sure Breeze will also hire a lawyer to fight me for it, but I'll battle you both with every ounce of breath in me."

Could Breeze be behind the financial problems at De La Brise? Her sudden appearance back in Hawaii was no coincidence; Craig was sure of it. Breeze being broke gave a lot more credence to his suspicions.

He tried to lose himself in the beauty of Sambrea's eyes. "Marry me. We'll fight this together. If you marry me, and it doesn't work out, in six months you walk away with De La Brise and all your other assets. I'll even sign a pre-nuptial agreement, but we must keep that part secret. We have to make a strong show of unity. I stand to lose the only woman I've ever loved. That would hurt like hell. But if we don't come to some amicable agreement, you stand to lose your very life, as you put it—De La Brise."

Though she hid it well, she was moved beyond description. "Let me sleep on it, Craig. I know I'm crazy for even considering such madness, but I can't gamble with what my father entrusted to me. It's been in his family for generations. I can't let it go. Can I sleep on it?"

"As long as I can sleep on it with you. Please don't send me away from you. I want to lie down next to you. I want to feel your heart beating in tune to mine. We don't have to do anything more than hold one another, Sam. I need to be with you. I love you, girl. Come back to my hotel with me."

Sambrea pressed her lips to his and engaged him in a lingering kiss. "Let's go, Craig. I need to be held. I don't need or want to be alone with my thoughts. I can't survive the pain that thoughts of the past bring to bear. I desperately need to believe in something good, in someone good. Can I believe in you, in your word? Can I really and truly trust you, Craig Caldwell?"

He crushed his mouth down over hers. Lifting his head, he looked past her tears, locking his midnight gaze deeply into her sand-and-sable eyes. "With your very life, Sambrea Sinclair."

SIX

Although it was only Sambrea's first day back to work, her desk was already cluttered with papers and file folders, along with a seemingly never-ending stack of pink telephone messages. Sambrea had been returning phone calls all morning and her voice was beginning to sound hoarse, but she vowed to get through the mountain of messages before day's end. Right now, though, she needed a short break.

Rolling the chair away from the desk and over to the window, she scanned the beach below with a calm but keen interest in the early morning beach-goers. Cruising through the rising waters at high speeds, wind-surfers, surfboards, and sailboats were plentiful. Sambrea loved most water sports, yet knew full well that she'd probably break her neck if she tried them. Snorkeling, sailing, and jet skiing were as daring as she was willing to get.

Closing her eyes, thoughts of Craig suddenly took over her mind. She looked dazed as the sudden turn of events on Maui came rushing back. The wedding ceremony had been brief, uneventful, with only the widowed Tai standing in as her matron of honor. Maui City Hall had been the site; a nondescript judge had performed the almost sad ritual. No wedding rings had been exchanged, traditional vows were taken, and the repeat-after-me segments had been recited. Afterward, only a dispassionate kiss had occurred.

No reception with family and friends was held, except the dinner shared with Tai. No honeymoon was forthcoming.

All the fire and passion she and Craig had shared since their first meeting seemed to have disappeared under the pressures and the realization of what they'd gotten themselves into. For Sambrea in particular, marriage seemed to have put them on an entirely different footing. Quietly, Sambrea reflected on days past.

She had married Craig, but she hadn't agreed to live with him in his home. Her tiny bungalow suited her just fine. This was only the hundredth time she'd told herself that. She was trying to convince herself that she was better off living alone. Familiarity had a way of breeding contempt. While Craig wasn't too happy with the living arrangements she'd suggested, he'd conceded. He reveled in the bigger challenge he saw himself faced with. He'd told her in no uncertain terms that he'd eventually make her see things his way, which meant they'd no doubt live under the same roof, as husband and wife.

Craig had wanted to get away from the business for a few days, but she had expressed other ideas that she now regretted. Getting back to the offices of De La Brise had been her top priority. She could've used some more time away, however—more time with her husband. When a light knock came on the door, disturbing her train of thought, she rolled the chair back to the desk and shouted for the visitor to enter.

Richard opened the door and walked over to the desk. Moodily, he sank his eyes into Sambrea's as he sat down. "What the hell is going on with you, Sambrea?"

She looked totally perplexed, yet she easily guessed what had probably brought on his foul mood.

"Why didn't you tell me you married Caldwell? How could you have kept something like this from me? How could you marry a man who's trying to steal your livelihood right out from under your nose? How could you go off and marry a man you hardly know—without telling the friends who love you anything about it?"

He sounded more hurt than angry. More than that, she saw that he was deeply disappointed in her, painfully so. She didn't like Richard having any negative feelings about her at all, but he'd get over them in time. He loved her too much not to.

She lowered her eyes for a fleeting moment. "I was going to tell you, Richard, but you weren't here when I came in. I've had so much to do this morning. I had rather thought we'd get a chance to talk over an extended lunch. Our marriage wasn't a planned affair." Feeling nervous about the whole thing, she slid her palms down her thighs. "It's not what you think. I only married him to ensure the future of De La Brise. A marriage of convenience, if you will. But no one must know that, Rich. Do I have your solemn oath?"

He shot her a look of exasperation. "That's the sorriest excuse I've ever heard, Sam. Given more time we could've saved the company ourselves. Why would you sacrifice yourself in this way? You're far too smart for this."

Unwittingly, the look in her eyes responded for her.

Richard slapped his forehead with an open palm. "Oh, no, Sam! You're in love with Craig Caldwell. I can see it in your eyes. He was telling the truth when he said he'd already met you, wasn't he?"

Her eyes spoke for her again. "It doesn't matter how I feel about him, or for how long I've known him. What matters is this company and its employees. Besides, we have a pre-nuptial agreement. De La Brise will stay mine no matter the outcome of the marriage."

Richard snorted. "Who are you kidding, Mrs. Caldwell?" he countered.

Sharply, Sambrea jerked her head up, meeting his concerned gaze. It was the first time she'd been referred to as "Mrs. Caldwell" since their wedding ceremony. It wasn't at all offensive to her. In fact, it actually sounded great to her ears. *Mrs. Caldwell.* She allowed Craig's surname, now hers, to completely sink into her brain. No, her new name didn't sound offensive at all. She even felt giddy with pleasure. She rather loved the sound of it.

"Craig Caldwell will never let you best him, Sambrea. Trust me on that point."

Revealing a bit of bad attitude, Sambrea cut her eyes at him. "We're living apart and I'll continue to be referred to as Sambrea Sinclair." Her eyes softened. "Rich, try to understand. Don't work against me. I can't stand for us to be on opposing sides of anything."

Smiling dispassionately, he nodded. "I promise I won't do that. But, Sam, you're not going to walk away from this unscathed. You can kid yourself, but you can't kid a kidder. You're in love with Caldwell and that's going to keep you tied to him for some time to come. I don't know how he feels about you, but if it's not the same as what you feel for him you can kiss De La Brise good-bye. On the other hand, if he loves you, you'd better move in with your husband and get on with your life. If you don't, you're going to lose him to someone else. I can't imagine Craig Caldwell living a life of celibacy. He wasn't satisfied with just a hostile take-over. He had to have the lady boss, too. It'll serve you well to remember that."

Oh, he was far from hostile when he took her over, she thought warmly. It was the gentlest takeover she'd ever known. Thoughts of him with another woman caused a deep fear to gnaw at her insides. Richard was right. Craig Caldwell would be considered an incredible catch by most. But then, so would she.

"Point well taken, Rich. But you know me. I always have to do it my way—my way is dictating for me to live separate from Craig. Celibacy is another matter entirely."

Feeling a little smug while thinking about the delicious couplings they'd shared on their wedding night, she tossed

Richard a mischievous smile. Their consummating wedding rituals had been sinfully delightful. They'd come together in a way that had nearly set her hair on fire.

"You need Jesus, honey. I'm going to pray for you. You're going to need it. Over the phone you mentioned you had something to tell me about your mother. What was it, Sam?"

Sambrea's mood turned somber as she chewed on her lower lip. "She's alive and well—and she's back in Hawaii."

Richard jumped up from his seat. "That's unbelievable, Sam! How do you know? Have you actually seen her?"

Unable to stop herself, Sambrea burst into a fit of rage. In answering his questions one by one, she told him all the things Breeze had said to her. Then she told him where Breeze had been living and why she'd returned to Hawaii after so long. Richard listened to her, utterly amazed by the whole thing.

Unannounced, Craig strolled into her office, causing Sambrea and Richard to look up. Craig looked like a man with a definite purpose, but the unmistakable pain in his wife's sand-and-sable eyes made him wince. "What's wrong, Sambrea?" He looked from her to Richard, as if he suspected Richard of causing her pain. He'd been so sure Richard would go through the ceiling when he learned of their marriage. It looked as though he'd been right.

Richard eyed Craig coolly. "She was talking about the sudden reappearance of Breeze Sinclair. This is a difficult subject for her. What do you know about all this, Caldwell?"

"Only what Sambrea has told me, Mr. Henry. I know you don't like or trust me, but you'll soon find out I'm not the enemy. I strongly suspect that De La Brise has a few adversaries, but I just don't happen to be one of them. Now if you don't mind, I'd like to speak with my wife. In private."

Richard bristled. "No, I don't mind, Mr. Caldwell. But don't you think you should check to see if your wife does?"

Sambrea saw the need to intervene. "It's okay, Rich. I need to talk to Mr. Caldwell, anyway. We have to get a few issues straight before things get out of hand around here." By the tone of her voice, her meaning came in clear to both men. Richard departed and Craig deposited himself on the leather sofa.

Craig smiled as Sambrea walked toward him. He only received a cold glare in return.

"I won't have you treating the staff this way, Craig. They've been loyal to this company for a long time. Try staying in your place for a change. I run De La Brise."

He chuckled at the fury in her eyes. "So you do, Mrs. Caldwell, so you do. From the looks of things, someone at De La Brise is running you. Right into the ground. I've ordered a financial audit so you can see the facts for yourself."

Suddenly, she felt tired. Releasing a resigned sigh, she sat down on the opposite end of the sofa looking as though she wanted to cry. This was getting too much for her to handle all on her own. Craig was much more experienced in this area than she could ever be.

Rapidly, he closed the distance between them. Pouting like a spoiled little boy, he laid his head on her shoulder. "How about a moonlit dinner cruise, Sambrea? I know a company that offers the finest ocean dining one can get. A sunset dinner cruise on the high seas can help soothe my wounded heart, since you refused my offer of a proper honeymoon."

Knowing his reference was to De La Brise, she allowed his compliment to touch her heart. Craig had a unique way of calming down her anger toward him before it could escalate into something major. As though it was the most natural thing for her to do, she ran her fingers through his hair. "Thanks, Craig. I'd like that. I try to make all the right decisions, but sometimes I think I'm too emotionally involved with De La Brise to be effective. Do whatever you need to."

"Is that all the thanks I'm going to get? I'd prefer a kiss." In taking advantage of her vulnerability, he thought it best not to give her time to think of a sharp retort. Smothering her lips under his, he kissed her sweetly, passionately.

Involuntarily, her arms wound around his neck. Losing herself in the sensational warmth of his mouth, she clung to him like a magnet to metal. She didn't offer any resistance when he pushed her skirt up over her thighs. When his fingers deeply caressed her, she nearly fainted with desire. Gently, he manipulated her with probing hands, his fingers weaving a magical web of sheer ecstasy inside of her.

Unzipping his pants, she freed him, touching the majestic tool pulsating in her hand. In one delicate motion, he pressed her back into the sofa, lowering himself against her. Her body riveted with one indescribable thrust after another, she clung to him. No longer able to hold back the powerful release surging through him, he muffled his cries of infinite pleasure into the gentle folds of her neck. She buried her pleasurable screams against his chest, and their bodies came together on a roller coaster ride to an explosive fulfillment.

The pleasurable sensations took them over completely.

Noticing the unlocked door, she felt her cheeks infuse with color. "Oh, no," she moaned. "Someone could've just walked in here. We wouldn't have known until it was too late. We can't ever do this again."

He grinned innocently. "Do what? What husbands and wives do all the time? Sambrea, let's get out of here. Let me take you home, our home. I want you there with me. We're back at work much too soon. I want us to stay in the honeymoon phase forever."

After standing up, she pulled her skirt down. "You're truly a sexual raider, Craig Caldwell, a corporate raider as well. You've also been raiding my emotions since that first night on the beach. When does it stop?"

She loved the idea of a forever honeymoon but she just happened to know better.

"It'll never stop. But it might let up a little when I have you right where I want you, in my bed every single morning and night. When are you going to stop fighting the inevitable, Mrs. Caldwell? We're destined to be together. You wouldn't have let me get that close to you the first night if you hadn't known it, too. You wouldn't have let just anyone in your home, either. I knew that then. We can have a wonderful life, Sambrea, if you'll just surrender. What have you got to lose now?"

"My sanity! Don't you need to be somewhere?" She walked into the bathroom.

Following her, he joined his hands with hers under the hot running water. "As a matter of fact, I do. Since I can't convince you to get out of here early, I'll pick you up at the bungalow at six-thirty. Dress to impress. The *Wayward Breeze* demands it." He walked over to the door.

Before leaving, he turned to her. "I love you, Mrs. Caldwell," he mouthed softly.

Trying to hide her feelings of euphoria, she picked up the paper clip dispenser and hurled it in his direction. Even if she'd really tried to hit her mark, she would've missed him by a large margin. The top on the dispenser broke open and paper clips scattered everywhere. Ducking out the door, he laughed at her bad aim. His laughter caused her own to surface.

Sambrea worked tirelessly for the next several hours, but erotic thoughts of Craig kept singeing her mind. Still, she managed to complete all of the monthly reports. After finishing up the last report, she rang for Joe to come to her office.

Wearing brightly colored clown make-up on his face, his cheeks painted a bright red, Joe entered, smiling. A big nose was attached to a band around his head and the dirty-brown wig he wore on his head only had hair on the sides. That tickled her to death.

Joyous laughter burst from her lips. "A little early for Halloween, aren't we, Joe?" She tried to stifle another burst of glee.

Joe's guttural laughter filled the room. "It's never too early for laughter, my dear Sam. Laughter is always right on time. You looked so unhappy this morning. I thought I'd cheer you up. From the looks of your cheeks and the gleam in your eyes, I'd say somebody beat me to the punch. What have you and Caldwell been doing in here, anyway?"

Wondering if the signs of her fulfillment were that noticeable, she felt herself blush. "He's my husband, you know." She was surprised at how easily *husband* had rolled off her tongue. Also, she couldn't believe she'd pretty much confessed to their afternoon tryst. Blushing still, she smiled, giggling gleefully inside.

"I've heard. Congratulations! He's not such a bad guy. I rather like him. He definitely has an arrogant aura about him, but he's confident as hell. You two should make an interesting pair. I just hope you don't end up killing each other with your arrogant and control-freaking ways." Joe looked thoughtfully at his lovely employer. In probing into her private affairs, he had to go at it gently. "Are you in love with him, Sambrea? I somehow sense that you didn't marry him just for the sake of convenience."

Joe was so perceptive. He always could read her like a book, she thought.

"I'm still trying to figure that out myself. Normally, I'm not an impulsive person, but Craig Caldwell is able to make me toss out all the guidelines that govern my life. Do you think he truly loves me, Joe?"

For a minute Joe seriously thought about her question.

"I don't know, Sam. But if he doesn't, he will. He won't be able to help himself. Sam, you're an easy person to love. Not only are you a great boss, you're a wonderful human being. If I weren't so crazy about Julie, I would've fallen in love with you myself." Joe laughed. "Oh, boy, Julie would strangle me if she'd heard that one."

Feeling a little embarrassed by his innocent-enough confession Joe crossed the room and pressed the fake nose into Sambrea's. As it made a loud, honking noise, she leapt out of her seat. Both dissolved into uncontrollable laughter.

After handing over the reports for Joe to type, Sambrea thought it would be a good idea to take the rest of the day off, just as Craig had advised. Before going home, she'd shop for a new dress. She hadn't purchased any new clothes for a while now. And she actually found herself looking forward to the evening ahead that she'd spend with Craig. They'd never had what one could call an official date—and here they were already married.

The reality of the situation amazed her. What would Craig lure her into next? Whatever it was it would be deliciously sweet and seductively thrilling. So far Craig had done everything in a unique way, at least everything that had to do with their personal relationship. He had been kind and gentle, showering her with warmth and genuine affection from their very first meeting.

A couple of hours before sunset the newlyweds boarded the *Wayward Breeze*, in great anticipation of a wonderful evening. Craig had an even greater anticipation of what might happen between them at evening's end.

Enticingly low-cut, Sambrea's sea-blue evening gown looked magnificent on her svelte frame. The slit up the side revealed a well toned, golden-brown thigh. Around her neck she wore a gold choker with a sparkling blue topaz stone in the center. Matching earrings dangled from her dainty ears. The sable curtain of silky hair was all that embraced her bare shoulders.

Craig looked lethal in a black custom-tailored tuxedo. A rich magenta-colored bow tie and cummerbund accented the ivory-white tuxedo shirt. Gold cuff links and a gold watch were his only jewelry. His dark hair had been neatly trimmed, and his midnight eyes blazed with romantic notions as he swept his ladylove aboard the *Wayward Breeze*.

Several employees noticed the beautiful couple when they first came aboard. The word spread quickly from one staff member to another that their employers had arrived.

Leading Sambrea by the hand, Craig chose a table dressed in baby-blue linens and candlelight softness. They would dine on the upper deck rather than in the spacious grand interior of the yacht's dining room.

"The live music will easily reach us via the outdoor speakers. It looks like you're the center of attention, Sam. Of course you are. Your dazzling smile lights up the night."

Sambrea saw the admiring glances cast their way. Women and men alike appeared envious of them. She saw the envious expressions of their faces. Admitting to herself that they were quite a striking pair came easy for her. As she thought of them having children together, she knew they'd be beautiful. Immediately, she pushed the disturbing thought away.

The smile she gave him was no less radiant than the sun. "You bring out my inner light. Your effervescence will take over if my smile should somehow lose its brilliance, Craig."

Quietly, the happy couple talked as they waited for their meal to be served. Her natural beauty enchanted him and she was positively enthralled by his humorous wit and vivacious charm. Drifting out into the sea breeze, their laughter transcended time and space. A soft, slow song struck his fancy. Standing, he extended his hand to Sambrea, and she took it eagerly. She was more than prepared to follow him off into the sunset should he but ask.

Instead of moving inside to the dance floor, they danced atop the open deck, up where the trade winds hummed a sweet tune on the cool night air. Sambrea snuggled into his arms, feeling as though she glided on the wind; he was such an excellent dancer. Locked in a hypnotic trance, their eyes stayed deeply connected.

How could she ever hide the fact that she loved him? She couldn't, not when her sand-and-sable eyes told him the very words she couldn't make her lips confess. Even as his midnight eyes echoed his love for her. That much she could see with crystal clarity. Feeling it right down to the ends of her feet, she basked in the sensuous friction and electric sparks flowing from their entwined bodies as he danced her around the deck.

She looked up into her husband's eyes. "Love on the high seas is terribly romantic."

Pressing his lips against hers, he kissed her hungrily. "Only if you're fortunate enough to be with the one you love. And if the one you love happens to love you back. I hope each touch, each kiss, and each smile I bestow upon you will always reveal the depth of my love for you. I want to be everything that you need me to be, Mrs. Caldwell. Don't ever doubt my love, Sambrea. Don't ever doubt our future."

Sambrea smiled. "Our love might be contagious since so many others have joined us here on the deck. They look as if they hope to catch whatever it is you and I are emitting into the atmosphere."

Laughing at her comment, he smiled back at her. "Having a good time?"

She shook her head. "No. I'm having a wonderful time." She paused briefly. "I'm frightened, Craig," she revealed breathlessly. She suddenly felt extremely vulnerable.

He frowned. "Of what, Sam?" he whispered tenderly. "Of what you're starting to feel for me, of what we're sharing, of what we induce in one another?"

"Yes, yes, yes," she whispered back. "Why do . . ."

He silenced her with his lips. "Not tonight, Sambrea. Hopefully not tomorrow either, but definitely not tonight. We can't possibly know what the future holds, but we know that God holds the key to our future. It's in His power that we must place our faith."

By the time the *Wayward Breeze* docked, Craig and Sambrea felt breathless with enchantment. Together they had discovered something powerfully overwhelming. A heck of a lot more than just sex was between them, Sambrea had learned. No longer able to fight her all-consuming love for him, she'd willingly go wherever he led. When he led her to his home, their home, she didn't falter for a second.

Why fight the inevitable? Why fight something she actually wanted, something she surely needed?

She'd seen the exterior of this palatial home many times over, but until that night on the beach, she'd never laid eyes on its handsome resident. She had always admired the impressive pagoda-style home, but now she more than admired its wonderful owner. The house stood out among the rest of the exquisite beach properties. It had a personality all its own, a personality matching that of the man who was now her husband. She saw that as he showed her around.

The interior was even more impressive than the exterior. Massive, airy rooms were elegantly decorated in red, ebony and ivory. An ivory lacquered baby grand piano was housed in a salon of its own, and dozens of theater seats faced the raised dais the piano sat upon. A magnificent stage was built into one wall, and an unbelievable crystal teardrop chandelier filled the room with a diamond-studded brilliance. Reflecting the engaging pinpoints of brilliant light, the walls were completely covered with beveled mirrors trimmed in gold. The room was as elegant and as brilliant as the man who had designed it.

Craig sat Sambrea on top of the piano, prepared to mesmerize her with a talent he never spoke of possessing. Not only was he a master of the ebony and ivories, he could sing beautifully as well. While he'd taken voice lessons, he'd gained most of his experience through singing in a church choir. He handed her a song sheet. Written on the paper were the music and lyrics to a song it had taken him only a couple of hours to compose. She was stunned by the love ballad he'd written just for her. It was simply called "Sambrea".

Out of the depths of the sea you suddenly appeared,

flooding my darkened life with dazzling light as you floated near.

Never in my life have I felt such a presence.

In every fiber of my being, I can touch your essence.

Sambrea, Sambrea, welcome to my heart.

Sambrea, Sambrea, don't keep us worlds apart.

The moment you touched me, my soul was reborn.

No longer am I a broken man, no longer forlorn.

Your kiss is as sweet as fresh morning dew.

How will I ever convince you that I love only you?

Sambrea, Sambrea, come soar with me.

Sambrea, Sambrea, we are truly destined to be.

Only our love for one another will set us free.

Tears filled her eyes as he sang the chorus over and over.

"That was beautiful, Craig. I can't believe you wrote that song just for me. Thank you," she said tearfully.

Sliding her across the sleek piano, he swept her into his arms. "You *are* my song, Sambrea. The lyrics came easy when I closed my eyes and envisioned the enchanting beauty that you are. The gentleness of your voice is the song I hear whenever you speak." Finding something else they both cared deeply for, music, the kisses passing between them were tenderly sweet.

If she'd thought the rest of the house was beautiful, she fell utterly speechless when he swept her into the master bedroom. It wasn't just a bedroom. It was the size of an apartment. Such elegant splendor would've been almost impossible to imagine.

What shocked her most was the color scheme of soft pinks and baby-blues. The decor had traces of a feminine touch. The pink satin comforter was heavily scalloped at the edges, as were the hems of the pillow shams. The satin draperies were mixed with panels of pink and blue. Pink and blue lace was used as accents throughout the room. The impressive, heavy bedroom furniture revealed a Spanish influence.

He kissed her on the nose. "I can assure you that it's my own creation. I designed it with the intent of one day sharing it with a woman I'd love enough to marry. Sambrea Sinclair is an exact replica of the woman I've fantasized about marrying. The house has been waiting for your exuberant and graceful presence."

She took his hand and put it to her mouth. "You are an extraordinary man, this is an extraordinary place, and this has been an extraordinary evening. Thank you for sharing it all with me. I'm still so moved by the song."

As a panic attack hit her, she fell into a few moments of silence. "Craig, I think I should go home now. We both should get some rest." She looked at her watch. "It's terribly late already."

His mouth fell open. Disappointment turned his midnight eyes into a whirlpool of sadness. "This is your home, Sambrea. This is our home. I know we've married under unusual circumstances, but, Sam, I married you because I wanted to. Because you're the only one I want to share every minute of my life with, because I love you. Please stay. We have to give this marriage every possible chance to thrive. Living apart will keep that from happening."

At this moment her love for him ruled out any foolish attempt to debate the point. What was there to debate, anyway? Almost timid, reaching over her shoulder, she fumbled for the zipper on her dress. Moving her hand away with the tenderness she'd come to expect from him, he unzipped the dress and slowly removed each and every article of her clothing. When all was bared, he helped her to remove his own attire. With nervous fingers, she removed his dinner jacket and shirt, marveling at the unbelievably healthy condition of his beautiful body.

Taking her by the hand, he led her to the huge bed. When he pulled the comforter back, she saw that the sheets were made of the finest linen. Inhaling her delicious scent, he lay down on the bed, drawing her down on top of him. As their lips connected in a fiery collision, Sambrea gave herself up to his magical powers.

Guiding her down onto his hardened length, he threw his arms back over his head, totally surrendering himself to whatever she wanted to extract from him. "Take me, Sam."

Responding to his request, Sambrea clenched her inner muscles around him, sending hot jolts of lightning bolts through his entire body. Shedding all restraints, she showed him what a woman was capable of when at the helm of passion. He wasn't disappointed in her style of command, nor did he have to fantasize about it.

Exercising her control to the fullest extent, Sambrea left nothing to his imagination. There wasn't a fantasy he'd ever had that could compare to the sensations now cascading through him. As they crashed into the end of the rainbow, a kaleidoscope of brilliant colors splashed in front of their eyes. Passionate screams enunciating their erotic climax sailed through the cavernous room.

Keeping him securely locked in the solitary confinement of her inner self, she shifted her body forward and laid her head on his chest. Burying his hands in her hair, he massaged her scalp and back until she fell into a dreamless sleep.

SEVEN

It was nearly noon when Sambrea and Craig finally awakened. Still lying on top of him, Sambrea was right where she'd slept the entire night through. Noticing the time as soon as she opened her eyes, she also saw that Craig was already awake. Since it was Saturday, neither of them had to go into work.

Happy that she was finally awake, Craig propped himself up in bed. "What about going sailing?" he suggested with enthusiasm. "We can have a picnic at sea, or find a deserted stretch of beach. After lunch, we can have one another for dessert."

She looked at him with a skeptical eye. "How good a sailor are you? I never go out to sea with an inexperienced limey."

"As good as I am at physically and emotionally satisfying you." He had a look of smug confidence. "Is that good enough for you, Mrs. Caldwell?"

Expressively, she closed her eyes, remembering how satisfied he truly made her. "All doubt erased. Do you have the makings of a picnic lunch?"

He swatted her in jest. *"We* have the makings. What's mine is yours." She rolled her eyes at him. "I know, I know. What's yours is yours, Sambrea. You're selfish, but I'm willing to share all I am and all that I have with you. In time, you'll feel the same way. If not, as long as I have you, I have all I need and desire."

Sambrea felt a flicker of guilt at the way she'd responded. She didn't like being called selfish, but she had to admit that she had been somewhat selfish with him. Craig had already shared so much of what he was and what he had with her. Would she feel the same way about him in time? *You already do,* came the soft voice inside her heart. Yet she still feared he'd end up irreparably breaking her already over-compromised heart. Just as Breeze had done to Samuel.

Was just them loving each other enough to build a life together? Breeze and Samuel had been in love once, but their love hadn't been strong enough to weather the storms of matrimony. At least, not for Breeze.

Guiding the sailboat across the water with confident ease, Craig hadn't lied about his expertise in sailing. Sambrea watched his rippling muscles as he kept the boat on a steady course. The light sheen of sweat on his body was sexy and it definitely turned her on. Just as he'd promised, he found them a stretch of deserted beach. Palm trees, a cascading waterfall, and a colorful riot of wildflowers made for a very romantic setting.

They left the boat, spread the blanket out on the sand, and placed their picnic lunch in front of them—fresh fruits and vegetables, along with a variety of cheese and crackers. Craig had mixed up a huge thermos of delicious and thirst-satisfying passion fruit juice and had selected several types of plastic utensils for the wicker picnic basket, while Sambrea had selected a small collection of CDs.

With the waterfall summoning them, they obeyed its crystal-clear, crashing command. After a brisk swim in the pool of cold water, they frolicked in the clear waters and then made love in the surf and on a smooth rock that was heavily covered with moss. While snorkeling in the cove, they discovered colorful schools of fish and plant life. Embracing each other beneath the cool waters, they marveled at nature's beauty. It was a captivating experience, one they wished they could have gotten on film.

The sun began its descent just as they coasted into the marina. Standing on the deck, they watched the sun fade into the distance. Craig kissed Sambrea as the sun bowed down, giving its last performance of the evening.

After securing the boat, they walked across the marina to an outdoor thatched-roof bar. Seated on barstools, Craig ordered two very tall, showy tropical fruit drinks.

Craig lifted his glass. "This is to a life of love and happiness."

Craig couldn't keep his eyes off his beautiful wife. He noticed that the other males couldn't either. The sun's brilliant rays had painted her skin a glowing bronze. The flowery sarong she wore showed off the gentle swells of her now-bronzed breasts. She'd been a lot different with him since they'd returned to Oahu. She seemed more accepting of their marital situation, more eager to give him his way— and less intimidated by the love he constantly confessed for her.

Last evening he'd kept awakening, half-expecting to find that she'd bailed out, but she'd been there beside him when his eyes opened. Her presence had made his heart burst with glee. Still, he wasn't sure if she'd return home with him again tonight and he was too afraid to ask. Afraid she'd once again become intimidated by him and bolt out of his reach.

He played with the tie of her sarong. "You don't look so peaceful, Sam. Want to tell me what you're thinking?"

She smiled delicately. "I was thinking about Breeze and what she might be up to. Craig, I'm really afraid of her. I know that sounds silly since she's my mother. You just might understand if you knew the hell she's put my father and I through. One morning we awakened and she was gone, leaving behind not a clue as to her whereabouts. If she could disappear on us like she did, what else is she capable of?"

He lifted her chin with one finger. "As long as I'm your husband, you're not to fear anyone or anything."

It almost sounded like a threat to her, as if he would only protect her as long as she was his wife. Wouldn't she always be his wife even if she were to become an ex-wife? Her eyes appeared to sadden. "If I weren't your wife, would you still be this protective of me, Craig?"

He kissed the inside of her palm. "Invalid point, Sam. You *are* my wife. I plan to keep it that way and I'll protect you at all cost. Breeze Sinclair wouldn't last a day in the trenches with me. I'm used to getting down and dirty. She may very well be a clever woman, but she's no match for your husband."

Melodic laughter cleared the lump in her throat. "You probably haven't had as much as a dirty fingernail in your entire life. It's my guess that you fight in the trenches with that mind of yours. You do have a brilliant mind, but at times it's frightening."

He scolded her with a wagging finger. "There's that word again. I have to teach you to master your fears, Sam. Fear is another useless emotion, unless there's really something to fear." He kissed her lips. "Now that's what I call frightening. Your hot kisses terrorize me." He hoped to lighten things up a bit.

"As yours terrorize me. We've had another fantastic day and a wonderful evening. I thank you for everything, but I'm really very tired. Though it's been a very satisfying day, it has been a very long one. Would you mind taking me home now, Craig?" She had a look of uncertainty.

Wondering what home she was referring to, he held his

breath. He had a pretty good idea it wasn't the one they'd shared last evening and this morning. "Whatever you want, Sam."

As the sparkle left his eyes, she felt saddened by the disappearance of midnight. Not wanting to be influenced in any way, she quickly turned her head away. Sambrea wanted to spend every waking moment with Craig, but she couldn't, not until she trusted him fully. She felt weak and needy in his presence. Loving him left her powerless and she needed all the power she could generate for her fight for De La Brise.

Ready to beg her to go home with him, he stood up and reached for her hand. Rather quickly, he changed his mind. He knew there was nothing he could say to change hers.

When they reached the bungalow, Craig came inside to use the bathroom.

Twenty minutes later, wondering why he was taking so long, Sambrea went in search of him. Finding him in her bed, fast asleep, no anger surfaced and no tirade surged forth. She didn't feel betrayed, nor did she utter any words that would send him packing. For several minutes she just stood by, quietly watching him sleep.

In the bathroom she stripped out of her sarong and climbed into the shower. Eager to slide into bed next to her husband, she decided to make it a quick one. How rapidly things kept changing. Like a fool, she'd been ready to forsake him for an evening alone just to put her head back on straight. But she had to accept that Craig Caldwell wasn't an easy one to abandon. There was nothing about him that came easy for her, with the exception of loving him.

Before she could get out of the shower, Craig was there beside her, fully aroused.

As her smile welcomed him, he felt relieved to know that he hadn't angered her with his latest prank. His eyes danced with light. "I'm ready to take whatever you're willing to give, Sambrea. I'd be satisfied with nothing at all if that's to be the case."

Her smile glowed. "Liar! Boy, if I don't take you out of your physical agony, you're going to be one hurting brother." Giving herself to him had become so natural for her, as natural as it seems to any newlywed couple who marry for love. In an instant she wrapped one of her legs around his.

He grinned broadly. "You can get into big trouble like this, girl." He nibbled at her ear.

"Promises, promises." She reached up and crushed one of his silken curls between her fingers.

As the water pelted over their bodies, intensifying the already steamy heat, neither one noticed when the shower ran out of hot water as they filled each other with one spasmodic delight after another.

Early the next morning Craig found himself alone again. Lying perfectly still, he thought about the woman he loved and how their lives had become entwined. De La Brise had brought them together, but that wasn't what he wanted to keep them together. He simply wanted Sambrea to return his love, wanted her to come to him, to surrender to him, of her own accord. But she still needed coercing from him. He was a patient man, he reminded himself, very patient indeed.

Although Craig Caldwell had made his fortune off the misfortunes of others, he didn't see it as his fault when others couldn't keep their businesses afloat, nor had he ever become personally involved in any take-over. There were some companies he'd backed away from, or helped, after he was made fully aware of their circumstances—special circumstances or unavoidable ones. But as for company owners known for bad business practices, he never gave them a second thought and he then would immediately order the wheels to be set in motion to obtain controlling shares of their company.

Once enough stock was acquired, Caldwell and Caldwell Incorporated moved in for the kill.

De La Brise had come under scrutiny by his team of experts. Financially, it looked grim for the company, yet when Craig found out who De La Brise actually belonged to, he did something he'd never done before. He got personally involved. The fact that he'd already come so dangerously close to making love to its beautiful, sexy owner played a large part in his decision, but his reasons went much deeper than that. Sambrea had been the woman in his fantasies from the first moment he'd laid eyes on her, and he'd fallen for her long before that momentous night on the beach.

Craig had watched Sambrea for months as she walked the beach looking lonely and forlorn. He hadn't even tried to find out her name. Seeing her on the beach at night had really concerned him, especially with a sexual predator on the loose. But what had preoccupied him most was how to make his fantasies about her come true. Although she'd always be his fantasy woman, he loved having her as his wife even more.

Getting out of bed, Craig walked to the front of the house, where he went over to the window and scanned the beach for his sea nymph. It was a rather hazy morning, but clear enough for him to see she wasn't on the beach. He looked at the clock. Only five A.M., yet he felt alive and alert. He seated himself in a chair to await her return. Little did he know that he'd have a very long wait.

The other offices were silent, except for the noisy humming of the printer. Sambrea sat in her private office, busy printing out financial documents she needed to study. She quickly noticed several large expenditures that she didn't remember signing requisitions for, yet they'd been approved by the board of directors. The signature of Tyler Wilson was affixed to each document.

Tyler had retired from the company, but it appeared the documents were dated after his retirement. In fact, dated very recently. Suddenly, a few things seemed to click for her. Before retiring Tyler had spent a good deal of time in France. Could he have been seeing Breeze? Could he have been helping Breeze in some way? After giving it serious thought, she doubted it. Tyler had been Samuel's best friend for over forty years and had been as anguished over the disappearance of Breeze as Samuel had been.

Still, she had to wonder about all the time he'd spent abroad.

Something flashed through the corridor, and though it was only caught by her peripheral vision, she was sure it had been the figure of a man. Glancing at her watch, she remembered it was Sunday. None of the staff was due in. Rarely did any of her employees come in over the weekend, but that might have to change, at least until the company was totally out of the woods.

Warily, Sambrea walked into the corridor, just in time to hear the front door click shut. Less than a second later, the security system went berserk. She covered her assaulted ears as she ran to the office housing the security equipment. Roving frantically from one camera to another, she tried to get a position on the intruder.

It was then that she saw him. The emotions in her eyes seemed to scream her disbelief and smoldering rage. Then she noticed something strange. Craig was heading toward the entrance, not the exit. No doubt trying to cover up his misdeeds, she assessed. With a flick of her wrist, she shut the security system down.

Shaking in her fine leather sandals, she went to wait at the elevator.

As Craig stepped out of the elevator, she attempted to land a full blow across his face. Catching her hand in mid air, he looked stunned by her sudden attack on him.

He gripped her shoulders. "What's this all about, Sam? We spent the entire night making love, now you look as though you want to kill me. What's wrong with you, girl?"

With a force akin to violence, she jerked away from him. "What are you doing here? Weren't you in these offices only moments ago? How did you gain access without reinserting the security codes?" Her eyes met with a blank stare. "You'd better 'fess up. I'm sure the police are on their way."

The mistrust in her eyes made him feel sick with grief. To ease the aching, he pulled her to him. "I just got here, Sam. I was surprised to find the doors standing open. Why would I go out and then come right back in? Why, Sam?"

She looked defeated. "Why do you do anything? Oh, Craig, if it wasn't you, someone was in here that shouldn't have been. Now I'm scared to death. How can I master my fears when they keep coming at me in such rapid succession?"

As tears sprang to her eyes, he kissed them away. Despite her anguish she felt his sensuality right down to her toes. "Come on, honey. You need a cup of hot coffee. You're shaking like a leaf in winter."

The police were in their faces before they had a chance to turn around. Satisfied with the identification given by Sambrea and Craig, they left to do a thorough search of the premises.

Craig led her to the employee's lounge, where he made a fresh pot of coffee. Once it was ready, he served it to her black. "Drink this, honey. It will help calm your nerves, or make you want to run a marathon. I'm not that great a coffee maker. I either underdo it or overdo it on the measurements, but I think you should drink it anyway. If it's not right for your taste, I'll simply make some more."

She laughed weakly. "I thought you did everything just right." *Certainly in the lovemaking department.* Waiting for the police to return, she calmly told Craig what she'd seen. She also showed him the questionable expenditures she'd run across.

When the police did return, all they had was a slip of white paper that read: "From the Office of Sambrea Sinclair." Several numbers were also written on it, which she immediately recognized as the security codes. The intruder must have been scared off by her unexpected presence. She was glad that she hadn't been physically harmed.

Sambrea was thoroughly shaken by the time the officers left. Craig could do little to comfort her, but one thing was for sure. He wasn't going to leave her alone at the office, or anywhere else, for that matter.

"Get your things, Sam. We're going home. It doesn't matter which one. Wherever you choose to stay, we'll be staying together. That's my final word on it. Another thing, I'm calling a staff meeting in the morning. I'm going to run it. For now, De La Brise *is* my responsibility. Have I made myself clear?"

She nodded. He wouldn't get an argument on that point. In fact, she was glad to have him take charge. She had to admit that she needed Craig—and that he'd been right about someone trying to run the company into the ground.

Much to his surprise, just as they reached the bungalow, Sambrea told him she'd decided to stay at his place for a while. She then packed a suitcase. A few minutes later, when they reached the Pagoda house, she went off to take a long nap.

While she slept, Craig looked over the financial documents she'd brought along. He took special notice of all the large expenditures that Sambrea had called to his attention.

A few minutes after one o'clock, she finally awakened.

Happy to see that she appeared much calmer, he smiled. He appreciated how good she looked in a simple pair of denim jeans and a plain white T-shirt. She looked like a teenager.

He welcomed her into the living room with a gentle but firm hug. "You were sleeping pretty soundly. I checked on you a couple of times. It was hard to keep from awakening you. Seeing you in my bed turns me on in a way I can't begin to describe. I wanted to devour you."

Her eyes flirted boldly. "You should've awakened me. Then we could've devoured one another. As you can see, I'm fully aroused now."

He looked down at the crotch of his pants. "That makes two of us. You are one delicious-looking sister. Shall we have dessert first and dinner later, Sam?"

The seductiveness that glazed her eyes electrified him. He could feel their powerful wattage lighting up his fantasy world, a fantasy world that had become a reality for him.

"I'm starving, Craig. Food first. Then we can take our time over dessert. I like to linger for hours over my sweets."

"A girl after my own heart. I love that we think so much alike. Are you going to cook for us, Sam?"

"No. But there is something I'd like for us to do together. I'm interested in going to Sea Life Park. Later we can go to Paradise Cove for a Luau. Last but not least, dessert served right in our very own bedroom. Monday will be here in a few hours and I have tons of work that'll keep me tied to the office for the next several weeks. Do my plans meet with your approval, Mr. Caldwell?"

He was speechless. The phrase *our very own bedroom* still burned in his mind. Finally he found his voice, but only after clearing his throat. "Mrs. Caldwell, anything you want meets with my approval. I am utterly under your command."

"Good! I'll go and grab a quick snack before I change clothes. Then we can be off to the park." She started to leave the room, but stopped and turned to face him. "Craig

Caldwell, I trust you." Smiling brightly, she disappeared down the marbled foyer, looking forward to their outing.

A huge grin covered Craig's face. *It doesn't get any better than this.* He hoped he'd never have to give her a reason to distrust him. If she'd learned to trust him, she could learn to love him as well. That is, if she wasn't already in love with him. Something in her eyes seemed to tell him that she was deeply in love with him. Things were suddenly looking up.

He felt like a young kid again. Emotionally and physically he was fit enough to go the distance for Sambrea Sinclair-Caldwell.

Sea Life Park Hawaii, located a scenic half-hour drive from Waiikiki, was overrun with tourists and local residents as usual. She hadn't visited the park in years, and she still wasn't sure what had prompted her to come here today. She rather suspected that it had a lot to do with the mesmerizing sea life that they'd encountered while snorkeling.

Craig slid his arm around her waist. "Let's take a walk through the informative exhibits. Then we can take in a few of the live sea-animal acts. The park closes in a couple of hours, which doesn't give us much time."

Sambrea frowned. "I wish I'd thought of it sooner than I did. Had I not been tempted to go into the office, we could've spent the entire day in the park. But then I wouldn't have discovered that something was amiss. Even though you knew the company was being robbed, I'm glad I saw it for myself. At any rate, what's done is done. We'll deal with things as they come up."

He hugged her tightly. "Let's not discuss any of that for now. I want you to concentrate on having a good time, Sambrea. I don't want you to worry about anything or anyone today. This is our special time together. We should take full advantage of every precious moment."

After visiting the exhibits, they went to Hawaii Ocean Theater, an open-air amphitheater with tiered seating. Trained dolphins, penguins, and sea lions showed off for visitors inside a 200,000-gallon glass tank.

Sambrea pulled Craig over to the Hawaiian Reef Tank. "More than 4,000 reef animals from Hawaiian waters live in this 300,000 gallon tank," Sambrea read from the sign.

Sambrea and Craig, both staunch supporters of animal rights, enjoyed spending time at the Monk Seal Care Center. The center served as a temporary home for injured or stranded monk seals.

"Before we go to the Luau at Paradise Cove, let's go to Whaler's Cove. That's where the park's star animal performers take the audiences on an exciting voyage through Hawaii's whaling history. Have you been there before?"

Smiling, Sambrea nodded. "Only a thousand times. As a teenager, my friends and I practically lived in this park over summer vacation."

As time passed, the thought of spending an evening at Paradise Cove was the only thing keeping Sambrea alert and on her toes. Dead tired after having gotten up so early, she hoped the short nap she'd taken would help her get through the next few hours. Just the thought of more time in the exuberant company of her handsome husband boosted her energy level tremendously. Once she got home, she'd be more than ready to sleep. But then again, the remembered promise of dessert in bed just might keep her awake a bit longer.

To be intimately involved with a man like Craig Caldwell a woman had to be ready for the expected and the unexpected. Since Craig never failed to surprise her, she hoped she'd always keep him as interested in her as he was now.

Reaching Paradise Cove, Craig parked the car and ran around to open Sambrea's door. Actually throwing herself at him, she kissed him deeply before they strode toward the entrance. That came as a pleasant shock. Paradise Cove offered a tour of a thatched hut village, a housing island, and many other attractions. One could step back in time while exploring the twelve-acre authentically created Hawaiian playground.

Noticing her lip-color all over his mouth, she smiled. "Everyone will know you've been kissing me. My lipstick is all over you." She tried to wipe it away, but he stopped her.

He kissed her forehead. "Leave it, Sam. I want everyone to know we're heavily involved. I don't want anyone to think I'm you're brother."

As she flashed him a golden smile, her eyes looked as if they'd been sprinkled with gold dust. "If you hold on to me the way you've been doing all day, there won't be any mistake as to who you are and what you are to me."

He pulled her closer. "I don't think having your lipstick on me will deter the hungry looks from the male wolves, but at least they'll know you're taken." He eyed her intently. "You look a little tired. Are you having a good time?"

Deeply touched by his concern, she smiled brightly. "It's been sparkling, love. But you're right. I am a little tired. Not to worry though, I'll get plenty of sleep tonight."

His laughter was mystical. "Don't count on it, especially if you're planning on sleeping in the same bed with me. And I hope that you are. If not, I'll be terribly disappointed—after all, we still have to have dessert."

"Sounds intriguing. I'm looking forward to it." She flirted openly with Craig. Feeling more and more at ease with him, she kissed him fully on the mouth.

Practically molded together, they sauntered through the village and several of the other attractions. Just before sunset, they dined on the sumptuous buffet feast. Afterward, at a *hukilau,* they pulled fishnets from the sea to the rhythm of a conch shell and island chants.

Craig later tested his skills at spear throwing. Seeing that he wasn't halfway bad at it, she spurred him on, cheering boisterously. Realizing he hadn't had such relaxing fun in a long time, he found himself looking forward to more of the same in the near future. He'd already made his fortune and now he had someone special to spend it on. But would she stay around that long?

Oh, God, help me. How he loved Sambrea, he reflected wistfully. He loved her endlessly. How would he ever manage to face life without her if she chose not to stay with him? She was here now, though, he realized, chiding himself for his thinking.

As everyone took their places at the traditional luau, Craig felt tears stinging his midnight eyes. Sambrea's sand-and-sable eyes enchanted him as she watched the fire dancer light up the night. He was sure the brilliant light in her eyes assisted in the illumination. She had the same thought about his eyes.

As if they both had cameras in their eyes, their inner vision seemed to capture the fascinating scenes before them. Craig was totally mesmerized by her gentle beauty and she was easily enchanted by his quiet but solid strength and drop-dead gorgeous looks.

It was all he could do to stop himself from untying her sarong and watching as it slipped to the sand. Loving her brought new meaning to his life. His mind went to work on the exotic, romantic scenario that would later take place. During the ride home, Sambrea snatched a few moments of sleep. There would be no slumbering once she and Craig got into bed.

When they finally reached home, Craig had other ideas, which kept them from making it to the bedroom, period. He coerced her into a midnight stroll, which didn't take much persuasion. Sambrea was as eager to share as many romantic moments as she could with him. They found a

perfect spot to sit and watch the tide roll in. Craig untied
her sarong, letting it slide to the ground, just the way he'd
earlier imagined. Placidly, he inveigled her down onto the
sand. As they set out on their slow and easy ride to ecstasy,
the stars shone down on two lovers in love. Two lovers
flying to the heavens. Two lovers flying to the heavens
above, two hearts soaring. Just when they thought they'd
reached the pinnacle an undiscovered stratosphere elevated
them to greater heights. As two hearts began to beat as one,
time stood still. With Sambrea wrapped up in the rapture
of his lovemaking, Craig was eager to love her in a way
she'd never known from him before. Although she'd experienced his method of loving in the past, this time was going
to be much different because he was surer of where he
stood with her. Before, he may have left a thing or two to
chance, but never again would anything be left to chance.
Never again would she have to wonder where she stood
with him.

By the time this night was over, there wouldn't be a di-
minutive grain of doubt left in her mind about his love for
her. He loved her. He married her. It was for keeps. He was
for keeps. She was for keeps. Their love was for keeps;
their marriage was for keeps.

It seemed like Monday's sunrise would never come, but
Craig and Sambrea could've cared less. They'd slept on the
beach the entire night, awakening before sunrise to partake
of an early morning breakfast featuring hot and heavy lovemaking.

With Sambrea asleep on his chest, Craig stroked her hair.
"De La Brise is calling us," he whispered in her ear.

Her lips pouting, she moaned softly. The sensuality of it
caused the fire to re-ignite in Craig's loins. "Do we have
to?"

He kissed her mouth hungrily. "No, we don't ever again

have to do anything we don't want to, but I want and need to have that staff meeting. Why don't you shower and get into bed until I return. When I get back, we can lounge around the pool and make each other laugh. Do we have a plan?"

She pondered his suggestion. "Yes, we definitely have a plan." Jumping up from the sand, she tied her sarong around her waist. "Come on, I'll help you shower and dress."

As she started up the beach, she noticed that he wasn't beside her. Looking back, she saw him still lying in the sand, a massive grin on his face. "Are you coming?" *So masculine, so seductive.* She smiled with pleasure. *A fine, black marble statue was he.*

"Within the next few minutes, I hope to be." He grinned like a Cheshire cat.

Burning a hot trail into her soul, his midnight eyes darkened the atmosphere. Catching his meaning, as it burned with yearning in her femininity, her cheeks infused with color.

As Sambrea kicked sand in his direction, he leaped up from the sand like a son of old Satan. Hotly, he pursued her. Like so many times before, he failed to overtake her as she ran at breakneck speed toward the Pagoda house.

EIGHT

Upon entering the office Craig saw that most of the staff was gathered around the spacious reception area. Each looked as if something dreadful was about to occur. As he passed through the spacious room, he heard the whispers circulating among the employees. Whispers weren't nearly enough to deter a man of his inexhaustible means. His confident stride relayed that to everyone present.

For Sambrea's sake, his arrogance would only surface if he deemed it necessary. Richard Henry was the only employee missing. Maybe it was just as well. Richard wasn't going to take kindly to his orders, but that wouldn't stop his mission. Eventually, however, he'd have to win Richard's trust, if only for Sambrea's peace of mind.

As Craig stepped into the center of the room, the whispers immediately went undercover. "Good morning to you all. I'm Craig Caldwell, the new joint owner of De La Brise. As many of you know, I'm also Sambrea's husband. I'm here to call an emergency staff meeting. It'll be held in the boardroom." He checked his watch. "I'll expect you promptly at nine-thirty. Tardiness is one of my pet peeves." He smiled. "It'll be appreciated if the word is spread to all those employees not present. Thank you and have a pleasant day."

Taking up residence in Sambrea's private office, he smelled her perfume as soon as he walked into the room.

Closing his eyes, he deeply inhaled her scent, the sweet gentle scent of the woman who made his life complete. Another familiar scent of hers came to mind, which nearly drove him out of the office and back to the beach house. Before settling in, he decided to call her. He really didn't want to disturb her, but he couldn't help himself. Hearing her voice would somehow make it easier for him to get through the staff meeting.

Floating lazily into his ear canal, her drowsy voice stimulated him. "I did awaken you." He felt utterly bewitched by her voice. "I'm sorry, but the truth is I had to hear your voice. Sambrea, Sambrea, you'll never know what that name does for me. Believe me, it's good. It's all good."

Her laughter was light and lilting. "I was about to get up anyway. What time is it?"

He looked at his watch. "A little after nine. The staff meeting is at nine-thirty. Hopefully I'll be back in your arms before noon. Miss me, Sam?"

She giggled. "Every inch of me does, Craig Caldwell. *I love you.* I've got to go to the bathroom. I always do when I first wake up." Without another word, she disconnected the line.

His heart rate careened. Laughter effervesced in his brain. Tears scrimmaged with the midnight darkness in his eyes. All of it was alarming, and he stood up, clapping his hands in the process. His legs felt weak and rubbery as he actually got up on top of the desk. While dancing atop the plastic blotter even his feet felt happy.

"She loves me, she loves me." He shouted it over and over again. "Sambrea Sinclair-Caldwell truly loves me. At last, she's confessed." The thought of her mentioning her love for him along with her need to use the bathroom sent gales of laughter flying through the otherwise tranquil room.

Looking highly agitated, Richard entered without knocking.

Laughing like an imbecile, Craig was still on top of the desk. Richard thought Craig had lost all of his toys; maybe Sambrea's rejection of him and his high-handed ways had pushed him over the precipice of sanity.

Richard's expression grew unreadable as he looked at Craig. "Would you mind telling me what's going on in here? Why wasn't I informed of this so-called emergency staff meeting? And where is Sam?"

Armoring himself with an extra shield of arrogance, Craig got down off the desk and sat back in the chair. He needed an extra dose of patience, too. "Since we're playing twenty-questions, why did you find it necessary to just walk in here unannounced? I do have an intercom, Mr. Henry."

Richard also saw the need to armor himself. "Mr. Caldwell, for your information, I've been walking in and out of this office at will for over fifteen years. This was Samuel's office long before it was Sambrea's. Always, their secretaries knew when they weren't to be disturbed."

The look on Richard's face revealed open contempt for his new employer. He thought his longevity deserved some show of respect.

Craig didn't care if he'd been there thirty years. This office was now his and Sambrea's. Richard Henry was just going to have to get used to the idea or find employment elsewhere. Rules always had a way of changing. If people could just learn to change with the rules, perhaps life wouldn't be so difficult, Craig mused, a brooding look on his face.

Trying to get a grip on his temper, Craig spun the leather swivel chair a full turn before turning back to face Richard. "One shouldn't dwell on the past. It's best left behind. Mr. Henry, since you know about the staff meeting, someone must have informed you. Do you think about what you're going to say before speaking? If not, it's a good habit to get into it. It helps to keep from making an ass of oneself. As for Sam, she's at our home, in our bed." If Richard had some sort of romantic fixation on Sambrea, Craig wanted his territorial rights clearly delineated.

Taking a seat on the leather sofa, Richard stared hard at Craig for several seconds. "This is no good," Richard uttered. Craig's eyebrows furrowed. "We can't run a company acting like this with one another. I do apologize for my part in this childish exchange." His tone was devoid of bitterness. Richard looked at the wall clock. "I think we have some people waiting for us, Mr. Caldwell. They're all probably half-crazed by now. Shall we go to the boardroom?"

Craig stood up and walked toward Richard. "I think you might have something there, Mr. Henry. It makes perfect sense to me." Smiling, Craig graciously extended his hand. "It would make me feel more at home if you'd simply call me Craig."

Without hesitation, Richard took the offered hand, shaking it firmly. "I hope you don't have an aversion to calling me Rich or Richard."

Though it wasn't spoken aloud, the two men had found some common ground. Neither would desecrate it without just cause. Both sensed it as they walked out of the office together ready to reassure and calm the employees. Entering the boardroom, they sat across the long table, each showing respect for the other's responsibilities.

Craig sat at the head of the table; Richard was at the opposite end. Craig quietly hoped that a strong alliance between them might be born. Samuel and Sambrea had obviously placed a lot of faith in Richard over the years. Craig decided it wouldn't do his and Sambrea's marriage any good to have them fighting over Richard's future with the company.

Craig saw that the employees seemed rather nervous. Using his charming wit and smile, he effortlessly put them at ease. Calling the staff meeting to order, he outlined the new policies to be implemented in the very near future. He also mentioned a few new benefits that seemed to make everyone extremely happy. All the men, married or single, were glad to know they could take sick time off to be with their families in a time of crisis and for maternity leave. Wanting children of his own someday, Craig took delight in making that particular benefit available to his new and old employees.

While Craig was grooming and winning over his new staff, Sambrea felt lifeless as she sat on the side of the bed. Telling Craig that she loved him had an unsettling affect on her. It was certainly true enough, but had she said too much too soon?

There was still so much that she didn't know about the man. Sambrea had never heard him talk about any family members, yet his company carried the name of Caldwell and Caldwell. Who was the other Caldwell? Could he have a son? Or was he the son? Had he been married before? Was the other Caldwell an ex-wife? She should explore all the possible scenarios.

It astounded her to realize how little she really did know about him. One thing for sure—she was going to find out. Continuing to play the game of Trivial Pursuit with herself, she thought of the personal questions she'd later ask of him.

Tired of the mental game, she propelled herself from the bed, deciding to discover as much about him as she could from his own habitat. She'd start here in the bedroom. Strolling into the walk-in closet, she examined what she thought was an excessive wardrobe for a male. It kind of reminded her of all the clothes she owned, which took up two closets, without counting the closet space in her office. There was no doubt that he had expensive and impeccable taste in wearing apparel. She gently fingered the fine silk of his vast collection of designer shirts and ties.

Moving through the house, slowly but surely, Sambrea familiarized herself with the layout of the rooms and their content. Spotting several leather photo albums in his lav-

ishly decorated retreat, she picked up one and settled down
in one of the plush recliners. The recliners were fashioned
after airplane seats but seemed far more commodious. The
entire room looked as if its design was based on another
of Craig's fantasies.

Inside the albums she saw pictures of numerous women.
Although Craig was in several of the shots, there didn't
seem to be anything terribly intimate between him and the
women. Feeling downright silly, she wrestled with another
bout of denial. As she looked at the pictures, the women
in them meant nothing to her because the only person she
could see him with was herself. The powerful image of him
and her together was all she wanted to see.

Suddenly, she stiffened, squinting her eyes at one of the
photographs. Removing it from its plastic protector, she
scrutinized it closely. A painful moan was torn from her
lips. *Breeze was the woman in the photograph.* Although
she wasn't exactly posing with Craig, she was close enough
to him to feel his breath on her cheek. Looking for a date,
she turned the picture over and saw that it had been taken
two years ago. It had been shot in Monte Carlo, the same
area where Breeze said she'd been living.

The pain in her gut was torture. It felt like a hot poker
stabbing her repeatedly in the mid-section. Was she jumping
to conclusions again, or did Craig in fact know Breeze?
Had he lied to her after all? Was he helping Breeze to take
De La Brise away from her? The questions came at her
relentlessly but with no answers in sight.

As she noticed Breeze in three other pictures, an icy gust
of air toyed with her stiffened spine. She trembled. Her
trickling tears felt as icy as the gust of air. Still, Craig wasn't
actually posing with Breeze. Yet they stood only inches
apart. How could he not know her? There were several other
people in the photograph as well; she saw that they were
standing just as close to him as Breeze was.

Her fingers shook as she placed the photos back in their

jackets. Feeling like someone prying into the private affairs of another without their permission, she put the albums away. Sitting quietly, she thought about what this could mean for her and Craig. Was it already over for them? Would their marriage end in a bitter divorce like so many others had?

What had Samuel always told her? A picture was worth a thousand words, but which thousand? Still, she wanted to give Craig the benefit of the doubt. Samuel had also told her to only believe half of what she saw and none of what she heard. Which part would apply here? Should she only believe half of what she saw in the pictures and none of what she'd heard from Craig? It would be so distressing to do the latter, she anguished.

Another serious warning from Samuel came to mind, the most profound and prophetic of all. If it looks, acts, feels, and sounds too good to be true, that's probably because it is. When you know in your heart you're dealing with a snake, don't ever make the mistake of putting it into your pocket, no matter how harmless it may appear. It will fill you with its venom the first chance it gets.

As she recalled the type of marriage Samuel had been so unfortunate to be saddled with, her laughter was chilling. Why hadn't Samuel applied any of his sagacious teachings to his relationship with Breeze? His wife had turned out to be a snake in the grass if there ever was one. She always did have to dress in the finest of leather. A female snake is the worst kind. *Once bitten by a poisonous female, death is absolute.*

Swearing to get to the bottom of what the photographs suggested, Sambrea moved into the mammoth, open-concept designed kitchen. Two skylights provided all the lighting she'd need. Desiring some fresh air, she slid back the sliding glass doors to allow the ocean breeze to drift through and cool the wide-open spaces.

Every modern convenience known to mankind was here

in this kitchen. All of them appeared untouched. She rather suspected Craig of rarely using the kitchen since he'd earlier asked if she was going to cook. If Craig had lied to her, she'd cook for him all right. But he'd never recover from the supper she'd prepare. It would be his last.

Oh, well, there wasn't much she could do about it now, except wait until he returned. She had to be a fool to even think of waiting for him. *Just like all the other fools in love.* It suddenly dawned on her that she didn't need to make excuses for staying. There was no need to wage a war against herself, nor was there any reason to deeply probe her conscience. She knew exactly why she was waiting for Craig. She loved him and he deserved a chance to defend himself. That is, if he truly needed a defense.

So far, Craig Caldwell hadn't let her down. But was that part of the plan? He wouldn't let her down if he were using her, at least, not until he'd used her up. She cringed as she imagined the pain and suffering she'd go through if that turned out to be the case. *You're much too mature for this type of mindless thinking.* She made a mad dash for the bathroom to shower and do all of the things that she normally did to prepare for the day.

It was eleven o'clock, she noted.

Fresh from her shower, she dressed in front of the mirror. Expecting Craig to walk through the door at any moment, she wondered if she'd be able to pull off questioning him without losing it. Could she truly be objective? Only time would tell.

Sambrea looked stunning in an emerald green sarong. Loving the easy, flowing style, she was most comfortable in uncomplicated attire. Craig had found another reason to love her in sarongs, which she owned in just about every color and design imaginable. They afforded him easy access to her most desirable flesh, he'd just told her a few days before.

Underneath the sarong, she wore a two-piece swimsuit

in the same color as the sarong. Since Craig had mentioned lounging around the pool, she wore the suit just in case she ended up lounging *in* the pool, unexpectedly. A pool was such a waste when one lived right on the beach, yet it did afford a lot more privacy during the daylight hours.

Although the pagoda house was secluded, now and then a neighbor would stray over the private property lines, but it rarely happened after dusk. Craig ignored most of the posted signs, but it was indeed a rarity for others to do so. Craig believed he owned the world and all that was in it simply because he was sure that that's what the Creator had intended, she recalled him saying.

Thinking Craig would be hungry when he made it home, Sambrea strolled back into the kitchen, unable to believe she was actually acting like a concerned wife; a wife wanting to make sure her husband was properly fed and properly bedded.

Looking into the refrigerator, she noticed the abundance of fresh fruit, vegetables, and many other delicacies, none of which had to be cooked. It appeared that Craig had on hand just the things he could prepare himself if he had to. Removing one of the pineapples, she split it with a large knife, coring and cutting it into large chunks. Having grown up on so much pineapple, she thought she'd grow to hate it. But the sweet, tangy taste of it still excited her palate, as did many of the other Hawaiian tropical fruits. Serving fresh fruit in Hawaii was akin to having salt and pepper on the table. It was always there.

Before leaving the kitchen, Sambrea cut two mangoes, a cantaloupe, and a honeydew melon into delectable chunks. Finding in the refrigerator what appeared to be a fairly recent roasted chicken, she cut it up, mixing it with celery, onions and herb mayonnaise. It turned out to be a great looking chicken salad. Craig had some fresh pumpernickel rolls and she lightly toasted them in the oven. Lastly, she prepared two garden salads.

* * *

Sambrea was busy setting the table out by the pool when she was pulled into his granite-like body. If possible, his eyes appeared to be a darker midnight, but not without the mystique of the moonlight. He taunted her with breathtaking kisses. And there was no way she could've resisted him. He was simply irresistible.

Looking right through to her soul, Craig sat her down on the chaise lounge. "You said something to me on the phone that I'm still not sure about. Please repeat your part of our phone conversation," he requested softly.

She feigned innocence. "Did I talk to you on the phone? I'm afraid I don't even remember the phone ringing, Craig. Perhaps I was talking in my sleep. Sorry, pal, I can't help you out on this one."

His eyes clouded with uncertainty as he shrugged his shoulders. "My mistake for waking you up." Barely focusing, he looked around the patio. Tears threatened. If he could've helped it, he wouldn't have allowed his emotions to show. He'd never been so disappointed in his life. It made him feel powerless.

Turning him around to face her, she cupped his face in her hands. His glistening tears severely stung her heart. Lowering his head onto her chest, she twisted her fingers in his carbon curls. "Every inch of me does, Craig Caldwell. I love you. I've got to go to the bathroom. I always do when I first wake up," she whispered across his lips.

His head jerked up in one swift motion. He transferred the now starry midnight of his eyes into hers. "I heard you right." His voice was barely audible as he tried to recover from the earlier shock. "You do love me, don't you, Sambrea? I haven't been just imagining what your eyes have been telling me for weeks now. Have I, Sam?"

Sambrea's tears fell onto his chest. "Yes, I do love you,

Craig. No, you haven't been imagining it. I love you, Craig Caldwell."

This was not at all what she'd planned to have happen. But how could anything else take precedence over her telling him she loved him, since it really seemed to matter. He appeared genuinely thrilled. The subject of Breeze Sinclair would just have to wait. If she had to leave him, she wasn't going to leave without one more memory to take with her. A memory to keep their love alive in her soul forever.

The sarong didn't stand a chance of being close to her body for one more delicious second. The swimsuit stood even less of a chance. Adeptly, he removed both and tossed them across the patio. "I love you, Sambrea. You love me. We'd be selfish to ask for more. Love me, Sam."

He carried her through the house. Rushing into the retreat, he deposited her in the captain's chair. Then he stripped away his clothes. Willingly, she assumed command, wrapping her legs up high around his waist.

Breathlessly, soaring into yet another uncharted zone, their lovemaking was even more sensuous, erotic, and tantalizing. The culmination of their love occurred with both lovers totally of one accord.

Sambrea and Craig showered together before finally taking up residence on the patio, where they feasted off the lunch her delicate hands had so carefully prepared. She wore a ravishing, hiding-very-little black bikini. He was clad in burgundy swim trunks that looked as if they'd been sculpted on his muscular body. A white towel was thrown loosely around his neck. His skin was deeply tanned from the recent sailing trip.

Sambrea watched as the pool waters swirled over the massive rock formations and out through the waterfall. At night the waterfall was lit up like a crystal Christmas tree. Absently, she plucked at the fruit, popping one kind after another into her mouth. As reality searched and seized her mind, burning questions regarding Craig's relationship to Breeze refused to be extinguished.

Reaching across the table, he caught her ear lobe between his thumb and a finger. Gently, he massaged it. "I have a big surprise for you, Sam. Would you like to see it?"

The little girl in her blossomed and her eyes grew wide with childish wonder. "I love surprises! Of course I want to see it. Can I have a clue?"

He laughed. "Not so much as a breath of a hint. Wait here. I'll be right back."

She was beside herself by the time he finally came back.

Using a silk tie, he covered her eyes and tied it loosely. He then carried her inside. As though a game of pin the tail on the donkey was about to ensue, he turned her around several times. That only added to her dizzy anticipation. All she could see were dark spots when he whisked the tie from her eyes.

Turning into a melting pot of fiery liquid, her eyes quickly refocused. Before her, hanging over the fireplace mantel, was the most magnificent hand-painted portrait of herself and Craig.

"When? How?"

He laughed heartily. "Look at the clothes we're wearing and you'll have your answer."

She eyed the portrait closely. *The Wayward Breeze*. She'd only worn the sea-blue gown that one time.

"Bravo, Sam!"

"But how, Craig? We certainly didn't pose for this portrait."

"Honey, we were posing all night—and didn't even know it. One of the staff members gave me the photos. They were taken while we floated off into God only knows where. I took them to a buddy of mine and this is what he came up with just by looking at the photographs."

"Amazing! It was only a short time ago. It's so life-like.

Gosh, we were dazzling that night. You and I look fabulous together. Look at all the fine detail. Please kiss me before I drown in my own excitement. Thank you, Craig. It's so very special!"

He wasted no time in honoring her request. He couldn't seem to get enough of this woman. Knowing that she loved him left his brain incapacitated but also gave him divine peace.

"Ready for a swim, Sam?"

"Not yet." Her tone was sobering. All the excitement left her breathless yet did little to wash away her fears. "Craig, since we're on the subject of photographs, I have some questions to ask you about a few pictures I saw in your albums earlier. Yes, I've been snooping. I remember someone telling me what was theirs was mine. Do you know who that someone was?"

He shrugged his shoulders. "Of course I remember. It was true. This sounds serious, Sambrea. What's on your mind? Before you tell me, let's look at the photos in question."

In the retreat, she sat the same place as earlier. Knowing exactly which album the photos were in, she turned to them without hesitation. "This is one." She pointed at the picture. "There are a couple of others. Do you know everyone in these pictures?"

He frowned. "I would imagine so, but not on a one-on-one basis. I can't even call them all by name. These are some of the people I hung out with when I visited France a couple of years ago. What do they have to do with anything? They were mere acquaintances."

She put her finger on the face of Breeze. "What about her? Was she just an acquaintance, too?"

He could barely make out the woman's face let alone tell her who it was. "I'm afraid you're going to have to use the direct-approach method. I don't play the game of cat and mouse very well. What is it, Sambrea? What has you so on edge?"

"That's Breeze, Craig. My mother is in several pictures with you. I want some answers," she stated in a matter of fact tone. Her voice started cracking under the stress.

He ran his fingers through his hair. "I don't have the answers, Sambrea. To me, she's just a woman in a picture. There were a lot of people there that day. I can't honestly say that I met every one of them. But if I'd met your mother before now, I'd surely remember her. The woman grated on my nerves the day she came to my office. I wouldn't easily forget her, Sambrea. To that I swear."

"I believe you. Sorry. I had to know. I still haven't mastered my fears, Craig. I hope you'll be patient with me."

He slipped his arm around her shoulders. "I have the patience of Job where you're concerned. There are a lot of things you have to learn about me, Sam, and I about you, but one thing you can be sure of is that I'm not a liar. Lying has no fringe benefits. It's destructive. I'm not about to destroy what we're just beginning to build here."

Hot tears poked at her eyes. Why was she so accepting of his answers? A short time ago she believed nothing he had to say. Was this what love did to people? It was the only answer that made any sense. Trust was not something she gave on impulse. Then again, hadn't she impulsively given Craig all that she was?

She placed her hand in his. "I don't mean to doubt you so much, but I have to be sure about everything and everybody. I'm beginning to be real sure about you. Is that a mistake, Craig?"

He felt the slight trembling of her fingers. "No mistake, Sam. I want you to be sure about me. I need you to be sure. Our relationship is important to me. Sam, have you ever wondered why I am the way I am? Why I possess a wealth of confidence, not to mention material wealth?"

Her expression was reflective. "I wonder about you all the time, Craig. Most people I can figure out relatively quickly. But I don't know that you can be figured out."

He grinned. "I like it that way, as far as my business dealings go. My relationship with you is another matter. Still, it would be no fun if we figured everything out all at once. You and I have the rest of our lives to figure each other out. As for my part, I promise to keep you intrigued."

She smiled wryly. "Why don't you tell me why you're so confident about everything, Mr. Caldwell. You seem to have a secret formula to success. I'd like to know what it is."

Placing his head in her lap, he looked up at her. "Sam, I simply believe that God will take care of all my needs. He's proven Himself so many times during my lifetime. I just don't worry about what I have or don't have because I believe without question in the promises of the Creator. Things haven't always been easy for me and no one ever said they would be. But I trust in the word of the Master. *Seek and you shall find. Try me and I'll pour you out a blessing you can't begin to receive.*

"My peace, confidence, and wealth simply comes from boundless faith. I can be happy with or without material wealth. I couldn't exist if I had nothing more to rely on than the almighty dollar. While I respect money and the things that can be accomplished with it, I don't worship it."

Astounded by his common-sense wisdom, her smile was bright. While she didn't exactly see him as a religious man, she was convinced that he possessed an incredible amount of faith. She almost envied him that. "Sometimes you just blow me away. You have the faith of newborn babies. They're completely helpless, yet their trust is implicit."

He kissed her forehead. "By the way, how do you feel about babies?"

"Whoa!" Her laughter was strained. "I don't know. I

mean, I love little children, but I'm not sure how I'd be as
a mother. I don't think I'm very well equipped for the role
since I didn't have a very good model. Can I think about
it a while longer?"

He gently tugged at a few strands of her hair. "Take all
the time you need. I don't plan on sharing you with anyone
for a long time to come. However, I'd eventually like a
couple of kids to nurture and spoil."

The question of children was only one of many questions
that needed answering, and she started firing away. "What
about your parents? Where are they?"

Thinking of his parents warmed his heart. "They're missionaries living in South Africa. They do what comes naturally to them, helping others. During Christmas and early
summer I fly to South Africa for a short visit. We always
have a wonderful reunion. Soon we'll go there together,
Sam."

"I'd love that. What does the second Caldwell stand for
in the company name?"

"For the son or daughter that will hopefully follow in
my footsteps. Now that we're married, you're the other
Caldwell. I plan to make the legal changes."

Butterflies flitted in her stomach. "That's a generous offer, but you should wait until the six months are up before
you go making any changes. In case it doesn't work out
between us."

"I won't let that stop me, Sam. My faith is not in *what
ifs*. Separate them—and they can be defined. Together,
there's no definition. They're not even linked together in
the dictionary."

"That's heavy, Craig, but what about the women in your
past? I know I said I didn't want to know, but I do."

He laughed at her contrite expression. "I'm not going to
go into depth over my past relationships. The past belongs in
the past, Sam. I live in the present most of the time, except
when I think back on the time I've spent with you." He

charmed her with a brilliant smile. "However, I've had plenty of other relationships. Only one was serious, but I never found it serious enough to commit on a permanent basis. I don't want to know all that much about your past relationships, Sam. It's not going to change a thing for me, but I'd like to know—have you ever had a serious relationship?"

"Lawrence and I grew up together. He was my one and only true heartthrob, too frivolous to be taken seriously. We've dated off and on and were doing so until recently." *That is, until you came along and swept me off my feet.* "I haven't had the opportunity to tell Lawrence that I'm married. I really don't think it'll matter much to him one way or the other. Lawrence is a playboy at heart. Where did you get your education?"

"Texas Southern University, Houston, Texas. I have a degree in mechanical engineering. Where did you go to school?" He didn't want to delve any further into her relationship with Lawrence.

"I graduated from the University of Hawaii with a degree in early childhood education. It looks like neither of us work in the fields we trained for."

Although it was late coming, for the next hour they learned of one another's likes, dislikes, ambitions, and dreams, along with a lot of other insignificant drivel.

Removing his head from her lap, he stood up. "Let's put a hold on the discovery issues for now. We have to save something for later."

Bending over the sofa, he picked her up and carried her through the house and back out onto the patio. Tossing her in the pool, he jumped in right behind her. Laughing, she remembered why she'd put the swimsuit on in the first place.

Yes, Craig will be true to his word—he'll keep me intrigued.

NINE

Located near Waikiki Beach, Scruples was a chic place, where the saddest of spirits could be lifted. This lively spot had a different theme every evening. Tonight was "Oldies-but-Goodies Night". The popular club stayed packed. Rarely did anyone leave Scruples feeling blue. No one had to leave alone, unless they chose to do so.

During a dreamy slow song Craig held Sambrea close as he guided her over the dance floor. He loved the black strapless dress. It outlined her sexy figure. The black onyx earrings and necklace she wore made her eyes appear much darker. The way they glittered fascinated him. With several of the buttons on his dark blue shirt open, her hand rested on the hairy expanse of his chest. Despite the blaring music they conversed through the poetic language of their eyes.

As the song ended, Craig led her to the table. He seated himself after she sat down. She seemed so happy and content with him. He hoped nothing would ever take her smile away. He held her hand across the table. "Do you want something else to drink, Sam?"

"Please. Another Mai Tai will incite me to do a striptease act in here, so make it a virgin."

He blinked hard. "A virgin is definitely in order if that's the effect it's having on you. Save the strip tease act for the privacy of our bedroom. I'll be looking forward to the late evening show." With mischief bright in his eye, he flirted with her. Smiling devilishly, he hailed the cocktail waitress.

The waitress appeared and Craig ordered the drinks.

Settling back in his chair, he stared at Sambrea, as if he expected her to up and disappear. His expression turned serious.

"What's happening in that head of yours, dreamboat? The midnight sun looks a little calamitous." She laughed at how serious he'd become.

"Nothing to worry yourself over, Sam. Sometimes I have a hard time believing you're no longer just a fantasy of mine. Every now and then I have to do a reality check." He cast her a bright smile to show her that everything was indeed fine. The brightness of his smile chased away the disturbing blackness in his eyes.

After getting out of her seat, she walked around the table and dropped down on his lap. "Do I feel like a fantasy, Craig?" she whispered. She coiled her arms around his neck. "Touch me, lover."

Grinning, his hand circled her waistline. "Yes, you do feel like a fantasy, Sam. You'll always be my fantasy, whether you're in my presence or not. That's one of the things I love about loving you. I can conjure up your image at will."

Pulling her head down, he kissed her hard on the mouth. Her lips, soft with the smoothness of satin, seared his mouth on contact and left him breathless.

Gasping for breath, she pushed him away. "Let's go home. We're making a spectacle of ourselves."

"One more slow dance and I'll honor your request. First, we finish our drinks. You look mighty thirsty, Sam."

"Hungry, too." She thought of later and all the delicious ways they'd feed their hunger and thirst. After kissing her again, he returned her to her original seat.

She stood right back up. "Got to go to the bathroom." He got to his feet. "No need to escort me. I can find my way back to you. I've bugged your crotch with a homing device. It's not like the natural radar you claim to possess, but it'll work."

Craig laughed at her colorful comment. He loved her more and more with each passing second. His eyes zeroed in on the seductive sway of her hips as she inched her way through the lively throng. The girl simply drove him crazy. When Craig finally turned his eyes from his alluringly beautiful Sambrea, the unruly, unpredictable Breeze had already set up housekeeping.

He eyed her curiously. "What are you after now, Mrs. Sinclair?" He had addressed her with a politeness that he didn't at all feel.

Her laughter was wicked. "The same thing you're after, Mr. Caldwell. Sambrea's money! I went to your office earlier today, but I was told you weren't in. Are you going to show up tomorrow for our scheduled appointment? It would be such a shame for you to miss out on what I have to say."

He raised an eyebrow. "I was sure my secretary would've phoned you by now. Our meeting is canceled, permanently. You and I don't have a thing to discuss."

Breeze snorted loudly. "Oh, but we do, Mr. Caldwell. We have plenty to discuss. I own the shares that could give either you or Sambrea the controlling percentage of De La Brise. For a smart man like yourself, I'm surprised to learn that you didn't know I was holding an ace or two. Of course, you couldn't have known the shares were in my maiden name. By the way, it was clever of you to sign that little pre-nuptial agreement using the name Jacob Ladder. You see, we do have something in common. *Deception.*"

Caught totally off guard by her announcement, Craig felt his heart slamming inside his chest. He felt like he was suffocating. Wondering how she'd seen a copy of the pre-nuptial agreement, his eyes narrowed with anger. The one Sambrea kept in her office? The break-in.

Breeze felt a moment of triumph. "It's obvious my silly little daughter didn't even bother to have her attorneys go over the agreement. Unless you have them in your pocket also."

Neither of them had noticed Sambrea's return. Stunned with shock and disbelief, she backed away. It felt as though her entire world had just been blown apart. She'd heard Breeze's statement regarding the pre-nuptial agreement. Remembering that she'd filed the document in the filing cabinet in her private office, she cringed. *Was that what someone was after when they broke into her offices? Apparently so.*

As far as she was concerned, she'd heard enough. With her mind in a state of anguish, she rushed toward the exit. Craig and Breeze were two snakes of one kind. She was now convinced of their alliance.

Craig smirked. "We'll never have to implement that agreement, Mrs. Sinclair. Sambrea and I are in love. We're in this marriage for life. Now that our cards are on the table—and I've been declared the winner—why don't you tell me what it will take to make you disappear for good?" he shouted above the blasting music.

Breeze had his rapt attention. She basked in the thrilling sensations that the victory brought. "For starters, I need money. Mind you, I live way above the clouds. And I have a few serious debts to pay. If I'm going to disappear, you're going to have to make it well worth my while."

Not at all surprised that she could be bought, Craig eyed her thoughtfully. She was as see-through as sheer nylon but hard as nails. Although she had exceptional outward beauty, inwardly, brittleness had turned Breeze into an ugly creation of mankind. Breeze Sinclair looked nothing at all like his beautiful Sambrea did.

Folding his hands, he placed them on the table. "Are you willing to sign over your shares and everything else you might think you have a right to? If not, we'll see you in court. Desertion of a sixteen-year-old child won't set well with most judges, especially women judges. You could come up against a female judge, you know." The look he gave her was menacing. "I'm sure you're aware of my strong influence with quite a few influential people here in Hawaii."

Breeze fidgeted in her seat. What a formidable opponent she had in Craig Caldwell. But then, he really didn't know her at all. And he certainly didn't have an inkling of what she was capable of when faced with desperation.

Unflinching even as his cold, darkened eyes stared at her, she held her head up high. "I'll sign anything you like. I'm afraid I'm not in any position to look a gift horse in the mouth. But I'm sure that you understand we're just exchanging gifts. I don't think you want me to make Sambrea the same offer I'm making you. You know what would happen if she somehow ended up with the needed fifty-one percent. Shall we say noon tomorrow?"

"Not tomorrow. I have a full schedule. Early next week works for me. I'll have my secretary ring your hotel with a time. One more thing. How can you do this to your daughter, your own flesh and blood?"

Knowing full well that she couldn't survive an entire week without adequate funds, Breeze looked horrified. In fact, she didn't even know how she was going to eat, let alone continue to live in a decent hotel. Her well-being came before anything or anyone, including Sambrea.

He read the look perfectly. The desperation flashing in her eyes touched off a spark of fear in him. He now realized her true potential for becoming extremely dangerous; not only to Sambrea but also to herself.

As Breeze pondered his question about Sambrea, her sable-brown eyes actually watered up. Stoicism quickly replaced whatever fleeting emotion she'd felt. "Mr. Caldwell, you've asked a question that you might not like the answer to. Sambrea would like it even less. For your information, Sambrea is *not* my biological daughter."

The remark clouded Craig's brain. Sweat swamped his brow. While looking at Breeze with certain contempt, his composure returned quicker than Breeze's had. This was one time he had to keep his cool. "How did that come to pass? Are you telling me Samuel gave birth to Sambrea? An *Immaculate Conception* perhaps?"

A profane laugh trickled from her. "Neither of the two. Sambrea is a direct result of Samuel Sinclair's biggest indiscretion. Sambrea is the daughter of a common street prostitute."

Not much different from you. Craig was reeling from the highly sensitive information. "Are you telling me Samuel got a prostitute pregnant and that you allowed him to bring their child into your home?"

"Surprise, surprise, huh? Maybe I'm not as bad as you thought. But I am. I allowed it because of his money."

Painful honesty. The only thing he could respect her for. "What proof can you offer me?"

She hissed. "I don't have to prove any of this to you. But let me tell you this. If you were to tell Sambrea the truth about her father it would outright kill her. Is it not better for her to have the likes of me for a mother rather than a sleazy tramp? Sammy already suffers from low self-esteem. Do you want to add to her mountain of grief and insecurities? If you become the bearer of this bad news, she'll come to hate you. She'll hate all men. She worshipped her father, you know. Samuel was her hero. Trust me, she's better off not knowing."

Craig's eyes blazed with unfriendly fire. "If that's the case, why did you see fit to reveal it to me?"

Breeze lowered her lashes. "So you'll understand her better. I love her in my own way, but my hunger and need for money is greater. I don't want to hurt her, but I will. She's a constant reminder of Samuel's indiscretion. That nearly killed me. We were still in love then."

Breeze's jeering expression turned pensive. "Somehow I get the feeling you truly love her. She loves you, too. She would've never married you just to save the company. But let her keep telling herself that she did, Mr. Caldwell. If it doesn't work out, she'll have that revelation to comfort her. It'll also help her keep her sanity."

Craig looked totally puzzled. "Do you hear yourself, lady? Your comments are so contradictory. You tell me not to tell her Samuel's secret. You say you love her. Then you talk about hurting her with the very information you want me to keep from her. Why don't you learn to say what you mean and mean what you say? As for my love for Sambrea, you couldn't possibly feel my love for her. You don't know the first thing about love," he ground out with uncontrollable fury.

Her dark eyes raged with disdain. "I know more about love than you give me credit for. Try to imagine this. You've prepared a wonderful candlelight dinner as a surprise for the woman you love. Then she comes home and tells you she's pregnant by another man. How would you feel?"

The look on Craig's face spoke of the hell he'd not be able to endure if something like that actually happened. Trepidation rumbled through him at just the thought of Sambrea carrying another man's child. He'd simply die from the indescribable pain.

Breeze laughed out loud. "Just as I thought."

"What happened to her birth mother?" Craig bridled his stampeding emotions.

"Who knows? Who the hell cares? She's probably still on the streets. Maybe she died in an alley somewhere."

Craig couldn't stomach any more. All he could think about was Sambrea. Breeze was right. Any negative knowledge re-

garding her father would kill her. Samuel was still her knight
in shining armor. He'd never be able to tarnish the armor Samuel had used to shield Sambrea so courageously. The same
courageous way in which he had to shield her.

After pulling out his wallet, he took out a wad of cash
and dropped it on the table. When Breeze reached for it,
he grabbed her hand. "One more thing. If you ever tell my
wife about our not-so-little secrets, you'll live to regret it.
Now if you'll excuse me, Mrs. Sinclair, this meeting is adjourned." Sure that he hadn't seen the last of her, he
watched Breeze disappear into the crowd. Never before had
he run across a more devious woman than Breeze Sinclair.

Glad Sambrea hadn't had to encounter Breeze, Craig
looked around for her. No doubt it would've spoiled her
evening. He wished he hadn't encountered her, either. Looking at his watch, he was unable to believe how much time
had transpired. He got up from the chair and moved quickly
in the direction of the restrooms. Near the entrance of the
ladies' room, he stationed himself in a spot that gave him
a clear view of the door.

After several minutes had passed, he asked a waitress to
check the restroom for him. When told that no one had
responded to the name he'd given, he looked worried.

Face to face with the fear gnawing at his insides, he
guessed that Sambrea had more than likely seen Breeze at
their table. Of course she had. Breeze had been sitting with
him forever. Or so it seemed. He wondered if she'd jumped
to the wrong conclusions. He hoped she hadn't heard everything. Just in case she hadn't left the club, he checked
out every nook and cranny. But he soon discovered that she
had indeed flown the coop.

Sambrea had hailed a cab to take her to the offices and
wait for her. She then went on to Richard's place. Crying
her eyes out on Richard's shoulder, badly disillusioned,

Sambrea was filled with anguish. Wildly, she waved a copy of the pre-nuptial agreement in the air. "How could I have been so naive? I never once looked at his signature. I was standing right there when he signed it. Oh, what have I done?"

Richard looked debonair dressed in a dark gray silk robe. He felt awful for Sambrea, but he truly didn't know what to make of the situation. He'd seen the way Craig looked at her. There was little doubt in his mind that Craig Caldwell had the look of a man in love. And he certainly didn't need her money, since the man was only filthy rich.

Richard removed the contract from her shaking hands and gave it a light once-over. "Calm down, Sam. You're going to have to get a hold of yourself. You may be wrong about him, you know. I realize the signature on this contract makes things look bad. But why would he meet with Breeze knowing you were there at the club with him? It doesn't make any sense. I'm sure if you give him the chance to explain it'll all become very clear. I don't know why he signed the pre-nuptial agreement this way, but you can't find out sitting here crying yourself sick. You need to go to your husband and get the answers you're seeking."

Angry beyond belief, she turned on Richard. "I can't believe you're defending him, Rich. When did you turn so loyal to the likes of Caldwell?"

"Sam," he shouted back, "don't you ever question my loyalties. I don't deserve that from you! De La Brise has never had a more loyal employee than myself. This is between you and Caldwell. Don't take it out on me."

Feeling so vulnerable, so hurt, Sambrea looked abashed through tear-drenched eyes. "I'm sorry, Rich. I know this isn't your fault. Can you ever forgive me?"

Richard had no choice but to take her in his arms. He loved her like a sister. "Come here, Sam." He held his arms open wide. Sobbing, she fell into his offered comfort zone. Together, they dropped down onto the sofa. "Let it go. I understand how you're feeling."

Minutes later, somewhat composed now, Sambrea stood up. "I'd better be going, Richard. It's really late. Will you call me a cab?"

"I certainly won't. I'll drive you home. Let me slip into some clothes. Make yourself comfortable. It'll only take me a few minutes." Richard exited the room.

Disbelief shining in her eyes, Sambrea sat back down on the sofa. As she looked around her, the warmth of Richard's apartment brought her a touch of solace. There was nothing spectacular about it, but it was homey and it smacked of his endearing personality. The earth tones and olive greens gave the place a touch of nature, along with live plants that seemed to grow right out of the walls. Richard had a serious green thumb. Sambrea often teased him about treating his plants like children.

Her thoughts turned back to Craig. How could a day that began so beautifully turn into a night of so much ugliness? Oh, how she'd come to trust Craig. And he'd let her down so bitterly. She cried inwardly, unable to reason this one out. She expected betrayal from Breeze, since she'd always managed to plunge the knife in her and turn it with undeniable pleasure. Breeze, who had no maternal instincts whatsoever, had always been able to intimidate Sambrea, often referring to her as her simple-minded daughter.

I'll bet Breeze is having second thoughts about me now, now that's she's practically broke. Her money was running out, or already had, Sambrea suspected. If she didn't contact Breeze within the next forty-eight hours, she'd probably have to find a cheap motel, almost an impossible feat in Honolulu. So things haven't changed at all, Sambrea concluded.

Sambrea allowed her mind a brief spin back in time, a time when money was just a gold card or a bank withdrawal away for Breeze. Samuel Sinclair had been a generous man and would've given Breeze the world, but it seemed she'd become terribly bored with him. Even with all the lavish parties, elegant dining, expensive gifts, and faraway travels

Samuel had indulged her in, she'd never seemed satisfied. She'd always wanted more.

Samuel was tired after he'd worked so hard amassing his fortune. An evening at home with his family around him is what he had considered time well spent, Sambrea mused with fondness.

He had loved the two females in his life. When he no longer had to put in long hours at the office, he'd sought out his peace at home. On the other hand, Breeze considered a night at home boring and unproductive, especially when she could socialize the night away. She was a society woman, a woman who needed to be in the spotlight. When the spotlight had shifted its glowing attention from Breeze to her blossoming daughter, Sambrea saw Breeze become restless and unpredictably moody.

As Sambrea began to grow into a shapely young woman, Breeze had begun to see her as the competition. Not only did Breeze have to share the doting Samuel with his daughter, she had to watch him fuss over her too. One person or another was always telling her how beautiful her daughter was. Because Breeze liked the attention of younger men, when those same men became innocently enamored with her effervescent daughter, she'd had a hard time handling it, Sambrea reflected.

Disappearing may have always been in the back of her mind, but she'd loved the things Samuel's money paid for too much to give them up. Somehow, someway, she must've managed to put a good bit of money aside for her to have actually executed her not-so-well thought out plans, Sambrea concluded.

Craig reached the bungalow only to see its darkness. No signs of life were visible from where he stood. No candle was in the window to flicker its usual welcoming light. On this night he knew his shouts and bangs on the door would go unheard. Feeling tired and lonely, the thought of sleeping without Sambrea hit him with a sickening thud. Too emotionally unstable to search for her, he knew he needed time to pull it together for himself and for his wife. Sambrea would need him more than ever.

Knowing Sambrea as he did, he wouldn't be surprised if she were already on her way to Maui. She would've had enough time to catch the last flight out. He suspected that she had a little of Breeze in her, in as much as she'd run away if life became too unbearable. That she might think of him as unbearable hurt like the dickens.

Craig hadn't been gone ten minutes when Richard's black Nissan pulled up to the back of the bungalow.

Inside, feeling as worthless as a penny with a hole in it, she stared out the window until Richard's car left. Fully dressed, Sambrea slipped into bed. Instant thoughts of Craig surrounded her. She could almost touch the clean-shaven smell of him, his wonderful, masculine smell. Her arms tightened around the pillow his carbon curls should've been resting on. Spilling down her cheeks like a Hawaiian waterfall, her tears came hard and bitter.

Later, when the phone rang several times, she ignored it. It was her husband whom she couldn't forgive. This was one night Craig Caldwell wouldn't have his way with her even if it killed her, she vowed. Crying long into the wee hours, sleep finally rescued her from the arms of anguish shortly before dawn.

A couple of hours after sunrise Sambrea undressed and showered. Donning a two-piece rose-pink suit and a baby-pink blouse, she slipped her feet into rose-pink pumps to complete her classy fashion statement. While struggling with her make-up, her hands trembled uncontrollably. She was in a hurry, and a stroke of blush and a hint of lipstick were all the cosmetic applications she had time for. After two aspirin and a glass of orange juice, Sambrea headed for the police department that was located closest to the offices of De La Brise.

Less than a half-hour later, after filing a restraining order that would keep Craig at least fifty yards away from De La Brise, or the bungalow, she walked out of the police department. Of course, she'd left out the part about him being part-owner of De La Brise. Since the merger wasn't quite completed, all legal documents weren't yet filed. If she had her way, they'd never be. The false signature on the prenuptial agreement should render the contract null and void. De La Brise was her company. She would manage it. It was time for her to take full charge of her life and her assets.

Since Samuel had been so well known and respected in the community, her motives went unquestioned by the officer who'd helped her. She had cited spousal abuse as the reason for the action, even if it was only mental and emotional abuse, another fact she'd left out. But he had hurt her far more than any physical abuse ever could. Craig Caldwell would soon find out how much power she wielded in this city, she thought with smug satisfaction. He wasn't the only person in Hawaii who had friends in high places.

While entering the office building, she prayed she'd get a chance to meet with her employees before Craig made an appearance. Although she'd alerted security, hoping to keep him from entering the building, she knew full well that nothing would stop him.

Headstrong and determined, Sambrea went straight to her office. The time had come to plan a new strategy. Craig Caldwell was in for one hell of a fight. Although she might lose, she wouldn't go down until the water covered her head, not until the last sweet breath of life was snuffed out by the tidal wave certain to engulf her.

While most of the employees came in early, there were a few stragglers who believed work began at ten-after-nine and ended at four-fifty. Eager to get on with the business at hand, she couldn't wait for those few. But she did make a mental note to talk with the tardy employees later.

A strong aura of confidence surrounding her, she walked to the boardroom podium. "Morning, everyone." She greeted her employees with as much cheer as she could muster. "I'm afraid there have been more new changes. I know Mr. Caldwell recently held a staff meeting, but some important changes have come about. That's why I'm holding this meeting." She noticed the employees were trading uneasy glances.

Hating to put them through so many changes, though it was necessary for now, she hoped to make them understand that each change was for the company's good. "I also know things are a little shaky around here. But if we all work closely together, I'm confident we can get things back on the right track. You'll continue to take orders from each of the assigned department heads and myself. Craig Caldwell will only be involved for a short while longer, if at all. I'll be managing De La Brise. Just as before."

Marlene Jackson, the receptionist, stood up. "Ms. Sinclair, are we in danger of losing our jobs? If so, I only think it's fair you tell us now. Many of us have families and other obligations. We can't afford to become unemployed."

Looking nervous, Sambrea folded her hands and placed them atop the podium. "That's a fair question, Marlene. I don't see any reason why anyone should lose their job. The merger with Caldwell & Caldwell stipulates that all employees are to be kept on. No, there's no chance of anyone losing their job. Quite the contrary. You may be asked to put in longer hours, for which you'll be paid overtime. De

La Brise is experiencing a few difficulties, but things can be handled without having anyone standing in the unemployment line."

Marsha Cohen, Richard's private secretary, stood to voice her concerns. "Are the new benefits Mr. Caldwell announced going to be withdrawn? As you all know, Mike and I are pregnant. With us both being employees here, we were happy to know Mike could take maternity leave, too."

"Absolutely not! I was thrilled to hear about the new benefits. Mr. Caldwell is a man of integrity." She wasn't believing a word of it. "He will keep his word." *Even if he hasn't kept his word to me.* Bittersweet yeast filled her, giving rise to impatient indignation as she momentarily pondered Craig's misdeeds.

Sambrea discussed her future plans for De La Brise and its employees before adjourning the meeting. She asked that everyone bear with her and have faith. As she led them in the Lord's prayer, practically everyone joined in. Those who didn't probably had serious misgivings about the power of prayer, Sambrea guessed. Very unfortunate, since they needed all the prayers they could get.

TEN

No sooner had Sambrea settled into her office than Craig burst into the room with a very readable expression on his face—hostile anger. Their eyes locked in pretty much the same way as when Sambrea first learned of his involvement in the take-over of her company: a fierce battle was ahead.

Glaring ferociously at her, he positioned himself in the chair next to her desk. Inhaling a deep, ragged breath, he dragged his fingers through his hair. "Do you always run when faced with an obstacle? If that's the case, I can see why De La Brise is in such a vulnerable state. Why did you run out on me again, Sam?"

"I was bored stiff." Her voice cackled with defiance.

"Yeah, right! You saw your mother talking to me at the club. As usual, you jumped to the wrong conclusions. When are you going to stop running and hiding from situations you deem unsolvable?"

A dead silence permeated the room, each one's eyes blatantly challenging the will of the other. No longer interested in the challenge, Sambrea pushed her chair back from the desk. Turning to face the window, she fixed her eyes on the rolling surf.

Feeling ignored, insufferably heated, his midnight eyes ignited a brushfire on her turned back. He hoped to cause her as much heated discomfort as he himself felt. "I guess

I'm getting the silent treatment now. We both know what happened the last time that you refused to open your lovely mouth! Are you going to sentence me to death without giving me a fair trial and the chance to clear myself?"

She gave a resigned sigh. "Craig, you're in this building illegally." She stole a glance at her watch. "As of eight o'clock this morning, I filed a restraining order against you. Once again, you're trespassing, Mr. Caldwell. While I can truly appreciate that all assets belong to the Creator, the Creator saw fit to put me in charge of De La Brise. I still own this company, since the merger hasn't been completed yet." Silently, she cursed security. They hadn't even seen him enter the building—they'd been busy with another serious matter.

The highly insulting piece of information sent him reeling. How could so much have changed between them in such a short time, so drastically? A restraining order! Did she really believe such a legal maneuver had been necessary? *Apparently so.*

He stood up. Bending over slightly, he placed both hands on the edge of the desk. "I'm not going to ask you why you felt the need to do such a thing, because I don't want to know. And if you were to explain, I know I wouldn't understand it for the life of me. Sam, you don't need a restraining order against me. All you had to do was tell me to stay away from you and De La Brise. I would've cooperated fully."

She sucked her teeth. "The same way you cooperated before, Craig? You never do anything that anybody tells you. I can't imagine you starting now. But if what you say is true, then I'm telling you to stay away from my company and me. I don't need or want your suave, deceitful presence in my life. You and Breeze can have each other. It has been said that birds of a feather flock together. Take flight, Craig. I'm sure your companion bat awaits you."

Another devastating emotion hit him like a tractor-trailer.

It nearly brought him to his knees. So stunned was he that he dropped down in a chair without much hope of ever being able to get up on his feet again.

"Unfair, Sambrea. None of it's true. If you really believe what you're saying, there's no damn hope for us anyway. Have you fallen out of love with me that quickly? Why the hell are you doing this to us? To our future?"

Just in case her eyes betrayed her, she lowered her lashes. No, she hadn't fallen out of love with him. She doubted that she ever would. But if she could help it, she would keep that knowledge from him until the day she died. As for their future, they had none—at least, not together.

"If you're not involved with Breeze, why were you discussing the prenuptial agreement with her? The one you signed 'Jacob Ladder.' That phony signature might not render our contract null and void, but you'll never have De La Brise. I'll burn it down to the ground before I let that happen!"

His heart felt as if a herd of stampeding cattle had trampled on it. Using painstaking care, he rose from his seat. "Sam, it was a joke. I signed it that way as a joke, because I no longer intended to take De La Brise. Because I knew we'd never have to execute our agreement. But I can see whatever I say won't matter to you. You've already made up your mind. Without trust, we have nothing." A lump arose in his throat. "I do love you." His voice was weakened. "I'm just sorry that you can't feel its burning intensity. I'll bring your things to you this evening. Good-bye, Sam."

"Don't bother. Donate them to charity!" she shouted at his retreating back. Refusing to dignify her childish behavior with a response, he simply walked out on her. That unexpected move spoke volumes to her. She hadn't expected him to give up the battle so easily.

As the door closed, she swiveled the chair around to face the window. Although no tears appeared on the surface, she was crying inside, crying for all she'd thought they'd become to one another, for all the passion never to be again, for the broken promise of happily forever after.

Richard and Joe entered her office at the same time.

She heard them come in but she didn't turn around. With her emotions so out of control, she feared they'd be able to see the inner turmoil she felt.

Joe approached her and rested his hand on her shoulder. "It's going to be okay, Sam. Is there anything I can get for you?"

Without facing him, she shook her head. There wasn't anything anyone could get for her. There wasn't anything she wanted. Anything other than Craig Caldwell, her now forbidden desire, her lover no more.

"Sam, you're acting like a fool." Richard gave her a scolding look. "All you have to go on is something you overheard. And you're not even sure you heard it all. The man that just walked out of here is hurting like hell. He looked as though a dagger had been plunged into his heart. What difference does the prenuptial agreement make when you two love each other so much?"

Sambrea wrung her hands together. "He's deceitful. That's what makes the difference. He's hiding something. I can feel it, Rich."

"There's such a thing as misguided feelings, Sam, but I don't think your feelings were misguided when you decided to marry him. You need to stop kidding yourself as to why you married Caldwell. It had nothing to do with saving De La Brise and we all know it," Richard charged. "You're not giving Craig a chance to prove himself. It's so unlike you to be unfair. Breeze has proved herself deceitful more than once. She's a very deceptive woman. I hope you know what you're doing. You need to hear your husband out. This time you need to listen. Don't put it off, Sam."

Joe turned the chair around and knelt down in front of her. "I think Richard is right, Sam. Craig's been doing all he can to salvage what's left of De La Brise. I believe it's because of you. The man is crazy about you. Before you completely shut him out, Sam, communicate with him. Use an open mind and an open heart."

After the well-meaning lectures, Richard and Joe left Sambrea to sort out her problems.

Finally, able to release the bottled-up tears, she reflected on how much she truly loved Craig. Never to feel his touch again was more than she could bear. Rushing into the powder room, she washed her face and struggled to put temporary bandages on her bleeding heart.

At the close of the day, without seeking anyone out, Sambrea rushed to the parking lot. She had to see Craig, one more time.

Inside the bungalow she showered and then dressed in the sexiest outfit she owned. After leaping into the Mustang, she drove the short distance to the pagoda house.

Pressing the bell with urgency, her breath came in short gasps as she waited and waited. Realizing that Craig wasn't in, she felt sick inside.

Remembering the delicate key case he'd given her, containing keys to his house, she fumbled through her purse and curled her fingers around the cold precious metal. Did she have the right to enter his domain after all the horrible things she'd said to him? Did she even have the right to be here at his doorstep? The dreary answers in her questioning mind sent her fleeing back to the car.

As the shadows of night crept into the bungalow, she paced the floor. Every now and then she turned to glance hopelessly at the ever-silent telephone. With so many sad things going through her mind, she wanted to scream out in anguish. If he loved her why wasn't he calling to tell her how wrong she'd been about him? Why wasn't he knocking down the door insisting that she listen to him? Had he lied to her about Breeze? Had she gotten all she was to ever get from him? Her questions were endless as burning tears scalded her cheeks.

The male scent of him loomed all around her and she felt his passionate touch in her heart. Closing her eyes, she could see him so clearly. She craved for his mouth to come crashing down over hers. Where was he? Was he with someone else? She didn't know, but she realized that she should be the one with him, wherever he was.

As the hours of darkness dragged on, her fears increased with an intensity that tore at her exposed nerve-endings. She trembled all over, a trembling she couldn't seem to control.

Craig sat on the patio watching the colors of the waterfall change. He felt tired, lonely, and troubled. Like Sambrea, he couldn't sleep. Thoughts of her disintegrated every chance he had at finding peace. If she still didn't trust him, then how could she profess to love him? Hadn't he done all that he could do to convince her of his love for her? "What does she want me to do to prove my love for her?" The stirring trade winds carried his question away within the breeze.

Sambrea clutched the gold key case to her heart. "Make love to her now," came the soft voice from behind him.

He turned around and was stunned to see her so near. Yet he'd somehow felt her presence. But then again, her presence was always with him. Her presence filled him. She looked frightened and more vulnerable than he'd ever seen her. He sensed her fear. Did she fear he'd send her away? Or desert her like Breeze had? Briefly, he considered sending her away, knowing the secret he carried inside him could never be told. No, he could never destroy her, especially with something like that.

"Come to me, Sambrea. I'd come to you, but I'm afraid you're only a vision. I don't want to make a fool of myself by chasing after an illusion."

The lights from the waterfall crossed her face, illuminating her in its bright colors. Willfully obeying his command, she stepped from the light and into the shadows of darkness. Lowering herself onto his lap, she instantly took delight in his fervent mouth.

"I'm crazy about you, Craig," she murmured between kisses. "I'll just have to take my chances. My heart keeps telling me you're not going to disappoint me."

"Listen to your heart, Sambrea. It only knows how to be honest. I love you, but I'm not going to make love to you. What I'd do to convince you of my love would free your spirit and unite it with mine forever. The problem is, I don't think you're ready to be convinced."

She sagged inwardly. As his eyes lit up her insides, bells went off in every direction inside her head. Then a tilting occurred, knocking her completely off kilter. Already feeling the heady affects of what he could do to her, she looked at him with undisguised longing. Did she have enough power over him to make him take her? Yes. Perhaps she did. Even if it was only sexual power, the power of the aphrodisiac.

Her eyes melded with his. "You could be right about me, Craig. If I let you convince me I'm loved by you, I may fear that I'm no longer a challenge to you. That's just one possibility. I may also fear that I might get bored with you if our lives became mundane, too predictable, too uninteresting. That's what happened with my parents. At least, for Breeze. I think they became too familiar with one another. What's the saying? *Familiarity breeds contempt.* I'm their daughter, you know."

He flinched from the tragic pain reflected there in her eyes.

"I bet I can seduce you," she taunted. Purposely, she'd changed the subject, something she was a pro at. Especially when she'd gotten herself in too deep.

His laughter chilled her. "I'm not a gambling man, Sam, at least, not with something so precious. If I had the desire to lay a wager, you would probably win. Hands down." Lifting her off his lap, he settled her into the chair beside him. "I've warned you about carrying excess baggage. It's an albatross around your beautiful neck."

Aching inside with heartfelt emotion, his voice had deepened.

"Go home, Sambrea. I've told you too many times that I'm not interested in being a fool. Just as you're not." She put up a hand to protest, but the foreboding look in his midnight eyes silenced her mouth. "If you should ever think of coming back here, Sam. Don't!"

Her body weakened as she gripped the arm of the chair for support. He was sending her away for good. Her biggest fear had come true.

"That is, until you've decided to make this your permanent home. You'll also need to lease out the bungalow. If there are to be any more escapes to Maui, we escape together. I hope I've made myself clear, Sambrea Sinclair-Caldwell."

Wanting to bring down his tongue-in-cheek attitude, she sniffed haughtily. Then she thought better of challenging him. Her desire to change his mind was strong, but if she insisted, his desire to send her away might become even stronger. He never made idle threats. She didn't think he was making one now.

Moving toward the door like an unraveling mummy, it was all she could do to keep from tripping over her exposed ego. Getting to his feet, he moved after her. She could feel him behind her as she opened the front door. Using both hands, he slammed it shut.

The thought of his changing his mind about making love to her brought moistness to her coveted secrets. She felt his hot breath on her neck as he moved closer, trapping her between the door and his body of granite. Feeling the coolness on her face from the metal around the door, she drew in a deep breath.

Fully aroused, his growing urgency pressed into the back of her upper thigh. Gently, slowly, he turned her around. "If you'll kindly lift the restraining order, we can get on with the business of strengthening De La Brise. I won't come there until you've done so. Sink or swim, Sam, it's your choice."

So strong was his desire to possess her, he had to quickly inch back from the heated contact. Disappointed that he hadn't given in to what they both wanted, needed from each other, she edged away, only to have him entrap her body once again.

"Are we going to work together for De La Brise or not? We've only been married a few weeks now, but there's five months or so left on our prenuptial agreement. What's it going to be, Sambrea?"

Irritated by the mention of the agreement, she pushed hard against his chest and he nearly lost his footing. "That damn prenuptial agreement is a joke, just like you said. Don't you ever mention it to me again." Scowling heavily, her eyes gave him a stern warning.

Funny, but she now believed it was the only deceitful thing he'd ever really done. At the moment it struck her as hilarious, but she fought the urge to laugh out loud. Craig could be just as amusing as he was complicated.

"What about the restraining order, Sam? Are you going to have that ridiculous ban lifted on me or not?"

"The restraining order has already been lifted. I used

poor judgment on that one, but I've been using poor judgment since the day you walked into my life."

"The night," her reminded her. "It was definitely night. I often do an instant recall. My, my, my, what a gorgeous body arose from the ocean that fateful night. Naked as a jaybird, as mystifying as the universe. Woman, if you leave me with nothing else, you've left me with the sweetest, most sensuous memories a man can have." His taunting of her was purposely done.

Before she could stop herself, she wound herself around him like a toy slinky, entangling him in her fervent need. It happened so quickly, she caught him completely off guard, making it easy for her get the upper hand. Just like he'd done her so many weeks ago on the beach, she brought him down to his knees. The floor felt much harder than the sand, but if she got what she desperately needed from him it would serve the same purpose. Anywhere she made love to Craig was heaven.

Could he stop her from her mission? No, he conceded. She had as much control over him as he had over himself. It was too late, anyway. Her hot hands had slipped inside his zipper and he already burned down where she heatedly stroked him. God, he cried inwardly, what awesome power over me you've given to this enigmatic woman.

Exercising the power she held, she worked fervently to render him helpless. Kissing, nipping, stroking every inch of his body, she sent him into uncontrollable spasms. Just when he expected to explode into a million fragments, she slid onto him, searing her body onto his eagerly awaiting manhood.

Her inner muscles clenched around him, squeezing his sexuality again and again. Enslaved by her thorough seduction and exquisite strokes, his sanity absconded. In a moment, she was deliciously naked, and he marveled at her beauty, wondering what magic she'd used to make her clothing disappear.

Entranced by utter fulfillment, without withdrawing, Craig rolled over. Securely, he locked Sambrea's body beneath him. Although she'd already exploded with him in ecstasy, he desired to retrace their impassioned journey.

Awakening hours later, still in the same spot on the floor, Craig found that his sea nymph had disappeared. Needing to release all the emotions holding him hostage, he didn't care anymore about holding back his sobs. If crying was the only way to free him of all the insanity that had entered his once-serene life, then let the hot tears flow. Maybe he'd shed enough tears to drown himself. Then he'd never again have to wonder how it could have been between them.

At any rate, Sambrea had won her bet. Maybe it had to be this way. Through no fault of his own, a dark secret had lodged itself between them. He knew something about her that she herself didn't know, something that would surely break her spirit, something bewildering. As for him, Sambrea's departure had left him bewildered for the very last time in this life, he vowed.

Sentimental tears fell as she did a final inventory check. As much as she loved the place, she loved Craig more. Having packed everything that meant anything to her, she'd lease the other things along with the bungalow. This place would never be the same if she stayed there and Craig was somewhere else. Finally, she'd found something that her place couldn't give her. In fact, there wasn't anything or anyone able to give her what she needed. Except Craig. She needed to be loved by a warm-blooded animal.

Craig was all that and much, much more. She was going home for good. If the marriage failed it wouldn't be because she hadn't given it her all.

* * *

By the time Sambrea returned to the pagoda house, Craig had showered and fallen tiredly into bed. Sambrea had made her choice. It just so happened that he wasn't it, he'd told himself before falling into the land of troubled dreams. She stripped out of her clothing and made her way to the bedroom, leaving a trail of garments in her wake, a trail that Hansel and Gretel could've easily followed. Craig could help her unload the car in the morning, which was only a few hours away. Maybe it would be afternoon before they got around to it. She laughed. She definitely had erotic plans for the last hours before sunrise. Who knows, it might take them weeks to get around to it. Snuggling up against his bare back, she nibbled at his ear, causing him to jump with a start.

He looked at her as though she were only starring in his dreams.

"Aren't you going to welcome your wife back home, lover?" she whispered in his ear, teasing his lobe with her tongue.

He groaned loudly. Turning over on his side, he pulled her roughly into his arms, sighing with relief. "You have indeed made a wise choice, Mrs. Caldwell." His flagging confidence had already been restored. "Welcome home, my precious sea nymph."

As though the night celebrated their reunion, unexpected fireworks lit up the sky, causing them to scramble to the bedroom balcony. Wrapped in the warmth of their love, they watched the dazzling show. As bright colors rained a myriad of fiery brilliance across the skies, they gasped in reverence.

All through their evening meal of tender veal, fresh vegetables and steamed rice, Craig's mood had been pensive, Sambrea noticed. Wondering if he now regretted them moving in together, Sambrea stole guarded glances at him. If she could read his mind, would her apprehension be allayed? Or would his thoughts only cause her increased anguish?

She took a small sip of guava juice. "I'm feeling left out over here." Her voice was soft and soothing. "Are we upset about something?"

Looking up from his plate, he cast her a sheepish smile. "It wasn't my intention to ignore you, but I do have a lot on my mind. Business stuff. You now have my full attention, my sweet Sammy. I'm sorry if I made you feel left out."

Always Sambrea or Sam, but never had he called her Sammy. Though she liked the way he breathed it, she didn't care much for the name itself. It reminded her of a slave name. Tai called her Samiko but it didn't have the same type of unsettling ring; it was more a part of Tai's native language than anything. Resisting the urge to ask him not to call her that, she smiled at him as though she'd never had the ridiculous notion to chastise him.

"I'm late, Craig."

He hunched his shoulders. "Late for what, my lady? You didn't mention you had to go anywhere this evening?"

Thinking him dense for missing such an obvious clue, she giggled inwardly. "My cycle, Mr. Caldwell."

Slowly, a macho smile stole across his face. His lips parted to show even white teeth. Then the smile dissipated all too quickly. "Is that good or bad news, Sam?" He feared that pregnancy could be a major problem for her.

"It all depends."

"On what, Sam?"

"If it's good or bad news for you."

Smiling with relief, he reached across the table and took her hand. "It's wonderful news for me, Sam! I want you to be the mother of my children. They'll adore you as I do."

Unexpected tears fringed her lashes. "Thanks. That's

sweet of you to say. I'm only a couple of days late. So maybe we should hold off the celebration until we're sure. I only told you because I don't want us to keep any secrets."

Her last sentence spun around in his head. *Keeping secrets*—exactly what he'd been guilty of. Until he got to the bottom of everything he wasn't going to broach the subject of what Breeze Sinclair had told him, or the fact he'd offered to pay her off. Nothing should upset Sambrea before he was sure of her medical condition. No, he couldn't tell her now. It was his duty to protect her, to shelter her from any more unpleasantness. If she was in fact pregnant, he felt even more justified in his actions.

"Let's go into the music room, Sam. I want to play something soft and sweet for you."

Leaving her chair at once, she ran out into the hall. Craig had to run to catch up with her.

As she sat beside him on the piano stool, the soft music made her heart sing along with his powerful voice. Once again, she got lost in the fantasy he so masterfully created. While he played and sang a few nursery rhymes, she laughed like a small child, loving every minute of being right here where she belonged.

This was now her home, in all its splendor, the home where her heart had come to roost. He was her husband, the husband who ruled her heart with a simple song. It wasn't exactly a celebration, but they shared in the joy of their love and happiness. If it were to be, they would share in the precious gift of their child.

Craig never could get enough of Sambrea's kisses and it puzzled him when she gently pushed him away. "Is something bothering you, Sam?"

"It's strange. I haven't heard from Breeze. The last time we talked she was desperate for money. Maybe she's found another sucker." Sambrea laughed weakly.

Craig held his breath, hoping to dodge the subject entirely.

"I think I'll call the hotel. Breeze cleverly managed to let Joe know where she could be reached when she moved from the Hilton. She knew that he'd tell me. But of course."

Alarm thundered in Craig's heart. "Why do you want to make contact with her, Sam? What would you possibly have to say to her?" He pulled her closer to him.

Putting a delicate hand inside his shirt, she laid her head against his chest. "I have nothing to say to her. I'm not going to talk to her. I'm just going to find out if she's still registered."

He frowned. "Oh? Playing Sherlock Holmes, are we? Why don't you just forget the whole idea? Breeze will contact you when she's in dire straits."

Ignoring his comments, she leaped off the piano stool and picked up the telephone book. Her eyes glazed over as she dialed. In an instant, the dazed look disappeared.

After being told that Breeze had checked out of the hotel, Sambrea cradled the phone. A thoughtful expression creased her brow. "She's checked out. Hopefully she's winging her way back to France. She's never had any problems taking off without a moment's notice. I can see that nothing ever changes with her."

Tears pushed their way to the surface and she didn't know whether to hold them back or release them. Either way, it would hurt. Breeze had done it again. She'd walked out of her life without dropping as much as a hint.

A woman with no conscience is no woman at all.

ELEVEN

Sambrea returned to Craig, who waited for her with open arms. Feeling her tension long before she reached him, he reached out for her, nestling her snugly into his arms. "Let it go," he whispered against her hair. "I can see and feel your need to cry. It's okay, Sam. I'm here for you. You'll never have to stand alone."

Blinking back the tears, she sniffed. "I'm glad you're here. Samuel Sinclair was always there, too. Every wrong turn I made, he steered me right. Every right turn I made, he cheered me on. After my mother disappeared, he comforted me. Did I ever tell you Samuel was my prom date?"

Astounded, Craig's eyes twinkled with sentimental glee. "You're kidding. How did you ever live that down?"

Smiling, she looked up into his eyes. "I didn't have to. Everyone at school thought it was the coolest thing. In fact, after hearing my plans, two of my closest friends got their fathers to take them to the dance also. We were a big hit that night."

"Couldn't you get a prom date, Sam? That's something I'd have a hard time believing. I can't imagine anyone as gorgeous as you without a date."

"Quite the contrary. That was part of the problem. I had too many requests and I didn't want to hurt anyone's feelings by turning them down. So when my father suggested that he be my date, I had the answer to my problem. Samuel was my official date, but of course he allowed me to dance with all my friends." She glowed at the memories of one of the sweetest nights of her teen years. "It turned out to be a wonderful evening."

"Samuel Sinclair must have been some man and one hell of a father. You were blessed, Sam. It seems that Samuel tried to give you back all that Breeze had taken away."

Her eyes danced. "He was everything to me and more, Craig. He tried to give me all that he thought I should have. But there was one thing he failed miserably at."

"What was that?"

"Being happy. With all the wise things Samuel taught me, he never practiced them himself. That made me wonder if he was really wise at all. He allowed Breeze to rob him of his happiness. I think that's why I'm always running away from everything. No matter what you tell a child to do, he or she will do exactly what they live and learn at home. Someday I'll know why my father let Breeze step all over him. I'm just not there yet. There were times when I thought he was weak. That's why I'm so determined to be just the opposite. I don't want to fall into doing what I saw him do. At an early age, I vowed that no one would ever rule me. My destiny would be a path of my own choosing."

Craig lazed a finger down her cheek. "You've accomplished that, sweetheart. You've laid down your own path. Keep it that way, Sam. No one has any right to choose or change your direction. As for Samuel, don't ever think of him as weak. He wasn't. Only Samuel knows why he took all the aggravation. Maybe it was because of you."

She frowned. "What do you mean by that?"

"Perhaps he thought it was the only way to protect you. If he'd left Breeze, God only knows what would've become of you. If he took you away with him, he'd be depriving you of a mother. Maybe there wasn't any other choice for him, Sam. I guess he did whatever he had to do to see that you were okay."

Her eyes glistened with tears. For the first time in her life she was beginning to understand why Samuel might have stayed with Breeze.

"Thank you, Craig. Some of it is starting to make sense now. If Daddy had left me, I would've been lost to him forever. He probably knew that. Breeze would've tried to poison my mind against him. It would've been impossible for him to visit me without a lot of drama. Wow! What power she possessed over him."

Knowing Sambrea had the same awesome power over him, Craig smiled. Though he thought his wife might be right regarding the reasons Samuel hadn't left Breeze, he now knew it went much deeper than that. Breeze had probably blackmailed him into staying, he guessed. She had a powerful weapon in her hands. *Adultery.* Samuel needed to protect Sambrea all right, but from what? From the unscrupulous Breeze or from the truth of his own indiscretions? Probably all of the aforementioned, Craig concluded.

Craig and Sambrea walked back into the dining room. As he started to clear away the dishes, she took the plates from his hand. "You go ahead and rest, Craig. I'll take care of the kitchen. Then I'll come and join you in the retreat."

He took the plates back. "We'll take care of the kitchen together. In this marriage we're equals. Meaning, we'll take equal responsibility for the chores. Can we at least agree on that, Mrs. Caldwell?"

"I concur, Mr. Caldwell." She smiled impishly.

Making quick work of the mess in the kitchen and the dining room, they retired to the den to watch the evening news. Sambrea walked over to the wet bar, where she opened a bottle of white wine. As she was just about to pour herself a glass, Craig came up behind her and took the bottle out of her hand.

His eyes scolded her gently as he returned the bottle to

the wine rack. "Are you trying to get little Craig or little Sambrea drunk?"

Looking terribly ashamed, she burst into tears. She placed a trembling hand over her flat abdomen. "How could I have forgotten what alcohol can do to an unborn fetus?"

Craig hadn't expected her emotional outburst. He felt horrible for his part in her pain as he looked at her with sympathy. "Come on over here and sit down, Sam. It's not as bad as all that. Is it?" As she sat down beside him on the leather sofa, he directed her head against his chest, stroking her back and arms. "Sam, I didn't mean to upset you. I didn't handle that with much sensitivity at all. I'm sorry, baby. Are you going to be okay?"

She did her best to get her sobs under control. "I didn't even think about the fact that I could be carrying our baby, Craig. I'm the one who's sorry. You did the right thing when you took the wine from me. I don't know for sure that I'm pregnant, but I promise not to touch another drop of alcohol unless it's been confirmed I'm not with child. You see? I told you I know nothing about being a mother." She hated what she'd almost done out of sheer ignorance.

Craig held her at arm's length. "Don't be so hard on yourself, girl. When it's time, you'll know everything you need to know. What doesn't come naturally for you, you can read about. For centuries women have given birth and raised children without all this modern technology and expert knowledge. I don't suggest it's not good, but I think it's highly overrated. You'll be a great mom."

She wiped her eyes with the sleeve of her sweater. "I'm not so sure about that. What do I have to go on? What if I treat our child like my mother has treated me? Emotionally, mentally, or physically abused children are said to become abusers."

He suddenly realized that her anguish ran a lot deeper than he first suspected. Sambrea was in sheer agony.

"Sam, you're not going to abuse our children. In no way

do I believe you're capable of emotionally bruising our babies. The cycle of any kind of abuse can be stopped. You'll stop it."

Sambrea had been abused in more ways than one by Breeze and her father. If what Breeze had told him was true, her natural mother had abused herself. Then she'd abused Sam when she'd given her up to a heartless woman. *What a mess.*

He kissed the tip of her nose. "Now, stop crying, Sam. A rerun of *Living Single* is about to come on in a few minutes. You know how much you love Overton and Kyle. They wouldn't want to see you so sad, not when they're in business to make you laugh."

She managed to smile. "You're just trying to make me feel better. Thanks. It worked. Do we have some popcorn? I love to eat popcorn when I watch the reruns of AA programs. The rerun of *Fresh Prince of Bel-Air* comes on after *Living Single.*"

"If it's popcorn you want, it's popcorn you'll have. None of that microwave stuff, either. I'm going to pop you the real thing, Sam. I'll be back in a jiffy." He laughed. "No pun intended."

She laughed too. "Jiffy Pop, huh? I love Jiffy popcorn. I like microwave popcorn, too. Don't go to a lot of trouble if we have the microwave version. The show's going to start shortly. I don't want you to miss any of it."

"No trouble at all. I got skills, native girl. Stretch yourself out on that sofa and get comfortable. Your man will be back before you know it."

"Plenty of butter, but not too much salt," she yelled at his retreating back. "We don't want our baby to be born with high blood pressure."

He stuck his head back in the doorway. "I told you it would come naturally, didn't I? We just happen to have some unsalted butter. So you're in luck. I'm going to take good care of you. Pregnant or not."

Sambrea stretched out on the sofa and closed her eyes. When a vision of a tiny baby, with a dark cap of silken curls, swept into her mind's eye, she smiled. The huge black eyes shone with the same midnight magic that Craig's did. She saw herself and Craig looking down into a beautiful hand-carved cradle.

"He looks just like you, Daddy," Sambrea told Craig.

"He does, doesn't he? But he's already given us an indication of how stubborn he's going to be. Just like his mama," he teased her.

Her mind's eye took her fifteen years ahead in time.

Standing face-to-face with her handsome son, she heard the anger in her voice as she berated him without mercy. *Can't you ever do anything right. You're so stupid. Where were you when brains were handed out? All you've got going for you is looks.*

Sambrea's eyes flew open, shutting out the painful scenario she'd created in her mind. Breeze hadn't been talking to her like that, for a change. Samuel had been the target of her vicious tongue on that day.

As far as the things she'd say to Sambrea, Breeze just criticized everything about her: her hair, her weight, her clothes, and anything else she could think of to make her feel inadequate, Sambrea reflected with deep sorrow.

Craig produced the popcorn in a jiffy, just like he'd promised. Setting the tray down on the coffee table, he removed the glass popcorn-filled bowl and put it in front of Sambrea. After removing the two glasses of iced juice from the tray, he set them down on coasters.

"Smells delicious." Taking a handful of fluffy popcorn from the bowl, Sambrea popped a few pieces into her mouth. "Tastes even better."

Craig sat down in front of her on the floor and she fed

him some of the popcorn from her hand. "It is good. Enough butter for you?"

Her lips slick with butter, she bent her head down, kissing him full on the mouth. Tasting the unsalted butter clinging to her mouth, he moaned. "More than enough butter. Native girl, you even taste good with butter and a tad of salt. Perhaps I should dash a little hot sauce on you and see how good you taste then." He laughed heartily. "Maybe that's not such a good idea after all. You're already too hot and spicy as it is."

She giggled at his comment. "No hotter than you, my transplanted native boy. You're going to have to be quiet in a very few minutes here. My two *main* men are about to entertain us. That blue-collar Overton sure turns me on."

Craig narrowed his eyes at her. "You better rethink that statement. Craig C. Caldwell is your main man. Your *only* man."

She hugged his neck. "Oh, how sweet! You're jealous," she cooed. "What does the *C* stand for? I didn't know you had a middle name. I've never seen it on any official documents, like our marriage license."

"No middle name, just the letter. My mother has a fixation with that particular letter. Her name is Candace. She told my father that she married him because both his first name and surname began with a *C*. My dad's name is Cameron Caldwell. Nice name, huh?" Sambrea nodded in the affirmative. "I wouldn't have minded being a junior to a name like that, but my mother had her mind set on Craig."

"Strong name. If we're pregnant, and it's a boy, we'll name him Craig Cameron Caldwell. How's that for strength?"

Pulling her head down level with his, he kissed her. "You're a girl after my own heart. That's the very same name I had in mind for my son. Do you have a middle name?"

She rolled her eyes. "As if *Sambrea* wasn't a mouthful

by itself, they had to add *Nicole*. When Breeze was angry or frustrated with me, which was most of the time, she called me *'Sambrea-Nicole,'* as if it was just one name. Shh," she told him upon hearing the opening music for *Living Single*. "It's show-time."

Craig got up from the floor. Snuggling up behind her on the sofa, he pulled her in close to his body, squirming about a bit until they both got comfortable. As usual, Kyle and Max were at each other's throat, yet the love they felt for each other came through to the viewing audience. The love she and Craig shared was also quite obvious to others. She laughed at the way Kyle rolled his eyes at Max.

Into the wee hours of the morning, Sambrea and Craig cuddled together while talking and sharing some of the most intimate details of their lives. It had surprised them both to learn that as children they'd had so many of the same interests. Their favorite thing to do back then was watch Saturday morning cartoons, something they still liked to do.

"Reading is another of my favorite pastimes, especially when it's raining. Knowledge is power, you know."

Craig grinned. "I love to read, too. We do have much in common, you see. We won't ever bore each other, Sam."

Craig later shared the details of the many places he'd traveled to with his parents, who were always on a mission of mercy. While telling her exciting stories about Turkey, Israel, and Greece, he talked about all the different types of people whom his parents had helped. He also spoke about the unusual types of homemade toys found in a lot of foreign countries.

"I can't wait for the elder Caldwells to meet my wife. They'll love the choice I've made in a lifetime partner. We'll go see them once De La Brise is running smooth again."

Nodding, she smiled. "I wish Samuel could've met my husband. He would've loved my choice as well. You're a lot like him. He'd be proud to have you as a son." With tears shining brightly in her eyes, Sambrea began telling Craig all the wonderful things Samuel had done for her while executing both parental roles.

"It was Samuel who brushed my hair till it shone. It was he that tucked me in at night. When I had a problem, Samuel helped to solve it. He was always there to keep me from needing a life raft." He kissed her chin.

"However," she continued, "Breeze did take me shopping. She bought me the finest things money could buy, but it wasn't enough for me. I wanted to be held by her, to be assured that she loved me. When I learned from my father about the changes that occur in a young woman's body, I wished it had come from Breeze.

"It was awkward for Samuel, but he was delicate in his explanations regarding the changes occurring in my body. He even discussed birth control with me, though he strongly suggested I wait for marriage to enter into such an intimate contract. Although I didn't wait, I'm fortunate enough to have married my lover."

Stroking her finger across his lips, Craig's heart swelled to near bursting. "I'm more than fortunate to have been chosen as your first. I wouldn't have loved you any less if I hadn't been though, Sambrea." He kissed the tips of each of her fingers.

"I know you said you don't want to know about my past, but I want you to know that I haven't told Lawrence Chambers I'm married yet. As I mentioned before, we dated off and on until I met you. He moved back to Maui a few years ago." She then told him how Lawrence had saved her life the day Breeze had reappeared.

Just the mere thought of her drowning sent shivers of fear up and down his spine. That Breeze had caused her such turmoil that day made him even angrier with her.

"Maui, huh? Is that who you've been running off to see when you just up and take off?"

"Not really. The last time I was there he just happened to be on the beach. Thank God. But he did mention that Tai had told him I was there. I asked him to dinner after he saved my life. We were supposed to dine on one of the yachts, but he called to cancel. It was when you were there in the suite with me. We know what happened next. You coerced me into going back to your hotel with you. The rest is history."

He smiled broadly. "Yeah! We became husband and wife. I suggest you tell Lawrence you're taken as soon as possible. In fact, I want the world to know we belong only to each other. Do we have a deal?"

"A deal."

Only seconds had passed when she found herself succumbing to her husband's lustful demands.

As Sambrea slept, Breeze Sinclair was all but forgotten in the mind of Sambrea. But hardly in Craig's mind. Breeze had most assuredly cramped his style. He'd given her an obscene amount of money hoping to rid Sambrea of her frightening presence once and for all. His wife needed to be stress free for health's sake. Breeze had promised to leave Hawaii and never to return, and she'd put her signature on the legal documents that signed away her shares and any other legal claims to the Sinclair estate.

How he was going to relay this bit of information to his wife was more troubling for him than Breeze's presence. He now wished he'd told Sambrea before she'd decided to give their marriage another try. Now the problem seemed larger than life. If he told her now, she'd only feel betrayed again. However, Sambrea had to be told—and by him. It would never do for her to find out in any other way. When would it be an appropriate time to tell Sambrea? For sure, sooner rather than later.

Awakening, Craig propped himself on one elbow. Smiling down at Sambrea, who was still asleep, intimate thoughts of their late-night lovemaking marathon sent bright flashes of light flitting through his midnight eyes. In a state of disarray, her sable hair fell loose and free, spilling out over the edges of the blue satin pillowslip. Clad in a shimmering bronze satin camisole and tap pants, she looked gorgeous and quite delectable to him. Though bare of lip color, she wore a contented smile on the mouth he loved to kiss. Taking a few strands of hair between his fingers, he lifted it to his nose and smelled its sweet scent.

Pitter-pattering of raindrops hit against the windowpane, causing Craig to snuggle in closer to his wife. Like a magnet, she curled into him, sighing contentedly. Her warm breath fanned his chest hairs, making his nipples grow taut and his loins ache with desire. In a haze of sleep, she looked over at him, offering her lips to him in a seductive manner. Craig groaned with lust as he lost himself to the rose petal softness of her mouth.

He drew the warmth of her breath into his lungs. "Did you sleep well?"

Purring, she heaved a deep sigh. "Always, when I sleep next to you. What time is it?"

Turning over on his side, he fumbled for his wristwatch. After glancing at it, he placed it back on the bedside table. "It's still early. We have plenty of time."

"Time for what, Craig?" She feigned innocence.

"Time for a repeat of last night's performance. Shall we play it again, Sam?"

"Play it again, Sam?" She laughed. "How unoriginal!"

"There was nothing unoriginal about last night, sweetheart. We wrote another exciting chapter on our love life, but I'm afraid I don't have a title for it."

"What about Hot & Silky or perhaps, White Hot Satin? It'll need an adult material warning label, of course."

"Either of those will do nicely. Are you ready to begin another chapter, Sam?"

"I can tell that you are." A slight shudder rippled through her body. "At least your newly sharpened pencil feels ready."

Laughing, Craig threw his head back. Pulling her on top of him, he smothered his laughter in the silky curtain of her hair, his joy tingling in her spine. A wave of intense heat traveled her inner thighs, turning her body into hot, smoldering liquid. As his tongue flicked at the inside of her ear, she glided herself across the rigidity of his thickened organ. Deft fingers removed the tap pants, replacing the flimsy satin with his silky-hot flesh. His mouth sought hers with an insatiable hunger.

There wasn't a flower in the world that could claim any sweeter scent or more tantalizing nectar than that flowing from his wife's body. Bodies, sleek and shiny, thrashed about in the huge bed, staining the smooth satin sheets with beaded drops of steamy sweat.

"Sweetheart, come fly with me," Craig gasped between insanity-inducing kisses. "Don't ever bring me down off this natural high you keep me on, native girl."

Temperatures in the hottest of deserts would be considered cool compared to the sweltering heat generated between the two of them. Wildly titillated, eager to obey his command, her legs gripped him tightly as she rode out the tempest of his intimate passion. A jagged cry tore from her throat as her body shattered and her world turned upside down. It seemed as if it would never again right itself.

Dizzy pleasure washed through Craig as he buried himself deeper and deeper into her heated, creamy moistness. With a lengthy shudder streaking through his entire being, he screamed her name without ever losing possession of her luscious, now swollen lips. Exhausted, he lay back against the pillow and snuggled her head onto his chest.

"Now that was some chapter," he moaned. "We'll have so many more to write before this novel is ready for publication. I imagine it'll be ready in about sixty or so years. What do you think, Sam?"

"Let's keep it under wraps until we die. We can leave it as a legacy to our children. Dead authors seem to get more play than those still alive."

"Sounds good to me, Sam. Now let's take a shower. I've got an emergency meeting to attend. I'd cancel it if it wasn't so important."

She rolled on top of him. "In a minute, lover. *This* meeting has yet to be adjourned."

TWELVE

Craig had called an emergency meeting so he could consult with the team of experts he'd hired to dissect all of the business affairs of De La Brise. Sitting at Sambrea's desk, Craig glanced down at his watch. He had ten minutes or so to finish preparing his own investigative report before everyone else arrived. Or so he thought, until Richard strolled into the office. With their troublesome clashes all behind them, the two men greeted one another like old friends.

"So what's up?" Richard took a seat.

Shaking his head, Craig stroked his chin. "There are so many discrepancies and inaccuracies in the accounting mechanism it makes me shudder with anger. De La Brise was being financially raped. I've all but figured out who the rapist was. My sharp investigators should be able to tell if I'm correct or not."

"Can you be more specific, Craig?"

Craig wrung his hands together. "Like Sambrea, I'm suspicious of Tyler Wilson, the board member who retired. It looks as though he receives several pensions from De La Brise, all under different names and in separate automatic deposit accounts. Two pensions are on direct bank deposit to a bank in the South of France. Similarities in personal information are uncanny, and the social security numbers are exactly the same. The pensions that make me feel so sure I'm right about Tyler are the ones in the South of France."

If he was right about Tyler, Craig had the sneaky suspicion Breeze Sinclair was somehow involved in this embezzlement hoax. If she were involved, Craig would have no problem prosecuting her to the full extent of the law. However, his wife might not be able to handle the woman she thought to be her mother facing such dire consequences.

Richard looked dumbfounded. "Do you think Breeze is in on this travesty? She's been living in France, too."

"That remains to be seen." Craig shrugged.

"If she is in on this elaborate scheme, why did she come here looking for more? She should be filthy rich by now."

"Samuel governed his own pension plan—with most of the company assets on hold, the pensions were stopped. According to the accounting figures, close to a half-a-million dollars a year has been appropriated illegally. I'm sure you can figure out the rest for yourself."

Richard whistled. "So the well ran dry. Though she didn't know about this at the time, Sam was smart to put everything on hold. I owe her an apology for getting all over her about it. I wonder if Breeze and Tyler are lovers who've decided to part company? When the money stalled, he probably had to cut her off—financially, at least."

"Maybe not. And she's as culpable as Tyler is if he's somehow forwarding monies to her personal accounts. The answers will all come. I'll see to that."

Craig sensed that he had a couple of tigers by the tail; both indeed seemed ferocious. At one time he'd thought the persons involved were stupid, but had to re-think that conclusion since they'd been getting away with it for several years. That added up to millions of dollars. Somebody had gotten rich off this intricate heist. He swore he'd find the guilty party or parties.

* * *

During the actual meeting, which had been moved down to the boardroom, Craig's hands flew in and out of his pockets with agitation as each troubling discovery was revealed. How this valuable company had so easily been led to slaughter angered him.

Richard marveled at how thoroughly Craig had launched the investigation into the financial woes of De La Brise. There were more private dicks in this one room than on ABC, NBC, and CBS combined. Each had been given a specific assignment. Each had delivered magnificently. Unsolved mysteries didn't get any better than this. Richard was beside himself with childish excitement. To watch Craig work was to watch a master expertly ply his craft.

Craig was extremely good at what he did. He addressed his colleagues with confidence and deliberate ease.

"It looks as though I'll be going to France." How he'd manage that feat without taking Sambrea along was more than he wanted to think about. Although Craig had been proved right about Tyler Wilson, he wanted more.

"I want you to uncover anything and everything that you can about anyone who might be involved in Tyler's bogus pension scam. I don't care if the paper trail leads to Timbuktu, follow it. When all the pertinent information is in, we bring down the house of cards. We'll meet the lions in their own den. Like Daniel, we'll walk out unscathed. Unlike these thieves, we have the power of the *Almighty* on our side." Craig sounded like a man with unwavering faith.

The boardroom's intercom line buzzed, interrupting Craig's animated speech.

Richard sat closest to the phone and he picked up the receiver.

"It's Sambrea," Richard informed Craig. "She needs to speak with you."

"Tell her to hold on, Richard. I'm going to take it in our office. Sam wouldn't call me out of a meeting if it wasn't important." Craig adjourned the meeting before taking off for the privacy of their office.

Hearing Craig's gentle voice call out her name, her eyes turned watery. "Sorry to interrupt you, but I needed to talk to you."

Taking his tie off, he laid it on the desk. "What's wrong, baby? You sound distressed."

"About the baby, Craig, I don't think we're pregnant." Her voice was weakened with stress and mixed emotions.

Concerned, he sat up straight in the chair. "How do you know that, Sambrea?"

"I saw my gynecologist and she did a pelvic exam. She also ran a pregnancy test, but the results won't be ready until late this afternoon. The pelvic exam proved negative. If the blood and urine tests come back negative, she'll run more tests to see what's keeping the monthly visitor at bay. Disappointed, Craig?"

"Disappointed, maybe a little. But as much as I want children, we could use more time alone. Time to really get to know each other's wants and needs. Does your doctor feel there could be something seriously wrong with you, Sam?"

"No, not really. She thinks I've been under too much stress. That in itself can cause the visitor to stay away. However, there is an injection that can be given and should bring my cycle around in about forty-eight hours. If the injection doesn't work, we'll have to explore other possibilities. I already have an appointment for next week."

"Good! I'm going to tag along."

"Why would you want to do that? All you'll see is a bunch of pregnant ladies and a bunch of other women who look distressed. Among us women, the gynecologist is the least favored medical office to visit."

"Because I care about you, because I want to know everything that goes on with you, the important and the unimportant. Everything, girl. Besides, I just need to be there with you, Sam. Is that okay?"

"Gee, if I didn't know better, I'd think you were a reincarnation of my father. He always went to my doctor appointments with me. I recall my first visit to the gynecologist. I thought Samuel would die from embarrassment, but he walked through that door with his head held high, looking as though he dared anyone to laugh or question his motives."

"I'm going to take that as a yes. As if I would take no for an answer."

"My appointment is next Tuesday at three o'clock. If you can fit it into your schedule, I'd be delighted to have you escort me."

He wished he could kiss her. "I wouldn't have it any other way. I'll have my secretary clear my calendar for the entire day. We can do some shopping and have a bite to eat. Now, my beautiful sea nymph, I have to get to another appointment. I'd like to see you take the day off. You could use some time to yourself, Sam. Everything's fine here at the office."

He made a kissing sound into the phone. "I love you. Can't wait to get back home to you, Sam. Miss you like crazy."

Sambrea listened to her husband's voice, letting it soothe her nerves. As he hung up, her eyes brimmed with love. Although it was in a very different way, it was almost like having Samuel around. That brought her undisguised pleasure. Yes, Craig would take care of her. Just as Samuel had. Most women would kill for men like those two, yet Breeze had seen fit to discard Samuel without any regard for how much he'd be hurt. For Sambrea, it just didn't add up.

Unable to bear the pain of her thoughts, she turned her face into the pillow and cried softly for all of those who have been seriously hurt by love. Sure in her heart that she wasn't going to be unlucky in love, she allowed a slight smile to creep across her lips.

Needing to be as professional looking as possible for what would more than likely turn into an ugly business confrontation, Craig dressed with extreme care. If Sambrea weren't involved in this mess, he wouldn't even take this meeting. His highly qualified staff members were well equipped to make light work of Tyler Wilson and those like him. In fact, had this been his company from the onset, there wouldn't be any need for a meeting of this sort.

Craig Caldwell knew everything about his company and his employees. He was deeply satisfied with himself and how he handled his professional responsibilities. It was his business to know everything about everything.

It had taken several weeks to complete the investigation of Tyler Wilson and the matter of the bogus pensions. As though in answer to his prayer, Tyler Wilson had come to Hawaii. That move solved a couple of problems for Craig. He wouldn't have to leave Sambrea, or have to lie about the reason for his sudden departure for Europe. One of Craig's lead investigators had called late the previous evening to inform him that Tyler Wilson had arrived in Honolulu a few days before. He was registered at the Waikiki Sheraton.

As he tied his dark blue Swiss dotted tie, he could see Sambrea's reflection in the mirror. Just the sight of her had him wanting to disrobe and climb back into the warmth of her all-encompassing womanhood. But then he'd have to put off this confrontation a bit longer, and he couldn't put it off. He had to get this over with.

Suddenly, he felt tired. It was time to get things out in the open, get them resolved, then relax and spend as many hours alone with his wife as he desired. A honeymoon was long over-due. A long, lazy Mediterranean cruise was more than just a little appealing right now.

Removing his navy blue double-breasted jacket from a wooden hangar, he slid into it with ease. A last glance in the mirror found him satisfied with his all-business-no-pleasure appearance.

Stopping at the edge of the bed, he leaned over and planted a kiss in the center of Sambrea's forehead. But she didn't stir. He scribbled her an endearing note, full of promises of things to come, then signed it and propped it against the alarm clock.

Armed with confidence, arrogance, and a strong yen to have this dirty business over with once and for all, he strode out to the garage and quickly settled into the black Jaguar. The rain had ceased and the sun had resumed its imperious position in the now clear blue skies. Craig was happy to see the change in weather. He watched as a silver plane sliced through the ether, leaving behind a trail of white pluming streaks.

The drive along the coast relaxed him, yet his mind worked through all the problems he was about to address. Tyler Wilson probably had no idea who Craig Caldwell was, but he was about to find out. Surely he didn't know that Craig knew about every minuscule detail of his life.

Pulling up into the Sheraton's driveway, Craig left the Jaguar with the valet and walked into the lobby. He didn't need to stop by the registration desk to ask for Tyler Wilson's room number. His people had taken care of that as well.

While riding upward in the elevator, he thought of all the things he and Sambrea were going to do together once this madness was over. First off, he had to tell Sambrea everything. Well, not everything, he decided. He'd never tell her the truth about Breeze.

Once Sambrea knew all that he could tell her, they could really start to live their lives without worrying about company business or Breeze's dirty laundry. If Sambrea refused to accept his honest reasoning for paying Breeze off, there might not be a life for them, at least, not as man and wife. Involuntarily, he shuddered. She had to understand, didn't she? He'd done it for her, for them, for what they could have together far into the future. Yes, Sambrea had to understand his motives, however selfish they may have been.

Before knocking on the door, Craig straightened his tie and put on his game face.

A slender, balding man opened the door wide. His smile was wide, as if he'd been expecting someone special. Craig was definitely not that someone special. He saw that from the questioning look in the older man's eyes.

"Yes? How can I help you?" Tyler believed the gentleman surely had the wrong room.

Without giving Tyler an opportunity to refuse him entry, Craig whisked into the room.

Tyler's confusion gave way to curiosity as he turned to face the young man who had so quickly invaded his space. "What is your business with me?"

"De La Brise," Craig charmed. "I understand it once was very much your main concern. As it is now mine. With that out of the way, I'd like to ask you some questions regarding your tenure at De La Brise."

Tyler stiffened. "How is it that De La Brise is your business, young man?"

Craig grinned. "I married its beautiful owner. Right before that delightful event took place, our two companies merged. My name is Craig Caldwell, CEO of Caldwell & Caldwell, Incorporated. I'm very surprised that you haven't heard about the marriage or the merger." Craig gestured toward a chair. "May I sit?"

Tyler studied Craig through wary eyes. "Suit yourself, but don't get too comfortable. I have a prior commitment."

Craig's smile was charitable. "I promise this won't take long. I have no intentions of beating around the bush. I'm a point man, one of few words. Now, to get right down to it, you've been ripping off my wife's company."

Taking on twenty years in a matter of seconds, Tyler's cocoa-brown skin turned ashy gray. Having seen pictures of the handsome, debonair Samuel Sinclair, Craig couldn't believe Breeze could fall for someone who looked as old and tired as Tyler. But then again, they had the same criminal minds.

"That's a strong charge, young man. One I don't take too kindly." Tyler scowled with great displeasure.

Craig nodded. "Very strong charge. Nor did I intend it to be kind. When someone is stealing from an innocent young woman, I find kindness an absurdity," Craig thundered.

The air grew thick with tension as Craig gave Tyler a few minutes to digest the unsavory meal he'd just served up. "According to all the collected data, you have bilked millions out of De La Brise. How does a man do that to the daughter of his best friend?"

Tyler bristled. "Young man, you should leave. I think I've heard enough of your offensive babbling. I think I shall call security and have you removed from the premises."

Craig reared up like an agitated stallion. That caused Tyler to step backward. "I don't recall asking you what you thought of my comments, sir. However, I did ask you how you could do this to someone you once called your best friend."

Trying hard not to forget what his parents had taught him about respecting his elders, Craig moved toward the telephone. Picking it up, he dialed the front desk. "The local police department, please. No, it's not an emergency." Craig talked into the dead silence on the other end of the line. "Ring me back when you have them on the line."

He turned back to Tyler. "What was it that you were saying, Mr. Wilson?"

Tyler Wilson had grown even paler. "Mr. Caldwell, it isn't necessary to get the police involved in this matter."

Craig raised his eyebrows. "Does that mean you're prepared to come clean?" Tyler couldn't have known that Craig hadn't spoken to anyone because his back had been turned during the call. However, Craig didn't want the police yet; he wanted a confession.

Raking his hands through what little hair he had left, Tyler sank into a nearby chair. "I'll do my best to cooperate." Tyler suddenly looked like a whipped puppy. "What is it you wish to know, Mr. Caldwell?"

Pretending to cancel the call he'd put into the front desk, Craig hid the triumph he felt inside. "Everything. You can start with why you got involved in something like this."

Looking relieved to have this all come to a head, Tyler blew out a ragged breath. "I fell in love with a woman. I did it for her. She'd been unhappy for years, thought she wouldn't stand a chance of getting a dime if she divorced her husband. I thought if I had enough money to take care of her in the style she'd become accustomed to, she'd somehow come to love me in return."

Craig lifted his hand in a halting motion. "You're not just talking about any woman. You're talking about the wife of Samuel Sinclair, your best friend. Is that not so?"

Wondering how Breeze had managed to keep him in the dark for so many years, about so many things, Tyler looked baffled. She had to have known about Sambrea's marriage, but she hadn't breathed a word to him. "Yes, I'm talking about Breeze Sinclair. I thought she was in love with me, up to this very second. Although I knew Samuel wouldn't deny her anything, I allowed my heart to overrule my common sense. Breeze has this crazy way about her. She's capable of causing quite a ruckus when she can't get her way. Breeze had become so jealous of her only child. It's a good thing she walked away from her family. Sambrea could've been hurt terribly had Breeze stayed."

Hadn't Breeze told Tyler the truth about Sambrea? Craig was amazed at how deceptive one small woman could be. "And you don't think Sambrea was hurt? Man, Sambrea trusted . . ."

The door suddenly flung open, causing the conversation to come to an abrupt halt.

Totally unaware of Craig's presence, Breeze whirled into the room, shouting at the top of her lungs. "We have to get out of this country, Tyler. Our indiscretions have been discovered. Sambrea's bastard husband is having us investigated."

"My mother was legally married to my father when I was conceived, Mrs. Sinclair." Craig leveled his cold gaze upon her.

"What . . . the . . . hell?" Breeze exclaimed.

Seeing Craig standing there was her worst nightmare. Knowing she'd already blown it, she saw no use in trying to clean up her act. What could he prove? It was her and Tyler's word against his. She knew Tyler's loyalty belonged solely to her, always had, always would. More importantly, it had to be that way, because Tyler had no choice in the matter.

She turned on Craig. "You can't prove a damn thing, Caldwell. Besides, Sambrea will never agree to have us arrested. She couldn't live with the guilt."

"Wrong again, Mother." Sambrea's strong voice had reached everyone from the doorway. "Guilt is an unhealthy emotion for a very emotionally healthy woman to carry around. At this very moment I'd agree to have you burned at the stake!"

Rushing across the room, Craig placed a protective arm around his wife—an arm she'd love to cut off. Sambrea didn't have to voice her anger at Craig. Feeling it in spades, he saw it in her eyes when she briefly looked his way. Her shoulders felt tense under his soft touch; the same soft touch that normally melted her like heated butter.

Turning to address Tyler Wilson, Sambrea moved away from Craig. "I'm shocked at your involvement in this despicable crime. My father died believing in you—and I'm your goddaughter. I hope Breeze was worth betraying us for. This is one pain I'm glad Samuel has been spared. If he wasn't already dead, this surely would've killed him."

"Do you want me to call the police, Sambrea? These two should be locked up." Craig looked at both Breeze and Tyler with open contempt.

"Not so fast, Mr. Caldwell. I have an offer to make to Tyler. Tyler, if you'll agree to become the state's evidence against Breeze, I won't press charges against you. I suspect you're just another one of her hand puppets. Someone at De La Brise has also been helping you in this crime. I need to know who it is. An intruder was in our offices a few weeks ago. I'm sure you both know who it was. What do you say to my offer, Tyler? You'll only get this one chance to save yourself."

Looking from Breeze to Sambrea, Tyler grew somber. Not knowing what to do, he looked to Craig, as though seeking his support. Tyler didn't want to betray Breeze, but neither did he want to spend time in prison.

Breeze, recognizing Tyler's dilemma, prayed he wouldn't betray her. "Sambrea, do you realize your husband is a party to all of this?"

Impatiently, Sambrea crossed her arms and rolled her eyes to the ceiling. "In what way is Craig involved, Mother?" Sambrea's coolness belied the way she felt inside.

Breeze placed both hands on her hips. "He's paid me a large sum of money for the sole purpose of having me leave town. I wonder why he was so eager to get rid of me? Do you have any idea, Sambrea? If you don't know why, I can tell you. He's trying to hide his own indiscretions. He had me sign over to him the few shares I owned; the shares that gave him controlling interest of De La Brise. You can't make any decisions for the company without him now. He has usurped all of your power. That's why he was so eager to get rid of me. You can't trust a man like him."

Bewildered at the horrific news she'd just received, Sambrea looked at Craig as though horns had just grown right out of his head. "Is this true, Craig? If so, what's your motivation?"

The very moment he'd dreaded now stared him right in the face. The pains in his stomach were overwhelming. "I did it for us, Sambrea. I thought if I could get Breeze out of our lives, we could get on with our marriage. Money seems to be the only thing she can relate to. Yes, I paid her off, but I can see it didn't work. I had her sign over the shares to me so no one else would buy them up. They were for sale to the highest bidder as long as they remained in her possession. Because it would only complicate matters more, I couldn't let her do that to you, so I paid her off. She was supposed to leave town and never return to Hawaii."

Craig wanted to bring his wife into his arms, but he knew he couldn't take it if she were to reject him. "I've been having these two investigated for some time now, but I couldn't tell you anything until I had concrete proof. I'm sorry it happened this way."

Sambrea felt sickened. Looking from one to the other, she didn't know what to believe anymore. Everyone seemed to be masquerading as something other than what they really were.

Sambrea was angry at Craig for keeping his findings a secret. She'd shared her suspicions about Tyler with him from the onset, yet he hadn't trusted her enough to do the same. They weren't the equals he'd said they were.

She'd deal with him later. She wasn't about to give Breeze the satisfaction of seeing her rip into her husband, so without bothering to respond to Craig, she turned her attention to Tyler. "Tyler, I have made you an offer. I'll give you twenty-four hours to make a decision. You know how to reach me. If I were either of you, I wouldn't think of trying to leave the country. You're in much too deep to escape this one," Sambrea threatened.

Without so much as a nod to anyone, Sambrea walked out of the suite. How had she ever allowed herself to be manipulated by these three people?

There was Breeze Sinclair, a wicked woman who just happened to be her mother. What a joke, she thought. She had often wondered if Breeze's pregnancy had been an accident or a freak of nature, since her mother had never taken any real interest in her. Breeze had been absent most of the time, anyway. And when she had been home, she'd constantly competed with her daughter.

Then there was Tyler Wilson, the caring godfather, who had seemed to love her as if she were his very own. Here was a man she would've entrusted her life to, but it was now abundantly clear his loyalties had always belonged to Breeze. His friendship with Samuel had somehow become a farce. She was sure that Samuel had gone to his grave believing Tyler Wilson was a man of integrity and strong moral values. Sambrea was glad Samuel had at least been spared the truth about his best friend. Such knowledge would have destroyed him.

How could a mother and a professed best friend end up so utterly betraying the man and the daughter who would've given them anything? If only they'd asked, Samuel would've given anything and everything within his power to give.

Last, but certainly not least, Craig Caldwell had entered her life bringing midnight eyes, smiles, champagne, roses, and hot sex. Love had introduced itself to her from the moment he'd appeared. After all she'd gone through to trust him, she was now faced with this new battle. Which wasn't new at all, she considered. It was like old times.

Why hadn't he just told her about the shares and the

money that he'd given Breeze? Had he wanted to get rid of Breeze for her sake, like he'd stated? Or did he have some other agenda? How would she ever learn to trust people when so many she thought to be trustworthy proved anything but? How many times had he lectured her about conquering her fears? Hadn't he just revived many of her old ones?

Knowing she'd have to face Craig sooner or later, she hoped it would be much, much later. Going off to Maui would give her the time she'd need to recover from all these betrayals. Tai would help her get through this one, just like she'd helped so many other times, before and after Samuel's death. Yes, Maui was where she needed to be.

Sambrea had no doubt where Tai's loyalties lay.

THIRTEEN

Just finishing up with her packing for Maui, she looked up at Craig as he strode into their bedroom. As he came near her, he touched her arm, and she pushed past him. Walking over to the dressing table, she sat down and picked up the hairbrush. Sambrea ignoring him only encouraged him further, since he was determined to make her listen to his side of things.

"Are you going to run away from me again, native girl? I thought you'd be tired of running by now. Don't you think your feet have plenty of blisters on them already?"

Scowling, she studied his reflection in the mirror as he towered over her. "I'm not running, Craig. I just need a break from all of this stress. I can't sort out my life with so much turmoil all around me. It's distracting."

Taking the brush from her hand, he ran it through her hair a couple of times. "I understand your need to get away from the stress, but you have a doctor's appointment tomorrow. I don't think you should miss it. You still haven't gotten your cycle. Even though the tests have all been negative, you still may be pregnant. Your doctor said it just might be too soon for accurate results. Every woman's body reacts differently, you know."

She lowered her head onto the table. "I pray to God that I'm not pregnant! It would be so unfair to bring a child into the world in our present situation. You know it as well as I do. With all the emotional stress I'm under, I might not even be able to carry a baby to term."

Fearing for her health, he sat down beside her on the stool. He put her hand in his. "That's even more of a reason for you to keep your appointment. Will you at least not go to Maui until after you've seen the doctor? I think you also need to consult her about your nerves. You're pretty fragile right now, native girl. I'm going to go with you. If you agree, I'll take you to the airport myself afterward. Though I really don't want you to leave here at all. Us being apart is not the answer."

She shot him a nasty look. "Why did you start calling me native girl all of a sudden? You knew I was a native of Hawaii from the start."

He grinned. "I liked the way it sounded the first time I said it. It fits you perfectly. You're wild and free like the beautiful plants and flowers that grow here. You dress like a native girl, you dance like one—and I love it when you wear fresh flowers in your hair. Especially white orchids and red hibiscus. You're simply a native girl, Sam."

"Whatever," she retorted. "I'll keep my appointment, Craig. Thank you for offering to take me to the airport, but I plan on parking my car there so I won't have to call for someone to pick me up or take a taxi when I return."

"Are you going to let me tell you why I did what I did regarding Breeze? There's so much you don't understand about people like her. I run into her kind more often than not."

Feeling too tired to fight with Craig, too defeated to listen to anything he had to say with an open mind, too vulnerable to keep her emotions out of it, she sighed wearily. "Not now, Craig. I'm not in the right frame of mind to comprehend anything you might say and I really don't want to misinterpret your remarks. Therefore, your explanation will just have to wait."

He gripped her shoulders. "For how long, Sam?"

Pushing him back from her, she sighed again. "For as long as it takes me to recuperate from all this madness. Any guess would be as good as mine."

He shrugged his shoulders. "I can wait. I came up here to the bedroom determined to make you talk to me, but I can see how exhausted you are. Are you hungry?"

She felt so worn out she had to actually think about his question. "Not really, but I should eat something just to keep up my strength. I'll go down in a few minutes and fix something for us. Right now, I just want to lie down for a bit. Do you mind?"

He kissed her forehead. "Of course not. You just get in bed. I'll go down and fix something to eat. Come on, Sam. Let me help you out of your clothes."

She knew she should protest his removal of her clothing, but she didn't have any energy to even voice an objection. Instead of making an issue of it, she lifted her arms up for him to take her sweater off over her head. Kissing each side of her face, he removed her top. Walking across the room, he took a silk nightgown out of the dresser drawer and carried it over to the bed. "Is this one okay?" She just nodded. After slipping it over her head, he pulled it down over her body.

Pulling the comforter and the top sheet back, he lifted her up and placed her in bed. Looking into her eyes, he nearly broke down and cried. He'd never seen his wife look more miserable than she did right now. Her sun-bronzed skin almost looked pale and her eyes were without their usual engaging sparkle. Though aching to kiss her, he knew the timing was wrong.

"Do you want the television on, Sambrea?"

"Could you just pop a sounds of nature tape into the cassette? *Sounds of the Waterfall* is a pretty restful one."

"Coming right up."

As the soothing sounds of water rushing down a mountainside breathed its relaxing melody into the room, Sambrea laid her head back on the pillow and closed her eyes. Her heart rate calmed as the music worked wonders on her irritable mood. Before leaving the room, Craig had turned down the ceiling lights until they glowed with moon-yellow softness.

Downstairs in the kitchen Craig tossed enough salad for two and set it aside. While the skinless, boneless breasts of chicken cooked on the stovetop grill, Craig heated sesame oil in the wok for stir-fry vegetables.

Then, as he worked, he smelled her perfume. As he turned to her, he smiled. His eyes meandered over the matching raspberry silk robe she'd put on over her nightgown. *So beautiful. Even when she doesn't feel so well, even when her hair falls in a cascade of unruly curls.*

"Couldn't rest?"

She frowned. "Afraid not. Too much on my mind. Besides that, I have a whopper of a headache. I came down to get some water to gulp down a couple of pain relievers."

Walking over to the table, he pulled out a chair. "Sit down, Sam. I'll get the water for you. Do you want anything else?"

I can get water for myself. She looked agitated, but she let him fuss over her without objections, and sat down at the kitchen table. "Nothing else, thanks. What smells so good?"

"The chicken you marinated last night."

Carrying the glass of water over to the table, he handed it to her. "Everything is just about ready. I need to stir-fry the vegetables for a hot second. Just the way you like them. Are you going to stay down here, or do you want me to bring a tray upstairs?"

"I'm going back up if you don't mind. Hopefully, my head will calm down by the time dinner's ready." Popping two white tablets in her mouth, she swallowed them with a long gulp of water. Just as Sambrea stood up, a wave of nausea surfed right through her stomach. Then a severe bout of dizziness nearly brought her to her knees. "Craig," she cried out in a panic, "I think I'm going to faint."

Before she could blink, he was at her side. With his arm securely around her waist, he guided her into one of the first floor bathrooms.

"Oh, God," she shouted. She bent over the toilet just as her guts raised up in her throat and emptied into the bowl.

Large beads of sweat dotted her forehead. As her hair fell down around her face, Craig pushed it back. He held her head steady as her stomach continued to empty itself. As the nausea began to ease, she lifted her head and rested it back against Craig's chest.

Holding her steady with one arm, he took a washcloth from the rack. Wetting it with cool water, he wiped her mouth and rinsed the cloth again and then laid it across her forehead. "Off to bed we go, native girl. I don't want you to move another muscle once I get you all tucked in again."

Sambrea made three more trips to the bathroom before Craig settled her back in bed. After making her comfortable, he placed a plastic-lined trash can on the side of the bed where she slept. Sliding into bed next to her, he cradled her in his arms. "No solid food for you. Should I call the doctor?"

Sambrea shook her head. "Not unless I get worse. We can discuss this problem with her tomorrow."

He stroked her hair with a gentle touch. "I know things are tough right now, Sam. There are a lot of things that need to be worked out between us, between you and Breeze. The problems aren't going to go away on their own. They have to be addressed by all parties involved . . ."

"Craig," she interjected, "I can't deal with any of our issues right now, or any of the issues between Breeze and myself. I'm too sick to care about anything. But I know I won't always feel that way. I don't know why I'm so sick. I just am."

Continuing to stroke her hair, his eyes sympathized with her quandary. "I think you're pregnant, Sam. I won't rule out stress as the culprit, but I think the stress is complicating the pregnancy. I'm no doctor, but you have all the classic symptoms of a mother-to-be." Nervously, he cleared his throat. "Would it really be so bad for you if you were carrying a child we created out of our love for each other?"

Smiling, she looked up at him, her expression soft and mellow. She loved him like crazy. So how could something so good be so bad for her? Just bad timing, she concluded. "Craig, if we're with child, we will give our baby the same kind of love from which he or she was created."

A light mist darkening his eyes, he looked down on the woman who made every day of his life worth living. Waking up with Sambrea every morning was like waking up to a perfect day, a perfect day in heaven. "Do you want me to sleep in another room, Sam, until you're feeling better?" Closing his eyes, he prayed that she'd want no such thing.

Scooting down in the bed, she placed her head on the pillow. "That's not the answer to anything. We promised never to go to bed upset with each other. I want us to honor that promise. I'm sure I have just cause to be upset with you, but since I don't know all the details of what I'm upset about, we can live in peace until I do. Besides, an expectant mother has to be careful not to pass her anxieties on to her unborn child."

Thrilled with her answer, even though it had surprised him, he never wanted to sleep alone again in his life. More specifically, he never wanted to have to sleep without Sambrea right there beside him.

Although it was still early in the evening, Craig stripped out of his clothing while making his way into the bathroom's walk-in closet, where his dresser was located. For the first time since he was a child, he put on pajamas—a

silk pair his mother had sent to him for Christmas several
years back. In fact, she'd sent him three pairs, in three different colors: navy, burgundy and brown.

Before climbing into bed with his wife, Craig lit a candle
and placed it in the window; just like Sambrea always did
at the bungalow. Her back was to him when he slid in beside
her. Feeling the cool silk against her feverish body, she
turned over to see what he'd worn to bed.

She laughed out loud. "You own a pair of pajamas? I'm
amazed. You look so handsome in them. Hot, too." She
smoothed her hand over the material covering his chest.
"Nice. Real nice." Without warning, a pang of jealousy
struck her right through the heart. "I know you'd never buy
pajamas for yourself. You like spontaneous skin games too
much to be trapped in swaddling bedclothes. Who bought
these for you? And I do want the truth on this issue."

Wanting to string her out for a bit, he looked crestfallen.
"Are you sure you want to know the answer to that question, Sam?"

Narrowing her eyes until they became dangerous slits,
she sucked her teeth. "Are you sure you want to suffer the
dire consequences that will surely come if you don't answer
it?"

He kept his game face on. "Well, she's about five-seven,
with a heart-stopping figure. An extremely beautiful
woman, inside and out. She's one of the sweetest women
I've ever met. Though she's another man's wife, I've spent
the best days of my life in her tender, loving arms."

Tears sprang to Sambrea's eyes, but she quickly brushed
them away. "You were right to think I might not want the
answer. But how could you sleep with a married woman?"

Sambrea's doleful expression kept him from bursting into
laughter, but he wasn't through with her yet. One day she
would learn not to threaten him with dire consequences, or
learn not to threaten him at all.

"It was easy. The three of us often shared the same bed.

At least, in the beginning—then it got kind of old. But we all still slept in the same house. Her old man wasn't a bit jealous. In fact, he applauded her for spending as much time with me as she did."

Sambrea was baffled as she put a little distance between them. "You all slept in the same bed? Are you trying to tell me you're bisexual? How would you feel if another man were to sleep with your wife?"

Wherever he'd expected her to go with the information he'd just fed her, he hadn't expected her to go there. Only Sambrea would've come up with that one. He was sure she would've guessed by now. As for the question about someone other than himself sleeping with her, the same question Breeze had asked of him, he didn't even want to entertain the idea.

She nudged him out of his thoughts. "Who the heck are this sick man and woman, Craig Caldwell?"

"My mother and father, Sambrea Caldwell." He burst into nearly uncontrollable laughter.

Sambrea had never felt so foolish in all her life. A moron could've put all the clues together. His parents! She was certainly happy that it wasn't a woman he'd been sexually involved with, delighted that Craig wasn't bisexual. It wasn't that she had anything against that particular sexual preference, it just wasn't her cup of tea.

"You really got me this time, Craig. This native girl feels like a first-class idiot. How could you be so cruel?"

"You asked the question. All I did was answer it when you insisted I do so. Everything I said was factual. I admit to leading you on a bit, but you led yourself so much farther afield than I could've ever led you." He laughed. "Girl, you have some imagination. Bisexual! Sam, only you could've come up with that."

Reaching for the trash can, she grabbed her stomach. Craig held her head once again as her insides spasmed with a force akin to violence. When her nausea eased, he got out of bed and retrieved another wet washcloth.

He got back into bed with her, drawing her into his arms. "Too much excitement there, native girl. Rest now. We can continue to intrigue one another later on." As she snuggled her head onto his chest, his grip around her waist soothed her.

"Sorry for spoiling your fun. I feel even weaker than I did earlier. I'm going to stay right here in your arms."

"Right where you know you'll be safe. Go to sleep now. My love sleeps with you. It's with you at all times."

Craig saw how scared Sambrea looked as they waited for Dr. Lindsey Gooden to enter the examining room. Small and vulnerable, she lay quietly on the cold leather table.

Getting up from the chair, he walked over to her. Smiling down at her, he covered her folded hands with his. "Remember what I told you about being afraid. With me by your side, there's nothing to fear." His expression grew somber. "Do you still trust me, Sam?"

Dressed in a dark double-breasted suit and gray silk shirt, Craig looked so good to her, smelled so good to her. He'd been good for her, good to her, she had to admit. She trusted him, but she didn't trust the things he'd kept from her. Nor did she trust the situation he'd gotten himself into with Breeze. She might be crazy to do so, but she had to trust the love for her she saw there in his eyes, the love that seemed unconditional, incontestable.

"Yes. I trust you, Craig."

"Thank you for that. However, I felt a silent *but* at the end of your response even though you didn't voice it."

"Let's just leave it at what I said, Craig. This isn't the place to discuss our personal matters."

Smiling, he tugged at the paper gown she wore. "This is some fashion statement you're making, girlfriend." Grinning, he fingered the unflattering gown. "Paper, expensive silks, or fine linens, your natural beauty enhances anything you have a mind to put on, but . . ."

She easily read his thoughts. "You look best in nothing at all," she finished for him.

They both laughed.

"You two seem to be enjoying each other," Dr. Gooden said as she entered the room.

A fairly tall black female who looked to be in her early thirties, Dr. Gooden had an olive-brown complexion. She wore her reddish brown hair in a short natural. Wire-framed glasses sat on the bridge of her small, well-formed nose.

"Good morning, Sambrea," the doctor enthused. "Hello, sir," she said to Craig. "You must be Mr. Caldwell. It's nice to make your acquaintance."

He smiled broadly. "My pleasure, Dr. Gooden. My wife speaks highly of you. And please call me Craig. Mr. Caldwell is a bit too formal."

"Thank you, Craig. That's kind of you." Turning to Sambrea, she smiled. "Well, young lady, I need you to tell me what's going on with you. Has your period come yet?"

Sambrea blew out a gust of trembling breath. "Not yet. Craig thinks I'm pregnant and that the stress I'm under is complicating my physical well-being. I had a terrible bout with nausea and dizziness last evening. It came on after a horribly distressing day."

Dr. Gooden looked at Sambrea with concern. "Your husband just might be right. Stress can complicate all sorts of physical stuff. Lay back, Sambrea. I'm going to do another pelvic exam. Maybe things have changed in your uterus since the last exam."

Sambrea looked totally uncomfortable. Craig sensed that she didn't want him to witness her dignity being usurped. She had mentioned that seeing the gynecologist was the most humiliating time of her life.

His smile was one of understanding as he bent down and

kissed her on the forehead. "I'll be right outside the door, Sam. I'll come back as soon as it's okay with you."

Grateful for his sensitivity toward her, Sambrea flashed him a smile that spoke of her feelings. "Don't go too far."

Suddenly, feeling as though she'd just shut him out of something that seemed so important to him, her expression grew pensive. For sure, if she were pregnant, he'd be there in the delivery room with her. The humiliation couldn't get any worse than when a woman gave birth to her child with a male in the room. But Craig wasn't just any male. He was her husband.

"Craig, wait," she called out to him, just as his hand turned the doorknob. "I want you here. I need you to hold my hand." She remembered all the thousands of times she'd asked Samuel to hold her hand.

He didn't try to rid his eyes of the tears that suddenly appeared. "Anything for you, Sambrea."

Moving behind the examining table, he took hold of Sambrea's right hand. Bringing her hand to his mouth, he kissed each of her knuckles. "Thank you," he whispered.

As the doctor examined Sambrea, Craig thought about love and what it truly meant. Very few people knew what it meant. He was one of the few that did; one of the lucky few; one of the blessed few. If it wasn't love he felt for Sambrea, his heart had seriously duped him. *Highly improbable!* His heart hadn't failed him yet.

Dr. Gooden directed the Caldwells to her private office once the exam was completed.

Holding hands, Craig and Sambrea sat in chairs in front of the doctor's desk. Craig leaned over, kissing his wife's cheek. "Don't look so worried. Together, we've got it all under control." The uncertainty in her eyes did very little to assure him that he'd gotten through to her.

"We'll see, won't we?" came her half-hearted response.

Why did he always have to make it seem like everything depended on their being together? It seemed to her that they'd done pretty well for themselves before meeting. For sure, Craig had made a wonderful life for himself. While De La Brise had its problems, she hadn't done so bad for herself, either. But they were better together, she finally admitted to herself. When Dr. Gooden called her name, Sambrea switched her thoughts to what lay ahead of her right now.

Dr. Gooden shrugged her shoulders. Stretching her palms out in front of her, she turned them face up. "The exam of the uterus was inconclusive, Sambrea and Craig. I'm sorry. I just don't have the answers at the moment."

Craig squeezed Sambrea's hand. "What does that mean? Is she pregnant or not?"

Dr. Gooden rubbed her hands together. "I just don't know yet, Craig. Her tests are all negative, but that doesn't necessarily mean she's not pregnant. There's been no change in the size of her uterus. We get a lot of false negatives in this business. Believe it or not, false positives occur quite frequently also."

Dr. Gooden looked at Sambrea with apologetic eyes. "We seem to be talking as though you're not here, Sambrea. You're so quiet over there. What are you feeling?"

Sambrea frowned. "I wondered if anyone was going to include me in this conversation. I'm the patient, you know."

The hard edge in her tone came through with crystal clarity to both Craig and the doctor.

"What am I feeling?" Sambrea repeated. "That's funny. I really don't know. Sometimes I want to be pregnant. Then I feel like I'm totally unprepared for this major responsibility." Sambrea sighed. "I guess that's something I should discuss with my husband in private. That shouldn't be your concern."

Lindsey Gooden smiled. "Everything that concerns you concerns me. When I know what's going on with you emotionally, it helps me to figure out the physical aspect. Let's do a hypothetical here. If you knew unequivocally you were pregnant, what would you do right now?"

Feeling powerless, Sambrea turned to Craig, unsure of how to respond. The truth was the best course of action, but she had to be careful of his feelings. If she somehow gave the impression she didn't want his baby it would hurt him deeply. But it wouldn't have mattered who the father was, the timing was wrong. The whole idea of being pregnant scared her to death.

Instead of voicing her thoughts, she put her head on Craig's shoulder. "This is something Craig and I should discuss in private. I can't answer your question without raising a bunch of other questions, questions I'm not prepared to answer. Can we table this until later?"

Trying to control his anger at Sambrea's ambiguous response, Craig got to his feet and stood over her chair. "Sambrea, it might be a little late for your indecisiveness. I hope you're not considering an abortion. I couldn't deal with that. I won't accept that as a solution. Maybe we should both pray that you're not carrying my child."

In her attempt to spare his feelings, she could see that her evasive remarks had done just the opposite. She actually saw fear in his eyes; fear that she might do the unthinkable.

After standing up, she attempted to take his hand. Frustrated, he jerked away from her. "We can't do this here, Craig. Let's discuss this at home." She turned to face the doctor. "I'm sorry about this, Dr. Gooden. This shouldn't have happened."

Dr. Gooden rounded her desk and stood before the unhappy couple. "None of this is good for your health, Sambrea. Craig, you shouldn't take Sambrea's feelings as a personal affront. Not once has she mentioned abortion to me. We don't even know if she's pregnant yet. Your wife needs your support, not your opposition. She's living in fear. For a reason that totally eludes me, or maybe it's just because Sambrea can't share it with me, this is a very difficult time for her. You two need to discuss your feelings about this situation in depth. You have some very important decisions to make. In the meantime Sambrea should not be stressed out like she is. Do you both understand?"

Craig couldn't stand to see Sambrea cry. He'd upset her without giving the slightest thought to her mental state. She'd been through hell and he'd just put her back through the wringer. *Talk about insensitivity.*

"Come here, Sam," he said, gathering her into his arms. "I'm sorry, Sam. I was wrong to lose my temper with you. Can you forgive me?"

Tears from her eyes splashed onto the back of his hand. "We need to get out of here and let Dr. Gooden get back to work. We're not her only patients. We'll talk at home."

"Dr. Gooden, I understand what you've said. I promise to keep Sam free of stress as best as I can. Hopefully, by her next appointment, we'll have worked through all of this. Sorry our first meeting turned out this way."

Dr. Gooden offered her hand to Craig then to Sambrea. "I'm going to hold you to that promise, Craig. Sambrea, I want to see you in two weeks. We're going to figure this all out. In the meantime, you're not to worry, but you do need to express your true feelings to your husband. And, Mr. Caldwell, you need to listen to what she's telling you. Don't make the mistake of discounting her feelings. Only she, no one else, knows what they truly are."

The formality with which she'd addressed Craig told him how serious she was. Softening the blow she'd dealt him, Lindsey called him by his first name before they parted company.

FOURTEEN

The ride home was made in complete silence. The moment Sambrea entered the front door, she went up the stairs to their bedroom. Feeling sick to her stomach, she threw herself across the bed. It wasn't exactly a physical sickness. It had more to do with nerves and the offensive things Craig had said to her. He entered the room only seconds later.

"Not feeling well?" He dropped down on the bed.

She turned over on her back. "How could you humiliate me like that in front of my doctor? Whatever gave you the idea I'd even consider an abortion? That erroneous barb really cut deep, Craig. I didn't expect that from you."

"I kind of figured when you didn't accept my apology I was going to catch hell over that stupid blunder I made. I lost control of my anger, Sam. What else can I tell you? I apologized and I meant it."

"You accuse me of contemplating murder and you think an apology is all I'm looking for. You know what I want? I want you to grovel. I want you to beg for my forgiveness. If that doesn't work, I want you to wallow in humility. I want you to eat that remark for breakfast, lunch and dinner. That's what I want!"

To make certain he understood her, giving him the finger came to mind. She refrained. That was just a little too crude for a refined young woman like herself to pull off. Still, she was lightly amused with the idea.

Enraged at her juvenile behavior, Craig got down on his knees. "Is this what you want, Sam? Are you happy with me crouched down here like some sick puppy?"

"As a matter of fact, I'm delirious with euphoria. Like praying, it does wonders for my soul. To see you on your knees is only the half of what I expect from you before I'll even consider forgiving you."

He got up from his knees and sat back down on the bed. "You really *are* angry, aren't you? Where's all that anger coming from, Sam? Are you really angry at me, or are you angry at your circumstances? Perhaps you're angry with Breeze for the way she's treated you all these years, for her rejection of you. Is that it, Sam? Tell me!" He was shouting at the top of his lungs, and it put the fear of the devil in her. Feeling compelled to bring her anger out, he knew he had to draw it out of her. It was eating her up inside.

"Tell me why you're so damn angry at everyone but the very people you should be angry at?" He continued goading her. "Breeze and Tyler betrayed you. Hell, maybe in some way you even feel Samuel betrayed you, too. Maybe you don't want to admit that you're angry as hell with a dead man. Is that part of what's killing you inside, Sam?"

As she leaped at him like a raging firestorm, he knew without a doubt that he'd hit all the release buttons. He hadn't just hit them, he'd smashed them. But could he withstand the raging inferno he'd knowingly unleashed? Her fists pounding into his chest matched the fury he'd seen in her eyes just before she'd pounced on him. But he just stood there, letting her pound away. Being the stronger of the two, he could let her pound on him, or let her continue to beat herself up. He could take more than she could simply because he knew how to let go and let his higher power take over. She would be able to do that one day too.

Everyone arrived at different intervals.

"Yes!" she screamed at him in her fury. "I'm angry as hell with Breeze. I'm angry at her for rejecting me, for rejecting my love for her. I'm terribly disturbed at Tyler. And I blame Samuel for all of it. That makes me angrier with him than anyone. He should've been stronger."

She wrung her hands together in anguish. "He was a coward, Craig. I said it before, but you changed my mind. Well, you're not going to be able to change it this time around. What type of a man lets a woman wipe her feet all over him? You tell me?"

He grabbed hold of her hands when she got too close to his face. He was strong, but not so strong he'd willingly take a blow to the face. "Perhaps a man in love, Sambrea. Love doesn't come with an operating manual. Other than I Corinthians 13," he amended. "We all react differently to that particular emotion. Love is not just an emotion, Sam. It's more of an action than anything. Samuel acted and reacted like a man in love."

She blinked hard. "You say you love me, Craig. Does that mean you'll do anything to prove it? That you'd take any amount of abuse from me to show me how much you love me? Would you let me entertain men much younger than myself right in front of your eyes knowing I had the hots for them?"

He tossed her a knowing look. "I don't know about all that, Sambrea. I hope I don't ever have to find out. But I did just get down on my knees and grovel at your request. I try hard to make your every wish my command, Sam."

"You also just let me beat the stuffing out of you." Her anger began to subside. "God, this is so complicated. You did this on purpose, didn't you?"

He feigned innocence. "Did what?"

Balling and unballing her tiny fists, she shot him an impatient glance. "You purposely goaded me into this rage. Don't deny it. Just tell me—why?"

He let go of her hands and pulled her down to the bed. "You needed to release all that rage. Rage can kill. More importantly, it can kill your spirit. Without a spirit, we might as well be dead. You were a powder keg ready to blow. I thought it was high time someone lit the fuse before it exploded inside of you. That would've been messy, Sam."

She stared at him incredulously. "How can you see in me what I can't see in myself? How's that possible?"

Shaking his head from side to side, he ran his hands through his carbon curls. "Because I'm on the outside looking in. Often we can't see the forest for the trees because we're afraid to look within. We're scared to death of what we might see there. Somehow, if our thoughts seem less than human, less than compassionate, we think we shouldn't have them. For us to admit anger for the dead challenges the very foundation on which we've based our character. We tend to think it falls right in line with having a warped psyche. But we wouldn't be human if we didn't entertain warped thoughts. It's just one of the imperfections of human nature, Sam. Humans will never be flawless in this life."

Sambrea eyed him curiously. "Do you know anything about being angry with the dead, Craig?"

Her question threw him for a loop. Suddenly engulfed up to his neck in the pain of his past, he gave serious thought to her question. "For sure. It's not something I like to talk about, but if it'll help you, I don't mind sharing. After this, I never want to speak of it again. It belongs to the past. I've dealt with it and I've moved on. Do you understand, Sam?"

She nodded. "It doesn't sound like you want to share. If it's that disturbing to you, we don't have to go there. The look in your eyes tells me it's a painful issue."

Walking into the bathroom, he stepped inside the massive closet. From the back of the closet, he pulled out a plastic hang-up bag. Carrying it back to the bedroom, he handed it to Sambrea. "Unzip it. It'll help me explain a few things for you."

Keeping her eyes on him, she unzipped the bag and pulled out its contents. As she looked it over, she could see that the military uniform appeared to be fairly new. The silver Captain's bars on the shoulders of the jacket shined like freshly minted coins.

He looked at his fingernails. "So you see, I have had dirty fingernails. I have fought in the trenches, muddy sand trenches. *Desert Storm.*" His calm exterior belied the quaking in his stomach. "That's also the reason I didn't want to talk about why I moved to Hawaii. Other than for business purposes, I left New York hoping to leave the past far behind."

She remembered telling him he'd probably never had so much as a dirty fingernail in his entire life. She'd been wrong about that, too, wrong about so much where Craig was concerned. The meaning of his comment, "It's a long story. I'll tell you about it one day," was about to be revealed.

"What does this all mean, Craig? What point are you trying to make?"

His eyes grew bright with mist. "You asked me did I know anything about being angry at the dead. Like you, more than I want to admit." He fought back his tears. When a tear ran rampant down his cheek, her heart broke at the nightmarish pain reflected in his eyes. "You see, I lost my best friend in that war. I was angry with him for years. He was like a brother."

Sambrea reached up and wiped his tears on her sleeve. "What was your friend's name, Craig?"

"His name *was* and still *is* Glen George. People don't lose their identity because they cease to exist, Sam. I hate it when people refer to the dead as 'the remains' or 'the body.' The soul has just gone back to the Creator, to be restored to its original owner at a later time."

She combed through his hair with her fingers. "I'm sorry, Craig. I didn't mean to offend your friend's memory. I don't like that reference either. What happened to him?"

Taking her hand from his hair, he kissed her fingertips. "I know you didn't, Sam. It's okay. He was blown up while he slept in the barracks. I'm sure you heard it on the news. It was an awful mess. One that I won't ever forget. We'd been through college together, where we played sports together. We joined the Air Force together. We'd been through a lot together. For a long time I felt like we should've experienced death the same way, together.

"I felt like he cheated me, that he ran out on our relationship. At a time when I needed him the most, at a time when all hell had broken loose around us. I felt that he'd left me behind so I could tell his wife and his four-year-old twin boys he wasn't coming home to them. That's why I was so angry with him. I think you know precisely what I'm talking about. The reasons for our anger with the dead are the same, Sam. We feel cheated and deserted because they left us behind, left us to face the world alone."

Sambrea dabbed at her own tears with her sleeve. "You're right about that. At least you've dealt with your anger, come to terms with, and finally moved on from it. Through your clever machinations, I'm just starting to recognize what I've been feeling is anger. When it's buried so deep inside of you, for so long, how do you rid yourself of it? How do you purge it? I can't just go around exploding like I just did for release. That would be awful."

Closely, he studied her features. He could almost touch the desperation in her sand-and-sable eyes. The quivering of her lips spoke to the pain deep inside of her. The nuance of frustration burning in her cheeks addressed her embarrassment. The wringing of her delicate hands called attention to her anguish.

Face to face with her, he propped two pillows behind his head and stretched out on the bed. "I can't tell you how to get rid of your pain, Sam. I can only tell you what I did to get rid of mine. My parents spent their entire lives teaching me the gospel truth. I knew what was right, but I fought against everything I'd ever learned. It didn't cast it's brightest light on me until after Glen got killed, when I felt helpless, felt out of control. Because I thought it was expected of me, I offered to marry Glen's widow and raise his children. That's when I began to wrestle with the devil. When I lost enough battles to his demons, I learned how to turn it over to my *H.P.I.C.* My Higher Power In Charge."

Sambrea looked more confused than she did before he'd told her his story.

"Any more questions, Sam?"

She had a question, but she wasn't sure she should ask it. She chewed on her lower lip. It might sound petty after the enormity of all he'd just shared.

"What is it, Sam?" he prompted.

She pursed her lips. "I hope you don't take this the wrong way, but did you and Glen's widow fall in love?"

Craig was intrigued by the way she lowered her lashes when she felt uncertain of herself. He couldn't keep himself from smiling. He could always count on Sambrea to come up with the unexpected. Of all the things he'd said to her she had somehow managed to zero in on his love life. The endearing innocence of his wife had a way of making him come unglued. "What difference would it make, Sam? It's in the past."

"It wouldn't, Craig. I was just curious."

"Just curious, huh? Why don't I believe that?"

"Why wouldn't you? Are you trying to say I'm jealous?" He grinned. "Are you?"

She sucked her teeth. "Whatever. I'm going to go and take a shower." She moved over to the edge of the bed.

He pulled her back to him. "No, Sambrea, we didn't fall in love. I didn't fall in love. I felt obligated. Michelle had the good sense to know exactly what I was doing—and she wasn't having any of it. She turned me down, but not before she kindly reminded me of what Glen used to say all the time."

"What was that, Craig?"

Craig smiled, remembering with fondness the man he loved like a brother. "I don't know if he was the originator of this or not, but here goes. *Yesterday is just a cancelled check. Tomorrow is a promissory note. Today is cash in hand. Spend it carefully and wisely.* And he did just that. He spent every minute of his days carefully and wisely. It works, Sam. I had the good sense to try it, along with all I've been taught over the years. Powerful combination."

Sambrea suddenly withdrew into herself. Craig had somehow put his finger right on the pulse of her pain, pain that was so deep, so raw, and so destructive. Like a zombie, she got up from the bed and started toward the bathroom. She looked back at Craig for one brief moment. Just long enough for him to see the torment in her eyes, torment strong enough to steal the light source from her beautiful sand-and-sable eyes. Craig followed her into the bathroom because he remembered being alone when his pain had hit him full force. He wasn't going to allow his wife to suffer the same fate, not when he was right there to hold her in his arms.

Sambrea tossed and turned in her sleep and sweat seeped from her pores as she wrestled with the silk sheets. In her dreams she recalled the things Craig had said, especially the reasons why he'd found it necessary to pay Breeze off. Awakening with a start, she looked over at her sleeping husband. Without warning, her tears came.

As though he felt her anguish, he awakened immediately. Craig drew her over to his side of the bed and into his arms. He kissed her tears away. "What's up, Sam?"

Although he'd asked, he already knew.

At his insistence, they'd discussed his short-lived involvement with Breeze before he and Sambrea had retired for the night. Besides wanting it off his chest, he wanted Sambrea to be armed with the truth about the viciousness of her so-called mother. He hadn't revealed Breeze's secret regarding Sambrea's birthmother because he couldn't bring himself to do it. He'd never be able to hurt his native girl that way. Even now, he wasn't sure Breeze had spoken the truth.

She bit down on her lower lip. "You're not going to like this, but I need to get away. I can't think straight anymore. I've got so much garbage to sort through. Can you give me some time to try and pull it all together?"

As though he had the power to look into her soul, his eyes peered into the depth of her being. "I can't comply with your wishes, not this time, Sam. I understand your need to pull it together, but you should do it right here where you belong. I'll give you all the support you need, but I can't give you anything if you're not here to receive it."

"And if I decide to go without your compliance?"

"I guess that's a risk you'll just have to take."

"What are you really saying, Craig? That you won't be here when I return?"

"I said it just as I meant it, Sambrea. I can't tell you whatever it is you want to hear because I don't know what you want from me. I just know I'm tired of you running in and out of my life whenever the mood hits you. Your feet should be extremely tired by now."

Getting out of bed, he sat on the side of it. Taking her hand, he placed it between both of his. "If I allow you to continue with this unpredictable behavior, you'll be running for the rest of your life, girl. One day you're going to have to face your demons just as I had to. I faced mine before it was too late. Are you going to wait until it's too late before you get up the courage to face yours? I hope not. I won't be an enabler, Sam. That's all I have to say."

"I don't think it's all you have to say. It's more like it's all you're willing to say. I think it's high time you stop withholding things from me. You want me to trust you, but you don't trust me enough to tell me the truth about everything that went down between you and Breeze. You won't even tell me how much money you paid her. I can't explain it, but you're keeping something major from me. I feel it in my blood. Whatever it is, it's a large part of the real reason you decided to pay her off."

Not only had she come close, she'd scored a bull's eye. He was sorry that he had to protect her from the truth about herself. If it was in fact the truth.

She cast him a defiant look. "Well, aren't you going to say something? If I'm wrong, you could at least defend your position."

Craig could see right through her, right through to what motivated her to keep this unrest alive. Sambrea seemed hell-bent on picking a fight with him so she could run off to Maui with a clear conscience. No, he wouldn't give her the excuse she seemed to need. If she ran off again, the liability for such an action would lie solely with her.

"Sambrea, I'm going back to sleep. If you still want to debate these issues in the morning, we'll do so. But I'm not adding any more fuel to this fire tonight. I love you, native girl. But like the beautiful butterfly that you are, I feel your need to fly free." Stretching his long frame out in the bed, he turned his back on her, pulling the comforter up over his head.

Infuriated by his decision to ignore her, she turned on her side and stared straight ahead at the wall. Regardless of what the consequences might be, she had to do what she had to do. Craig Caldwell would do the same.

* * *

The sun was not shining at all in Maui, nor was it shining in Sambrea's heart. In fact, it hadn't rained this hard in Maui for quite some time. For as far back as she was able to recall, she couldn't remember her heart feeling darker or stormier than it felt at this very moment. For some strange reason she had expected Craig to appear in Maui, yet an entire week had passed without so much as a lousy phone call. It wasn't as if he didn't know exactly where she was.

Much to her surprise, Tyler Wilson had called and said he'd made the decision to accept her offer. She couldn't believe he was willing to sell Breeze down the river. That was exactly the reason she'd made him the offer. She simply hadn't believed he had the stomach to accept her offer or the willpower to oppose Breeze—pretty much like herself.

Tyler truly loved Breeze. That much was very clear to her. Love seemed to make bigger idiots out of already self-proclaimed fools. She felt rancor within.

As Craig descended into her thoughts, the same old questions she'd asked herself for days popped up in her mind. Not so long ago she'd been sure of the answers, sure of Craig. It hadn't come easy for her, but it had finally come. Now she wasn't so sure anymore about anything.

Did Craig love her without question or thought? The way she loved him? Was he satisfied at making her his wife—as satisfied as she was at becoming his wife? If he did love her, was it strong enough to last all of eternity? Would his love for her pass the test of time? She could only guess at the answers, since he hadn't made any new attempts to prove his love for her.

Maybe he was tired of proving it. Maybe she'd walked out on him once too often, failed to believe in him once more than he could bear, refused to hear his explanations a time or two more than he cared to accept. His explanation regarding his reasons for paying Breeze off hadn't gelled for her. It still hadn't.

Tai entered the glass-enclosed alcove of her suite.

"Samiko, you have a phone call. Would you like to take it in here?"

Sambrea smiled tenderly. "No, Tai. I'll come into the main salon. Do you know who it might be?"

"Your secretary, Mr. Joseph. He says it's urgent that he speak with you."

Sambrea followed Tai into the other room. After handing her the phone, Tai slipped out of the room quietly.

"Joe, what is it? Tai said it was urgent. What's happened?"

"Calm down, Sam. I can hear your heart pounding right through the telephone wires." Joe hesitated briefly. "It's Breeze, Sam." He heard her impatient intake of breath. "She's in the hospital. Her attorney, Ed Nellis, called. He wants to speak with you. I have his number, Sam. Do you want it? He's expecting your call."

"Do you know what's wrong with Breeze, Joe? Is it serious? Is it life threatening?"

"It seems she's having severe chest discomfort. This morning while she and Ed discussed the criminal charges you and Craig might bring against her, she took ill. She's still in the ER. Once she's stable, they want to move her to a private room. Ed Nellis wants to know if the company will pay for her medical bills. She's flat broke."

"Broke? According to Craig, he'd given her more than enough money to allow her to live the way she's always lived. Of course, Craig never did reveal the amount he'd given her. That's one of the things that has me so infuriated with him."

"It's my understanding that Craig stopped payment on the check the minute he learned Tyler Wilson was in Hawaii. He suspected that Breeze hadn't left the country. The check was on a thirty-day hold, one of the stipulations Breeze had agreed to. However, Craig had given her enough money to live on until she could draw off the funds. It appears he played his hunch right."

Sambrea was astounded. "Joe, how do you know so damn much about the agreement between Craig and Breeze? Where are you getting all your information?"

"From Craig, Sam. He told me everything before he left the country. Richard and I are the only two people who really know what's going on around here."

"Left the country?" Sambrea's stomach became queasy. "Did he say where he was going, Joe?"

"No, he didn't, but I overheard him talking on the phone. He made mention of South Africa. What the hell is in South Africa, Sam?"

Sambrea choked back the tears and her rising panic. "His parents live there, Joe. They're missionaries." Her voice began to crack. "Enough about Craig. Let's get back to Breeze. I need time to think, Joe, before I call Ed Nellis. But I need you to make sure that Breeze gets the proper medical attention. Craig might not like this, but we'll be responsible for her medical expenses. I need to talk to Richard. Is he there?"

"No, Sam. He's taking care of some company business on the big island. Sergio summoned him. He'll be back in a couple of days. Any other instructions, Sam?"

"Yes, keep an eye on Marsha Cohen. According to Tyler, she's the one who's been helping them. Raschad Ali, in the accounting department, has also been implicated. I don't know if Breeze has talked to them yet, but don't arouse their suspicions just in case she hasn't. However, you need to have the security codes changed. I know this will be an inconvenience to everyone, but make up some excuse. Just don't let on what's really happening. If we're going to get things solved, we have to use discretion in every action we take. We've already jumped the gun here."

"Sam, I hate to be the bearer of more bad news, but Marsha and Mr. Ali have both resigned. They left letters of resignation on my desk. Fear of the company folding and too much corporate unrest were the reasons given. Now we know the real reason, but I wonder if Mike knew. Richard doesn't know yet. He's going to feel responsible, since Marsha is his secretary."

"So, Breeze *has* contacted them. She's so clever, or so she thinks. I'm not going to worry about Raschad, Marsha, or Mike. I suspect they're small potatoes in this pot of stew, but we will get them sooner or later. We also have to investigate everyone else at De La Brise, especially those in the accounting department. We have to make a clean sweep. Joe, contact me immediately if Breeze takes a turn for the worse. At any rate, I'll be returning soon. Please hold down the fort. Talk to you soon."

Sambrea hung up the phone and returned to the alcove, where she watched the storm grow in intensity. There hadn't been any severe storm warnings, but that didn't necessarily mean there wasn't imminent danger. She was well aware that tropical storms could do as much damage as hurricanes did on the mainland. In some cases, more damage.

So, Craig is in Africa. That was an unhappy thought. At the same time, she hoped his parents were okay. Sambrea regretted the fact that she wasn't with him. She hated that he hadn't bothered to contact her to inform her of his departure, especially because they'd planned to go to South Africa together one day.

Why should he have contacted me after I walked out on him? Admitting that she loved Craig deeply was not a problem at all for her, but admitting she'd been wrong about him so many times was a big one. That she may have been wrong about him again only made matters worse.

It was possible he'd paid Breeze off for exactly the reasons he'd stated. He simply wanted his wife to be rid of Breeze and her threatening presence once and for all. Perhaps he'd purchased the shares from her to keep her from selling them elsewhere, to the highest bidder, which is what Breeze surely would've done.

Thinking of Breeze made her heart sorely ache. Was she

really ill, or was this just another of her attempts to manipulate? There was really no way of knowing. At least not until she heard the medical reports on her condition. However, if Breeze was really ill, she didn't want her mother to suffer and she would do anything to keep that from happening.

FIFTEEN

As the doorbell pealed its Hawaiian interlude, Sambrea arose from the sofa to answer the pleasant appeal. "I'll get it for you," she called out to Tai on her way to the door.

Lawrence Chambers smiled lazily at her. "Hi. Sorry it's taken me so long to get over here. Tai told me you were in town. She said it would be nice if I was to drop in on you. How's it going?" He stepped into the foyer.

"Come into the alcove, Lawrence. You're just the person I've wanted to talk to. I was going to call you." Sambrea saw Lawrence comfortably seated and then she went into the kitchen to ask Tai if she could make some tea and a light snack for herself and Lawrence. Returning to her guest, Sambrea sat across from Lawrence in one of the Papasan chairs.

"Lawrence, I'm going to get right to the point. I'm married."

Without even cracking a smile, he stretched his eyes in disbelief. "Excuse me, Sam? Married . . . married to whom? When?"

"Some gorgeous guy who sports midnight eyes. He swept me right off my feet, Lawrence. I've never met anyone like him."

"Does this gorgeous guy have a name, Sam?" He sounded impatient. "And where the hell is he?"

Sadness assaulted Sambrea's eyes, giving them the appearance of a raging desert sandstorm. "His name is Craig Caldwell. He's in South Africa."

"Why aren't you with him? Your honeymoon isn't over already, is it?"

"I'm not with him because I don't deserve to be. The honeymoon was over the day I deserted him and the marital bed one time too many. I'm so confused, Lawrence."

"You're telling me? I can see how confused you are. You couldn't have known this guy for very long, so what possessed you to marry him? And what did he do to make you take off so soon after marriage? You're impulsive, but not that impulsive, not without just cause. Give me some answers."

"I wish I knew all the answers, Lawrence. Breeze is mixed up in this. She has caused so much pain in my life. She claims to have been intimately involved with Craig, but he was able to convince me otherwise." She went on to explain all the important details to Lawrence, hoping he could steer her in the right direction. She thought that men made better judges of other men, since most of them seemed to think alike.

Quietly entering the room, Tai served them and then departed for work.

"Whew, Sam, you sure get yourself into major fixes. As much as I hate to side with the man who stole your heart from me, I think he's innocent. However, he's guilty of trying to protect you from the heartless woman you call mother, guilty of trying to save your company." Studying Sambrea intently, Lawrence scratched his head. His brows furrowed. "I always thought you were going to marry me someday. Was I that far off the mark?" Keeping his eyes fixed on her, he picked up the cup of tea.

Sambrea laughed at his boyish expression. Her heart melted under his warm, probing eyes. "You knew I'd vowed never to marry. Besides, you didn't seem to be slowing down any on the fast track of life. You have more women than you can possibly handle. I just didn't see myself fitting into the marriage mold—I was never any good at playing house. I've always thought I deserved more than marriage could ever give me. I was so sure I'd found that *more* in Craig Caldwell."

"And now you're not so sure about him? Sam, I think you *are* sure about him. I think you've been inventing excuses to keep this marriage from working. You're sabotaging your own chance at happiness. When you speak his name, the passion in your eyes tells me that you really love him. May I have the honor of booking your passage to South Africa?"

Sambrea smiled wistfully. "I can't go to Africa. I wouldn't know where to begin to look for him. Besides, my mother is ill, and I should go and see about her. I don't have to like the awful things she does, but she'll always be my mother. I can't change that and I wouldn't want to. Samuel wouldn't want me to, either. But I have to find an effective way to deal with her. Otherwise, she's going to drive me out of my mind. I wish I had someone to show me how to cope with her."

"You have several someones, Sam. You have your husband, you have Tai, and then, there's always me. It's up to you to decide which one of us you're going to let in. Craig Caldwell seems to know how to deal with your mother quite effectively. Keeping him around will help keep Breeze in check." He laughed. "I can't believe I'm campaigning for my arch rival. What is wrong with me?"

"There's nothing wrong with you, Lawrence. You just happen to be one of the most fair and honest guys that I know. I'll give everything you've said some serious thought."

Stroking her cheek with his forefinger, he kissed her forehead. "You do that, sweet girl. I'm going to miss our nights out and the times we've spent just talking and watching television. We've always managed to keep coming together, especially after we'd chased everyone else away from us with our fear of commitment. Think we could have an illicit affair?"

Chastising him with a mere look, she reached up and kissed him lightly on the mouth. "I want so much to believe in 'till death do us part.' "

"That's exactly what you're supposed to believe in. Craig Caldwell is one lucky man. I somehow get the feeling he already knows that. Be happy, Sam, but don't forget about me. We'll always be best friends." He got to his feet. "I've got to run. Don't want to be late for this date. It's our first. I think you might like Reyna. The next time you come to Maui, I'll bring her around to meet you."

Sambrea grinned. "That is, if her name's still in your little black book. You change girlfriends like you do your underwear—often." Standing on tiptoes, she kissed him again.

After walking Lawrence to the door, Sambrea went into the guestroom and packed the important items she'd brought along to Maui. In the morning, she'd return home. Once her packing was all finished, with the exception of her toiletry items, she grabbed a sweater and headed for the door. She looked out the window. The storm appeared to have passed over.

Tai came in just as she was going out. "Are you going out, Samiko?"

"A walk on the beach, Tai. I won't be long."

"Shall we have dinner when you return, Samiko?"

"That will be fine, Tai. I'm glad I took you up on your offer to stay here in your suite. Here with you, I don't have to eat all by myself. Or talk to myself," she joked.

"I'm always delighted to have you here. I will see you upon your return. Be careful, Samiko. More rain is not far away."

As the cool breeze whipped around her head, she made her way to the sandy shore. The clean air felt good against her skin. Inhaling deeply, she allowed the fresh air to seep into her lungs, hoping it would also clear up the garbled thoughts in her head.

The familiar sound of a distant ship's horn delighted her. Though it wasn't dark enough to see the flashing lights guiding and warning the ships, she could see the lighthouse from where she stood. Despite the hour, a few swimmers were in the water, along with many sailboats whose white sails gleamed on the water's dark blue horizon.

At sunset, Sambrea found a comfortable place where she could watch the sun go down. The sun's dimming rays added splashes of golden highlights to a sky already streaked with deep purples and pale lavenders. Creating a mystical scene of poetry in motion, several large birds swooped across the darkened skyline. Doing their best to diminish what was left of her fighting spirit, the shadows of evening closed in on her ominously. Her spirit was in dire need of rejuvenation, but only one person could bring that event about. Craig Caldwell.

How many nights had they quietly sat through the sunset, made love under the setting sun while whispering how much they loved one another as the sun arced downward? Not nearly enough. She felt grief as she wondered if they'd ever have those wonderful experiences again.

Reminding her of a seductive hula dance, the full branches of the palm trees bowed and swayed in the breezy trade winds. Enchanting her with its musical softness, the whispers of the wind seemed to speak only to her. She missed Craig more than anything in the world; his absence hurt like hell. If only he could share this impassioned moment with me, she wished, crying inside. "Craig, I need you here with me. Is it too late for us? Have I lost you for good?"

The only sound came from the whispers of the trade winds as they dried her tears.

* * *

Tai ushered Sambrea into the magnificent dining area. She had laid a marvelous table. That made Sambrea think of all the times she and Samuel had dined with Tai over the many years that Breeze had been absent. This would be the first time Sambrea had dined in this room since Samuel's death, yet she would dine there many times more.

Tai pulled out a chair for Sambrea. "You get comfortable, Samiko. I'll serve the food."

Sambrea took Tai's hand. "Let's bring everything in here. We can serve ourselves. That's what we did when Samuel and I ate dinner with you."

Bowing at the waist, Tai nodded. Moving aside, she allowed Sambrea to precede her into the kitchen. After gathering all the covered dishes, they carried them into the dining area. Once everything was on the table, they sat down. Tai passed the blessing in her native Japanese and then in English.

Sambrea uncovered the largest of the covered dishes, She squealed in delight at its contents. "Oh, Tai, the duck looks scrumptious! How did you manage to keep me from smelling it? It has a smell like no other."

Tai grinned. "I knew you would smell the duck so I had to use one of my secret cooking techniques. I wanted to surprise you. I know my Chinese recipe for Peking Duck is your favorite. When you are back with your husband, I will share some of my cooking secrets with you. That way, you can keep him in suspense and his palate in paradise."

Sambrea bit down on her lip. "Do you think that will happen, Tai? I've made such a mess of things. My distrust may have cost me what matters most in my life. I do love him, Tai. I love him more than I thought I was capable of loving anyone or anything."

"It will be love that will bring him back to you, Samiko. You've not had much experience with love. There were not enough living examples to guide you in the affairs of the heart. Samuel did his best but you needed a mother to guide you in these delicate matters. Do not be so hard on yourself. You could only work with what few tools you had."

"I know Samuel did his best, but he couldn't help me, especially when he didn't know what to do with the love he felt for Breeze. He gave her so much love, so much of himself—and she threw it all back in his face. So many times my heart bled for him. He never learned how to cope with her rejection of him. He died loving her. Had he lived to see her return he would've taken her back. I know it. What a miserable waste that would've been."

Tai knew that Samuel would have never taken Breeze back but remained silent on the issue.

"It is done, Samiko. Let it go. Samuel Sinclair is resting in peace. Breeze Sinclair will never know that kind of peace."

"Dead or alive," Sambrea interjected.

"Finish your meal. It's possible you are eating for two now."

Sambrea zealously dug into the steamed rice and oriental-style vegetables. The pearl onions, mushrooms, water chestnuts, bamboo shoots, carrots, and broccoli cooked in a lightly spiced peanut sauce tasted heavenly.

When Sambrea finished her meal, Tai handed her a fortune cookie. Sambrea's thrilled laughter showed her delight in the traditional gesture, although it was a Chinese tradition, not Japanese.

"See what is in store for you, Samiko. May all your wishes come true."

After breaking open the cookie, Sambrea pulled the small piece of white paper from the shell. "Love and Happiness Is Yours For the Taking. Seek and You Shall Find," she read aloud. Craig had said that to her once. "Oh, Tai, if I believed in this tiny piece of paper, I'd go in search of my husband." Sambrea's voice crackled with emotional stress.

"It is not the paper you must believe in, Samiko. It is the belief in what you feel for Mr. Caldwell. Love and happiness is only what you make of it. What is worth seeking is worth finding."

"You could be right, Tai. I'll never know if I don't find the courage to face my husband. I just hope he'll listen to me whenever he comes back home. If he comes back."

"Hasn't he always?" Tai remembered the things Sambrea had told her about Craig's patience with her.

Smiling, Sambrea nodded. Feeling better than she had in days, she got up and helped Tai clear the table.

Within minutes of her plane landing, Sambrea had hired a taxi to take her to the private hospital, located in downtown Honolulu, where Breeze was a patient. Stopping at the front desk, she inquired of Breeze's room number. Taking the elevator to the fifth floor, she tried to relax as the elevator moved up the shaft with a quiet ease.

Her legs shook as they carried her down the long corridor. What would she say to her mother? She still didn't know how ill Breeze really was. She shouldn't have come here—at least, not alone. Breeze still had a strong hold on her, the kind of hold she wasn't sure she could ever break free from. It was a silly notion, but she was still hoping for them to become close.

Sambrea came to a halt at the entrance to the private room that Breeze occupied. Bowing her head, she whispered a few words of prayer. Erecting a wall of courage, she entered the room, only to find an empty bed stripped of its linen. Fearful that she might be too late, panic hit her with a force that nearly knocked her off her feet. All sorts of wild scenarios passed through her head before she got a grip on herself.

Calmly, she walked out of the room and over to the nurse's station. After explaining her relationship to the patient, she inquired of Breeze's whereabouts.

"Mrs. Sinclair is downstairs in the cardiac lab. She's having some special testing done and should be back in her room at any minute," a cheerful nurse instructed. "Would you care to wait in her room?"

"Thank you. That's a generous offer, Nurse Andrews," Sambrea said as she looked down at the nurse's name tag. "However, I'm mainly interested in knowing my mother's medical status."

"Your mother is doing just fine, but Dr. Wylie wants to keep her here for another few days. She has a mild case of angina pectoris; pain in the heart caused by a spasm of the coronary artery. It can be serious but can also be treated effectively," Nurse Andrews told her.

Sambrea smiled. "Thank you for enlightening me. I feel much better. I'm going to go now, but I'll be back later. Don't mention to my mother that I was here. It will only cause her to become anxious. I don't want that to occur."

"Whatever you wish, young lady. You have a good day. And don't worry about your mother. She's in good hands."

Waving goodbye, Sambrea smiled again. Quickly, she headed for the elevator. She would come back but she couldn't come alone. She was sure that Richard or Joe would be happy to accompany her.

Glad she hadn't driven herself to the hospital, her hands shook as she called for another cab to take her to the offices of De La Brise. She couldn't wait to be in the comforting presence of her friends and employees, yet she would much rather be running into the comforting arms of her sexy husband. *Craig, if you only knew how much I need you.*

Find him and tell him, a disquieting voice in her head commanded.

Richard spotted Sambrea the moment she entered the reception area. "Hello there, you! We've missed you." He reached for her and enveloped her in his arms.

She kissed Richard's cheek before walking toward her

office. "I've missed you, too. I called to talk to you, but I understand you were on the big island. How did that go?"

"It was a piece of cake. Sergio always panics even when there's nothing to panic about." Richard took her overnighter. Opening the door to her private office, he let her go in ahead of him. "If Sergio wasn't so brilliant at his job, I'd recommend that we fire him. No, not really. I'm just joking. But Sergio just needs to calm down a bit. He gets so out of control."

Without commenting, Sambrea settled herself on the sofa. Richard and Sergio were always into it. She didn't expect that to ever change. "Where's Joe? He wasn't at his desk."

"Who knows? He's around here somewhere. As soon as he catches the scent of your perfume, he'll be in here. Isn't that the perfume he gave you last Christmas?"

Amazed that Richard knew exactly what perfume she wore, Sambrea laughed. "Not many men pay such close attention to the thousands of different feminine scents. How can you possibly know it's the perfume Joe gave me?"

"Are you kidding? Joe sprayed that perfume all over these offices trying to find out if you were allergic to it or not. When you said that someone's fragrance sure smelled good, he knew he'd made the right choice. Joe is weird!"

"I resent that!" Joe entered the door. "There's nothing weird about me. Sam, you're back." Smiling joyfully, he rushed over to give her a big hug. "How are you doing, honey?"

His arms felt so good. It made her realize how much she loved the warmth of human contact. "I'm doing fine, Joe. Thanks for holding down the fort. Are there any important matters needing my immediate attention?"

"Not really. Richard and I have handled all the important stuff, but there's still the problem with Breeze. How are you going to handle her, Sam?"

Sambrea frowned slightly. "I just came from the hospital,

guys, but I didn't hang around to see her. She was having some tests done. I'm not strong enough to see her on my own. Will one of you go back there with me after work?"

"I'll go," Richard quickly responded. "Breeze can't stand Joe. We wouldn't want to cause her anymore discomfort, now would we?"

"She can't stand me because she knows I can see right through her. She's as transparent as Saran Wrap. She also knows how loyal I am to Sambrea. That old girl is no fool!"

"I think you're right," Richard commented. "Breeze can't take anyone who knows her next move before she does. You always were good at reading people, Joe. I wish I had that kind of a gift."

"He is good at it," Sambrea concurred. "I'm afraid he reads me pretty good, too." Thinking of that *someone else* who could also read her pretty darn good, Sambrea grew silent. She wanted so much to ask the guys if they'd heard from Craig, but she didn't want to make her feelings too obvious.

Joe read the wistful look on her face. "No, Sam, we haven't heard from your husband. But don't worry, you'll hear from him. He won't be able to live without you. Trust me."

She scowled. "That transparent, huh? Oh, well, it doesn't matter. I've screwed up, now I have to live with it. Gee, how I'd love to have that boy right here in front of me. I miss him more than I want to admit. But I'm afraid I've mistrusted him once too often . . . and he hates it when I run away from him and our issues. Africa, how I envy you. You have him where I'd love to have him. Right at your fingertips."

"It's not like he's going to be there forever, Sam," Richard advised. "He still has that incredible house on the beach. Speaking of houses, where are you going to live, since you've leased out the bungalow and have now left your man?"

Shrugging her shoulders, Sambrea looked troubled. "I guess I'll stay in a nearby hotel. I love to stay in hotels and have a host of other wonderful amenities at my disposal. But I'll probably tire of it after a few days. My stay in Tai's hotel suite was altogether different, since it's her home. I preferred being anchored. I'd begun to think of the pagoda house as my permanent residence. So much for wishful thinking."

"Is there a good reason why you can't stay at the pagoda house?" Joe questioned. "You may be pregnant, you know."

With a deep sadness in her eyes, she frowned. "It wouldn't be right. I don't think Craig would want me there while he's away."

"Sam, if I'm not mistaken, Craig gave you the right to be there when he married you. That house is as much yours as it is his. I believe Craig would want you to stay at the house while he's out of the country, especially if you're carrying his child," Joe counseled patiently.

"I hate to keep giving Joe this much praise, Sam, but he's right," Richard interjected. "Why should you pay to live in a hotel when you would be more comfortable in your own home? Besides, all of your things are there."

Having heard enough, she threw up her hands. "Okay, okay, I get it. Jeez, you two should have been lawyers. Your opening arguments have been impressive, but I don't want to hear your closing remarks. I'll tell you my decision when I make it. Now can you two get out of here and let me get some work done. Those phone messages aren't going to return calls on their own," Sambrea quipped. "If they could, we'd all be out of a job."

The two men laughed at her off-handed comments. They walked out the door and closed it behind them.

Joe quickly stuck his head back inside the door. "How about something hot to drink? Say tea or hot milk?"

Sambrea sweetly declined.

Here in the solitude of her office she found everything

but solace. There were too many things reminding her of Craig. The times they made love on the office sofa were right at the top of the list. Even now, she blushed as she relived those tantalizing moments. There wasn't anything she wouldn't give to have him back in her arms. She missed him. In fact, her entire body ached for his riveting touch.

Sambrea looked through the phone messages but pushed them aside. She wasn't interested in returning any of the unimportant calls, or the important ones, for that matter. There were no messages from Craig. Had there been she would've immediately returned them, would've been glad to return them. No matter how disinterested she was in returning phone calls, there was one she had to return.

Tyler Wilson had called several times. One message was marked urgent, yet Joe hadn't mentioned it to her. While tapping her fingers on the desk, she waited for Tyler to answer the phone in his hotel suite. She was just about to hang up when his voice came on the line. "Tyler, its Sambrea. I'm returning your calls."

"Ah, yes, Sambrea. How are you and how was your trip to Maui?" Tyler's voice cackled with stress.

"I'm fine. So was my trip. Tyler, is there something wrong? Your voice sounds terribly strained."

Tyler sighed heavily "I'm under a tremendous amount of stress, Sambrea. I'm so worried about your mother's illness and what might happen if I testify against her. It's wrong of me to save my own hide at her expense. Sambrea, is there another way? I can pay some of the illegally obtained money back, but I don't know if I can sit by and watch your mother go to prison while I go scot-free."

"Tyler, we had an agreement," Sambrea admonished. Though her heart wasn't in it, she couldn't let him know that. In fact, Tyler was doing exactly as she'd hoped he would do in the first place. Prosecuting her mother had never set very well with her. But her anger at Breeze had somehow overruled her sense of fair play and her strong affinity for family loyalties.

"I know we did, Sambrea," Tyler debated wearily. "But I can't bring myself to sit in front of a court room full of people and point a finger at the woman I love so dearly. You may not agree with me, Sambrea, and I may offend you, but Breeze truly believed she should have the money I received through the fake pensions. I did it because I thought she deserved it, too. I was never in it for the money. Samuel never would've wanted Breeze to have to barely eke out a living when he had so much. I admit that we went about things the wrong way, but, Sambrea, please have some compassion for your mother. Simply because she is your mother. "

"I do have compassion for her, Tyler. But I have to ask you this. Where was her compassion for me? Why didn't she think of how much I would be hurt? Hell, why didn't you think about it? You knew what you two were doing was wrong."

"Does this mean you're never going to forgive us, Sambrea? I'm so sorry for what has occurred. Yes, of course I knew it was wrong. Breeze knew it was wrong, but we did it anyway. You have every right to feel the way you do, but I'm begging you to have mercy on your mother. I will not testify against the woman I love. I'd allow myself to be cast into hell before I'd ever betray Breeze."

"Meet me at the hospital in an hour, Tyler. We need to settle this once and for all."

Disconnecting the line, Sambrea turned her chair around to face the window. Looking out over the ocean always calmed her nerves. It offered her the ability to think more clearly. The ocean afforded her that type of serenity. It made her feel closer to God.

Could she forgive Breeze and Tyler? What if she could? Would the Board of Directors go along with her if she decided not to prosecute? How would her employees look upon her? Would they lose respect for her? Would she be opening herself up to more heartache?

There were too many questions without answers, yet she wasn't sure she even wanted to begin to sort things out. Craig would know what to do, but he was on the other side of the globe. Craig always knew what to do, she reminded herself. If only she could've believed in him from the start, there was no telling what heights their relationship might have reached by now.

All he'd ever asked of her was that she put her trust him. She had failed to do so, and now he was unattainable, out of reach . . . and she didn't know if she'd ever be able to reach him again. Physically or emotionally.

SIXTEEN

Walking out into the corridor, Sambrea stopped to chat with Joe. She then moved on to Richard's office. After knocking on the door, she waited for him to call out.

Richard had his head in a large book. He looked up from his reading as she came into the room. "Hi, have you had enough time to think through everything? That's why you're here, isn't it, Sam?"

"Actually, no. I haven't even had a chance to think about where I'm going to sleep tonight. However, I have talked to Tyler Wilson. And I'm not at all sure how I feel about our conversation. He's refusing to testify against Breeze. What do you make of him, Richard?"

He summoned Sambrea to sit in the chair next to his desk.

Beautifully polished, the large beech-wood chair matched his rather large beech-wood desk. Just like his apartment, his office was filled with healthy green plants and cheerful silk flowers. A variety of pictures featuring aesthetic scenes of nature hung on the walls.

Richard pushed his chair back from the desk. He turned slightly to face his guest. "I don't know what to make of Tyler, Sam. I never suspected he'd be disloyal to Samuel and the company. He's not the type of man that can be easily persuaded, yet Breeze was able to do just that. I've given the entire matter a heap of thought. I've come to the conclusion that Breeze must have something on Tyler, something he fears more than a long prison term."

"What?" Sambrea shook her head in disbelief. "You think Breeze has been blackmailing him?"

"As a matter of fact, I do believe just that. Your mother has a way of getting a strong hold on the people in her life. She had a strange hold on your father. I'm not suggesting that she blackmailed Samuel, but I never could figure out how a powerful man like Samuel Sinclair allowed a shallow woman like Breeze to lead him around by the nose. Sam, you have to admit it, she even has a strong hold on you."

Sambrea nodded in agreement. "She does get a strong hold on people, but I think it's made possible because we've loved her so much in spite of her devious ways. All of the people you've mentioned love her. I love her. Tyler admits to loving her. That's the reason he can't speak out against her. I don't think it's anything more than her being loved by those she exploits. And she does do one hell of a job at it."

With troublesome thoughts flickering in his eyes, Richard stroked his chin. "Maybe, Sam, maybe not. I think there's more to it for Tyler than love. He's hiding something. This may come as a shock, but Craig thinks the same as I do."

Sambrea's mouth fell open. "Did Craig tell you that, Richard?"

"Not directly, but he mentioned it in one of the meetings we had with the investigative team. He's not going to stop his investigation until he finds out what Breeze has on Tyler."

"I find it so interesting that my husband has confided in everyone but his wife. He's never mentioned any of this to me. Why? Do you know why that is, Rich?"

"Probably because you have enough to worry about. Craig feels that it's his job to lessen your burdens, if not completely annihilate them. Sam, Craig does the things that he believes a man should do. Incredibly well, I might add.

Shielding you from anything that might bring you harm or stress is his job. That's the type of man he is. Face it, Craig strongly believes that chivalry is alive and well."

Sambrea shook her head in bewilderment. "I'm amazed. Craig has gotten down and very personal with me, yet I can only think of one time that he truly bared his soul to me. But it seems to me that he's holding so much more back. What am I lacking in that keeps him from baring his all to me?"

Richard scratched his head. "Do you think if he'd bared his all to you it would've kept you from running out on him? What if he'd bared all and you still ran out on him? How do you think he would've felt? Sam, he may have been a little more open with you if he'd been sure that you trusted him. Craig's just as prideful as you are, Sambrea."

"I see your point. Oh, God, where does it end? I guess he's kept me in the dark because he wasn't sure of what to expect from me." Tears sprang to her eyes, but she fought the urge for release. She pushed them aside, along with her and Craig's personal issues. "I came here to tell you that I'm meeting Tyler at the hospital. Can we leave now?"

Richard nodded. "Give me about twenty minutes and we can be on our way. I have to make a couple of phone calls first."

Sambrea somehow got the impression that Richard didn't want her around while he made his phone calls. Wanting privacy was understandable. His strange behavior wasn't. Eyeing him suspiciously, Sambrea stood.

Leaning over the chair, she planted a kiss on Richard's cheek. "I'll be in my office, guy." He had already dialed the phone number. It seemed to her as though he hadn't even heard her last comment. Frowning, Sambrea quietly slipped out.

Joe wasn't at his desk when she passed by. As she crept into her office, tears crept from her eyes. She was learning more and more about her husband's character. She now suspected Craig of being a lot more sensitive than he'd originally told her. Although he'd admitted to being sensitive about some things, he certainly hadn't elaborated on *how* sensitive. How she must have hurt him by denying him her trust. She felt deep regret.

Hadn't everything bad that had come into their relationship come about because they really didn't know each other at all? If they'd taken the time to get to know each other, perhaps they would've developed a deeper understanding. But did they really need to know anything more about each other once they'd fallen so deeply in love?

Craig hadn't wanted to know anything about her past. But, yes, they did need to know more about each other. If she somehow got the chance to continue on with Craig in their marriage, she'd see to it that they got to know each other. And it would be more than just on an intimate basis. She needed to know more about what made him tick, wanted to know more. In fact, she wanted to know everything there was to know about the mysterious Craig Caldwell: what his favorite color was, how he liked his eggs, his pet peeves, his hobbies, his social likes and dislikes, his political views. There were also so many things and places that she wanted them to discover together.

She already knew he was intelligent, a shrewd businessman, handsome, and passionate. He also loved her and he was capable of giving so much more on a personal level. But she'd robbed him of the chance to share it all with her. Mistrust had resulted in destruction.

Richard had been right. Craig would've bared all to her had she opened her heart and her mind to receive all he had to offer. If she got another chance, not only would she know everything about her husband, she'd be able to count the hairs on his head. She'd be able to see into those unfathomable midnight eyes and know his thoughts long before he himself knew them.

Her thoughts were interrupted when the door swung

open. Strolling across to her desk, Richard extended his arm. Getting to her feet, smiling affectionately, she looped her right arm through his. In the reception area, they bid the staff a good evening as they left the offices.

The hospital floor Breeze resided on seemed eerily quiet to Sambrea when she and Richard exited the elevator. Sambrea took a deep, calming breath while guiding Richard to her mother's private room.

Again, Breeze was absent. Again, Sambrea panicked. "What's going on now, Richard? Could she be having tests run this late in the evening?"

Richard shrugged his shoulders "I don't know, Sam, but why don't we ask one of the nurses. I'm sure there's nothing to worry about."

Remaining patient with her, Richard led Sambrea to the nurse's station.

"We're here to see Breeze Sinclair, but she's not in her room. Can you please tell us where we might find her?" Richard inquired politely.

The nurse flashed the couple a nervous glance. "Are you family?" she asked rather brusquely.

Sambrea raised her hand. Immediately, she felt silly. *This isn't elementary school.* "I'm her daughter. My name is Sambrea Sinclair-Caldwell." She almost giggled over the names she'd dared to use so proudly.

"I see . . . Mrs. Caldwell, is it?" Sambrea nodded. "I'm surprised someone didn't inform you that your mother has been moved to the ICCU unit. She's had a mild heart attack."

Sambrea would've crashed to the floor had Richard not been there to break her fall. Richard grew concerned as Sambrea's eyes rolled to the back of her head. "Sam, Sam," he called out anxiously.

The nurse quickly summoned Richard into an empty patient room. "Lie her down over there." She pointed at the far bed. "I want to take her vital signs. But I'm sure it's nothing more than shock at hearing about her mother. Has she ever had any heart problems?"

"No. Sambrea is healthy, but she might be pregnant. However, her father died of a heart attack. Now it appears that her mother has heart problems. Heart problems are genetic, aren't they?"

"They can be, but other family members don't always end up with the same problem. However, it is good to know her family's medical history," the nurse told Richard.

Looking up at the nurse, Sambrea smiled weakly. "I'm okay. I just haven't eaten a thing today. When I heard about my mother, I guess everything came down on me at once."

Sambrea sat up, but Richard gently lowered her head back down on the pillow. "Sam, rest for a couple of minutes, at least, until the nurse has checked your vitals. We'll go see Breeze as soon as I'm sure you're okay."

With no energy to mount a protest, Sambrea nodded and closed her eyes.

Seated on the side of the bed, the nurse raised the sleeve on Sambrea's sweater and took her blood pressure and pulse. The nurse smiled as the results came back favorable. "You're just fine, missy," the nurse told her with kindness. "However, I do suggest that you get something to eat, especially if a baby could be on the way. There's a cafeteria on the first floor. I know about the terrible reputation that precedes hospital cafeterias, but the food here is actually pretty good."

"As soon as I see my mother, I'll have my friend here feed me. I won't be able to eat a thing until I see her. Thank you for your kind concern." Sambrea had made a valiant attempt at gaiety. She then turned to Richard. "I'm ready to see my mother now, Richard. Shall we go?"

After helping her get up from the bed, Richard waited as she straightened her clothes and fiddled with her hair and makeup. Taking her by the hand, he led her out of the room and back to the elevator.

Sambrea was sweating pebbles by the time they reached the I.C.C.U. area. Her nerves were stretched far beyond understanding—and she knew that things were only going to get worse for her. Physically, she'd reacted the same way when Samuel had suffered his heart attack. Samuel's had been fatal. Would her mother die, as well? That was the burning question uppermost in her mind.

Stopping at the nurse's station to inquire about Breeze's health, they were given the information that her condition was stable. When they were given the cubicle number where Breeze rested comfortably, they also learned that only fifteen minutes was allowed for visitation. Those were the rules that governed the intensive care unit.

Using Richard's arm for support, Sambrea inched her way to where Breeze lay.

Unprepared to see her mother so pale and gaunt-looking, Sambrea let out a muffled cry. Richard squeezed her hand in a reassuring manner. Sambrea's hands, weak and trembling, reached out to touch Breeze's face. She was startled by how cold and dry her mother's skin felt.

"Mother," Sambrea whispered, "can you hear me? It's Sambrea. Richard is here with me, too."

There wasn't as much as a flutter of an eyelash from Breeze.

Sambrea's panic surged. Breeze's chest arose and fell in rapid successions. It appeared to be an abnormal breathing pattern. Placing her hand over Breeze's heart, Sambrea felt the erratic beating smashing against her trembling hand as she prayed for her mother's life to be spared.

Breeze needed to live, needed to have another chance to repent, needed to mend the fences with her daughter and all the others she may have harmed. Sambrea needed her mother more than she'd ever needed her before.

She desperately needed her mother's love and also her approval.

"Mother, squeeze my hand if you can hear me," pleaded Sambrea. Breeze's hand lay lifeless and tears welled in Sambrea's eyes. "I'm going to speak as though you can hear me. I love you, Mother. I'm sorry if I've hurt you. I want you to get well. We need each other. Samuel would want us to be a family. We're all the family each of us have."

No, that's not a true statement, Sambrea confessed inwardly. Craig was her family, too. He just wasn't around for her to lean on because she'd run away from him once too often. Interrupting the emotional moment, a nurse came to the doorway to say their time was up.

Bending over the bed, Sambrea touched her lips to her mother's, whispering her love for Breeze with hot tears barreling down her cheeks. "I'll be back. I promise you."

Sambrea cried brokenly as she left Breeze's side.

Putting his arm around Sambrea's trembling shoulders, Richard led her from the room. "She's going to be fine, Sam. I'm sure she heard you and that she was probably comforted by your words. You'll have to do plenty of soul-searching when prosecuting her comes into play. I'll be here for you every step of the way. Joe will be there, too."

"Oh, Richard, if my mother gets another chance at life, I couldn't possibly prosecute her. She's my mother. The only family I have left."

Richard hugged her tightly. "You still have a husband, Sam. He's as much a part of your family as your mother is. I hope you won't hate me for this, but I know how to get in touch with Craig. Shall I try to reach him?"

Sambrea couldn't believe her ears. "You know how to reach . . . Craig? Why didn't you tell me this before now? Did he tell you not to tell me?"

"To be honest, I really wasn't sure you wanted to know.

Yes, I heard what you said earlier, Sam, but you've been so wishy-washy through this entire relationship. You need to make up your mind about your marriage one way or the other."

She gave him an impatient glance. "Richard, did Craig tell you not to tell me how to reach him?"

"Not at all. In fact, he didn't say one way or the other. He told me if he was needed to contact him at the number written on the card that he handed me before he left that day."

"Does Joe know you have Craig's number?"

"If he does, he didn't hear it from me. All Joe said is that we hadn't heard from Craig. We haven't, Sam." Richard sighed. "I guess I'm going to have to confess. The phone call I had to make earlier at the office was to Craig, but he wasn't in. I did leave a message. He should call me later. Should I tell him to come home, Sam?"

Snatching her arm from Richard's grasp, Sambrea had the look of murder in her eyes. "This is out of control! Do you know who signs your paycheck every two weeks? I consider your actions treasonous!"

Richard was completely taken aback by her anger. "It's not like that, Sam. Of course I know who signs my paychecks, but have you forgotten that Craig now owns part of De La Brise. Your two companies *did* complete the merger. So that also makes him my boss. Doesn't it, Sambrea?"

Sambrea felt sincere regret over her petulant remarks. "I shouldn't have said that, Rich. I'm just upset that Craig has taken you and Joe into his confidence. He's left me completely out in the cold. I'm truly sorry, Rich. It seems I keep putting my foot right smack dab into it."

An approaching Tyler Wilson stopped Richard from making further comments.

He looked tired and thin to Sambrea; she could easily

see the toll that all the unpleasantness had taken on him. She only hoped that he wasn't going to take sick, too.

Tyler kissed Sambrea's cheek and shook Richard's hand. "I've been waiting for you in the lobby, Sambrea. When you didn't show, I decided to come looking for you. I thought I might find you up here. How's your mother?"

"She's stable, Tyler. I haven't had a chance to talk to her doctor, but I will before this evening is over."

"Tyler, would you mind accompanying us to the cafeteria? Sambrea hasn't eaten today and she nearly fainted because of it. I don't think she should wait much longer," Richard said.

Tyler looked at Sambrea with concern. "Of course, I'd be delighted. We have some important matters to discuss and they shouldn't be discussed while you're in a fragile state. Young lady, you shouldn't go without eating," Tyler scolded.

The three concerned-looking souls took the elevator down to the first floor, where the cafeteria was located.

There was only a handful of people seated inside. Tyler chose a table while Sambrea and Joe went through the line to choose the foods that interested them. After paying for their purchases, they joined Tyler at the corner table.

Richard handed Tyler a cup of coffee. "It's black, just the way you like it."

"I'm flattered that you remember, Richard."

"You were only around the office for several decades. Everyone knew how you liked your coffee, which brings me to something else. After having been so loyal to De La Brise for so many years, how did you get caught up in such a distasteful crime? What does Breeze have on you, Tyler?" Richard had gotten right to the point.

Sambrea gasped as Tyler turned gray. She gave Richard a threatening glance. "Richard, not now. Tyler has enough on his mind."

Tyler looked ashamed. "It's okay, Sambrea. I deserved

that. Breeze has nothing on me, Rich." Tyler had denied
the charge but without much conviction. "I've just made
some pretty poor choices in my life—and I know I'm
going to have to pay for them. I won't allow Breeze to
take all the heat. She's pretty fragile right now, too. Sambrea, we need to discuss your mother's future. Are you
feeling up to it?"

"That's why I asked you to come here." Sambrea took
a sip of her herbal tea before continuing. "I'll never understand what you two have done, but I realize I can't hold it
against you forever. We're going to have to come up with
a way for you and Breeze to make restitution without being
imprisoned." She looked Tyler right in the eye. "There's
nothing written that says you'll be convicted, especially with
a shrewd lawyer. But eventually your conscience will do
what the courts might fail to. It won't be very pleasant for
either of you. If we can work something out that we can
all live with, I'll consider not filing the embezzlement
charges."

"Sam, are you going to be able to live with your decision?" Richard asked. "These people have committed a serious crime. What message are you sending to the rest of
your employees if you let them off? Also, Tyler has refused
to name the others involved, except for Marsha and
Raschad. We both know someone higher up than those two
were involved in this scheme."

"I've thought about all that, Rich. Maybe no one else is
involved. Raschad is a genius with figures. At any rate, I've
no intentions of letting anyone walk away from this without
them taking serious responsibility for their actions. I think
both you and Breeze need to seek professional help before
you do anything else, Tyler. That is, if Breeze lives."

"Breeze *is* going to live, Sambrea. She's too stubborn
not to. Besides, the Lord's work is not nearly done. He's
going to turn Breeze around and I'm going to ask Him to
work on me, too."

"Oh, boy," Richard harped loudly. "Now we're on the Jesus bandwagon. How come everybody calls on the Lord when they're in trouble, yet no one ever calls on him to help them from getting into trouble in the first place? Spare me the sermon on repentance!" Richard sounded thoroughly disgusted.

Tyler arose from his seat. "Young man, I can understand why you feel the way you do. This is not an easy thing to sort out. I'm ready to face whatever it is that you decide, Sambrea. But I stand behind Breeze one hundred and ten percent. I will *not* testify against her."

"We'll talk later, Tyler." Sambrea looked so tired. "We all need to concentrate on Breeze's health. We can sort the rest of this out later. Thank you for coming, Tyler. I thought we could resolve this here and now, but I see it's much too complicated for that to happen. Good night, Tyler."

"Good night, both of you. I'll be in touch. I'm going to go up and see your mother before I go back to my hotel. Drive safely."

Richard tossed daggers into Tyler's back as he departed. "I can't believe the nerve of that old geezer. Tyler just walked away from here as though he hasn't done anything wrong. He's made me angrier than I've been in a long time. I'm sure that the old man wouldn't have been so self-assured had Craig been here. Compared to Craig's raging anger, thunder and lightning would appear harmless. He wouldn't have been nearly as understanding as you were. Craig wouldn't have even considered not filing any charges. In all your strength, you still have a lot to learn about the cutthroat business we're in."

"I know. But right now I'm too tired to even care."

During the drive to Sambrea's home, Richard saw no point in further discussing her decision about Tyler and Breeze. She had shocked him when she'd asked to be taken to the pagoda house but it also pleased him. The thought of her staying in an impersonal hotel didn't feel the least bit good to him. He would wait until she was inside to back out of the driveway.

As she hesitated, he expected her to run back to the car. Proving him right, she did.

Stopping short of getting into the car, she turned around and went back to the door. She opened it and disappeared inside. When he saw the inside of the massive house light up, he sighed with relief. Whistling a delightful tune, he backed out of the driveway.

Timidly, Sambrea walked through the house and up to the bedroom where she and Craig had spent so many sensuous nights, so many wonderful mornings, afternoons and evenings. While clicking on the lights, a tidal wave of sweet memories rushed at her from every corner of the room. All of the spots where they'd made love seemed to come alive to taunt her.

Feeling overwhelmed, she dropped down to her knees and allowed the memories to completely overtake her. Craig's presence could be strongly felt. His cologne still wafted through the air and his warmth engulfed her.

With her heart in mourning over the love she'd lost, his absence was felt even more.

From her position on the floor, she surveyed the entire room. Spotting one of Craig's silk T-shirts thrown over one of the reclining chairs, she had the urge to pick it up, just to smell it, hoping his scent would still be embedded there.

Getting up off her knees, she walked to where the T-shirt lay. She noticed a large envelope stuck in one corner of the dressing table mirror. Drawing closer, she saw that her name was written on the envelope. The handwriting was Craig's.

Sitting down at the dressing table, she opened the envelope with care and took a deep breath before unfolding the lengthy letter. Suddenly, feeling nervous, she wondered about its contents then started to read: "Dear Sambrea, if you're reading this it means you've either come to the house for your things or you've come home to stay. I hope for the latter. Do you remember what I said the last time you ran away? I do, painfully so. Sambrea, I want you to have the house. The title transfer will be taken care of. I couldn't stand for you to live in a hotel. Your security is too important to me. I don't know how long I'll be out of the country, but you can rest assured that I won't disturb you. However, I desperately need to know if there's a baby. And you need to know that I won't be kept away from my child." It was signed: "Sincerely, Craig."

"Sincerely, Craig," she screamed. "Is that what our relationship has come down to, a formal closing? Or was it just a business arrangement all along?"

The anger she felt was not at Craig but rather at herself.

No matter how she sliced it, she had single-handedly orchestrated the breakup of her marriage, a marriage Craig had seemed willing to see through to the end of eternity. It had never been a formality or a business arrangement for him, she mused, answering her own question. He'd loved her. But she'd been too caught up in the anguish of her parents' marriage to see that love didn't necessarily have to turn out the way theirs did.

No, it wouldn't have turned out that way. If only she . . .

Finding it was no use to beat herself up over the mountain of mistakes she'd made, she placed the letter back in the envelope. Though she refused to cry over spilt milk, the pain in her heart couldn't be ignored. It was much too deep, much too abrasive—much too empty to ever be filled again.

A long hot shower failed to produce its usual relaxing benefits. Her shoulders and head still ached, her back muscles felt tightly drawn, her nerves frayed. How could she sleep all alone in the love nest built for two? More to the point, how was she to sleep at all?

SEVENTEEN

A loud noise, which seemed to be coming from downstairs, caused Sambrea to arouse with a start. Adrenaline flowing at a high rate, she sat up in bed and trained her ear on the noises that had grown louder. Leaping out of bed, she made her way to the double doors and opened one side as quietly as possible. Hearing footsteps on the staircase, she ran back to the nightstand and opened the lower drawer. Craig's gun wasn't there. Just as she pulled open another drawer, the door was flung back wide. Ripples of fear streaked through her rapidly beating heart as she tried to decide what her next move would be.

"Good morning, Sambrea," Craig greeted cheerfully.

Too stunned to respond, she could only watch him deposit on the table the breakfast tray he held. "I hope you're hungry. I prepared all your favorites."

Crossing the room with long strides, he took her hand and gently drew her toward the bedroom's dining table. "It's a beautiful morning. Would you care to eat on the terrace? It'll be nice to have the birds sing for us while we eat."

Am I dreaming? "Craig, I thought . . ."

Two of his fingers placed over her lips silenced her. "I don't want you to think. I've done enough of that for both of us. I need to talk and I need you to listen. Okay?"

Taking her briefly in his arms, he grazed his fingers tenderly over her lips. Waiting for her answer, he bent over to retrieve the tray.

Although she hadn't responded to his question regarding her dining preference, he carried the tray outside to the sweeping terrace, which gave them a magnificent view of their very own private seascape.

Before sitting down, Craig pulled out a chair for Sambrea. Reaching for the pot of decaffeinated coffee, he poured two cups and slid one in front of her. "Isn't this a wonderful day?" He deeply inhaled the fresh sea air.

Eyeing him strangely, she nodded, wondering if he'd lost his mind. Hadn't he said he wasn't going to ever disturb her again? But then, he wasn't disturbing her, not the least bit. Dressed in a silk robe, revealing his sexy chest hairs—she couldn't believe he actually sat across from her. *Of course, I'll wake up in a few minutes, only to discover he'd been a figment of my creative imagination.* If he wasn't an illusion, when had he gotten there?

The previous night Sambrea had dressed in a close-to-see-through black nightgown. She thought it was most appropriate for a woman in mourning. While the gown left little to the imagination, Craig wasted no time in using his memory to recall those beautiful body parts he couldn't quite see. His memory served him well as he drank in her cover-girl beauty.

"Sambrea, you're not eating. Are you feeling okay?"

Tossing the linen napkin into the center of the table, she pushed her chair back. "What the hell is going on here, Craig? Have I missed something?" Though she was happy he'd come back, she had to fight hard to keep herself from doing something crazy again. Like walking out on him before hearing him out.

"I hope you've missed me, Sam. I've missed you. Sit back down, native girl. Like I said before, I need to talk."

Reluctantly, she returned to her seat. Putting her elbows

on the table, she placed her face between her hands. "Speak, Craig, or forever hold your peace."

His eyes flashed with genuine compassion. "Honey, I know what I said in the letter. But, Sam, that's not what I want, definitely not what I need. I want *us*. I want us to be together. I realize I've gone about things the wrong way. We met one second and became intimate the next. Believe me, I've never done anything like that in my entire life. I couldn't help myself. I fell in love with you the first night I saw you on the beach, ages ago. I want to go on loving you forever. But we can't go on if you don't trust me."

Removing her face from her hands, she clapped her hands together loudly. "Did you talk to Richard yesterday, Craig?" She was suspicious that Richard had called him and that Craig had come back to her only because her friends had persuaded him. Or perhaps he had returned to her out of pity.

"If he tried to reach me yesterday, I was long gone from the number I gave him."

She felt like breathing a sigh of relief but held it within.

"It was really difficult to keep up with the time changes and all. I imagine Richard had a hard time with it also. I've been flying for two days. I had to see you, Sam. I couldn't stay away any longer. I want us to start all over again. I want to date you, to romance you, to do it the way it should've been done at the outset. We need to learn so much more about each other. "Will you go steady with me, Sambrea Sinclair? Will you wear my class ring?"

Holding out his hands in front of him, he turned his palms up. "I want to build all of our dreams with these two hands, Sam. Will you let me?"

Sambrea could see the reflection of her tear-filled eyes in the mirror of his midnight ones. He still wanted her and she felt so utterly overwhelmed by it. As tears broke free from her eyes, he lifted her from the chair and embraced her with all the tenderness he was capable of. His tenderness was quite immeasurable, in her opinion.

Undoing the clasp on the gold neck-chain he'd purchased for her, he slipped the ruby-stoned class ring onto it. Turning her slightly, he fastened the clasp. "Will you be my girl, Sambrea?"

She laughed through her tears. "If I'm going to be your only girl. I don't want to share!"

He kissed her temple. "You're my only girl and you'll never have to share. I want to take you out tonight. We're going to do it right this time. Shall I pick you up at seven?"

Her laughter was playfully hypnotic. He prayed that they'd always possess the ability to make each other laugh, from this day forward, for forever more.

"Seven, it is. But what are we going to do in the meantime?" Suggestively, she licked her lips. Flirting with him, she batted her eyelashes seductively.

"We're going to finish our breakfast. Then I'm out of here. I'm staying at the Seven Seas Hotel. I'm going to remain there until we have accomplished all that we need to. Trust is the first order on the agenda. We're going to take things slow and easy. The next time we make love, we'll be inseparable. I'm going to enjoy courting you. You're going to enjoy it too, Sam. Have you talked to our doctor?"

"Not yet." She sighed, touched by the words "our doctor." "I just got back into town. Now she's away. She'll be back next week. I have an appointment next Thursday."

"I'm glad to hear it. I want to go with you, but only if you want me there."

"We can get into that later, Craig. I'm dying to get into this wonderful food right now." After seating themselves, they dug into the meal with gusto.

The scrambled eggs were fluffy and moist and the fried potatoes were soft and flavorful. The silver-dollar-size buttermilk pancakes smelled and tasted heavenly.

"It's funny, Craig, but I had the same kind of thoughts that you've mentioned having. I blamed all our problems on us not knowing each other very well. Do you think we'll still want to be together after we find out everything about each other? I have some horrendous habits." Frowning, she popped a potato into her mouth.

He eyed her intently. "Not knowing each other is only part of the problem, Sam. I want to see you get over your hang-ups regarding your parents' marriage. They just didn't have the kind of staying power that it takes to make a marriage work. It takes a commitment from both parties for it to work. We're going to work it, Sam, apart at first, and then together. Baby or not, we have a future, Sam."

She scowled heavily. "I'm not sure I like the bit about being apart, but I know where you're coming from. I guess I don't have to like it, but I'm willing to go along with it. Craig, can we talk about what happened before I escaped to Maui?"

"Are you sure you want to go into that now, Sambrea? It could stir up some unpleasantness for you." His eyes held a warning.

"I'll be fine. I'd like to rehear your justifications regarding the way you dealt with my mother, though I doubt I'll understand them any better." She smiled to soften her rising indignation. "I'm waiting with bated breath."

"Sweetheart, Breeze was hurting you terribly. I couldn't stand to see the pain in your eyes or the sadness in your voice, especially when you talked about her not being there for you and your wanting her to be. I gave her the money so you'd be rid of her. I need you to understand that."

"Did you ever think I might not want to be rid of her, Craig? Did you ever think I might need her like crazy?"

Her questions shocked him. "I hadn't thought of it like that at all. Why would you want someone around who constantly reminds you of all the pain you and your father went through, especially when you thought she was deceased?

Needless pain, I might add. Don't tell me you enjoyed the painful remarks and unbearable actions she inflicted on you. You don't ever have to need anybody. You have me. A lifetime supply."

"Don't be coy, Craig. You're in enough hot water as it is." Knowing she couldn't fault him no matter how hard she tried, she nearly smiled. "Craig, maybe I wanted her around, needed her around, because she's all the biological family I have. She's my mother, Craig, regardless of how she's treated me. One day I expect her to regret all the hurt she's caused. It might come sooner than I expected, though the circumstances are unfortunate. She's had a heart attack."

Craig was visibly shaken as he got to his feet. "A heart attack? When? Is she going to be okay?" he rattled off without taking the slightest breath.

"She's stable, Craig." Sambrea tried to force back the broken sobs. Moving swiftly to her side, Craig swept Sambrea into his arms. "I feel so guilty." Her anguish was apparent.

Gently, he stroked her hair "Guilty? Not that again. What do you have to feel guilty about, sweetheart? You did nothing to cause her medical problems." He realized that his comment was a tad too harsh. "I'm sorry. I don't mean to sound so insensitive."

"When I first heard about her condition from Joe, I thought she was just being manipulative again. But when I found out she really was ill, I felt guilty for what I'd thought. She's now in intensive care. I've tried but I haven't been able to reach Jeremy Wylie, her doctor. I really don't have a lot of sound information about her condition."

"Does this mean you're not going to prosecute her?" He regretted asking the question the moment it left his lips. "There I go again, being insensitive. I'm just not as emotionally involved with Breeze as you are. But she's your family," he said, though he knew he'd been told differently.

"I owe her respect for that reason alone. Forgive me, Sam." He tenderly kissed the tip of her nose.

"Breeze will have her day in court, Craig, but putting her behind bars is not what I have in mind. I can't even think about anything like that while she's so ill. Understand?"

"Understood, Sambrea." He gave a resigned sigh. "Are you going to the hospital this morning? She is in the hospital here in Honolulu, isn't she?"

"She's still in Honolulu. As soon as I shower and get dressed, I'm going to pay a visit. I'll need to call Richard to go with me. Craig, I just can't face her alone. I've already tried. When I did see her, she didn't know I was in the room. I was glad Richard was there with me."

"I'm going to be with you this morning. May I take a shower and get dressed in your home, Mrs. Caldwell? I promise to clean up after myself," he joked. "I will leave everything just as I found it."

Sambrea couldn't keep herself from laughing. "I didn't say that to blackmail you into coming with me. I said it because it was true. You don't have to go with me, Craig. I'll certainly understand."

"I never do anything I don't want to, Sam. You should know at least that about me," he gently censured.

"In that case, you may go shower and dress. By the way, what time did you get here? If you're staying at a hotel, why aren't you dressed?"

He grinned. "I got here about four A.M. I had to know if you were staying here. When I got home, I found you asleep. I was too tired to drive so I slipped into this robe and took a nap in one of the guestrooms. I'm glad you were here, Mrs. Caldwell."

She wrinkled her nose. "I'm glad I was here, too. I'm even happier that you decided to come home. I missed you. Is it against the rules to give your only girl a kiss?"

She had more than just a kiss on her mind.

Craig felt reborn the moment his lips made contact with the moistness of hers. This is what he'd hoped for, had longed for, and had dreamed about. This was the only woman in the world who could fulfill his hopes, his dreams, and his longings. His arousal was uncontainable. Breathing raggedly, he had to pull himself away. She clung to him, making it even harder for him to drag himself from the heated embrace.

"No, Sam," he moaned against her parted lips, "don't do this to me. We need to do this right." He groaned, wanting her even more than he'd ever thought possible. He thought he had to be crazy not to take what she so wantonly offered.

As hard as it was, she released her hold on him, but not before tempting him with another tantalizing kiss. Her touching him in all the special places nearly drove him into abandoning the entire getting-to-know-you idea.

"You're too hot, Sam. I've got to run for my life, native girl."

Despite voicing his desire to run, he pulled her back into his arms and allowed her to do with him whatsoever she desired. Loving the idea of them really getting to know one another, she found the strength to restrain her amorous advances. Enamored with the idea of them going steady, she couldn't wait for the "dating game" to begin. She could be pregnant—and here they were talking about dating one another. She laughed with glee.

Craig began clearing the table. He then carried the soiled dishes down to the kitchen. With him and Sambrea working together, they made short work of putting everything back in order. Though showering in separate bathrooms, their torrid thoughts kept them erotically and emotionally connected.

Craig straightened the guestroom and then went in search of Sambrea. He found her in the master bedroom sitting at the dressing table. She was putting on her lipstick. When Sambrea looked up at Craig, she thought he looked great in the heather-gray dress slacks and the gray and burgundy pin striped shirt he wore.

Walking up behind her, he wrapped his arms around her waist. "Hmm, you smell good. You look good, too." His eyes took in the dark green jeans and the mint green light-weight sweater, all of which appeared to have been hand-painted on her.

Taking the lipstick from her hand, he outlined her full lips. Then, with slight strokes, he filled in the center, tasting her lips as he went along. "Hmm, you taste good, too. Too bad we've already had breakfast." He moaned while nibbling her ear lobe.

Sambrea nuzzled her head back against his chest. "I don't pet on the first date. You're going to have to take things very slo-oo-ow, Mr. Caldwell. I'm one of those old-fashioned good girls." She laughed at that, knowing how close they'd come to doing a lot more than just pet on their first encounter. And that hadn't even been a date.

"You're an old-fashioned naughty girl!" He brought a strand of her hair up to his lips. "We'd better be going." He found it hard to distance himself from her intoxicating sensuality.

Sambrea put her make-up items back in the pearl-covered makeup kit. As she stood, she gently pushed Craig away. "I'm sure Breeze is waiting for me to make an appearance. Boy, how am I going to face her? What am I going to say to her? I'm just glad to learn from the phone call that she's finally come around."

Craig tilted her chin, looking deeply into her sand-and-sable eyes. "You can face her, Sambrea. You can face any-thing with me by your side. You'll know exactly what to say when the time comes. Remember, you're not the one who has done something wrong." Kissing her cheek, he rapidly moved away, wanting desperately to do more than just kiss her.

Walking over to the closet, Sambrea pulled out the jean-jacket that matched her pants and slipped it around her shoulders. "Are we going in one car?"

"I think we should take both cars, Sam. The next time I come back here will be to pick you up for our date. Is that okay with you?"

"That's fine!" Walking over to where he stood, she slipped her arm into his. "Shall we go?"

He tenderly covered her hand with his. "As you wish, native girl!"

Breeze was actually sitting up in bed when Tyler Wilson entered the room. Happy to see her looking much better, he rushed to her side and dropped down in the chair next to her bed. "Oh, Breeze, I'm so glad to see that you're doing much better. Welcome back, darling!" Bending over the bed, he kissed her forehead.

Shrinking away from him, Breeze stared at him with a blank expression. "How could you betray me?" Her voice had a drug-induced, scratchy sound to it. "How, Tyler?"

He looked as though he'd just been stabbed in the heart. "I haven't betrayed you, Breeze, at least not entirely. I'm not going to testify against you. I've already told Sambrea as much."

Her eyes blazed with anger. "What made you change your mind? A few days ago you were ready to allow Sambrea to burn me at the stake." Her voice was raw with disgust.

Tyler rocked back in the straight-back chair. "I didn't have a change of mind, but rather an abrupt change of heart. I couldn't do it knowing all that we've meant to each other, been through together. I am ready to take all the heat, Breeze. I don't know what made me think it could be done any other way. Fear perhaps, or temporary insanity? I just don't know."

"I can tell you what it was," Breeze screeched. "You're afraid of my retaliation. You know I have you by the short hairs. If I tell Sambrea the truth about . . ."

Movement at the door caused Breeze to cut her sentence short.

Having heard most of the conversation, Sambrea stepped into the room. "Don't stop on my account, Mother. I'd really like to know the rest of it, especially about the truth. I'm sure Craig would also like to hear it."

Sinking down into the bed, Breeze pulled the sheet up under her chin. "Hello, Sambrea. It was good of you to come." Briefly, Breeze glanced at Craig, but she couldn't find anything appropriate to say to him. Quickly, she looked away from Craig's steady gaze.

Craig had plenty to say to her but refrained.

Sambrea moved closer to the bed. Shocking Breeze, she reached for her hand, and rubbed it gently. She allowed her eyes to make direct contact with the pale woman. "Your doctor says you're doing much better. We just ran into him out in the hall. He's confident that you'll have a full recovery."

Breeze pulled her hand away. "You're not really interested in how I'm doing, so why don't you just tell me why you're here, Sambrea? We don't have to pretend with each other. We both know exactly where we stand." Breeze practically hissed at Sambrea.

Wincing inwardly from the sharpness of Breeze's tongue, Sambrea managed to smile. "I'm here because I care about you despite all that you've done. I may know where I stand with you, but you couldn't possibly know where you stand with me. If you did, you wouldn't act the way you do. I can assure you that my motives are pure and fraught with concern for you."

Unexpectedly, totally out of character for her, Breeze

burst into tears. She pressed her head against Sambrea's chest. "How can you have concern for me when all I've done is hurt you?" Breeze sobbed. "I could be dying and I'm still hurting you." Breeze trembled uncontrollably.

"Oh, Mother," Sambrea cried, "you're not dying. I have concern for you because I love you! You're my mother, Breeze, and I hope you haven't forgotten that Samuel is my father. Samuel had a very forgiving heart, which I inherited."

With tears racing down her cheeks, Sambrea stole a glance at Craig. His heart went out to his wife, but he watched Breeze with a skeptical eye. He couldn't tell if Breeze was sincere, or if she was putting on the performance of her life. Either way, Sambrea's vulnerable heart was at risk and he couldn't stand to see her hurting so badly. Was Breeze really capable of changing, capable of loving Sambrea, of being there for her? He had serious doubts.

Dressed in a crisp white uniform, a smiling nurse sauntered into the room, interrupting the emotional exchange between Breeze and Sambrea. "Sorry, but your visiting time is up. Mrs. Sinclair has to retain her strength. There are several more tests that have to be run. You all can come back tomorrow."

Sambrea squeezed Breeze tighter. "I'll be back. We have a lot of catching up to do, but it can wait until you're out of here. Have a good rest, Mother."

Out in the hallway, Craig pulled Sambrea close to him, hugging her tightly. "It's going to be all right, Sam, but I still want you to be careful of Breeze. Her claws may be retracted right now, but you know how quickly she can disclose them. You already know how sharp they are."

Sambrea pushed a stray curl back from his forehead. "I understand your warning, Craig, but I think things are going to be different for us. My mother could've died. That seems to have sobered both her and me. Breeze can do as she likes, but I have to forgive her. I don't know any other way to do this."

Sambrea seemed to be apologizing for having such a forgiving heart, which Craig thought ludicrous, since it was one of the things he loved most about her. How many times had she forgiven him? Even if he hadn't been guilty of anything except loving her too much.

"I guess you have Samuel to blame for your serious heart condition, Sam. If he was as loving and forgiving as you've said, I can see why you turned out the way you are. Don't change. It becomes you. Come here," he commanded softly. He pulled her closer against him, kissing her mouth fervently.

Parting ways at the front entrance of the hospital, Sambrea and Craig promised to be in the best of moods for their date. Neither spoke about the things Breeze had been about to reveal when they walked in, yet both felt that Tyler was somehow very much in Breeze's debt.

As the doorbell pealed, Sambrea slipped into a robe. She looked over at the clock on the nightstand. *Way too early for Craig.* Only an hour had passed since they'd left each other at the hospital entrance. "Maybe he forgot to take something he needs," she mumbled to herself on the way to the door.

Upon opening the door, she found Richard standing there looking worried and burdened. "I don't like the look on your face." She frowned. "Is something wrong at the office?" She moved aside so he could enter the foyer.

Facing her, he placed soothing hands on her shoulders. "We just received a call at the office from a nurse at the hospital, Sam. It's Breeze. She's taken a turn for the worse. The nurse suggested that we get in contact with you immediately. Apparently she got worse right after you left.

That's probably why they didn't find you at home. I rushed right over here to take you to the hospital."

With sweat popping out on her forehead, Sambrea felt slightly faint. "I need to sit down. Did they say she had another heart attack? Did they give you any idea as to her condition?" She lowered herself down on the sofa.

Richard sat in a plush chair facing the couch. "They didn't go into any detail. With my not being family and all, legally, they really couldn't divulge too much. The privacy act was designed to protect our rights, you know. That is, before the Internet. All I know is that she's not doing so hot and that they need to talk to you as soon as possible."

Slightly woozy, Sambrea wobbled a little to the side as she got to her feet. "You're family to me, Rich, but I understand their position. I'm going upstairs to put my clothes back on. Be back in a second." She walked out of the room, only to turn around and come right back. "By the way, thanks for coming here to tell me about Breeze. I might not have taken it so well over the phone. Thanks for being such a loyal friend."

Richard wrinkled his nose. "Friends are great, Sam, but I think we need to get in touch with your husband. He'd want to be here for you at a time like this."

Sambrea smiled. "He *is* here. I'll tell you about it on the way to the hospital. So as not to keep you in suspense, we're going to work our marriage out. We love each other."

Richard grinned. "Now, those are the kind of stories I love to hear. I can't wait to hear all the juicy details."

Upstairs in the master bedroom Sambrea chose a simple dark-blue linen dress to wear to the hospital. Uncomplicated in design, the knee-length dress buttoned all the way down the front, making it easy for Sambrea to slip right into it. Instead of the usual pumps she wore, Sambrea slid her feet into navy-blue leather flats.

The sound of the phone startled her so badly it felt as though her heart had pumped its way right into her mouth. Panic-stricken, she stared at the ringing nuisance. Fearful of what she might hear from the other end, she let it ring two more times before actually picking up the receiver.

"Sambrea, it's me, Craig. Are you alright?" He wondered why her breathing sounded so shallow and labored.

She drew a quick breath of air into her lungs. "I'm afraid I'm not doing so well. Where are you?"

"I'm at the hotel, but what's going on over there? What's happened to you since I left? You sound so distraught. Are you physically ill, Sam?"

"It's Breeze, Craig. She's taken a turn for the worse. Richard's here to take me to the hospital."

He sucked in a deep breath. "I called to let you know an important meeting has been called and that I might be a little late in coming to pick you up for our date. Instead, I'll cancel the meeting and meet you at the hospital. How soon before you and Richard leave?"

"I'm ready to go now, but I want you to take your meeting. Is there a number where I can reach you should I need you?"

"Are you sure about this? There's nothing in this world that's more important to me than you, native girl."

Sentimental tears glazed her eyes. "Ditto, Craig. But I'll be just fine. I don't even know the real situation yet. Once I've summed things up, I'll contact you if necessary."

"Grab a pencil. It's a private number, Sam. But I'll alert my client to the fact that you might call."

Sambrea picked up a pencil off the telephone stand. She wrote down the number as he gave it to her. "Got it. I'll call you only if I need to."

"Love you. My thoughts and prayers are always with you, sweetheart."

EIGHTEEN

Hospital personnel bustled busily about the corridor as Sambrea and Richard made their way to the Cardiac Intensive Care Unit. At the nurses station Sambrea inquired about her mother.

Remembering Sambrea from the previous visits, Nurse Andrews came from around the desk and took Sambrea's hand. "It's not good, young lady. The doctor will see you in a few minutes. He wishes to talk with you about your mom's condition."

A bout of dizziness assailed her, and Sambrea groped for Richard's arm. "Here we go again. I feel so sick, Rich."

"Steady, Sam." Richard braced her with an arm around her waist. "Let's go over here and sit down." He guided her to the visitors' seating area.

Looking at Sambrea with deep concern, the nurse followed them into the waiting area. "Can I get you something, young lady?"

Sambrea smiled up at her. "A glass of water would be just great. Thank you kindly."

The nurse came back quickly with the water.

"Here you go, young lady." She handed the paper cup of water to Sambrea and returned to the nurses' station.

Removing a small piece of paper from her purse, Sambrea turned to Richard. "I need to call Craig. This is more serious than I thought. He'd offered to meet me here, but

I told him to wait for my call. Do you have your cell phone with you? Mine is at home, in my car."

Removing the extremely slim phone from the breast pocket of his sports jacket, he handed it to Sambrea and stood up. "You're going to need some privacy. I'll be out of earshot, but right in the line of vision." He leaned over to kiss her forehead.

She gave him an adoring glance. "Thank you, Richard. I don't know what I would do if I didn't have you here to anticipate my every need." Craig's voice came on the line barely a moment after she asked to speak with him.

"How's it going over there where you are, Sam?"

"Simply spoken, I need you."

"Say no more. I'm on my way, but I need you to do me a huge favor, native girl."

"What's that?"

"Hang on to happy thoughts of us as you dig down deep and tap into the wellspring of courage within you. It's there. But you have to grab on to it and hold on to it with all your might, my beautiful Sambrea."

She smiled. "If I can't, you have enough courage for the both of us. I don't know why I couldn't see it before, but I now know you don't mind sharing all that you are and all that you have with me." Without further comment, she disconnected the line.

With a wave of her hand, Sambrea summoned Richard, who watched her from his seat on the leather sofa located on the other side of the room. He immediately got to his feet and took the few steps across the room.

After sitting down in the chair next to her, he turned to face her. "Is he coming?"

She grinned. "Did you really need to ask? Of course he's coming."

Richard smiled "How quickly things change."

"I've certainly changed a lot since Craig came into my life. Though the changes haven't all been for the better, I think I'm finally headed in the right direction with my marriage. Can you believe he wants us to date each other?"

Noticing the tall, ruddy-complexioned man towering over their seats, Richard didn't attempt to respond.

The man extended his hand to both Sambrea and Richard before taking a seat directly across from them. "Dr. Paul Wylie at your service." He greeted them with an anxious smile.

Sambrea nodded her head. "My mother. How is she, sir?"

Dr. Wylie flipped open the medical chart he held in his left hand. "Your mother has an obstructed coronary artery. She's going to need bypass surgery, but this last attack has left her dangerously unstable. If we can't stabilize her within the next few hours, we're going to go ahead with the surgery. With your permission, of course."

"Of course." Sambrea had a certain degree of apprehension. She didn't at all like the fact that Breeze's very life seemed to be in her hands. "Is surgery the only alternative?"

He outlined the sides of his mouth with his forefinger and thumb until they came together. "Afraid so. Our decision was based on the outcome of the heart X-rays that we recently took. We also closely examined the blood vessels."

"Can you explain the surgery to me?"

"In simple terms," the doctor offered, "it's a heart operation in which a vein graft taken from the leg is used to bypass an obstructed artery."

Removing a graphic chart of the heart from within the medical chart, he pointed to the aorta with his finger. "The graft is attached at this end of the aorta. At the other end it's attached to that portion of the coronary artery located beyond the obstruction," he explained. "It's very helpful in the treatment of angina pectoris."

"The success rate?" Richard queried.

"An extremely high success rate," the doctor responded

with undeniable confidence. He got to his feet. Taking a business card from the pocket of his white lab coat, he handed it to Sambrea. "Please feel free to call me at any time. Though I may not be available right away, I'll get back to you as soon as I'm able to. We're going to do all we can for your mother."

Sambrea smiled up at him. "Thank you."

He looked down at the chart again. "Mrs. Caldwell, as next of kin, we're going to need you to sign all the necessary forms that will give us permission to go forward with our treatment. Each form will be explained to you in great detail. You can see one of the nurses at your convenience, but I suggest that you take care of it as soon as possible. We can't afford to be held up."

Craig, followed by Tyler Wilson, turned the corner just as Dr. Wylie disappeared behind the glass enclosed wall of the intensive care unit. Craig shook hands with Richard and then he rapidly made his way to his wife.

Bending over, Craig gathered Sambrea against his chest. As she got to her feet, he pulled her limp body into his. "Are you okay, Sam?"

She kissed him full on the mouth. "I am now." She motioned for Craig and Tyler to take a seat. "Let me fill you both in on the details."

Sambrea told the two men exactly what she'd been told. As she explained things, she couldn't help noticing how pale Tyler had turned. This man, regardless of what he'd done, had once been her father's best friend. Though she didn't care for what he'd done, as her godfather, she loved him dearly. He'd been good to her long before and long after Samuel's death. She believed that there had to be more to what he'd done than he was willing to admit to.

Tyler stood up. "This is an unbearable situation. God, what an awful thing to have happen to someone so vibrant."

As though he suddenly remembered he wasn't in this alone, he turned to face Sambrea. The agony in his eyes made her flinch as he took hold of both of her hands. "I'm so sorry, sweetheart, but I can't adequately express how much I regret the pain I've caused you."

Giving Tyler a gentle hug, she squeezed his hands. "I think you already have."

Protectively, Craig pulled Sambrea's head against his chest. "We're in this together, Sam. You know that, don't you?"

She nodded. "I only wish I'd realized it a lot sooner. I could've spared myself so much anguish. How can I thank you for hanging in here with me?"

Hoping to make her smile, he wiggled his eyebrows suggestively. When it worked, he felt a sharp intake of breath. Her smile simply took his breath away. "I can think of many ways for you to thank me, Sam. But I'll save them for later. When we're alone together." He rested a balled fist under her chin. "Have you eaten anything, Sambrea?"

She looked slightly abashed. "Afraid not. Am I now in for a lecture on proper dietary management?"

Soft as a whisper, he glided his fist down the side of her face. "Not at this time. However, we're going to march right down to the cafeteria and replenish your bread basket."

She started to protest but quickly changed her mind. She had to eat, no matter what. Besides, Craig wasn't going to have it any other way—and she was through fighting him on every issue and at every turn. So far, he hadn't told her one thing that hadn't been for her own good. So far, he'd really been nothing less than good to her.

She grinned. "I'll second that."

She had surprised him with her hasty concession.

"Good girl." He gave a dazzling smile.

* * *

The moment the small group returned from the cafeteria Tyler asked to speak to Craig in private. Before agreeing, Craig made sure it was okay with Sambrea for him to leave her alone for a short time. With Richard there to keep her company, she told him she'd be just fine.

After leaving the room, the two men found their way to a small, comfortable lounge located at the end of the hallway. Craig allowed Tyler to precede him into the lounge.

"What's on your mind, Tyler?" Craig was more curious about this private meeting than he wanted to let on.

Tyler clamped his hands together. "Young man, you've got to do something about this threat of prosecution hanging over Breeze's head. It's what's causing her condition to worsen. She's scared out of her mind. A woman like Breeze won't last a day in jail. And I'm sure Sambrea doesn't want her mother to go there. It has to be you that's pushing this thing," Tyler accused Craig. "Why do you have to force this power trip on your wife if it's not her will?"

Without removing his relentless gaze from Tyler, Craig took a seat in one of the leather armchairs. He studied Tyler with an intensity that made the older man burn beneath his shirt collar. Craig could almost smell Tyler's discomfort.

"As far as I'm concerned, you've pushed this loyalty-to-mother thing down Sambrea's throat long enough, Tyler. You and I both know Breeze isn't Sambrea's natural mother. Don't we, Tyler?"

Craig didn't know if Breeze had ever told Tyler what she'd told him regarding Sambrea's birth mother, but the time had now come for him to find out. The horrified look on Tyler's face told Craig he'd been right to reveal his hole cards. He did know about it and a heck of a lot more. Tyler had been Samuel Sinclair's best friend.

Recovering from the shock Craig's words had stunned him with, Tyler forced his hackles into commission. "Where did you get such nonsense, young man?" he growled.

"From your nonsensical friend, Breeze. When she came to me to ask for my help, she planned on using the information as a weapon against my wife if I didn't see things her way. She figured I'd do anything to protect Sambrea from the truth about her father's affair, like paying her off. She figured right. Is it true Samuel involved himself with a prostitute?"

Once again, Tyler looked horrified. "Is that what Breeze told you?"

Craig raised an eyebrow. "Are you saying it's not true?"

Tyler looked like a man at war with himself. "Breeze can be so dramatically creative. She's always been a drama queen," he told Craig. "Sambrea's birth mother was not a prostitute. Far from it. Davina Davis was Samuel's administrative assistant. Not only was she loyal to De La Brise, Davina loved Samuel dearly."

Though his insides shook like a bowl of jelly, outwardly, Craig appeared as his usual calm self. "Do you know where Davina is now?"

Tyler's eyes grew blank. No expression crossed his face. Then his shoulders slumped, as though he'd just suffered a major defeat. "She's dead, son. She died in a car crash when Sambrea was just four weeks old. The day she died I was driving the car she was killed in. Samuel and I escaped the burning car without so much as a scratch."

Craig leaped to his feet. "What are you saying, man? Why were the three of you in the car together? I can't believe this nightmare. It keeps getting more tragic."

Tyler wiped at his sweaty brow with a plain white handkerchief he'd removed from the back pocket of his pants. "It was right after work." He looked a little more composed now. "Sam and I were taking her to pick up the baby from her home. She had a private sitter who came in to take care of little Samantha. . . ."

"Samantha?" Craig interjected, startled at the mentioned

name. "If that was the baby's name, where did the name Sambrea come from?"

Tyler moaned. "One of Breeze's brilliant ideas; Sam/ Breeze. You see, she'd blackmailed Samuel and Davina into allowing her and Samuel to raise the child as their own. Breeze had threatened to go public with their affair if Davina didn't give the baby up. Not only would she have gone public, she would've fought for custody of the child as well. It had nothing to do with Breeze wanting to keep her marriage to Samuel intact. This all came about because Breeze was incapable of giving birth to a child. She's sterile. Samuel never knew that about her. She only told me about it in a moment of deep despair."

Craig shook his head in disbelief. "This doesn't make sense. Samuel could've fought this thing and won. He was the one with all the money."

Tyler paced back and forth in the small lounge. "He wasn't going to take any chances. Not when it came down to the possibility of losing the most precious person in his life. His child." Tyler shrugged his shoulders. "A win wasn't a guarantee for a man who was involved in an extramarital love affair. Besides that, Davina's reputation would've been destroyed in the process. He would never allow that to happen. He loved Davina far too much for that."

Craig looked totally perplexed. "Samuel wasn't in love with Breeze? Sambrea seems to think just the opposite."

"He did love her, once upon a time. She destroyed the love he felt for her simply by being herself. Breeze is a very self-centered woman. Her greed for money drove Samuel into the arms of Davina, a woman totally unlike the woman he'd married. Davina gave up Sambrea to protect the man she loved and adored. She didn't give a damn about her own reputation. Breeze was a force no one could reckon with at the time. Samuel could've offered her every dime he had—and it wouldn't have mattered, could've promised her her very own planet, and it wouldn't have done any good. He could've satisfied her every whim—and it would've been meaningless.

"Breeze was barren. For that reason alone, she would've fought to the death to get custody of Sambrea. But that wasn't the only reason, of course. Little Sambrea was the sole heiress to Samuel's vast fortune. Why take a small slice of the pie, when you can control it all?"

"Exactly," Craig seconded. "Sambrea's the one who ended up with the whole pie, but she also got the heartburn that came with it. What I want to know is how Breeze explained having a child without ever having been pregnant?"

"Being reed thin was one of her strongest allies. A trip to Europe in the last trimester of Davina's pregnancy kept Breeze out of the public's eye. The day she came home from Europe is the very same day we were bringing the child to her. Everyone at the office was told that Davina had lost the child during the birth. There were a lot of rumors and innuendoes flying about the office, but I'm the only one who knew for sure that Samuel and Davina were involved. Most people thought it was just a coincidence that Davina and Breeze were pregnant at the same time. At any rate, the mendacity was pulled off without a hitch."

Craig had heard a lot of abominable stories, but he couldn't even begin to rate this one. He probably couldn't count that high. This scenario was way over the top. Craig looked worried. "Are you sure no one else knows about this, Tyler?"

Tyler nodded. "I can't say that with certainty, but Sambrea is now twenty-five years old, and not a single word of this has ever been breathed to her, as far as I know. Of course, there's Samuel's old friend, Tai. But if she does have this knowledge, she'd never cause Sambrea a moment of pain. She loves your wife like a daughter and she knows how much Sambrea adores Samuel. Tai would be the last person to bring this burden to Sambrea."

Craig's worry grew tenfold. "You know, my wife might be pregnant, and her background is important if she is. I swore I'd never tell her any of this, but I'm not so sure I can avoid it. If there were to be complications in her pregnancy, or in her health in general, I wouldn't be able to keep this knowledge from her. If I wait until an emergency arises to tell her, I'll lose her altogether. Getting her to trust me has been one colossal feat."

Craig paced back and forth in front of his seat. "Until today, I never understood how deep her fear of love and commitment ran. She grew up in a house with two people who didn't know the first thing about love and devotion. Breeze loved money and Samuel loved the other woman. It all makes sense now."

Tyler came over and stood in front of Craig. "I don't envy your position. But I don't think you should be the one to tell Sambrea about this tragedy. She'll hate you for it."

Craig grimaced. He recalled Breeze saying the same thing. He understood it more now than he did at that time. She might not hate him, but he had no doubt that she might try to convince herself that she did, thus creating an excuse to go back to being the runaway child, running wild.

"If it offers you any comfort, I know who Davina's doctor was. In fact, Dr. Laramie Gooden is the mother of Lindsey Gooden, the doctor Sambrea sees. Though they might be on microfilm by now, I bet Davina's medical records are still obtainable. That means we could obtain her medical history for Sambrea. Would you like me to find out for you, Craig?"

"None of this offers me any comfort. I wish I knew none of this story. You say I shouldn't be the one to tell Sam this story, but someone has to—and Breeze is in no condition to. Pray tell, man—you tell me who that someone should be."

With Craig looking dangerously close to hitting something, Tyler put a safe distance between them. He didn't want to find his nose on the other end of Craig's rather large fist.

Tyler aged another couple of years while pondering Craig's question. "I'm her godfather. I'll be the one to tell her, but not until after Breeze's surgery. That would be too much on her all at once. Besides, she'll have a lot of questions and I'm the only one who can answer them for her. Even if Breeze gets well and Sambrea asks questions of her, we both know Breeze may not answer them honestly. She's already lied to you about Davina's reputation. We need to calm down here and deal with one crisis at a time."

Without so much as a snort of a response to Tyler's offer, Craig strode from the room. Keeping Sambrea out of crisis was the only thing he had any intentions of dealing with. Lindsey Gooden might be able to steer him in the right direction where Sambrea's health and welfare was concerned. He'd have to tell her the truth about his wife's birth. But patient and doctor confidentiality was a guaranteed protection. He was as much Lindsey Gooden's patient as Sambrea was simply because he shared this pregnancy with her. Sambrea hadn't gotten pregnant by herself. If in fact she was with child.

Feeling sorry they'd had to cancel their special date, Sambrea rushed through her nightly ritual of cleansing her face and lavishing it with moisturizers and invisible under-eye night creams. Normally she brushed her hair for several minutes, but she'd skip that for now.

Craig was downstairs in the kitchen making them a late night snack. Much to her dismay he'd be returning to his hotel for the rest of the night. She made a mad dash for the staircase, hoping he'd stay on a while after they'd consumed their snack. With what she had to tell him, she thought the chances of him staying on just might be excellent.

As she swept into the room, the rustling of the white satin robe and gown she wore caught his immediate attention. She looked like a princess out of a fairytale. Her perfume aroused a longing in him that he wasn't sure he'd ever be able to quell.

She practically threw herself into his open arms "Hi, darling," she cooed. "What smells so good?" She looked around to see what was on the stove.

"You, my fair lady." He continued to flirt with her while kissing her eyelids. "What's that fabulous scent you have on? It smells wonderful on you."

"Sinful!"

His eyes smoldered like hot coals "Quite an appropriate name for what's on my mind. What *sin* do you have in mind on this beautiful, balmy night, Mrs. Caldwell?"

"For starters, overeating. I'm hungry. We'll go into the other sins in depth, after we have our snack." She flirted back while moving out of his arms.

Disapprovingly, he clicked his tongue. "I think I'd like to have that discussion first. It just might help me decide on something I've been pondering." He flashed her a wicked grin.

"Don't you want to go into a little more detail than that, husband?" She tried to thwart Craig as he kept her from poking her nose into one of the pans on the stove.

"No, I don't. I'll leave it to your imagination, just as you've done to me. Let's get this snack over with. It sounds like we've got some important and exciting challenges ahead of us."

He pulled a chair out from the table. After pulling her away from the stove, he deposited her in the seat. "Want some orange juice?"

She smiled. "I'd love some if it's freshly squeezed."

He shifted his eyes at her. "Aren't you the spoiled brat. Do you think I'd serve you anything less than fresh? If you do, you'd better think again. Nothing but the finest of everything for my native girl."

Blushing, she grinned. "Ease up on the charm, lover boy.

You already possess the master key to my heart." She laughed as he pulled a funny face.

As he placed the cheese and mushroom omelet on her plate, followed by a bowl of grits, a plate of hash browns, potatoes, and a platter of fresh fruits, she squealed with delight. "Is this what you call a snack? Boy, this is a four-course meal. Are you planning on getting me fat so no other man will look at me?"

His eyes and the quick drop of his chin put her in check. "They can look all they want. In fact, I'd be flattered by it. I don't have a problem with that at all. But when it comes to touching . . . don't even need to go into that since you already know what the outcome would be. We both know it won't be pretty."

Sitting down across from her, he saw that her eyes burned with something akin to mystery. "What's that look about, Sam?"

"Mr. Caldwell, how do you expect your wife and our child to fend for themselves while you serve time in prison for attacking someone physically?"

Something about her statement caused him to think that she knew something she hadn't decided to share with him. When she caressed her stomach with infinite tenderness, he guessed at what that something was.

"You're pregnant, aren't you? How . . . when?" He looked stunned.

She threw her head back in laughter. "If you don't know how and when, I'm not sure I can educate you in the ways a child is conceived, not at your age. But then again, maybe I could. I hear it's never too late to teach an old dog new tricks."

Getting up from her chair, she deposited herself on Craig's lap and entwined her arms around his neck. "Yes, husband, wife is pregnant. Dr. Gooden left a message for me to call her when I got in. Her answering service put me through to her home and she told me the results of my last pregnancy test. We are going to have our very own child to love and spoil!"

Without giving him a chance to respond, she covered his mouth with her own, kissing him as though there were no tomorrow. His fervor matched her own as he kissed her back. When thoughts of what Tyler had told him tried to push through his euphoria, he shoved them back. There'd be time enough to deal with them, time enough to deal with the lies, time enough to make things right for his beautiful wife. But for now, a joyous celebration was in order.

He was going to become a father.

Looking dazed, Craig pulled his head back slightly, allowing his eyes to come to rest in hers. "Sam, you seem excited about the baby, but I know how apprehensive you've been about becoming a mother. Are you really okay with it?"

Taking his breath away, she gave him an encore of the last kiss. As she brought the kiss to an end, he looked even more dazed. She slid her hand into his. "I am ecstatic about having your baby, Craig." Her answer was truthful. "I only wish that the circumstances could've been different. And I wish the news hadn't come during a period of crisis."

His eyes deeply probed hers. "The crisis with Breeze? Is that the only thing that you wish was different?"

She rubbed his cheek with the back of her hand. "Don't look so anxious over this, Craig. I think what you're trying to find out here is if I'm ready to take on the responsibility that comes with being a wife and mother. I'm ready for all of it. I'm deliriously happy with what my fate has turned out to be. Is it a son that you desire most, Craig?"

He kissed her to show how much he appreciated her candor. "Every man wants a son, but a healthy daughter would bring me no less joy. And if she were to look exactly like her mommy, I'm afraid I would lose myself in her, as I've lost myself in you."

Sambrea looked puzzled. "Lost? I don't like that word.

Do you feel lost when you're with me? Does that mean you don't know who you are or what you are when you're with me?"

Seeing how serious she was, he chose to laugh inwardly. "Sam, you may have misinterpreted things a little here. Losing myself in you is a good thing. When I'm working, I lose myself in my work, but that's not necessarily a good thing to do. It can be stressful. But when I lose myself in you, I feel relaxed. I'm able to cast all my troubles aside. It allows me to enjoy our time together, to enjoy that wonderful sense of humor you possess. It just means that I don't need to define myself when I'm with you. I become one with you. I simply become a part of you."

Her hot tears grazed his cheek. "You have a logical answer for everything, Mr. Caldwell. And I love the answer you just gave. It was deep, just as you are."

He shook his head. "I don't have an answer for everything, Sam. If I did, I would've figured you out by now. But I've decided that I don't want to figure you out. You're not an equation to be solved. You're not a Rubik's cube either. I love the way you keep me intrigued. I love the challenge of loving you and having you love me back. I don't ever want you to change a single thing about yourself. You keep all my hopes and dreams alive. I love you, Sambrea. Congratulations to us on the creation of our first child! May this be the beginning of us becoming one big happy family."

"Thank you, darling! I pray for the very same."

Moving her off his lap, he stood up. "It's time for me to go. My pregnant wife needs her rest. As soon as Breeze is out of the woods, we'll really celebrate on our special date."

The look in her eyes turned solemn. "Speaking of Breeze, as I held her in my arms, there at the hospital, she whispered something to me that made my blood run cold. I've been worried over it ever since. She said that we needed to talk; that it was important, and that what she had to tell me would change my life forever. That's the part that has me upset. Do you happen to know what she has to tell me, Craig?"

NINETEEN

Craig felt sick inside as he kissed her forehead. He wished he didn't have any secrets to keep from her. "Breeze says a lot of things and we both know she's a stranger to honesty." He had responded, but without giving a direct response to her question. He didn't want to lie to her, but neither could he answer her question. In time, he would make everything right for her.

Sambrea smiled up at him. "No matter what Breeze has to tell me, I'm not going to let it affect me. I have you in my life. You love me and that's quite enough for me. You're my equalizer, my strength, my bond. We're going to have a child together. Therefore, we've become a family. If Breeze chooses to be a part of our family, I'll welcome her with open arms. Whether Breeze decides to be a part of our lives or not, our family circle is complete. She can't hurt me anymore. I won't let her. Like you said, she can't do anymore to me than what I allow."

Oh, God, how he wished that were true. He knew exactly what Breeze had to tell Sambrea—and he'd move mountains to stop her. What Breeze had to tell Sambrea would undoubtedly have a serious domino effect on her emotions. Learning about her father's infidelities could only do harm to his wife and possibly their unborn child. It wasn't that Sambrea shouldn't ever be told, he just didn't think it should happen before the baby was born.

Sambrea looped her arm inside of his. Vulnerability shone in her eyes as she looked up at him. "I know I'm being silly right now, but I don't want to be alone tonight. I need you here with me, Craig. Before, it was always you begging me to stay with you, now I'm begging you to stay with me. I just need to be held, need to feel safe and secure. No one does that for me better than you do. Will you stay here with me tonight?"

Holding her tightly, he lifted her off her feet. This woman filled him up. His love for her had completely runneth over. "You don't ever have to beg me for anything. All you have to do is let me know what it is you desire. If it's within my power to grant you what you're in need of, you'll have it. As for my staying here tonight, I'll grant your request—but on one condition."

Perplexed, she looked into his eyes. "Name it."

He grinned. "After I put you to bed, and you've fallen off to sleep, I'll retire to one of the guest rooms. No more hanky panky until after we've pulled everything together. What do you say to my conditions?"

She smiled wryly, but the look in her eyes said *yeah, right*. "Whatever you say."

"Come on, Sam, let me tuck my sweetheart in. Do you want anything before we go upstairs?"

"Yeah, this." She kissed him hard on the mouth. "And this." She planted kisses on his neck and ears. "Oh, yes, this," she breathed, touching his intimate zone.

Standing her on her feet, he held her away from him. "I can see that you've decided to make this a real big challenge for me. Am I right?"

"You figure it out." She stretched her arms high over her head. "I'm ready to go night, night, lover. Are you coming?" She bolted for the stairs before he could respond. Running after her, he took the steps two at a time.

* * *

For the second time in his adult life, Craig dressed in a pair of pajamas, another one of the sets his mother had given him. Sambrea liked the navy blue ones on him better than the burgundy ones he'd worn before. With the gold crest, the navy blue silk looked rich.

"Don't you look debonair and cute."

He ruffled her hair. "Come here and get close to me. Scoot down in the bed so you can relax. I'm going to sing you a lullaby. What would you like to hear?"

Sambrea's heart grew full. " 'Daddy's Little Girl,' " she requested. "My father used to sing that to me when he tucked me in. He came to my room every night before he went to bed."

Craig pressed his lips into the palm of her hand before singing.

He sang so sweetly to her until he finished every verse of the song.

"Are you okay, sweetheart?" He brought her into his arms. "I don't like to see you cry. It's the memories, huh? Powerful stuff, I guess."

Trying to control her quivering lower lip, she nodded. "I'm a sentimental jerk, but that song is so very special to me. I was Daddy's little girl and I'm not ashamed of admitting it. We were crazy about each other and I miss him terribly." She began to sob. "I'm sorry for acting so childish, Craig. Sorry for all the tears, but I can't help feeling sorry that our child won't get to interact with the most wonderful grandfather he or she could ever hope for."

"Don't be sorry, beautiful. It's good for you to release your emotions." Gently, he cradled her head in the well of his arm. "Go to sleep, love. I'll be right here beside you. I wish you pleasant dreams."

"Thank you, Craig. You are my dream come true."

Craig got up from the bed. "I'm going to put the *Wind Chimes* CD on. I'll be right back."

Sambrea fell into a deep sleep while her husband's arms held her all through the night.

Dressed in dark blue Dockers and a lemon-yellow polo shirt, Craig sat in a chair in front of Dr. Gooden's desk, his legs crossed. Normally he had nerves of steel, could face anything or anybody, but something about discussing Sambrea's situation with Dr. Lindsay Gooden had him a little unnerved.

Dr. Gooden came into her office. She greeted Craig cheerfully as she took a seat behind her desk. "It's nice to see you again, Craig. I was a little surprised to learn that you'd be coming in without Sambrea. Is everything okay between you two?"

Craig stroked his chin. "As far as Sam's health is concerned, she's fine, but still has bouts with morning sickness. The medicine you called in to the pharmacy has helped a lot." His face took on a pained expression. "I'm here on an entirely different matter, but I don't know how to say what I need to say, which is a rare thing for me. I'm used to getting right to the point. As your patient, I do believe I have the doctor-patient confidentiality privileges. Am I correct?"

Dr. Gooden laughed. "Well, I've never heard one of my patient's husbands refer to themselves as my patient. But since you made an appointment to see me, and you're a paying customer, I guess that makes you my patient, too. Are you having some medical difficulties?"

He shook his head in the negative. "I do share in Sambrea's morning sickness from time to time, but nothing more than that. I also get emotional when she does, but I guess that's natural, especially when a man loves his wife as much as I love mine. However, the reason I came here is because I'm concerned about Sambrea's medical background. You see, Sambrea really doesn't know all her history . . ."

"It's okay, Craig," Dr. Gooden interrupted. "I know what you're trying to say and I'm not going to make you go through the hell of telling me Sambrea's tragic story. I can only imagine what this must have cost you to come here today. I already know that Breeze Sinclair is not Sambrea's birth mother."

Craig jumped to his feet. "Did Sam tell you that? Does she know?" He lowered himself back into the chair.

Folding her hands, Dr. Gooden placed them on the desk. "No, not Sambrea. She doesn't know. My mother told me the whole story when I went to her out of concern for Sambrea. She's never told another living soul about this. Because of the things I told her Sambrea was experiencing, she felt compelled to share her medical knowledge of Sambrea's natural mother with me. My mother was Miss Davis' doctor. It seems that Miss Davis' pregnancy couldn't be confirmed for several weeks either, much like Sambrea's. The stress of becoming a single mom complicated things for Ms. Davis, the same as it has done to Sambrea. But at least we have a firm diagnosis now."

Craig sighed in relief.

She looked Craig right in the eye. "I would venture a guess that you're here to ask my advice on whether you should tell your wife the truth." Craig nodded. "As far as her medical history goes, I've got that covered. I have access to Ms. Davis' medical records. At her request, my mother kept her files in our home. If I were in Sambrea's shoes, I'd want to know. She has the right to know—and that's why I've made the decision to tell her the truth. I plan to tell her at her next appointment."

Craig felt awful inside. "This story gets more incredible each day. The discoveries are so amazing. I want to be the one to tell my wife, but I've been told that she'd hate me for it. While I don't believe she'll hate me, I do believe she'll use this as an excuse to run away again. Sambrea had vowed never to marry because she was scared to death of failing at it. But I guess she found me irresistible." He tried to lighten his own somber mood. "So why do you think you should be the one to tell her?"

Lindsey briefly pondered his question. "Because I'm not emotionally involved with her on the same level that you are. This may come as an embarrassment for her and her dignity will be severely taxed. Her anger may even become unmanageable for a period of time. From what my mother tells me, Samuel Sinclair was bonkers over his daughter. Just from the things that Sambrea has told me about him, I know the feelings were mutual.

"Not only do I think she shouldn't hear it from you, I don't think she should hear it from any male figure. We're talking about infidelities here. To have the man she loves divulge sordid secrets about the man she worships would be her undoing. I'm a professional but a woman first. I'll do it in whatever fashion you suggest. But I think my telling her will preserve her dignity, considering the sensitive nature of the subject we're dealing with."

Craig was blown away by Lindsey's insight into the situation. What she'd said made perfect sense to him. He'd never be able to handle it from a woman's perspective, he was sure of that, no matter how sensitive he was.

"Now, that brings us to another point. You're going to have to decide if you want her to know that you possess this knowledge. I can't tell her that for you. Patient-doctor confidentiality," she reminded Craig.

Craig stood up again. "You're right. I'll let you handle it the way you see fit. Though I feel like a coward for letting you take the bull by the horns. However, I do have one request. I want to wait until Breeze is out of danger to tell her. Sam's already got enough on her plate."

Lindsey got to her feet as well. "I don't think we should wait. I'll explain myself. If for some reason, God forbid,

Breeze Sinclair doesn't survive this ordeal, Sambrea will never have closure. She's going to have a lot of questions, and two of the most important players aren't here to answer them—her biological parents. Through my mother's knowledge of this case, I'll be able to give her some solid answers. My mother has also agreed to talk with Sambrea should that be her desire."

She propped herself on the corner of the desk. "My mother thinks Miss Davis would want her to be there for Sambrea. She says Davina Davis was a wonderful person, with a great deal of humanity, and a sparkling sense of humor, much like the wonderful characteristics that Sambrea possesses. Except Davina fell in love with someone who belonged to someone else. If you don't mind my asking, how did you come by this extraordinary information?"

Craig snorted. "Straight from the horse's mouth, with Breeze Sinclair being the horse. I didn't much believe her, but it was confirmed by Samuel's best friend: Sambrea's godfather, Tyler Wilson. He also happens to have a sick relationship going with Breeze. He's no less than up to his neck in this thing. He suggested to me that he'd tell Sambrea the truth, but I totally rejected that idea. I didn't even respond to him when he made the suggestion. He's already betrayed her in the worst way. In fact, he was the one driving the car Davina was killed in. Plain and simple, the man's a perpetrator."

Lindsey gasped. "Oh, no, he definitely can't be the one to tell her. Do you think you can trust me with this one, Craig?"

"Explicitly."

Lindsey smiled. "Thank you for that. You can rest assured I'll have in place all the professional support systems that she might need to get her through this crisis."

Craig looked concerned. "Sambrea's heart is fragile. She may very well feel that it's broken beyond repair after she hears this story."

"With you there for her, she'll come around in time. But she's going to need you like she's never needed you before. She's going to wear what's left of her heart on her sleeve. But she might very well start by carrying around a chip on her shoulder the size of an iceberg. I hope you're strong on patience."

Craig's pager startled him when it went off. He hadn't believed in carrying one around until he'd learned that Sambrea might be pregnant. He thought that no one but the Creator, and now his wife, had a right to access him twenty-four/seven. It was his wife paging him because she was the only one with the number.

"Dr. Gooden, may I use your phone. It's Sambrea paging me."

"Be my guest. I'll give you some privacy. I have other patients to see. Just close the door behind you when you're finished."

Craig thanked Dr. Gooden as he dialed his home number. "I'll wait to hear from you."

"Have a good day, Craig. I know it's going to be tough on you, but I don't want you to come to her next appointment. If there are any complications, I'll know how to reach you."

Sighing heavily, he nodded.

"It's me, honey. Is everything okay?" he asked Sambrea.

"Breeze's doctor called a few minutes ago. They're ready to go ahead with the surgery. He feels that now is the time since she's somewhat stabilized. It's scheduled for tomorrow, early morning. I paged you to let you know I'm leaving for the hospital now. This is a good chance for me to spend some time with her before the surgery. I'll keep you informed of my movements."

Craig panicked. He didn't want her alone with Breeze, at least not until Dr. Gooden had a chance to tell her everything. Breeze seemed to have a thing for hurting Sambrea. Although his wife thought Breeze's illness had suddenly brought her to seek redemption for her evil soul, he didn't believe Breeze was capable of seeking atonement.

His sigh was audible. "I don't want you going there alone. I'm on my way to pick you up. It'll take me approximately twenty minutes to get there."

"Craig, that's not necessary. I'll be fine. Besides, I want to hear what Breeze has to tell me. If you're with me, she'll probably clam up. Neither of you tries to disguise the contempt you feel for each other. That can't be good for her in her condition. Let's get together at home for dinner. I've got a tri-tip roast marinating in the fridge."

Now what do I say? If he pressed the matter, she'd become suspicious of his motives, but he just had to give it one more try. "Sam, honey, just let me meet you there. I want to be there for you. I'll only go into her room long enough to say hello and to wish her well. Then I'll go and run some errands. You can page me when you're ready to leave the hospital to return home. Please don't say no to me."

She couldn't stop smiling. "You're too dang charming for words. You win. See you at the hospital."

"Sam, one more thing before we hang up."

"Yes, Craig." She readied herself for the truckload of charm to come her way.

"I love you, native girl."

As he walked into the hospital room, the look on Sambrea's face seemed to tell him he was too late to save her from her worst fate, Breeze Sinclair. With his heart pounding inside his chest like a jackhammer, he drew near the woman he loved more than anything in this world. With his eyes filled with adoration for Sambrea, he didn't seem to notice that Breeze wasn't in the room.

Jumping to her feet, she waited for his comforting arms to secure her in their strength. The trembling in her thighs came from the anticipation of the serenity that would come the moment he embraced her. The moment she made contact with his hard body, as though they had a will of their own, her arms went around his neck and her hands came together at his nape.

He kissed her softly on the lips. "What is it? What's happened, my love?"

She could barely breathe. Looking up into his eyes, she made the connection leading to the door of his soul. Without uttering a single word, she entered his spirit. "Dr. Wylie decided he couldn't wait until tomorrow. She'd started to lose ground again and he felt that they needed to go in now. Before she became so unstable that the surgical risks would become much higher."

Although concerned with the present situation, he felt relieved to know he'd possibly misinterpreted the reason for the look of devastation he'd seen on her lovely face.

"I'm sorry, Sam, sorry I wasn't here with you when the doctor told you what needed to be done. I'm sorry that you have to go through any of this. I . . ."

She touched his lips with the pads of her fingers. "Please don't, Craig. You're here now, and that's what matters most to me. I'll admit that this has been an extremely trying ordeal, but what I've gleaned from it has made me a better person, a better woman. There's not too much that I feel I can't face. I've really grown up within the past few months. Just a short time ago, when Daddy was no longer there to shelter me from the troubling places in the world, I had to learn how to fly on my own. Still, I'm not exactly flying solo. You've become the wind beneath my wings. Thank you." A sob came, followed by a hiccup.

Tears brimming in his eyes, he drew her quivering lower lip into his mouth. How did he ever manage to earn this beautiful creature's love and trust? *By showing and giving her unconditional love,* came the whispering voice from way down in the depths of his heart.

The seconds flew by as they just stood there staring into one another's eyes, thinking of the many reasons why they loved each other. The language their eyes conversed in was easy to translate.

"Oh, Sam, how would I ever get through a day without having you to hold? Everything I do, my work, my play— everything, has become so much easier for me because I know you'll be waiting for me at the end of the day."

She smiled at him. "That's such a good feeling, isn't it? I know what you're talking about because I feel the same way. No matter how tired I get, or how frustrated I become, all I have to do is remind myself that you'll be there at day's end. Presto chango, it's all made better. Could it be the magic in your eyes?"

"Not hardly. It's the magic in our love, in the belief that we can conquer anything as long as we do it together. Apart, we're just two ordinary people. Together, we're explosively extraordinary. Our love can take the world by storm. We personify the love man was created from in the beginning."

She suddenly felt sad. "Yeah, too bad everyone isn't as fortunate in love as we are. I can't imagine being married to someone when I know my heart belongs to another. How very sad that would be."

Her statement earned a curious look from him as he drew her in front of the window. Standing beside her, he wrapped his arms around her waist and rested his chin on her shoulder. Whether she knew it or not, she'd pinned the tail right on the donkey. Samuel had been married to Breeze, but his heart had belonged to Davina. *How sad, indeed.*

Had Breeze talked to Sambrea after all?

Turning her around to face him, he tilted her chin upward. "Did you get a chance to talk to Breeze before they took her to surgery?"

Briefly, she averted her eyes from his gaze, hoping to

hide the pain she felt at just the mention of Breeze's name. "We talked for a short time and then she grew very tired. Then the pre-op shot was administered. From then on she just more or less babbled. A few minutes later she was whisked away by two orderlies and a nurse. Dr. Wylie expects the surgery to take several hours, at the least. If complications should arise, he said it could take longer."

"Sam, do you want to go home and rest for a while? I'll bring you back in a couple of hours. Intermittently, we'll call the hospital from the house."

She frowned. "It sounds like a good idea, but maybe I should stay here just in case an emergency does arise. I'd never get over it if something happened to her and I wasn't here."

He shook his head from side to side. "No, we're not taking that trip. If anything happens to Breeze it'll happen no matter where you are. God is running this show and *His* will shall be done. This thing is out of the doctor's hands. For sure, it's out of ours. We have a baby to think about, Mrs. Caldwell. This is too stressful an atmosphere for an expectant mom. We can wait this out comfortably, in our home, where all is familiar. Shall we go home, Sam?"

She blew out a ragged breath. "There's that common sense wisdom of yours at work again. But I know this is not a contest with you. We can go but I'd like to go by the hospital chapel first. Okay?"

He smiled. "We can go by the chapel, but I want you to remember that He resides right here, inside the chapel in your heart." Gently, he pressed his palm against her chest. "It's open for prayer twenty-four hours a day, seven days a week. And He will hear you. He's a glorious, loving Father."

Hand-in-hand, they walked the few yards to the small chapel.

Reaching the altar, they both knelt down and closed their eyes. With their hands still entwined, Craig led out in prayer. Sincere in his supplications, he asked that Breeze be kept safe from hurt, harm, and danger, if it was the Father's holy will.

During Sambrea's prayer she asked that her mother's life be spared and that her and Craig's union be blessed until death do them part. She then said a few words of prayer for their unborn child.

While Sambrea relaxed in the shallow end of the pool, Craig was in the kitchen talking to Dr. Gooden. As he filled Lindsey in on the latest developments, he poured a frothy concoction of blended fruits into two tall pineapple, lime, and powdered sugar garnished glasses. With that done, he placed a red Maraschino cherry in each glass.

"I'm going to come over there, but I need you to disappear while I talk to Sambrea."

Craig sighed. "I don't think that now is a good time. She's a lot more relaxed than earlier, and I don't want to see her all tense again. I think we should wait until after the surgery."

"What if Breeze doesn't survive the surgery, Craig?"

"Then she doesn't survive. But if we tell Sam this now, and she gets the kind of call you're talking about, she'll go crazy with grief. She could lose two moms within the course of one day. No, I can't let that happen to her. I will put a call in to you the moment we get word on Breeze's condition. I'm sorry, but that's the way it has to be."

"Have it your way, Craig. I just hope this decision doesn't backfire on you. I'll be looking for your call."

"Thanks for your time and your concern, Dr. Gooden. I'll be in touch."

Holding a snack tray in his hand, Craig quietly observed Sambrea from the French doors leading out onto the patio. She appeared more restless than before he'd gone inside to fix them drinks and a snack. He could see the worry blazing in her eyes.

The royal blue polka dot bikini she wore hugged her body like a leather glove fits a hand. Her hair was pinned up on top of her head and his fingers itched to loosen the mountain of unruly curls and let them slip through his fingers. The knitted cover-up matching the swimsuit was thrown over the back of an umbrella-striped lawn chair. Resting beside her cover-up was his navy blue terrycloth robe.

Craig sat the tray down at the edge of the pool. Stripping himself of the trunks he wore, he slipped his nude body into the sun-warmed water, where he joined Sambrea on the lower step. Pulling her onto his lap, he removed her top. Bending his head, he drew a bronzed mound of flesh into his mouth.

She moaned with pleasure. "Oh, that feels so good." He brought his head up. "Don't stop," she pleaded. "I need to forget everything for just a few minutes. Touch me, Craig, before I go insane with longing." She breathed kisses against his lips.

Kneading her breasts with gentle hands, his tongue found refuge inside the warmth of her delicious mouth. As their kisses grew intense, he removed the bikini bottom. His hands left her aching breasts and came to rest between her creamy thighs.

Hungrily, his mouth took over hers, his tongue probing deeply into the sweet recesses of her mouth. Each time she purred it was like music to his ears. His hands rubbed and kneaded her body as he touched every inch of her flesh with dexterous fingers of fire. Pulsating against her burning flesh, his manhood was rock-hard.

Turning her around so that her back was to him, he ran his tongue up and down her spine, causing a spine-tingling reaction in her entire being. Gently, pressing his finger pads into the small of her back, he massaged her with erotic tenderness, until she called out his name with wild abandon.

"Craig," she cried out, "I need you inside of me. I can't take anymore. My body is on fire. I'm a human inferno."

Keeping her firmly planted on his lap, with her back facing him, he reached his long arms around her hips and glided his fingers in and out of her moist abode. Ripple after ripple of torrential ecstasy washed through her like a speeding projectile. The spasmodic trembling of her inner-self told him she'd been physically fulfilled. As he turned her around to face him, the hot tears running down her cheeks spoke to her emotional release.

She pressed her cheek into his. "What about you? I want you to feel the same wonderful feelings, too."

"I do feel them, sweetheart. As I've told you've before, you satisfy me in so many ways. I'm complete just being in your presence. Did I make you forget?"

"Forget what? My mind has been a complete blank from the moment you laid your divine hands on me."

He spread his arms out wide, tightening them around her waist. "May you always find the security of Fort Knox in these here arms. We may have come together under unusual circumstances, but I know we were meant to be. I think you know it, too." He captured her lips again.

Smiling mischievously, she wrapped her legs around his waist. "What happened to the no hanky-panky rule?"

He grinned widely. "I decided to give you a little bit of the panky. I'll give you all of my hanky in the near future." He looked down at his throbbing sex. They both burst into laughter, then jumped with a start as the sharp jangle of the phone bell pierced into the joy of their capricious moment.

"I'll get it." Craig reached for the portable phone.

Against her will, Sambrea immediately tensed up, fearing what was being said on the other end. She closed her eyes for a moment of silent prayer.

"Thank you. My wife and I will be right there."

TWENTY

In one fluid motion, she got out of the pool. "Was it the hospital? Is everything okay with my mother?" She was unable to stop the panic that suddenly assailed her calm.

He took her into his arms. "Calm down, Sam. Your mother is in the recovery room. The surgery is over, but Dr. Wylie wants to see you right away. I'm afraid that's all I was told by the nurse. Once we're dressed we can be on our way. You go on upstairs. I'll follow you in just a few minutes."

Picking up one of the glasses of fruit juice, she drank deeply from it. "Ah, that's better. My throat had gotten extremely dry. I'll be ready in a flash. I'm going to take a quick shower before I put my clothes back on. The heady but delicious scent of our lust clings to me still."

She laughed to quash the fear she felt inside.

Seated in the passenger seat of the black Jaguar, Sambrea looked over at her husband, who seemed to have a lot on his mind. She wanted to talk about Breeze but wasn't sure he'd want to hear what she had to say, at least not on the matter of not prosecuting her mother at all.

He sensed her need to talk. "You look like you want to say something, native girl. I'm all ears for you, baby. There's nothing you can't share with me."

Though doubting his comment, she decided to take a stab at it anyway. "It's about Breeze. I've decided not to bring charges against her."

She waited for his reaction. When none whatsoever came, she saw it as a sign to continue. "We'll never recover all that money and what good would it do to put a woman with a heart condition behind bars? Tyler's getting old and I don't want to see him spend the next twenty years or so locked away from the world. I don't think Samuel would've prosecuted them either."

Silence settled between them for several minutes. It seemed a lot longer to Sambrea. When he still offered no comment, Sambrea grew frustrated. She saw that her suggestion bothered him by the way he chewed on his lower lip.

"Is my husband giving me the silent treatment?"

He glanced over at her. "Not at all. I'm just wondering if you've made this decision based solely on Breeze's health. Putting her behind bars may not be the answer, but you're going to have to do something if you want to save face with your employees. I also think you're right about Raschad being smart enough with numbers to pull this off on his own. With Marsha involved in the payroll department as well, I think it's safe to say they acted alone in implementing Breeze and Tyler's elaborate scheme.

"This has been going on for a very long time. Now that you know it was going on before Samuel died, you don't have to hold yourself entirely responsible. At any rate, the investigative team hasn't been able to come up with a shred of evidence implicating anyone other than those we already know about. I have a few suggestions as to the punishment phase, but we should wait until later to discuss them. And, Sam, I'm behind you no matter what you decide. I won't fight you on it."

She reached over and stroked his thigh. "I think that's what I wanted to hear from you. I don't intend to let her go unpunished for her crimes, but I just don't think jail is the answer. I'm considering talking with the DA's office just to see if they might have any suggestions for me. Whatever we decide as punishment, I hope to implement it through the courts. That way, they'll have to abide by the conditions set forth."

Craig pulled into the hospital's underground parking garage. After cutting the engine, he exited the car and walked around to open Sambrea's door. "There'll be plenty of time to discuss these issues. They're not going away. For now let's just concentrate on seeing Breeze through her illness. Is that okay with you, Mrs. Caldwell?"

"I couldn't ask for more, Mr. Caldwell. Thanks."

Sambrea and Craig took the elevator up to the floor where Breeze's room was. Sambrea didn't know if Breeze would return to the same room, but she couldn't find that out until after she talked to the nurses assigned to the floor.

Reaching the nurses' station, Craig took a seat in the waiting room, while Sambrea approached the desk. Though she'd expressed a desire to handle things on her own, she wanted him standing nearby should she need his support.

Sambrea smiled at the duty nurse. "I'm here to inquire about Breeze Sinclair. I was also called at home by one of the nurses here. My husband was told that Dr. Wylie needed to speak with me right away."

The red-haired nurse smiled back. "Yes, Mrs. Caldwell, we've been expecting you. I will page Dr. Wylie immediately. You can have a seat in the waiting area if you'd like."

"Can you tell me anything about my mother's condition? I'm pretty anxious to know how her surgery went."

The nurse smiled sympathetically. "I'm afraid I'm not at liberty to discuss Mrs. Sinclair's condition. Unlike most doctors, Dr. Wylie likes to talk to the family personally. It's better that way. Sometimes information gets mixed up, especially when there's too many mouthpieces involved," she explained patiently.

Sambrea nodded her understanding. "I'll just go and join my husband in the waiting room." Before Sambrea reached the area where Craig waited, she heard someone call her name. Turning around, she saw Dr. Wylie, and walked back to meet him.

"Hello, Mrs. Caldwell," he greeted her politely. "Let's have a seat over there."

He pointed at several chairs lined against the far wall. Sambrea followed him to the chairs and he waited until she was seated before he joined her. "Is your husband here with you?"

Sambrea wrung her hands together. "Do I need him to be?"

He patted her hand. "Not necessarily. I just thought you might want him here. But I can see you're anxious to get this over with. First of all, the surgery went well. We encountered no complications. Your mother is still in the recovery room and should be brought back to her room fairly soon. It's going to be awhile before we know if the surgery was a success, but I feel confident. I know it's too soon to be talking about discharge plans, but your mother's going to need someone to look after her when she's released. I could send her to a rehab center, but she has no insurance and very little money. The reason I needed to talk with you is to see if you're willing to have her in your home once she's released from the hospital. She's going to need a lot of attention during her recovery."

Of all the things Sambrea had expected to hear, this wasn't one of them. In fact, she hadn't even thought about where Breeze would go once discharged. More than that, the subject had never crossed her mind. She was completely taken aback by the suggestion.

"Is there a problem, Mrs. Sinclair? You seem stunned."

Sambrea's laugh was weak. "It's not really a problem for me, but it might be for my husband. I'm embarrassed to admit this, but my husband and my mother don't get along very well. And that may very well be an understatement. Our family story is a complicated one, an unusual one. All I can say for now is that I have to discuss this with my husband before I can give you a definitive response."

"That's okay, Mrs. Caldwell. Mrs. Sinclair told me she wasn't your biological mother but that she raised you—and that she was the only mother you knew. I'm faced with this more than you can imagine. It's not that unusual of a story at all. You don't have to be embarrassed by it."

Sambrea was speechless. All she wanted to do was find a private spot and scream her head off, but she had to keep her composure in front of the doctor. So, Breeze was telling her the truth when they'd talked earlier. If Breeze had confided in the doctor, then surely there must be some truth to it. She'd thought it had been all the medication doing the talking. Therefore, she hadn't given any thought to what Breeze had said to her.

Sambrea felt her insides curl up in a tight ball.

"Mrs. Caldwell, are you okay? You're looking mighty pale."

Sambrea shook her head, as though she was trying to clear it. "I'm fine," she lied. "I'll get back to you on this matter as soon as possible. When do you think I'll be able to see my . . . mother?"

Dr. Wylie looked at his watch. "She's been in recovery for some time now. I expect the recovery room team to return her to the I.C.C.U. at any minute. However, it may be hours before she'll be coherent enough for you to converse with. I expect her to sleep quite a bit over the next twenty-four hours."

"Thank you. I'll wait around until she's back in the room. I'll get back to you on that other matter as soon as possible."

Dr. Wylie looked at Sambrea with concern. "Are you sure you're okay? You don't look as though you're feeling very well."

Sambrea released a shaky breath. "Just a little overwhelmed, that's all. I'm relieved to know everything went well. I've been dizzy with anticipation for hours. I'm glad it's all over."

"Okay, now. You call me if you have any other questions. Good evening, Mrs. Caldwell."

Feeling as though a volcano had erupted inside of her head, Sambrea rubbed her temples with her fingertips. Oh, God, she cried inwardly, what does this all mean? *If Breeze isn't my mother, does this mean that Samuel isn't my father? Am I an adopted child? This is absolutely crazy.* But maybe it wasn't so crazy, after all. How many times had she wondered if Breeze was her real mother? She certainly hadn't acted like one, except on a few rare occasions. Completely disoriented, Sambrea dropped back down into the chair she'd been seated in.

Craig found Sambrea in the same spot twenty minutes later.

He dropped to his knees in front of her. "What's going on? Why didn't you come back to me? Have you already talked to the doctor?"

Leaning forward, she dropped her head on his right shoulder. "I'm sorry, Craig. I've just been trying to pull it all together. I've seen the doctor and all is well. I'm feeling overwhelmed here. Breeze should be back in the room shortly. I'd like to wait so I can see how she's doing for myself."

Craig eyed her strangely. "That sounds like good news, Sam, but you don't look like a person who's just received good news. Is something else going on?"

Forming a steeple with her hands, she covered her nose and mouth. Entwining her fingers, she removed them from her face. "Breeze is going to need a place to recover when she leaves the hospital. The doctor has asked if we can take her in. She's going to need someone to look after her."

"And?"

"And what?" Her tone was riddled with impatience.

"What did you tell him?"

"That I'd have to discuss it with you first."

"What do you want to do, Sam?"

"What any compassionate human being would do."

"We'll set the wheels in motion. We can hire a live-in nurse. This isn't something I want you handling on your own. You don't need that kind of stress. It won't be good for either you or the baby. You can be there to oversee the day-to-day management of her health care, but you don't have to be directly involved. Breeze can occupy the suite of rooms downstairs. There's plenty of private space for both her and the nurse, but I rather expect the nurse to be in the same room with Breeze at the onset."

All she could do was to stare at this incredible human being she'd been fortunate enough to marry. Craig never ceased to amaze her. Closing her eyes for a brief moment of prayer, she thanked the heavenly Father for the wonderful, gracious man he'd placed in her life. "That easy for you, huh?"

"Any decision that speaks to your happiness and well-being is easy for me. I'm not without compassion, Sam. I'm sure you know that much about me. Breeze is your family and you're mine. Therefore, we have to take care of each other. We'll get through it. Together."

If only you knew, she mused. Knowing she wasn't ready to discuss what she'd just learned about Breeze she turned off the voices inside her head, voices prompting her to confide in the man she loved.

Not now. She didn't have the presence of mind to deal with the cruel hand she'd been dealt. She didn't know if she'd ever be able to deal with it.

The bitter bile arising in her throat tasted like soured

milk. She fought the nausea, unsuccessfully. "I need to go to the ladies' room," she told Craig. "I feel really sick right now."

Craig rested his hand under her elbow. "There's one right across the hall. Can you make it on your own, or do you need me to go with you?"

She smiled weakly. "Just help me get to the door. I can manage the rest."

Worry lines creased his forehead. "It seems that every time you get too much excitement the nausea rears its ugly head." He opened the door for her and held it until she disappeared inside.

Inside the stall, Sambrea emptied the contents of her stomach, sure that this bout of nausea had little to do with her pregnancy. The nervous stomach had come on her in the same instant Dr. Wylie had mentioned what Breeze had confided in him. She was surprised that she'd held back her sickness for this long.

Was that why Dr. Wiley had told her early on that she need not bother to donate blood for storage in the event Breeze might need a transfusion? She didn't know how the blood issue worked in conjunction with mother and child, but she was almost sure it was the father's blood that got passed on.

If Breeze wasn't her biological mother but Samuel was her natural father, then who was her real mother? That scenario would somehow imply that Samuel had to have been involved sexually with someone other than Breeze. Unless she was adopted. She had to be adopted.

The Samuel she knew and loved just wasn't capable of cheating on his wife.

When she didn't emerge from the bathroom after fifteen minutes had passed, Craig stormed inside. "Sambrea, which stall are you in?"

Flinging the stall door back, she stepped out. "I'm right here. I was about to come out."

Relieved to see that she was okay, he put his arm around her waist and guided her over to the sink. After turning on the hot water, he took her hands and placed them under the running water. Squirting a good amount of the pink liquid soap into his hand, he lathered it over hers. Taking several paper towels from the roll, he dried her hands thoroughly.

She couldn't stop the laughter streaming from within her. "You're spoiling me way too much, lover. A girl could get used to all this special treatment. You sure you want to continue in this vein? I could end up rotten through and through."

He kissed her forehead. "That's okay by me, as long as I keep you happy. They brought Breeze back to the room while you were in here. Are you ready to see her?"

Before Sambrea could respond, an elderly lady entered the restroom. She screeched when she saw Craig. "My word! What's the world coming to?"

Laughing, Sambrea and Craig apologized, darting for the exit.

Breeze's room was as quiet as death, devoid of light and cheer, when Sambrea and Craig came into the room. Pale as the white blanket that covered her, Breeze lay deathly still. Seeing her like that caused Sambrea's heart to cry out with torment. How a woman so beautiful, so lively, but so viciously mean and nasty, could be reduced to a state of nothingness in such a short span of time was a mystery to Sambrea.

The worn, torn sight of Breeze had her quivering inside, praying for the wisdom to understand how these things could happen. This woman had stolen the light right out of so many eyes—and now it seemed the light had been stripped from her own. *What goes around surely comes around*. Immediately, she hated herself for such a churlish thought. With bitter tears falling from her eyes, Sambrea turned around and headed for the door in haste.

Craig grabbed a hold of her arm before she reached the corridor. "What's going on, Sam? Talk to me about what you're feeling."

Lying her head against his chest, she breathed in deeply. "I don't like what I've been thinking. It's not right for me to think so badly of her when she's lying there with a broken, torn heart. But I can't help remembering all the horrendous things she did and said to my father and me over the years. I could easily hate her, but I really don't want to bring myself down to that level. I pray so hard over this, constantly, yet I still have black thoughts about this woman who never even pretended to give a damn about me. Craig, I've got to release these feelings or have them destroy me."

Guiding her over to the visiting area, he sat down and positioned her comfortably on his lap. "What you're feeling is natural. The fact that you keep praying about it says you don't want to or like to have these dark thoughts. Breeze may not deserve what's happening to her right now, but she has irrefutably earned your feelings of wrath. Give yourself some more time to sort this all out. Don't let her win again by returning your power back to her."

Tilting his head back, she kissed his throat. "Thanks. You're a Godsend. I beat myself up far too much. Sometimes I forget that I'm humanly flawed. Let's get this visit over. I'm glad we won't be able to talk with her right now."

Unable to figure out what had been going on with Sambrea over the past week, Craig felt compelled to keep a close eye on her. He didn't like what was happening to his wife. To make matters worse, she kept denying that anything was wrong. But he knew better. For the last few days she'd been listless, temperamental, weepy, and sensitive way beyond the norm.

Though he wanted to blame it on her pregnancy, something told him it was much more than that. *But what?* He sat on the bed watching Sambrea toss and turn fitfully in her sleep. It could possibly be the burden of knowing that Breeze would be coming into their home in just a couple of weeks, which was enough to make anyone who knew the maddening woman terribly apprehensive.

While he hadn't ruled out the possibility that Breeze had told Sambrea about her birth mother, he just couldn't imagine her not sharing it with him by now. She'd come to trust him as much as she professed to love him. He'd convinced himself that she wouldn't keep something so important a secret from him.

Opening her eyes slowly, surprised to see Craig at her side, her eyes widened with curiosity. "Hey," she said softly, "what's up? Was I talking in my sleep again?" She stretched her arms high above her head.

Smoothing her disheveled hair back, he kissed her lightly on the mouth. "I wish. It might help me figure out what's bothering you. You're not sleeping peacefully, native girl. You keep saying nothing is wrong, but your actions indicate otherwise. If you're sick, you need to let me take you to the doctor, Sam. I can't stand not knowing what's wrong with you."

She laid her head in his lap and looked up at him, something she hadn't done in the last couple of days. She'd been avoiding making direct eye contact with him because he had a way of reading her through her eyes. "I'm not sick, Craig. Haven't you ever been just plain old tired? So much has been going on. There's my pregnancy, Breeze's surgery, the problems at De La Brise, so on and so forth." *And there's that not-so-little problem of who I am and who my parents are.* "I'm physically and mentally exhausted."

"Come here, Sam. Climb up here in my lap. I want to

hold you for a minute or two. I need to make the connection with you that always reassures me."

Climbing into his lap, she drew her knees up toward his chest. "What would you say if I told you I needed to get away for a short time, before Breeze comes here to stay? Would you be terribly upset with me?"

Wearing a poker-face, he narrowed his eyes. "I would think you were running away again. When things get tough, you tend to take flight. I know Breeze coming here to stay in our home is weighing heavily on you. However, Sambrea, we've got a live-in nurse lined up. Her care is not going to fall on your shoulders. What would you say to us getting away together? We could go to Maui, or to one of the other islands. We could go on a cruise, or even take off to the mainland for a few days if you'd like."

Frowning, she wondered how she could tell him she needed to go alone without hurting him. "Craig, it's not that I don't want to go away with you, I just need some time to myself." Seeing the hurt in his eyes made her regret having brought the subject up. "Listen, I've got to go into the city today. I'll stop and pick up a few travel brochures from the travel agency we use for our business trips. Maybe we should get away together. If we're both going to go away, we'll do it after Breeze is settled in and on her way to a full recovery. I have several errands to run, but I promise we'll have a long talk about everything when I get back. Okay?"

"I've never known you to break a promise, so I'll be counting on you to keep this one. What would you like for dinner? It's my turn to be the chef tonight."

"Why don't we have something delivered, Chinese, Japanese, Italian, Hawaiian? You order it and I'll eat it. As long as it's nothing fishy."

"Are you sure about that? You've become such a finicky eater. What about an old-fashioned Southern fried chicken dinner. Mashed potatoes, thick brown gravy, fresh green beans. Fresh applesauce cooked in brown sugar and cinnamon will go great with my special buttermilk chicken recipe. I'll even make some homemade rolls."

"He bakes, too!" Sambrea looked down at her stomach. "All that grease can't be good for our baby. Let's stick with the fresh vegetables and fruit—and I'd love to try some fresh applesauce. What about grilled Teriyaki chicken, with slices of grilled pineapple, along with grilled zucchini marinated in balsamic vinegar and various herb seasonings?"

"That sounds way too healthy, Sam, but I also think it sounds delicious. I've never cooked Zucchini that way, but I can work with the other items."

"A friend of mine, Matt Hansen, taught me how to cook it. Leave the zucchini for me to take care of. I'll marinate it before I leave. It's a very good dish. I think you're going to love it."

He tousled her hair. "I'm sure I will. Are you ready to hit the shower?"

"As long as you're going to hit it with me."

He pulled her into his arms. "Welcome home, Sambrea. I've missed you terribly. I'm glad your spirit's back."

While kissing him full on the mouth, her hand wandered down the front of his briefs to show him that more than just her spirit had returned.

Three hours after leaving the sanctuary that she often found in her husband's arms, Sambrea drove the Mustang through the wrought iron cemetery gates. A gripping chill made her realize nothing but death surrounded her. Spotting the live flowers and trees scattered throughout the grounds, she felt a little less disconsolate. Somehow the natural beauty of the well-kept grounds shadowed all the depressing things she often associated with death.

On weak and rubbery legs, she got out of the car. Carrying two baskets of fresh flowers, she walked up the hill to where Samuel had been laid to rest. Just as Tyler had told her, when she'd met with him earlier, Davina's final resting-place was only a few yards away from Samuel's. Amazed by the reality of what Tyler had told her, her eyes filled with bewilderment.

Apparently Davina had been resting there when she'd attended Samuel's funeral, but she didn't know then what she knew now. According to Tyler, Samuel had purchased the burial plot closest to Davina's resting-place immediately after her death. If Samuel couldn't be near her in life, he wanted to be with her in death, Tyler had told her. Her father had also paid all the expenses for Davina's funeral. Breeze had forbidden him to go to the service, but Sambrea was delighted to learn that, in no uncertain terms, he'd stood up to her on at least one occasion.

Kneeling down in front of Samuel's headstone, tears flowed freely from her eyes. With shaking hands, she lovingly fingered the gold marbleized letters of his name. "Oh, Daddy," she sobbed, "you did find some happiness. Though I wished you'd been the one to tell me about my birth mother, I'm glad to know that somebody loved you the way you deserved to be loved. I hate to admit this, but I've found sweet comfort in the fact that Breeze isn't my biological mother. However, I freaked out when I thought you might not be my father.

"Because of Breeze's cruelty towards me, I've been so afraid I might turn out to be just like her. I'd never want to hurt my babies the way she's hurt you and me. It's easy for me to accept she's not my real mother because she's never really treated me like I was her daughter. However, it's been hard for me to accept that you were an unfaithful husband.

"After Tyler explained your affair with Davina, my mother, I understood it a lot better, but that still doesn't make it right. It violated your marriage vows. You see, Daddy, I'm married now—and you're going to be a grandfather. If a man as honorable as you could cheat on his wife, it makes me wonder if my husband will remain faithful to me. I love him so much, Daddy, and I couldn't bear the thought of him with another woman. He's been good to me, good for me.

"He's helped me to grow up. A few months ago this whole revelation would've put on a collision course with destruction. But Craig has shown me I'm strong where I thought I was weak. He's also done wonders with De La Brise. We're strong and solvent again because of his expertise. De La Brise is finally back in the game."

She wiped at her eyes with the heels of her hands. "I can only imagine what you must have gone through being married to one woman and in love with another. For whatever reason you decided not to be with the one you loved, I'm sorry you never got to feel the joy, joy way down in your heart on a permanent basis. I miss you, Daddy."

Taking all the blooms out of one basket, she placed them in the water-well located in front of the headstone.

Moving over to Davina's headstone, she bent her head down and kissed the engraved name. "Hi, I'm Sambrea, but I know you named me Samantha. Though I like the name you gave me, I'm so used to being called Sambrea that I can't imagine changing it. But I'm most comfortable with just plain old Sam. I don't know much about you, just what Tyler Wilson has told me, but I'm going to learn a lot more. Tyler told me you have some relatives on the mainland, a sister and two brothers. He's going to help me locate them so I can pay our family a visit. I'm sure they miss you as much as I miss what it might've been like to have you and Daddy raise me together."

Removing the flowers from the other basket, she arranged them before placing them in the water-well.

"I'm not going to stay long on this visit because my husband, your son-in-law, Craig, is probably a little crazy about now. He probably thinks I've run away again. You see, I used to run away from complicated stuff, but that's before I grew up. Before I found a wonderful man to love me unconditionally, before I learned I was worthy of love, before I learned how to fly. You know what? I wasn't even looking for someone when he happened into my life. Because of Samuel's horrific marriage, I had decided to live my life all by myself. Sad, huh? But no more sadness for me, the truth has set me free."

She kissed the engraved name again. "I'm going to go now, but I want to thank you for loving Samuel. Like me, I don't think he knew he deserved love either. That is, until you happened along. Much like what happened to me when my Craig came along and showed me what true love feels like. Good-bye, Mommy and Daddy. I love you both. May you always rest in peace."

As though her loved ones were responding to her, a pure white pigeon swooped down from nowhere, landing on Samuel's headstone. As if he had every right to be there, he hopped down from Samuel's headstone. With his head held high, he strutted over to Davina's grave. Flapping his marvelous wings, he fluttered in mid-air, then he was gone in the blink of an eye.

Unable to believe her eyes, Sambrea laughed through her tears. Standing there in wondrous awe, she chalked the divine experience up to possible wishful thinking on her part. Whatever it was, it left her with a peace that passed all understanding.

TWENTY-ONE

"Craig," Sambrea yelled as she went from room to room looking for her husband. "I'm home and I'm hungry."

Coming behind her, he wrapped his arms around her, startling her in the process. "So you are." He nuzzled her neck with his nose. "I'd started to worry about you. I expected you back long before now, Sam. Where have you been all this time? It's almost dark outside."

"It's a long story. I'll tell you all about it over dinner. Want to help me slip into something a little less encumbering?"

"I'd love to." Picking her up, he carried her upstairs to their bedroom.

In front of the dressing table mirror, he stood her on her feet. "Before I help you slip into something comfortable, let me help you slip out of these."

Sambrea watched him in the mirror as he made an art form out of peeling her top away. Kissing her neck, he slowly unbuttoned the top of her white linen slacks. Seeing and hearing his sharp intake of breath, she smiled as he inched his hand inside the waistband. As his hands came to a brief rest at the top of her silk panties, he stuck his thumbs in each side and slowly lowered the silk inch by inch down her trembling thighs. He didn't have to remove her bra simply because she wasn't wearing one.

Taking her by the hand, he drew her nude body into the

walk-in closet, where he selected a flowery, red and white full sarong, which he wrapped around her. He then tied it halter style around her neck. The design of the sarong afforded him a full view of one bronzed leg, along with the upper portion of her well-toned thigh.

"You're now dressed for dinner, Sam. For my dessert, I'm going to have the pleasure of removing this baby so I can feast off the sweetest pastry I've ever tasted." He smiled flirtatiously, wickedly. He held out his arm. "Dinner awaits us, darling."

As he kissed her all the way down the stairs, Sambrea didn't think they'd manage to make it through dinner if he kept enticing her appetite for his heated flesh. Taking her into his arms before stepping outdoors, Craig made her appetite more voracious as he kissed her passionately.

He led her out to the patio. "All for you, native girl."

Clapping her hands together with glee, much like a small child would do, Sambrea was in awe of the delightfully romantic table Craig had set out by the pool. A crystal vase filled with red and white Hibiscus flowers served as the centerpiece. Although it was nowhere near Valentine's day, Craig had chosen Valentine decorations as a symbol of his heartfelt love for his stunning wife. Graffiti cut into tiny red-foil hearts were scattered all over the stark-white linen tablecloth.

Breathless, Sambrea stood quietly, looking up into the midnight eyes of the man she adored. "You've made this so special for me!"

Nodding his head, Craig looked a little smug. "It is kind of special, isn't it?"

Plucking one of the flowers from the vase, he broke the stem off. After sticking it in her hair behind her ear, he secured it with the bobby pin he'd stuck in his pants pocket for that very reason. "I know how much you love to wear the Hibiscus flowers in your hair."

While inhaling the scent of the lipstick-red flower resting

behind her ear, he pulled out a chair for her to be seated. "It smells almost as good as you, Sam. I'm going to serve dinner now. Everything is all ready. I've just been waiting for you to come home." Before going back into the house, he pecked her cheek. He didn't trust himself to kiss her any deeper than that.

With all the love Craig has shown me how could I ever think he might just up and leave me for someone else? But if Samuel had been capable of infidelity, what made Craig any different? Her father had loved Breeze. She'd seen it with her very own eyes, yet he'd ended up betraying his wife. *Are all men inherently unfaithful?* Just entertaining the thought of Craig cheating on her made her scared stiff.

Craig pushed a serving cart over to the table. Unloading the serving dishes one by one, he placed them on the table. After taking the seat next to Sambrea, without comment, he bowed his head and said the blessing.

Sambrea bit into a Teriyaki chicken breast. "Hmm, this is heavenly. It's so tender." She held the chicken up to his mouth for him to taste a bite of hers. "It's great, isn't it?"

Licking his lips, he nodded. "It *is* good. I'm eager to taste your zucchini."

Enjoying the soft Hawaiian music floating from the outdoor speakers, Sambrea and Craig eagerly feasted off the delectable meal. When the tempo of the music picked up, Sambrea stayed seated but moved her body to the tune of the faster beat.

Biting into the grilled zucchini, Craig closed his eyes expressively. "You were right, I do love this. How did you learn to cook it?"

She wiped her mouth on a red linen napkin. "I told you earlier. Matt, a friend of mine, taught me. Tai also has taught me how to fix vegetables all sorts of ways."

Craig snapped his fingers. "I remember that now, but I forgot to tell you that Tai called. She's excited about the baby. She wanted to know how you were doing. She told me something interesting about you, something I didn't know."

Sambrea laughed out loud. "News update, Craig. There's a lot you don't know about me. However, was it good or bad?"

"It all depends."

"On what?"

"How you feel about it. I hear you do a mean, seductive hula dance. Since you're dressed like a hula girl, don't you want to give me a private show while we're having this fantastic island interlude?"

"Honey, we've being having an island interlude since the night you walked into my life."

Without needing anymore prompting, Sambrea got up from her seat and walked over to the waterfall, where the colored lights filtered softly through the water. Craig had put the flower on the side single women used to boast their availability, so she changed it to the side married women wore theirs on. Moving her hands in tune to the music, swaying her hips gently, she gave herself up to the rhythm of the melody entering her soul.

Completely under her spell, Craig watched Sambrea bewitch him with one of the most romantically seductive hula dances he'd ever seen. She was darn good at it. While Hawaiian women danced the hula it was the hands that were responsible for weaving the magic into the fabric of the story.

With her eyes growing bright with moisture, she continued to dance. She thought of the love that Samuel must have felt for Davina to risk his marriage and reputation for her. Imagining how he must've felt at losing his love in a tragic car accident only a few short weeks after she'd become mother to his only offspring, she broke down and cried like an abandoned, wounded child. Lowering herself to the ground, she balled her body into the fetal position.

Her anguished cries rent the air with loud groaning and desperate moaning.

With his brows furrowing with concern, Craig grabbed the portable phone. Thinking she had suddenly taken ill, he made it to his wife's side and knelt down beside her. "I'm going to call an ambulance, Sam. Hold on, sweetheart."

She reached her hand out to him. "That's not necessary. I'm not physically ill. I'm just plain heartsick. Hold me, Craig. Hold me until the pain in me subsides."

Sitting down beside her, he pulled her onto his lap and cradled her in his arms while she sobbed her heart out. She clutched at Craig as if he was her lifeline. He didn't know what had caused her unexpected emotional eruption, but it was serious. He'd heard Sambrea cry, had seen her tears, but never had he heard cries from her that sounded so desperate, so forlorn and bitter.

Without looking up at him, she reached up and touched his face. "I talked to my mother today at the cemetery. She was right there with my father. I feel so bad for them . . ."

Looking alarmed, Craig held her away from him. "What are you saying, Sam? What's this about a cemetery? Breeze is still in the hospital, isn't she?"

Unable to look him in the eye, she pressed her head back against his chest. "I'm talking about my birth mother, Davina Davis. The woman my father had an illicit affair with. The same woman my father fell madly in love with and had a child with."

Oh, God, she knows. Who told her? He prayed that it hadn't come from Breeze, knowing she would've enjoyed inflicting undue pain on his precious wife.

He saw no use in pretending shock at her statements. "I'm glad you finally know the truth, Sam. I've wanted to tell you myself, but I was convinced not to. Can you forgive me?"

With her ears still roaring, she finally looked up at him. "There's nothing to forgive. It was never your place to tell me. My father should've told me this long ago, long before he died."

"How did you find out, Sam?"

"I got some of it from Breeze. I thought it was the drugs talking, that is, until Dr. Wylie made mention of Breeze not being my biological parent. I can't tell you how stunned I was to hear that from him, of all people. But I managed to keep my composure. I'm sure that he didn't know he was telling me something I'd never heard before. I went to see Tyler today and he told me everything that he knew. But he didn't tell me that you knew. He must have been trying to protect you."

Trying to soothe her shaking limbs, Craig rocked her back and forth in his arms. "Maybe so. I talked to him about the authenticity of the information Breeze had given me. I don't have to tell you that I didn't believe a word of anything she'd said. She was trying to blackmail me, which made her capable of anything. She knew I loved you and I'd protect you at any cost. She was right but wrong to assume I'd let her get away with it. Did you see her today?"

Fresh tears pooled in Sambrea's eyes. "I did. It looks like we're going to have to put our vacation on hold. She's doing so well that Dr. Wylie wants to discharge her in less than a couple of weeks from now. So we've got to get busy and push all of our arrangements up. I just hope the nurse can come here that soon."

He looked at her in amazement. "You know that Breeze is not your mother and you still want to bring her here to live?"

She kissed him softly on the mouth. "I'm a compassionate woman, Craig Caldwell. I would do this if she were a perfect stranger if it were asked of me. I'm not accountable for her actions, only mine. Isn't that what you've been trying so hard to teach me? Isn't compassion something that you've come to expect of me?"

He hugged her fiercely. "Yes, yes. You've been a great

student, Mrs. Caldwell. And you've been a remarkable teacher. I've learned a lot from you as well. Your heart is a forgiving one and your compassion runs deep. Don't ever change, my precious sea nymph."

"Craig, I'm sorry we're not going to do all that dating we've talked about. With Breeze coming home much sooner than we expected, we're going to have to put our private lives on hold. Christmas is just around the corner, so maybe we can get away during the holidays. That is, if all goes well with my pregnancy."

He chucked her under the chin. "Everything is going to be just fine and we're not going to put everything on hold. We're going to have that special date day after tomorrow. I'm going to stay here with you for now, but I'm going to go to the hotel sometime soon. After our date, I'll be coming home for good. Do we have a plan, Mrs. Caldwell?"

"We have a plan. Should we discuss how we're going to handle the crimes Breeze and Tyler committed?"

"That will all fall into place in time. Right now we have other serious matters to discuss. Like the dessert I spoke of having earlier."

They both fell into laughter.

Wearing a pair of denim jeans and a simple white shell, Sambrea was looking down on Breeze. She saw that Breeze was still very pale, practically lifeless, even though five days had passed since her surgery.

As Breeze's eyes slowly fluttered open, Sambrea was assailed by the urge to run out the door again. Now that she had knowledge of their true relationship, this woman frightened her even more. With no blood between them, no real affection to speak of, Sambrea saw Breeze as more dangerous to her now than ever before. Knowing Craig was right outside the room gave her the courage to remain.

With her lips dry and cracked, Breeze managed a weak

smile. She pointed toward the glass of water on the bedside table. Understanding her gesture, Sambrea lifted the glass and positioned the straw between Breeze's lips for her to drink. After a few seconds of sipping water through the straw, Breeze pushed the glass aside and Sambrea returned it to the table.

Smoothing Breeze's hair with her palms, Sambrea smiled. "How are you feeling? You're certainly looking a little better today."

Breeze blinked hard. "I'm much better," she rasped painfully.

Sambrea scowled lightly. "Maybe you shouldn't try to talk. It looks like it hurts to do so. However, I need you to listen to what I have to say."

Hoping to quell her emotional agony, Sambrea took a deep breath. "According to Dr. Wylie, you're going to be discharged fairly soon. I've been asked to assist in the discharge planning. In view of your current dire circumstances, you're going to need a place to stay until you recover fully. Craig and I have made plans to bring you home with us since we have plenty of room. For your comfort, we've made arrangements for you to have a live-in nurse."

Extremely agitated at Sambrea's suggestions, Breeze looked horrified. Flailing her arms about wildly, she hit the glass and the water pitcher and knocked them over. Water splashed all over Sambrea's jeans and top, causing her to gasp loudly. The crashing sound of glass brought Craig running into the room.

Looking as if she could kill death, Breeze sat straight up. "I don't want to live with you. It will never work. I can't live with you. I won't live with you. You look too much like that tramp of a woman that gave birth to you. Davina Davis was a tramp. She stole my husband."

Hurt beyond reason, beyond definition, Sambrea stood stock-still, staring down at the pale, sickly woman, a woman who should've been weak as hell. Yet she'd somehow found the strength to plunge serrated daggers into the dead center of Sambrea's fragile heart.

Craig hated the cutting words Breeze had spewed out at his wife. The agony he saw in Sambrea's eyes was almost too much for him to bear. "What's happened, Sambrea? What's going on in here? Are you okay?" Craig wiped off her clothes with the clean towel he'd picked up from a nearby chair.

Before Sambrea could respond to her husband, Tyler popped inside the room. Looking unhappy, seemingly upset, he carried a large envelope in his hand.

Deeply saddened by Breeze's sudden outburst, Sambrea nodded her greeting to Tyler. "Everything is fine, Craig. Breeze is just having a nasty temper tantrum, which indicates to me she's feeling a lot better much sooner than I would've ever expected. In fact, it appears she's feeling a hell of a lot better. She doesn't want to come live with us while she recovers."

Forgetting Breeze's recent surgery woes, Craig snorted. "As if she somehow has a host of other attractive choices. Perhaps she does. Where will you go, Breeze? Back to the south of France? More to the point, who's going to provide you with the type of specialty care you're going to need? How are you going to pay for those special services?"

Sambrea placed a soothing hand on Craig's arm. "Not now, Craig. She's not feeling *that* good. Let's not make this situation any worse than it already is. Enough has been said for now."

"She felt good enough to label people with malicious and unattractive names." He shoved a hand through his hair. "Sorry, Sam. Let's get out of here. You don't have to take this insensitive woman's insults ever again. Obviously she's found a way to fend for herself."

Tyler stepped forward. "Breeze, I don't see how you can turn their generous offer down, unless, of course, you do have alternative plans. Or perhaps you have it all worked out since you've stockpiled quite a handsome sum of money over the past several years."

Turning to Sambrea, Tyler handed her the large envelope. "I think you'll find the contents of this packet very interesting."

Not knowing what Tyler had handed Sambrea, looking a tad bit uncomfortable, Breeze peered at the mystery envelope as if it was a hangman's noose. If Tyler's remarks were any indication as to what was in the envelope, it would mean a noose around her neck.

Sambrea looked puzzled. "What is this, Tyler?"

"Take your husband somewhere quiet so you can read the documents inside. It's not going to be very pleasant for you, so brace yourself. Craig, get your pregnant wife out of this nauseous, aggravating atmosphere. Don't worry, Breeze isn't going anywhere for a long time to come, no matter how well she may seem. She also has a lot of explaining to do for me."

Taking the packet from Sambrea's hand, Craig led her from the room and out into the corridor. Guiding her to the waiting area, they sat down next to each other. After opening the mysterious envelope, Craig removed its contents.

For several minutes he gave each document his undivided attention. Though eager to know what the documents were all about, she patiently waited for Craig to finish his reading.

Looking up from the papers, Craig turned to Sambrea. "Most of these are bank statements, which are of great interest to us. But the list of what's in the safety deposit boxes is unbelievably enlightening. It appears Breeze has had tons of money all along—and jewelry."

Taking some of the papers from Craig's hand, Sambrea looked them over. Understanding very little of what these papers actually meant, Sambrea looked perplexed. "What does this mean for us, Craig?"

"It's probably your money you're looking at, Sam. According to the dates on those bank statements, she's been hoarding money even before she disappeared from here. It looks as though she was practically robbing Samuel blind while still sleeping in the same bed with him."

"That surely didn't happen too often. Feigning illness, Breeze slept in one of the guestrooms on many occasions. There were seven bedrooms and five baths in our house."

"What happened to the house, Sam?"

"Dad sold it just before his death. I was already living in the bungalow. He thought there was way too much room in that house for only one person, so he moved into a suite of rooms at a hotel close to the offices. Besides, the house was full of bad memories for him."

Eyeing Sambrea strangely, he touched her forehead. "Are you okay?"

"I'm fine. Why do you ask?"

"A lot of stuff has gone down in the last few minutes, but you're as cool as a cucumber. I expected you to be terribly upset over the things Breeze said to you. I'm proud of the way you've handled Breeze's last nasty episode."

Sambrea sighed heavily. "You wouldn't be so proud if you knew what went on inside of me during her tantrum. In fact, you would've been worried sick about the baby and me. For a minute there I wanted to curl up and die. Then I thought about all the wonderful things I had to live for. You and our unborn child were at the top of the list. I couldn't let either of you down. You both mean too much to me. I survived her hateful intentions for sixteen years. I suspect I can live through another sixteen. Now, back to these papers. What do we really have here?"

Craig shook his head. "Just lot and lots of money on paper. Getting our hands on it is going to be the problem. What I find so strange is that Tyler's name is on these accounts along with Breeze's, yet he acted as if he didn't know about the money until now. I guess we'll have to wait for him to fill us in on the details. I don't see any recent withdrawal activity, which may mean that all this money is still deposited in these accounts. But we can't rule out recent electronic transfers. However, nobody gets rid of this amount of money that quickly. Let's go and see if Tyler is still in with Breeze."

Trembling slightly, Sambrea's brow creased with worry. "I don't think I can go back in there right now. I don't like the way I feel when I'm around Breeze. I become too anxiety-ridden, which can't be good for the baby. Perhaps you could have Tyler come out here. It would be much easier for us to talk candidly outside of Breeze's presence."

He kissed the end of her nose. "I agree with you whole-heartedly. You gonna be okay until I get back?"

"If you promise not to take too long. I sometimes feel so lost without you. I don't like that feeling either. Before you rescued me, I'd been feeling that way since Daddy died."

"In that case, I'm not going to leave your side." Taking out his cell phone, he called the hospital switchboard and asked them to put him through to the nurse's station responsible for Breeze's care.

In his most charming voice, he asked the answering nurse to deliver a message to Tyler, who was in visiting with Mrs. Sinclair. "Tell him he's needed in the waiting lounge around the corner from the patient's room. Please use discretion so we don't upset Mrs. Sinclair."

Sambrea smiled. "You're very clever, Mr. Caldwell. I would've never thought to do that."

"I remember some very clever things you've done that I would've never even thought of doing. Does the name *Neptune* bring to mind one of your brutally clever stunts, darling?"

Sambrea laughed heartily. "That wasn't very clever. It was absolute cruelty. I'll never forget the look on the restaurant manager's face. I think he really wanted to arrest us. I'm glad you were able to bail us out." Remembering the incident brought them both to laughter.

Looking concerned, Tyler approached the laughing couple. "I wish I could find something to laugh about. That woman in there is damn near impossible. I don't know how I got myself into this mess with her."

"Greed!" Craig stated, as a matter of fact.

Looking shocked, Sambrea swiped her fingertips across Craig's lips. "Honey, please don't. We need Tyler to help us figure this all out. We can't do that by offending him."

Wearily, Tyler dropped down in a chair. "Your husband is right, Sambrea. Greed is at the root of all of this evil Breeze and I have been involved in. What do you need from me?"

Craig palmed Tyler's shoulder. "I apologize for that remark. It wasn't necessary, though nonetheless true. I work hard at being nonjudgmental, but I've failed miserably throughout this case. As a spiritually driven man, I've learned a lot more about forgiveness from my wife. I hope I can forgive and be forgiven in this situation."

"There's nothing to forgive. You and Sambrea are squarely within your rights. I often ask myself what I'd do if the shoe were on the other foot. I've yet to come up with an answer. You two had something in mind when you summoned me to the area. Would you like to get on with what it is you wanted?"

Craig cleared his throat. "We'd like to be enlightened regarding these documents you handed Sambrea. Think you're ready to do that for us?"

Looking anguished, Tyler wrung his hands together. "It seems that Breeze has made a fool of all of us. Those bank statements represent all the money she's hoarded over the years. She's been telling me she's broke for years now. Claims to have incurred a lot of serious debts while she was with Samuel."

With her eyes directly on Tyler, Sambrea leaned forward

in her seat. "This doesn't make sense to me. With so much money, why come here looking for more?"

"Why indeed?" Tyler remarked. "I think Craig summed it up quite accurately. Breeze has never been satisfied with a little or a lot of anything. Sambrea, I'm sure you know that much about her from living in the same house with her for sixteen years. As sick as this may sound, I personally think she's still trying to get back at Samuel for what she believes he did to her. Sambrea, do you remember the large sum of money Samuel lost when the European deal fell through?"

"I do. But what does that have to do with anything?"

"Breeze was behind the deal. She orchestrated the entire setup. Samuel never knew she was behind the European Corporation that practically led him to bankruptcy court."

Outwardly distraught, Sambrea gasped loudly. "How long have you known about this?"

"I'd love to hear the answer to that one, Tyler," Craig interjected.

Tyler blew out a ragged breath. "Just a few days ago. After I got these papers, I started doing a little investigating on my own. Breeze opened these accounts in both our names, but I never knew about them. She's somehow managed to forge my name and use my social security number to open these other accounts. It appears that she had all the accounts transferred to one bank, a bank where she had quite a bit of clout with the manager. The problem came when the bank changed management. When she tried to withdraw large sums of money, the new bank manager insisted on adhering to the bank's very old policy, which the original bank manager had been in serious violation of. Your team didn't discover the accounts because of all the movement."

"What was the policy?" Sambrea inquired.

"In some European banks, when an account has joint owners and large sums of money needed to be withdrawn, the joint owner has to sign the withdrawal slip as well. Since I didn't know about the accounts and she never wanted me to know of them, she found herself in a real dilemma. Realizing she could no longer move large sums of money around the way she wanted to, she came here looking for more to start an individual account with only her name on it. She began using my social security number because she was presumed dead. Nine years had passed since she disappeared. She probably thought using her own was too risky."

Standing now, Sambrea paced back in forth in front of Tyler and Craig. "You mentioned the safety deposit box earlier. What's in it?"

Tyler pounded his right thigh with a closed fist. "The most important is the account number to your trust fund. I don't know why she has it, or how she got a hold of it, but she did. I remember Samuel moving your trust account to another bank not long after she disappeared.

"Sambrea, I'm afraid Breeze intended to completely wipe you out financially. She was probably going to have Raschad go to work on your trust fund next. She already had him working on the problem she'd encountered with the bank. Remember, he's an accounting and computer whiz. Perhaps she figured you wouldn't touch your trust fund until De La Brise was on its last leg. Then, when you did try to use it, there'd be nothing left of it. Before you ask, yes, she hated Samuel and Davina that much. And you look just like your mother."

"This sounds like a lot of speculation on your part, Tyler. What solid proof do you have, if any?" Craig asked.

"Those papers I gave you will prove a lot of what I've said. The rest I got from Raschad Ali, but he'll never testify in court. I was lucky to track him down before he left the country. Scared of being prosecuted for embezzlement, he's going back to the Middle East to live. Figure that one out.

I would've thought that prison in the U.S. had to be better than going back there."

Beyond irritated, Craig got to his feet. He shoved his hands in his pockets. "You're sitting here talking about this grave situation like it's no big deal. These are serious crimes we're discussing here. Millions of dollars are involved in this heist you and Breeze illegally contrived. We all know what the problem is here, but now we have to figure out the solution. If you're not going to be a part of the solution, you're still a major part of the problem. What do you suggest we do in light of this new information you've given us?"

"I want you to give me a few days to work on Breeze. She needs to get more strength back before I hit her with both barrels. I'm going to ask her to return all the money she has stockpiled, including the interest, which adds up to a lot of money. It appears she can't do anything with it without my signature, and I will remain adamantly against giving it to her. Sambrea, you and Craig are going to have to give me something to offer her in return. Full immunity from prosecution is what I have in mind in exchange for the return of monies we've obtained illegally. I take full responsibility for both our actions. If prosecution is the only thing that will satisfy you, I'm your man. I'll take the rap for the entire scheme. I just don't want to see Breeze hurt anymore."

"See Breeze hurt?" Craig bristled. "Doesn't anyone think about what this has done to my wife? The woman you're so concerned about protecting just got through attacking my wife with a vengeance. Sambrea is not responsible for Davina and Samuel's indiscretions. Why is it that she's the only one paying the price for something that happened before she was ever born?"

Taking her husband's hand, Sambrea squeezed it gently. "Tyler, let us think about your suggestions. The tensions are mounting here—and that won't help any of us get through this ever-growing nightmare."

"I agree, Sambrea. One more thing before we end this. Are you still willing to take Breeze into your home until she recovers? She's going to need someone, Sam. I can't think of a single person other than you who would even consider having her in their home. I've already talked to Nina Chambers, Lawrence's mother—Breeze's good friend. But she seems to want nothing to do with any of this. She hates what Breeze has done to you and Samuel. Nina was the only true friend Breeze ever had, but she's managed to ruin that relationship as well."

"Is it any wonder? You sound surprised about her friend's reaction. Look in the dictionary under *betrayal* and you'll find Breeze's picture there." Craig looked to Sambrea. "Do you still want that devious woman in our house after what you've just learned?"

Sambrea scratched her head, looking overwhelmed. "The offer I made to Breeze still stands, as far as I'm concerned, Craig. But are you still willing to have her there? It's your house, too. Having her there will affect both of us."

Taking Sambrea into his arms, he kissed her nose and chin. "I never go back on my word, Sambrea, no matter how much I would like to in this instance. But I can't talk the talk without walking the walk. The spiritual side of me tells me I must do this for all our sake. God has a plan and I won't know what it is if I don't follow his instructions. However, she's already said she won't come to live with us. So how do you propose to make Breeze do something she's not willing to do?"

Tyler cleared his throat. "I've already convinced her to accept your offer. Now I have to work on getting her to see the light where the money is concerned. Breeze is not half as bad as you all seem to think she is. This is a woman who's been badly abused and hurt. She thought Samuel would love her forever. She's never gotten over losing him to another woman. It kills her inside to know how much he loved Davina."

Sambrea began to tremble. "Are you saying my Dad just up and had an affair on Breeze? I know there's no excuse for anyone to cheat on a spouse, but I don't think Samuel was that kind of man. Something must have prompted him to behave in this manner. If he was getting everything he needed from Breeze, why did he turn to my mother?"

"He *wasn't* getting what he needed from Breeze most, her respect. She didn't treat him with the kind of respect a man needs from the woman he marries. She respected him until she got him down the aisle, but that's where it ended. Samuel somehow found out that Breeze had purposely set out to get him to marry her, only for his money."

Tyler's eyes filled with water. "However, Breeze finally realized what a good man she'd snared, and she later fell head over hills in love with him. But it was much too late. Deeply hurt by what he'd learned, Samuel had turned to Davina for comfort. One thing led to another. Davina always had a thing for Samuel, from the day she came to work for him. But she never set out to break up his marriage. She was there for Samuel just as a caring friend. Fate stepped in and they fell madly in love. Only death could've torn them apart—and did, but only for a short time."

Sambrea's heart was breaking for her parents. She wished they could've been together other than in death. While she felt bad for Breeze, she didn't think she deserved any of the things that Breeze had taken out on her simply because she could no longer hurt Samuel and Davina.

"It seems as though everyone involved in this has been hurt in some way, but Sambrea will no longer be a victim of Breeze's cruel intentions. I can assure you of that. My wife and I will discuss how we're going to handle this situation and get back to you in a couple of days."

"I can't ask for more than that. Thank you both for even

taking my suggestions into consideration. You two have a good evening. I'll look to hear from you soon."

Sambrea practically cringed as Tyler kissed her cheek. She felt instant sorrow for reacting that way to his affection. Deep down inside she knew he'd been badly used, just like everyone else in Breeze's life. "Good evening, Tyler. Craig and I will be in touch soon."

Burrowing her head into Craig's comforting chest, she began to sob. "Let's go home now so I can rest. I've had more than enough of this situation for one day. I'm sure you've had your fill of all this drama as well."

"Baby, I can't begin to tell you how much I've had of this weird scenario. We'll deal with all of it in due time, but not tonight. We're going to get into bed and just hold one another until we fall asleep wrapped up in one another's arms. How does that sound to you, native girl?"

"Like a little touch of heaven!"

TWENTY-TWO

Sambrea knew exactly which dress she was going to wear for her date with Craig. The same dress he'd shown a special interest in when she'd moved her things into the pagoda house. As she'd handed it over to him to hang in the closet, Craig had gotten off a loud wolf-whistle. She recalled him saying that he couldn't wait to see her in it.

Wrapped in a plush velour bathrobe, Sambrea rushed from the bathroom to the bedroom closet. She pulled out the spicy, full of attitude, fire-engine-red knit dress that boasted a mandarin style collar and mock wrap-around skirt, with a right, thigh-high slit. The sleek red banded pumps she'd chosen had a strappy, nubuck upper with open toes and a two-inch heel.

Deciding to try the dramatically sexy, wavy hairstyle she'd recently seen in a hair fashion magazine, Sambrea took the lid off the jar of ultra-light styling gel. Dipping her fingers into the gel, she evenly distributed it through the crown of her hair, using just enough gel to give it a soft wave pattern. Setting the blow dryer on low heat, she lightly dried the waves and sprayed all of her hair with an oil-free sheen.

Done with her hair, and satisfied with the seductive, sophisticated style, Sambrea retrieved from her jewelry box a pair of sassy triangle-shaped earrings cut from Austrian crystal. Pulling on her pantyhose with extreme care, she was mindful of her ability to go through several pair of silk hose before ever leaving the house. Her fingernails usually caused the snags.

Looking stunning, softly seductive in her spicy red dress, Sambrea walked to the top of the stairs. She peered down on the beautifully decorated spaces below. The rooms were all so Craig. She suddenly felt a brief pang of sadness. He should be here in the space he'd created for himself and the woman he'd love enough to make his wife, not in some hotel suite, no matter how lavish the rooms might be. Even if it had been only for the day.

Descending the stairs, Sambrea walked slowly toward the music room. As she stepped into the room, Craig's creative energy surrounded her. This was his own special place, a place where he discarded the worries of the day, where he lost himself in the sweetness and peacefulness of the music he wrote and played.

Sitting at the piano stool, she lifted the cover. Freeing the keys, she fingered the ivories with gentleness, causing them to tinkle lightly. Oh, if only she could play, she'd score a most beautiful song for her husband, a song that would reach into the core of his very being and illuminate his heart and soul for the entire world to see.

She smiled when she noticed the hand written sheet music to *"SAMBREA"* still on the music stand. Had he played it before he'd left for Africa? Had his midnight eyes misted when he sang it? Had his voice been full of fiery passion, the same way it had been when he'd sung it to her for the first time?

The doorbell rang, dragging her from the sweet revelry she'd fallen a willing victim to. With her heart acutely aware of who stood on the other side of the door, a huge smile lit up her sand-and-sable eyes.

Outside the door, waiting for Sambrea to come and rescue him from the bout of loneliness he'd suffered through the entire day, Craig put away the key he'd almost used. It was second nature to him, since this was his home, too. But not tonight! This was the home of his date, he reminded himself: he had a date with a goddess. Knowing his voracious appetite for something so delicious had nothing at all to do with food, he grinned widely.

After opening the door, Sambrea just stood there smiling, her eyes heatedly traveling the length of her flawlessly suited marble statue. The autumn-brown double-breasted suit jacket, exuding class, matched the neatly, impeccably creased pants. The chocolate-brown silk shirt stroked his muscled strength. In various shades of autumn, his silk tie offset the darker shades of brown.

Drinking in the beauty of the red dress, Craig grinned like a shy schoolboy. "You remembered! However, that dress could get you into real hot water tonight, Sam. But I've got a feeling that I'm the one that's going to need water to put out the fire you're igniting under my skin. You look fabulous, Sambrea!"

Sambrea touched his face tenderly. "It's not fire-engine-red for nothing, Mr. Caldwell. If there are any fires to be put out, I'll be the one to douse them. But not before I set your entire body and soul ablaze!"

Her wiped his brow in jest. "Okay, enough of that kind of talk. I don't need to sweat anymore than I already am." His palm swept downward toward his car. "Your chariot awaits, Mrs. Caldwell, uh, that is, Miss Sinclair for now. She's polished and ready to sweep us into another dimension. Shall we get our first date started, beautiful? Our island interlude?"

"Absolutely!" Stepping back inside the door, Sambrea removed her wrap from the banister post. She held it out for Craig to take. After securing the doors, he held his arm out. She slid hers into his and squeezed it affectionately.

Once he saw Sambrea seated in the car, he deposited himself into the driver's seat. Leaning across the seat, he stole a quick kiss from the beauty beside him. After starting the engine, he drove down the circular driveway.

Inside the Lalani Towers Suites, Craig and Sambrea entered the elevators and took the car up to the penthouse. Sambrea's curiosity had gotten the best of her, but her desire for being surprised kept her from asking questions of Craig. He probably wouldn't have given her a clue anyway, she guessed.

At the door of the penthouse Craig possessively slipped an arm around Sambrea's waist. "This is an obligation I had to keep, but we won't be here long. I promise."

A slender, mid-twenties female with ivory-beige skin smiled broadly as she laid eyes on Craig. She frowned when she noticed Sambrea on his arm. "Hello, darling," Isa Tanner crooned. "Sooo glad you could make it!"

"Hello, Isa. You're looking quite well." Craig pulled Sambrea closer to him. "Isa, this is Sambrea Sinclair."

With jealousy settling in Isa's ebony eyes, she coolly summed Sambrea up before extending her hand. "Nice to meet you, Sambrea Sinclair. That's a very unusual name. Where did such an odd name come from?"

Isa's prying tone sounded as if sugar instead of poison dripped from her tongue.

Rankled by the use of her maiden name by someone so rude, Sambrea forced a smile. "It came from my parents." Immediately regretting her impatient insolence, Sambrea bit the end of her tongue. Although something more than Isa Tanner's rudeness rubbed her the wrong way, she promised to keep her retorts to herself. She didn't want to be an embarrassment to Craig in front of his friends. "My mother's name is Breeze and my father's is Samuel."

"So they came up with Sambrea. How charming," Isa responded dryly. She then took hold of Craig's other arm and directed her guests into the spacious living area. "We have so much business to discuss, Craig, so I suggest we get started."

Looking as if she wanted to be kissed, she puckered up her bow-shaped mouth. That gesture drew a fleetingly nasty glance from Sambrea. As the trio walked into the dimly lit living area, bright lights flooded the interior rooms. Then a bunch of people jumped out yelling "Surprise!"

Craig looked positively stunned. Sambrea had no idea what was going on until she looked up and saw scores of balloons on the ceiling and a wide gold banner that read: "Happy Birthday, Craig" in huge, bright red letters.

Oh, squat! Sambrea cried inwardly. She didn't even know it was her own husband's birthday. That they didn't even know that much about one another was a travesty. *Isa had certainly known it was his birthday.*

"Hello, everyone!" Craig smiled broadly. "This really *is* a surprise. Thank you so much for wanting to make my birthday special." He turned to Sambrea. "Honey, most of these people are employees of my company. Everyone, this is Sambrea Sinclair." He hated using her maiden name solo, but it was only a temporary measure for now.

Feeling embarrassed, insecure, and downright silly, Sambrea nodded and smiled. Lowering her lashes for a fleeting moment, she prayed for strength to get her through this awkward moment. She'd never met the people that worked for Craig, with the exception of the two men who'd come to her office with him to make an offer for De La Brise.

In fact, she'd never even graced the door of Caldwell & Caldwell Incorporated. Now, she stood amidst a group of people who looked at her with strange curiosity. The fact that no one seemed to know that she was his wife brought no pleasure whatsoever.

So much for an intimate date for two! She hated the unenviable position that she suddenly found herself in.

When Craig got swept away by one of the numerous well-wishers, Sambrea felt alone and intimidated until a slightly familiar face stepped forward to rescue her from total embarrassment.

"Hello, Mrs. Caldwell," Mike Arlington said. He was careful no one overheard the name he'd used in his greeting, since Craig hadn't officially announced his marriage.

So, someone here does know we're married. "Hello . . . oh, I've forgotten your name, but I remember your face." Sambrea felt grieved at not knowing his name. "You're one of the men who came to De La Brise with Craig. Am I right?"

He smiled broadly. "You're absolutely right, Mrs. Caldwell. Does the name Mike Arlington ring a bell?"

Laughing, she nodded. "Yes, of course it does. You were the quiet one of the three. Your partners were the overbearing loudmouths." She smiled delicately.

He gave her a wry smile. "Since you ended up marrying one of those loudmouths, I can only assume you weren't too awfully offended," Mike teased. "Can I get you something to eat or drink? There's plenty of refreshments in the dining area."

Sensing that she somehow had an ally in Mike, Sambrea thought of a few questions she hoped he'd answer for her. "No, thank you, but you can help me out in another way. If you don't mind, I have a couple of questions to ask of you. Starting with, why doesn't anyone but you seem to know I'm Craig's wife?"

Mike cupped his hand under Sambrea's right elbow. "Come out on the terrace. It will be easier for us to talk and to hear one another. The music is practically deafening."

Stepping out onto the marbled terrace, Sambrea's breath caught. The view of the city was breathtaking from thirty floors up. *Some spectacular view!* She wished that Craig had been the one to introduce her to the sky-high, mesmerizing city lights.

Mike leaned against the iron railing. "Now what was it you wanted to ask of me, Mrs. Caldwell?"

"Sambrea, please," she solicited sweetly. "I want to know why you're the only person out of all these people who seems to know I'm Craig's wife?"

"I'm not the only one. Paul Rochelle knows, along with a few other important powers. Craig likes to keep his private affairs private, Sambrea. Believe me, he's not ashamed of being married to you. He's quite proud of the fact. Craig is just a very private person. That's all. He's always been one who likes to keep his private life separate from his business."

Casting Mike a charming smile, she heaved an inward sigh, glad that she'd gotten the preliminaries out of the way. "That's certainly nice to know. What's this poison-tongued Miss Isa Tanner all about? Who is she? Does she work for Caldwell & Caldwell? And does she have the hots for my handsome husband?" She hadn't taken a single breath between questions.

Smiling, Mike pulled a patio chair out for Sambrea to be seated. "I can see that you still don't mince words." He seated himself. "Isa is the daughter of one of Craig's very wealthy clients. She has the hots for him all right, but he's never been interested in her. In fact, it was Isa's idea to throw this birthday bash. Her father owns this penthouse. Had Craig known of her intentions, he never would've agreed to it. As I said before, he's a very private man."

"Hmm," Sambrea breathed. "You've made me feel much better, Mike. I wasn't very comfortable being here until now—since I've never had the good fortune to meet any of Craig's employees. Maybe we should go back and join the others. I don't think I'll feel intimated by anyone in there now, especially Miss Tanner."

"Perhaps Mike should go and join the others." Craig walked onto the terrace. "Mike, do you mind? My wife and I need some private time."

Acknowledging his employer's request, Mike gave a slight nod. "Not at all, Craig. Sambrea, it was nice to see you again. I hope to see you again real soon. Happy Birthday, man!"

Craig extended his hand to Sambrea. Standing, she placed her hand in his. Leading her over to the railing, he gently pressed her body against the cold metal. Taking up a cozy place directly behind her, he nuzzled his head against the nape of her neck. "If I could, Sam, I'd give you the universe." His voice was husky with emotion. He pointed at the millions of stars above. "I feel so inebriated when I'm with you. If we could, would you fly to the moon with me, Sam?"

Pressing her head back against his chest, she looked up at him. "We *are* on the moon, Craig. Look how close it is. We can touch it. Go ahead," she softly persuaded.

Tilting her face up to him, he bent his head and inundated himself in the tenderness of her sweet mouth. "Yes," he whispered. "We can touch it. Hold me, Sam, and never let go of me."

Squirming around in his arms, she molded herself against him, gasping with pleasure against his lips. Her tiny hands reached up and pulled his head further down. While holding him captive, her tongue plunged in and out of his mouth. Craving the sensational taste of her, his mouth wandered over her neck and ears and came to rest at the base of her throat. Desiring another taste of her sweetness, he nibbled on her ear.

Plying her throat with moist kisses, Craig's hands roved up and down her back, feverishly liquefying her entire body. "I'd love to take you right here and now. The things you make me want to do to you, Sambrea, are practically sinful. I desire you every time I come near you."

Lost in each other, neither of them heard Isa when she entered the terrace. As she cleared her throat, they pulled apart with a start.

As if Sambrea were invisible to her, Isa looped her arm

through Craig's. "Sorry to interrupt your little rendezvous, Craig, but you have other guests inside. They're dying to sing 'Happy Birthday' to you." Cattily, she tossed Sambrea a chilled glance.

"That was nice of you to remind me, Isa. We'll be right in," Craig responded with impatient politeness.

Isa tugged at his arm. "I want you to come now," she pouted. "My favorite song is playing and I want to dance with you."

Craig looked helplessly at Sambrea, who watched Isa with wry amusement. "Isa, since this party is for me, I get to choose who I dance with and when. Okay?"

"By all means, Craig. I just thought I should have the first dance since this is my party as well. However, I don't want to have words with you. Still, your guests are waiting."

She stormed back indoors.

"Looks like you've ruffled the feathers of the hostess, Mr. Caldwell. She doesn't have any ferocious dogs to sic on us, does she? That girl there seems to have a nasty temper and she also growls like a rabid dog."

"Isa is all bark, Sam. Much like you." He moved out of reach of harm's way. "Both of you bark loud and ferociously, yet you're harmless. Don't let her get to you. She may be a beautiful young woman, but she's far too spoiled and immature for me."

All Sambrea could do was laugh. He was right, at least where she was concerned. She had barked plenty, but she hadn't bitten. And he hadn't despaired once, despite it all.

Moving indoors with Sambrea on his arm, Craig meandered to the center of the room. Unbeknownst to the Caldwells, the style and grace they seemed saturated in drew everyone's immediate attention.

"I understand my presence has been requested in here. I wasn't trying to be rude, but I had some important matters to discuss with the stunning lady here on my arm. I trust that I'm forgiven." He had a knowing way of being charming.

Everyone clapped. When someone began singing "Happy Birthday," the others joined in. Looking on, Craig beamed his approval.

As soon as the singing ceased, Craig blew out the candles on the huge birthday cake. Pulling Sambrea into the space cleared for dancing, his hands rested on her back. Feeling like the luckiest woman in the world, she snuggled herself deeper into his arms. Using only her sand-and-sable eyes to relay her deepest feelings, she looked up into his midnight orbs, sending him messages fraught with genuine love. The sexy smile he cast down on her in response made her knees quiver and left her body trembling with desire.

"In the next thirty minutes we're going to blow this party. I promised you an intimate date and I intend to keep that promise. I hate surprise parties, Sam. So don't ever think of throwing me one."

"Well, there's two more things I've learned about you. This could get real interesting. I kind of like discovering new things about you, Mr. Caldwell."

"Besides my hating surprise parties what else did you learn about me, Sam?"

She giggled loudly. "That today is my husband's birthday! Something I'm very embarrassed about. How could I've not known it was your birthday?"

"I guess because we never discussed it. But don't feel bad. Until we came here, I wasn't aware of it either."

"You forgot your own birthday?" Grinning sheepishly, he nodded. "Will wonders never cease? This is a really nice party they've thrown in your honor." She thoroughly checked his palms and then scanned the hair on his arms.

He gave her a puzzled look. "What are you doing, Sam?"

"Checking your anatomy for third degree burns, what else? Since Miss Isa Tanner is sizzling in her silk panties, I just wanted to make sure that she didn't burn you too badly when she was fondling you."

A little flattered by her remarks, Craig buried his deep

laughter into her hair. "Do I sense a little jealousy here? Don't tell me you feel threatened by Isa, Sam?"

Feigning surprise, she raised an eyebrow. "Who me? I don't have a jealous bone in my body. What does she have that I don't have? Besides this penthouse suite, of course," Sambrea joked with casual ease.

"Me! Sam, Isa has had on a crush on me since forever, but she knows I don't take her seriously. Isa is in no way pining away for me. She has plenty of male suitors. Millionaire suitors."

Placing her hands on the back of his head, she kissed him fully on the mouth. "That's good to know. Now I can cancel that call I just made to my hit man."

The announcement she'd made with a straight face caused Craig to burst into a gale of raucous laughter.

"I didn't mean for that statement to tickle your funny bone, Mr. C. I wanted to let you know exactly what I'm capable of, especially when I'm annoyed." Her smile was sinister.

"Oh, Sam, I know quite well what you're capable of. How well do I know! And I love you just the way you are."

Directing her head onto his chest, he wrapped his arms more tightly around her waist. Wishing he had wings, Craig floated her across the dance floor. At the moment, flying them back to the moon seemed like a magnificent idea.

Sambrea already felt like she'd landed on the moon. Being in Craig's arms was just like the imagined journey to seventh heaven she'd once had—arms she'd once feared would never, ever hold her again.

It suddenly dawned on her that he really had come back to her, in spite of her mistrust in him, in spite of all the times she'd deserted him and their marriage. It wasn't a dream. She was helplessly meshed against his granite body. It felt so wonderful, so right. Was she the most blessed woman on the planet, or what?

With the song ending, Craig made his way back to the center of the room.

"May I have everyone's attention," he shouted above the din.

As commanded, everyone turned their attention to the handsome man in the center of the room. Craig had a presence like no other, as far as his wife was concerned.

"I want to thank you for coming here this evening to celebrate my birthday. It was an immeasurably warm gesture from all of you. I've enjoyed myself tremendously. Unfortunately, with much regret, I have to leave. I have a prior commitment that I must honor."

Placing his hands on Sambrea's shoulders, he positioned her in front on him. "Before I leave, I would like to make a very important announcement and a formal introduction. Earlier I introduced this beautiful woman as Sambrea Sinclair. However, she's in fact Mrs. Craig Caldwell, the woman who stars in all my fantasies. We were married a short time ago and we'll be happily married for the rest of our natural lives." Before anyone could pass comment, Craig swept Sambrea toward the front door, eager to have her all to himself.

Shocked at Craig's speech, Isa was just quick enough to catch up to him when she saw him rushing toward the door. Nearly knocking Sambrea over, she grabbed Craig's hand.

"I'm a little peeved at your announcement and this rudely hasty departure." Isa looked over at the mountain of presents stacked on the foyer table. "Oh, well, what's a few presents to a man that can buy himself anything he desires? In view of your recent marriage, you're now a man who has everything! You win some, you lose some."

Before turning away, Isa winked at Sambrea.

Smiling with understanding, Sambrea winked back at her.

Inside the car, Craig lifted Sambrea's wrist and planted butterfly kisses up and down her forearm. "I guess I stunned you by announcing our marriage. I hope you don't think it was a mistake."

Sambrea laid her head on his shoulder. "I couldn't have been more pleased, Craig. I wondered how you'd managed to keep it a secret for so long, since everyone at De La Brise knows we're married. Gossip has a way of crossing any and all boundaries. Have you ever heard that the tongue is the lightest of all the organs, but it's the hardest and heaviest to hold?"

"I have heard that. It's very true. My employees know how much I detest gossip and those who indulge in it. I'm sure there are many who knew already, but they wouldn't dare discuss it at the office. I've been known to fire some-one for a lot less."

"Oh, my, you are some taskmaster, Mr. Caldwell! I cer-tainly hope you have no plans to fire me. I don't relish the idea of standing in the looking-for-a-new-husband line." Her statement was meant as a joke yet it caused fear to settle in her stomach.

"Remember that when you get the urge to run off again. The next time you won't get off so lightly. I will punish you in ways that'll make you beg for more. You'll be the happiest and most satisfied abused wife in Hawaii."

"Ooh, is it too late for me to be punished for my last crime? I did skip out on my parole, you know. From the sound of it, I'll love being an abused wife. What type of abuse do you have in mind?"

"I'm better at demonstrations." Taking her into his arms, he punished her lips with the most brutal, sweetest, sensu-ous kiss she'd ever laid claim to.

Craig had driven for several miles before he finally pulled through a set of iron gates, onto what appeared to be a private stretch of beach. After parking right on the sand, he jumped out of the car and ran around to the passenger-side to assist Sambrea.

As she kicked off her shoes, her breath caught at the grandiose surroundings. She was standing on one of the most beautiful stretches of beach she had ever seen; the white sands felt as soft and as fine as dusting powder under her stocking feet.

One could probably see for miles and miles across the ocean in the daylight. While Craig toyed with something inside the trunk, Sambrea took a short stroll on the deserted sands, enjoying the warm trade winds blowing through her new free-spirited hairstyle.

When she returned from her short trek up the beach, Craig had an impressive picnic laid out under a magnificent swaying palm, where he'd already spread an Air-Force-blue blanket over the white sands. Coming to an abrupt halt at the end of the blanket, she reached under her dress and stripped away her pantyhose. After tossing her unmentionables off to the far corner of the blanket, she sat down.

"This is so romantic, sweetheart. I love it here." Her eyes were ablaze with the mystique and magic of midnight.

"I'm glad you think so. A friend of mine owns this little piece of paradise and he's given us permission to be here. He had these white sands installed. Imagine the cost of that."

Taking the wrapping off a platter of cheese and crackers, Craig held it out to Sambrea. "Do you care for a glass of non-alcoholic champagne, Sam?"

"Not right now. I only want to drink in my perception of this unmitigated beauty. When you say private, you mean private, don't you? I feel like I've stepped into an uncharted universe. It's certainly out of this world!"

"I'm glad you feel that way, since I plan to purchase a piece of land very similar to this one. Together, we'll design the plans to build our own private hideaway. Would you like that, Sam?"

Moving over closer to him, she laid her head in his lap and peered up into his eyes. "Very much so, Craig. However, I love where we live now. It doesn't make sense to have two houses so close together. Even though it's leased out for the time being we also have the bungalow."

"Since the land I'm purchasing is in the Mediterranean, I don't think the houses will be all that close together." He smiled.

"The Mediterranean! Oh, Craig, that sounds marvelous. Where in the Mediterranean?"

"Somewhere in the Greek Isles, or perhaps the Cote d'Azure. It's a surprise. I made a bid for the land when I was traveling to Africa. In fact, I'll take you there to see it in the very near future. We haven't had a honeymoon yet. We have to do it before the baby comes."

Looking melancholy, she traced his lips with the tip of her fingernail. "Breeze's illness has really turned our lives topsy-turvy. Look at what's happened to all of our plans. We've also had to back out of the idea of dating so we can get to know each other better."

Bending his head, he kissed her forehead. "By the time we leave for our honeymoon, I plan to know everything there is to know about you—and then some. I'm going to spend all of my free time with you. We're going to talk, talk, and talk some more."

Her expression turned serious. "I need to talk now. I have some things I'd like to clear from my head. Would you mind terribly if I got a few things off my chest?"

"Not at all, as long as you leave those two bronzed mounds intact."

He had hoped to make her smile.

Rewarding him, she smiled brilliantly. "I have no intentions of eradicating any of your pleasures, my star-quality lover."

"That's comforting. All jokes aside, Sam, go ahead and say what's on your mind."

Licking her lips, Sambrea appeared nervous. "I know I've not always trusted you, but I do now, explicitly. In light of the disturbing information that I've learned about my father, I've become worried about marital infidelity. As you know, I never intended to marry. Not because I knew my father had cheated on Breeze, although I suspected her of cheating on my father with men much younger than she was. I never wanted to marry because they didn't have a very happy marriage. I don't know how it started or who started it. At this point, it's passé, yet it happened.

"Our lives together are just beginning, Craig. I don't like myself for thinking this, but I've been asking myself what makes you any different from Samuel. What's going to keep you faithful to me? Maybe if I always know what it is that you need from me, and vice versa, perhaps we can keep the same things from happening in our marriage."

He felt so sorry for her. Although she'd tried hard to hide if from him, this thing with her father had hurt her tremendously. The situation with Breeze had everything to do with her strange behavior over the past days, he'd come to realize.

He stroked her hair. "What's going to keep you faithful to me, Sam? To take it one step further, what makes you any different from Breeze?"

His thought provoking questions were ones she'd never considered before. "I don't know. How do you expect me to answer that?"

Studying her expression, he gave her a thoughtful glance. "I guess the exact same way you expected me to answer it." He took her by the hand. "Honey, males don't have a corner on the infidelity market. It's not an exclusively male club. You could cheat on me just as easy as I could cheat on you. Marriage is about commitment. I feel as though I'm committed to you beyond marriage. Can I honestly say it'll last through eternity? I don't know. All I know is that I want it to. When I asked you to marry me, I was asking for forever. I'm going to do everything in my power to keep our love as fresh as the first day I realized I was in love with you."

He wiped a runaway tear from the corner of her eye.

"Sambrea, like everything else in life, love and marriage is a risk. It's a risk I was willing to take simply because our love is worth it. Besides, you know I'm the type of man who commits himself to anything I take on. I don't mess with anything in my professional or personal life that I don't feel a strong commitment toward."

His sincerity brought more tears to her eyes. "I never thought about it like that. You have a way of making things so clear for me. It must be a gift from above. I wish my mind worked just as yours does. But then again, our different gifts are what keeps us so intrigued with each other." She sighed. "Craig, can we make the commitment to talk with each other when we're not having a happily-ever-after attitude toward one another? Can we promise to keep the communication lines open, no matter how bad things get? I don't want to make the same mistake Samuel and Breeze made. I don't want our marriage to just survive. I want it to blossom like wildflowers on a country hillside. I want it to be just as colorful as a field of tulips and daffodils in the spring."

"I've already made those commitments to you, to us, Sam. The day I stood before the Justice of Peace and said 'I do.' I meant those two little words with all my heart."

"So you did." She breathed in shakily. "So you did. But I need to tell you one more thing, Craig. One of the reasons that I've been afraid of having Breeze in our home is because she intimated that you and she had an intimate liaison. I know better than that now. I know I can trust you, but I'm not sure I can trust her. She likes to stir up problems. She suffers from a classic case of misery loves company. Seeing us so happy just might make her more miserable than she's already shown herself to be. Any suggestions on handling that?"

He laughed. "We could always lock her up and throw away the key." His joking made Sambrea smile. "We're simply not going to own her problems. If she gets out of hand, she has to go away. There will be no ifs, ands, or buts about it. We're going to live in a stress-free environment. We're not going to allow anyone else to bring any outside disturbances into our peaceful home. I'll have a talk with her before she's discharged. If she can't behave herself, we'll buy out the lease on the bungalow and banish her to living there."

Lifting up her head, she captured his lips in an impassioned embrace, kissing him fiercely. "Thank you. We've resolved the major issues. We can . . . save the . . . rest of this talk for . . . later," she muttered between kisses.

"Yes, later."

Getting to his feet, he pulled Sambrea up from the sand.

With the silver moonlight lighting up the sand and the bright stars twinkling merrily, Craig danced with his barefooted wife. The only music they heard came from the melody of their thundering hearts.

Stretching out on the blanket, Craig pulled her alongside him. Slipping his hand up past the slit of her dress, he gently massaged her thighs. As she arched against him, his manhood sprouted forth. Rolling her onto her back, he covered her with a blanket of warmth, tenderly pressing his trembling body into hers. "How's this for conversation, Sam?"

Afraid of breaking the magical spell they'd fallen under, Sambrea didn't respond.

Instead, she kissed him urgently, bringing him back to the place where she longed for him to be: lost in the ecstasy of their passion, as she was. Disregarding all the rules that had been set, unzipping his pants, Sambrea reached in to stroke him, hoping to make him forget the silly rules they'd made.

After all, they were man and wife.

Even if they didn't know each other as well as they should, their bodies had become more than well acquainted. Why should their bodies go through withdrawal, especially when they'd grown so harmlessly and permanently addicted to one another? Finding himself in yet another hopeless situation, Craig allowed Sambrea to strip him of every article of clothing. He further encouraged her with passionate, sexual murmurs.

As her lips traced his chest with balmy kisses, he began disrobing her, touching her in all the most erotic places. He was ready to lure her into the fiery furnace of his ecstasy.

As their much-fantasized union became a reality, Sambrea moved under him. Tenderly, she drew him deeply inside of her. With the issues of trust and commitment settled between them, they concentrated on each other.

Filling each other with the magic of midnight, they lost their souls and minds to a newly discovered mystical kingdom. Unadulterated gratification was attained much too soon.

Insatiable, Sambrea and Craig seemed determined to rediscover the magic they brought to each other's soul. Over and over, all through the rest of their island interlude, which would last through the rest of their lives.

Dear Readers:

I sincerely hope that you enjoyed reading ISLAND IN-
TERLUDE, the romantic saga featuring Sambrea Sinclair
and Craig Caldwell, from cover to cover. I'm interested in
hearing your comments and thoughts. Without the reader,
there is no me as an author.

Please mail correspondence to: Linda Hudson-Smith,
2026C North Riverside Avenue, Box 109, Rialto, CA
92377. Please enclose a self-addressed, stamped envelope
(SASE) with all your correspondence if you would like a
return letter. You can also e-mail your comments to me at
LHS4romance@yahoo.com. Please also visit my Web site
at http://www.lindahudsonsmith.com.

ABOUT THE AUTHOR

Born in Canonsburg, Pennsylvania, and raised in the town of Washington, Pennsylvania, Linda Hudson-Smith has traveled the world as an enthusiastic witness to other cultures and lifestyles. Her husband's military career gave her the opportunity to live in Japan, Germany, and many cities across the United States. Her extensive travel experience helps her craft stories set in a variety of beautiful and romantic locations. It was after illness forced her to leave a career in marketing and public relations administration that she turned to writing.

Romance in Color chose her as Rising Star for the month of January 2000. ICE UNDER FIRE, her debut Arabesque novel, has received rave reviews. A.A.O.W.G. voted Linda Best New Author, presenting her with the 2000 Gold Pen Award. She has also won two Shades of Romance awards in the categories of Multi-Cultural New Romance Author of the Year and Multi-Cultural New Fiction Author of the Year. SOULFUL SERENADE, released in August 2000, was selected by Romance in Color readers as the Best Cover. She was also nominated as the Best New Romance Author at Romance Slam Jam 2001. Her novel covers have been featured in such major publications as *Publisher's Weekly, USA Today,* and *Essence* magazine.

Linda is a member of Romance Writers of America and the Black Writer's Alliance. Though novel writing remains her first love, she is currently cultivating her screenwriting skills. She has also been contracted to write several other novels for BET/Arabesque Books.

Dedicated to inspiring readers to overcome adversity against all odds, Linda has accepted the challenge of becoming National Spokesperson for the Lupus Foundation of America. In making Lupus awareness one of her top priorities, she travels around the country delivering inspirational messages of hope. She is also a supporter of the NAACP and the American Cancer Society. She enjoys poetry, entertaining, traveling, and attending sports events. Linda is the mother of two sons; she and her husband share residences in both California and Texas.